Witches' Bane

Susan Wittig Albert

Witches' Bane

CHARLES SCRIBNER'S SONS
NEW YORK

MAXWELL MACMILLAN CANADA
TORONTO
MAXWELL MACMILLAN INTERNATIONAL
NEW YORK   OXFORD   SINGAPORE   SYDNEY

Copyright © 1993 by Susan Wittig Albert

Charles Scribner's Sons
Macmillan Publishing Company
866 Third Avenue
New York, NY 10022

Maxwell Macmillan Canada, Inc.
1200 Eglinton Avenue East
Suite 200
Don Mills, Ontario M3C 3N1

Macmillan Publishing Company is part of the Maxwell Communication Group of Companies.

ISBN 0-684-19636-0

Printed in the United States of America

Acknowledgments

Thanks go to Bob Tyrone, of Bob Tyrone Automotive, Austin, Texas, for technical help with automobile details; David's Auto Parts, Bertram, Texas, for access to their wrecking yard; John Webber, for editorial comments and brotherly reassurance; and Molly Ficken of the Austin Jung Society for encouraging me to teach tarot. The New Braunfels *Herald-Zeitung* is a valuable and interesting source of small-town doings, and *Texas Monthly* helps to re-create Texas as a state of mind. Also and again, thanks to Anita McClellan and Susanne Kirk for their continued energetic support.

Most of all, grateful thanks to my husband and co-author Bill Albert, whose active and ongoing engagement with the China Bayles series (and all my work) makes it as much his as mine.

Author's Note

This series is set in the imaginary Texas town of Pecan Springs, which includes such fictitious elements as the campus of Central Texas State University and the Pecan River. Readers familiar with the central Texas hill country should not confuse Pecan Springs with such actual towns as San Marcos, New Braunfels, or Fredericksburg. (These real settings appear now and again in their own special identities.) The author has created the fictional characters and events for the reader's pleasure, and intends no connection to real people or happenings.

Witches' Bane

1

"Sometimes you almost have me convinced, China."
McQuaid squatted on his heels to admire the stone fountain he'd
just installed in the garden in front of my herb shop.

"Convinced of what?" I was on my knees with a trowel, set-
tling a rosemary transplant behind the fountain.

"That maybe Pecan Springs isn't such a bad place. Maybe I
should settle down here, after all."

"Ha," I said, under my breath. "I'll believe that when I see
it," I said, out loud.

I straightened up and took a deep breath of the fresh morning air. It was a late-October Monday, my day off, and the
warm, hazy-gold sun spilled over the silvery mounds of
artemisia and lambs-ears around the new fountain. Behind me
was Thyme and Seasons, the herb shop I own and operate. Four
years ago, I called it quits with the Houston criminal law firm
where I'd worked for a decade and a half, cashed in my retirement, and went looking for a small town. I found it halfway
between Austin and San Antonio, bought a marvelous two-
story, century-old stone building with space for two stores in
front and living quarters in back, and went into business. I love
it here. I aim to stay.

The problem is, I also love Mike McQuaid, or I think I do,
and I think he loves me. How many guys would give up a weekend with their toys to put in a fountain? But neither of us are

kids who believe we can have everything we want. We're adults. We have to accept the reality of one another's lives, and a central reality for McQuaid is his career, which he loves. He's an ex-cop who is now an assistant professor in the criminal justice department at Central Texas State University—a tall, dark, sexy, and almost handsome ex-cop with slate blue eyes, a jagged white scar across his forehead, and a nose that's been broken more times than it deserves. McQuaid is bright and ambitious, with fourteen years experience in law enforcement, fine academic credentials, and two years of full-time teaching. At thirty-eight, he's on his way up the career ladder to a big-time professorship in some high-powered criminal justice program in a large university in a major city. He's also a single parent.

And that's the rub. I'm forty-four, and I've never accommodated myself to a live-in lover, much less a lover-plus-child. I enjoy my privacy. I cherish my personal space. I enjoy my small-time herb business and my small-time life in this small-time town. That's why I shut down whenever McQuaid says something that sounds even remotely long-term. I'm keeping my emotional distance.

McQuaid splashed his hands in the fountain to wash off the dirt. "Yeah, well, I have to admit that there's something to be said for the quiet life—if you don't mind being bored now and then."

"Who's bored?" I stood up for a stretch. When I left the rat race, I wanted to leave the rats behind, get away from the superhype, the constant push, the unrelenting pressure. But there's plenty of big-city cop left in McQuaid. The more action, the better.

"I'm bored," McQuaid said. "But not for long." With a Draculan leer, he lunged at me and stuck his cold, wet hands under the front of my tee shirt.

I swatted him with the flat of my trowel. "Stop it, McQuaid! This is a main street. People are watching!"

"Good. Let's sell tickets." McQuaid pinned my arms behind me and gave me a long, hard, and extremely satisfying kiss.

Resumé Workshop

Tuesday, August 8, 2023 6:30PM
WACL Conference Room 2

Are you new to the workforce and need help creating a resumé?

Or are you back for a second career, and need to update your old one? This workshop will demonstrate the basics of using a template to create a resumé from scratch, as well as tips for editing and updating. Further individual assistance may be requested by appointment. Stop at our circulation desk for details on personal appointments.

Western Allegheny Community Library
362 Bateman Rd
Oakdale, PA 15071
724-695-8150
www.westernalleghenylibrary.org

INFORMATION
LITERACY

"I'd make that a ten."

It was Ruby Wilcox, my best friend and tenant. She owns the Crystal Cave, Pecan Spring's only New Age shop, which occupies the other space in my building. Ruby is six feet tall in her flats, with orangy-red hair and freckles. Usually, she looks like Cher outfitted for a show at the Sands, but with her body and charm, she gets away with it. Monday is her day off too, so she was wearing something casual—a wide-shouldered blue-gray jersey and skintight white calf-length pants. With her height and those giant shoulder pads, she reminded me of a Cowboy linebacker.

McQuaid released me and grinned at Ruby. "Gotta go. I've got a class at one, and I haven't finished grading the quizzes."

"Give 'em hell, McQuaid," Ruby said. As he climbed into his old blue Ford pickup, she gave the new fountain a critical look. "Cool," she said. "But don't you think it needs something? Lilies, maybe? A stone frog?"

"Rome wasn't built in a day, Ruby. Give it time to grow moss." I turned to see Constance Letterman coming up the walk.

"Is that your new fountain?" Constance asked. She's short and round, her tight brown curls courtesy of Bobby Rae's House of Beauty, where perms are half price on Wednesdays. Squeezed into a bright orange-and-yellow checked pantsuit, she looked like a plastic pot scrubber. She scrutinized the fountain. "Looks kinda empty."

"That's what I was just saying," Ruby said. "It needs lilies and a stone frog."

Constance looked at Ruby. "Hate to tell you, Ruby, but Arnold won't run that ad for your fortune-tellin' class. He says it's a bad idea right now, what with people all upset about this Satanic stuff."

Constance is half gossip, half native philosopher, and holds a lifetime membership in the moral majority. She writes a column called "News Roundup" for the Pecan Springs *Enterprise*, which belongs to her cousin, Arnold Seidensticker. I think people read the column mainly to see their names in print. At fifteen thousand, Pecan Springs is small enough that the grapevine does a pretty fair job of keeping people informed. By the time an item makes the "Roundup," it's already made the rounds of the Doughnut Queen, Lillie's Place, and half the churches in town. Everybody who wants to know, knows, including some who don't.

"It isn't a fortune-telling class," Ruby said. "It's a tarot class. And it has nothing to do with Satanic cults."

"You know that and maybe I know that," Constance said judiciously, "but a lot of the folks readin' the paper don't know that. It's for your own good, Ruby. People get it into their heads you're a witch, you could be in deep, serious trouble."

"Nobody burns witches anymore," I said. "It's against the law."

Constance folded her arms across her chest. "It's not burnin' that's at stake here." Ruby groaned and I winced. Constance didn't appear to notice. "And it's not the law you got to think about, either. People in Pecan Springs just plain don't like witches. Especially these days, what with the grand jury investigatin' the old Ellis case and diggin' up poor old Leota."

Constance was talking about the mysterious death of Ralph Ellis, a sixteen-year-old boy whose body was found hanging from a horse apple tree out on Cotton Gin Road one summer evening two years ago. In the absence of witnesses, and since the school counselor testified that Ralph was despondent over a girl, the death had been ruled a suicide. But that wasn't the end of it. The stories were quietly passed around, every telling more terrifying than the last. The Ellis boy, it was said, had been murdered by devil worshippers, thirteen of them. He wasn't the only one, either, so the stories went. The transient found six months ago under the bridge and Leota Rainey, who wandered away from the nursing home last spring and ended up in a ditch— every mysterious death for the last few years, every incident of cemetery vandalism, every midnight sighting of shadowy figures was being attributed to one or more secret cults of devils and witches.

The grand jury got in on it when Leota Rainey's daughter (spurred on by Leota's cousin, who works part time at Bobbie Rae's and part time as a cosmetician at Watson's Funeral Home) began insisting that the peculiar marks on her mother's forehead looked an awful lot like the scratches on the transient's forehead and the marks on the Ellis boy's arms. She demanded an investigation. Bubba Harris, Pecan Springs' police chief, reluctantly opened all three cases and took his findings to the grand jury. Nobody knew the details, but rumor had it that Leota and the transient were about to be dug up. The whole business had people nervously looking over their shoulders for a Satanic cult on the loose, corrupting children and lying in wait for old ladies.

Ruby was firm. "I am *not* a witch."

Constance made a noise between a humph and a snort. "It don't matter whether you're a witch or not. What counts is whether the ladies at the beauty parlor *think* you're a witch."

I'd have let the matter drop, but Ruby's flammable disposition matches her flaming hair, and Constance was about to light her torch. "You're way off base, Constance," she said angrily. "This is the nineties, for crying out loud. Nobody's going to get bent out of shape about a little thing like a tarot class. It's not like I'm charming snakes or casting spells on children."

Constance shuddered. "Don't say thangs like that, Ruby." In Nacogdoches, where Constance comes from, they say things like thangs and nobody laughs. "You got to be more careful. You never know who might be listenin'."

She darted a nervous glance across the yard. Vida Plunkett, my neighbor on the other side, was standing on the front walk, arguing with Duane Redmond, the owner of Duane's Dry Cleaners, over whether the city council should make Crockett Street one way. Duane was making the point that one-way streets frustrate the tourists. Vida, a sharp-tongued, suspicious woman who hates almost everybody, replied tartly that somebody needed to do *something* about the traffic, she didn't care what, and since tourists are already seventy percent frustrated and twenty percent lost, a little more certainly wouldn't hurt. It's the sort of argument people here get into. Pecan Springs, at the edge of the Hill Country, makes a healthy living off tourists, and most people (including me) are willing to suffer an inconvenience or two if it makes for happy tourists. Vida doesn't make a living off tourists. She owns the Washateria on Houston Street. She makes her living off people who make their living off tourists.

Ruby's eyes (ordinarily hazel, green today because she was wearing tinted contacts) narrowed at Constance's remark. "The last I heard, Constance, Texas is a free country." She appealed to me. "There's no law against tarot, is there, China?"

People who know that I used to be a lawyer ask all kinds of odd legal questions—only some of which I'm equipped to answer. The firm I worked for specialized in baddies with big bucks: corporate presidents with their fingers in the till, stock-brokers trading on inside information, drug kingpins. Once in a blue moon I got assigned to a case I cared about, but that didn't take the bad taste out of my mouth. I could have switched to another firm or gone out on my own or even changed my speciality, but by the time I figured it all out, I'd stopped believing that the legal system can be counted on to create justice. I'd had to make so many deals that I'd almost forgotten how to tell the difference between right and wrong. If I hung around any longer I might not have any self left, at least, any self I could respect.

So I bailed out. Herbs had fascinated me from the time I helped my grandmother China harvest basil in her New Orleans herb garden. As a child, I'd wanted to be a botanist, and when I lived in Houston I crammed my tiny window greenhouse with herbs, read everything I could find about them, and made weekly stops at the local herb shop. Getting out of the law and into the herb business seemed like the right thing to do, especially after I located Thyme and Seasons. I still pay bar association

dues and keep up the other requirements, in case I have to fall back on the law. But my old life seems a long way back—until somebody asks me a legal question. Then I'm reminded of what I used to do for a living.

Ruby's question was easy. "No," I said, "there's no law against tarot." I picked up a pot of santolina and trimmed off some broken silvery foliage. "The First Amendment gives you the right to free speech."

Ruby turned to Constance. "See?" she said. "Anyway, I don't need to advertise in the paper. My class is already full. It starts tomorrow night."

Constance's mouth pursed into a tart round *O*. "You're teachin' tarot cards *now*, with Halloween comin' up? Ruby, I hope to tell you, you are *askin'* for it."

I set the santolina into the ground two feet away from the rosemary and stood back to admire the effect. I wasn't sure what Halloween had to do with anything, but Ruby didn't appear threatened. She lifted her chin with a benign smile.

"Life is a learning experience, Constance. If trouble comes, it's just one of those lessons the Universe has assigned me for my own good." It was a statement straight out of Ruby's New Age philosophy. When she talks that way she sounds very Zen-ish, but the fact is that Ruby hardly ever takes any lesson lying down.

Constance shook her head. "Well, when the universe lets fly, just remember I said it first. No telling what people'll do if it gets around that you're a witch."

Ruby was not perturbed. "So let them," she said with a shrug. "I'm ready."

A rattletrap pickup loped up to the curb and honked. "It's Lester Kyle," Constance said, "come to install the lights for that new photographer who moved in last week." In addition to writing for the *Enterprise*, Constance owns the Craft Emporium on the other side of Thyme and Seasons. It's a big old Victorian, remodeled into small shops and boutiques. "The Grand Openin'

is Wednesday mornin', right after the Mayor's Prayer Breakfast." She opened the straw tote she was carrying and began to fish around in it. "Speakin' of the prayer breakfast, I understand that the speaker is an expert on Satanic cults. He's goin' to tell people how to tell if their kids are into stuff like that. And Chief Harris will be talkin' about that information the state sent him—thirty ways to tell if there's a cult in town, or somethin' like that. If you haven't got your tickets yet, I can fix you up." She pulled out two tickets and held them up.

"Thanks, Constance, but I think I'll skip the prayer breakfast." I didn't have an overwhelming desire to shell out sevenfifty for the privilege of sharing my huevos rancheros with a witch hunter. "But I'll be at the opening."

I glanced at Ruby, who smiled slightly. Andrew Drake, the new photographer, was her newest boyfriend. She'd been seeing him for about a month, and from the hints she'd dropped, I guessed that the relationship was beginning to gather momentum.

"How about you, Ruby?" Constance asked.

"I've already bought my ticket," Ruby said. "I've got a theory that nobody'll suspect you of being a witch if you're a regular at the Mayor's Prayer Breakfast."

✳ ✳ ✳

If it hadn't been for all that stuff about witches, I might not have let Ruby talk me into going to her tarot class Tuesday night. I'm not your basic New Age type. I'm not big on symbols and I usually forget that my rising sign is Gemini and that my Capricorn sun is in the tenth house until Ruby reminds me that it's significant. I like digging out the facts, marshaling them in logical order, and putting them to work. I'm right-brained, Ruby says, which in New Age terms means I'm too analytical. Ruby has decided that the Universe has given her the mission of switching on my left brain.

"I'm really not interested in fortune-telling," I said, when Ruby came into my kitchen that afternoon to invite me to her class. Living behind the herb shop is wonderfully handy and even life-preserving (I no longer have to make a daily kamikaze commute down the Houston freeways), but it does encourage drop-ins.

"Forget fortune-telling," Ruby said. "The tarot's really a mind-expanding tool. It will help you break through your linear, rigid, cause-and-effect thought patterns. It will strengthen your Inner Guide."

I pushed myself away from the computer where I was working and Khat jumped off my lap and onto the floor. Khat is a seventeen-pound narcissistic Siamese who for the past year has permitted me to sleep in his bed and supply him with chicken livers, cooked until they are just slightly pink. When he first came to live with me I called him Cat. Ruby complained that the name was too mundane for such a splendid beast. We compromised with Khat, pronounced Cat.

Displeased at the interruption, Khat flicked his tail, glared at Ruby, and stalked to the bathroom to sit on the sink and admire himself in the mirror. Khat is not anybody's pet, least of all mine. He only lets you stroke him as long as you do it in just the right way, in just the right place. Otherwise, he nips. He does not answer to "kitty, kitty."

My computer sits on the desk in my kitchen, so I can work and keep an eye on whatever's cooking on the old green-and-cream Home Comfort gas stove I found in a garage sale in Pipecreek, Texas. This afternoon, several things were cooking. I was boiling down a pot of tomatoes to make catsup, brewing a tea of tansy leaves to water my houseplants, and baking a peach pie. At the moment, I was taking a break from cooking to bring some order to last month's profit-and-loss sheet. I didn't like what I saw. Things had been slow lately, with the economy still struggling to stay afloat, but I hadn't realized they'd been that slow. The bottom line was a definite reality-check. I had to do something to beef up sales—quick. Teach a class, maybe, or develop that mail-order catalog I've been thinking about.

"Anyway," Ruby added, tasting the catsup, "I need you." She rolled her eyes appreciatively. "What's in this, China?"

"Cinnamon and mace, among other things." I got up to check on the pie. When I was working fourteen-hour days, six days a week, I scarcely took time to eat, let alone cook. Now, I'm collecting my favorite recipes and various herbal home brews for a cookbook. "What could you possibly need me for, Ruby? I don't know the first thing about tarot."

Ruby sniffed the tansy tea, brewing in a saucepan. "What's this?"

"Tansy, for my houseplants. The leaves are full of yummy potassium. What do you need me for?"

Ruby sat down at the table. "Well, to tell the truth, my class isn't quite full. I just said that because Constance was being such a jerk about witches. It would be nice to have another person. To sort of fill out the group."

"A warm body, you mean."

"So to speak."

I opened the oven. The crust was beautifully browned. "What's the magic number? Thirteen?"

"Smart ass. So far, there's six, not counting you. Pam Neely is coming. You know her, don't you? She teaches psychology at the college." Central Texas State University, on the north edge of town, now boasts an enrollment of twelve thousand, but to the natives, it's still the "college."

"Sure, I know Pam," I said, reaching for a potholder. "I didn't know she was into tarot."

"I keep telling you, China," Ruby said patiently. "Tarot is not for flakes. It is a complex system of symbols that opens a way deep into our nonrational thought. Serious investigators of the unconscious understand that the cards help expand our intuitive capabilities."

I had to smile. When Ruby wants to defend her New Age practices, she dresses them up in polysyllabic words. "Who else is coming?"

"Judith Cohen is signed up, and Mary Richards, and Dottie Riddle and Gretel Schumaker." Ruby frowned and ticked the list off her fingers again, as if she'd lost one. "Oh, yes, and Sybil Rand."

"Isn't six enough?"

"Seven would be better. We're having dessert afterward. You could bring your pie." She inhaled deeply. "Smells wonderful."

I put the pie on the table and turned back to the Home Comfort to stir the tomato catsup. To me, tarot was just another of Ruby's spacey interests, like crystals and rune stones, which I can take or leave. But I like Pam Neely, and Judith Cohen keeps herself so busy that I almost never see her. I didn't know Mary Richards, but I'd seen the fascinating gold and silver jewelry she made, and I'd been wanting to meet her. I was hesitating when Ruby added the clincher.

"You wouldn't stay away just because somebody might call you a witch, would you?"

When I moved to Pecan Springs, I was enticed by the sweet, clean air, the limestone ridges of the Edwards Plateau, and the lovely cypress-shaded Pecan River. It seemed like a delightful haven from Houston's smog and noise and constant rushing. But Pecan Springs is a typical small town. A big night out is barbecue with the neighbors or slow dancing at the Greune (pronounced Green) Dance Hall, which opened for business in 1878 and has never closed since. The people, while they are often warm and friendly, can also be narrow-minded, as you can see for yourself by walking over to the Book Nook and looking at the books Madeline Martin puts on the shelves—and those she doesn't. As Constance says, people here have a tendency to distrust outsiders' ways. It's understandable, when you think about how small towns work. It can also be frustrating, even a little frightening.

But the women who gravitate to Ruby's shop and classes are different. They have a kind of tangential relationship to the town, both complementing and questioning it. They believe they have something inside that hasn't yet emerged, something worth discovering. They remind me that there are spaces within me that haven't yet opened up.

So when I rode my bike over to Ruby's on Tuesday night, it was more because of the women than the tarot. Still, I have to admit that the class turned out better than I expected. We spent an hour getting acquainted with the cards and arranging them in various patterns. To explain the symbols of the suits—Cups, Wands, Swords, and Pentangles—Ruby showed us what she called her "ritual tools": a crystal chalice, a willow wand with an eagle feather, a bone-handled ritual knife with her name etched on the blade, a pottery bowl filled with coins.

As I watched Ruby's ritual, it dawned on me that we were practicing what a lot of people would call witchcraft, and that they'd undoubtedly accuse us of being witches. Despite that, I was intrigued by her theory—that playing with symbols taps an unconscious part of us that our everyday minds don't want to deal with, that our minds are afraid of and want to keep repressed. There are plenty of dark places inside me, and I'd probably be healthier if somebody turned on the lights. I keep Leatha—my mother—in one of those dark places. My childhood memories of her are blurred, as if I were seeing her underwater, but my adult anger and bitterness are sharp and painful. All that stuff you read about dysfunctional families? That's mine, dysfunctional to the core. Leatha was a lush and my father was on a perennial power trip. He went out of my life when he died ten years ago. She's still in it. At least, she'd like to be. I'd rather she wasn't. It's all very dark.

When the class was over, Pam Neely was the first to speak up. Pam is the first black woman to teach in CTSU's psych department, which doesn't give her an easy row to hoe, as we say in Texas. But she handles herself with grace and panache. Her classes are crowded and even the faculty lounge lizards act like humans when she drops in for coffee. She's also hung out her shingle as a psychologist.

"My unconscious has an urgent question to communicate," she said. "Is it time for dessert?"

"Rumor has it that somebody brought a peach pie," Mary Richards said. From Mary's introduction, I had learned that she teaches part time in the CTSU art department and devotes the rest of her time to jewelry-making. She was wearing a silver pendant in the shape of an ancient goddess symbol—a voluptuous female figure cradling a crescent moon.

"I brought the pie," I said. "Ruby and I picked the peaches in Fredericksburg last summer." Fredericksburg is a small town about eighty miles deeper into the Hill Country, famous for its pick-your-own orchards.

"I taught stretching classes at a nursing home there last year," Judith Cohen told me as we followed Ruby down the hall toward the kitchen. Judith is fifty-something, but you'd never know it from her lithe shape—a great advertisement for the yoga classes she teaches. She wears her graying hair pulled into a tight bun, giving her face an austere, sculptural look. "What I was teaching was really yoga, but no one figured that out."

"Right," Dottie Riddle chimed in. Dottie is the cat lady of Pecan Springs. Dozens of cats live with her, and she feeds countless strays around the university. She's one of Judith's students. "Some people think yoga is the devil's work, but if you call it stretching, they go for it."

In the kitchen, Ruby took out a stack of plates. "You can get away with murder as long as you don't say exactly what you're doing."

Sybil Rand gave a deep-throated laugh. "There are some things you can never get away with, around here at least."

Sybil had been a regular customer at the herb shop for the past year, but she'd never invited friendship. She was remote and disdainful, as if she wanted to be sure that people around her understood that she was different, special. She was in her late forties, with unruly dark hair and dramatic makeup that accentuated her hooded, deep-set eyes. Of all the members of the group, she looked most like the kind of person who might be interested in the occult. She was wearing black slacks, a black cowlnecked tunic, and a striking African necklace of carved wooden beads, animal teeth, and polished fragments of bone. I didn't know much about her, only that she lived at Lake Winds Resort Village—an exclusive, upscale development about five miles outside of town—and that she was married to C. W. Rand, the managing partner of the resort. I knew that she and Judith were friends, and that she collected unusual plants. I wondered if there was any connection between her interest in plants and her interest in the tarot.

Pam took a plate and headed for the kitchen table, which displayed the desserts. Pam is a petite woman with skin the color of a rich chocolate mousse. She speaks with a soft Georgia drawl that conceals an inner resourcefulness. "What couldn't you get away with, Sybil?"

For a moment, Sybil didn't answer. Then she lifted her chin and spoke in a throaty voice, cool, amused. "Poison," she said. The word dropped like a pebble into a quiet pool, and the silence widened in rings around it. Pam's eyebrows went up.

"I heard about that," I said after a moment. Sybil had entered her garden in the annual Pecan Springs Garden Club contest. When the jurors showed up to see it, they were horrified to learn that all those lovely plants were poisonous. I had the sneaking suspicion that they wouldn't have known if Sybil hadn't told them.

"I read in the paper that they gave you a prize anyway," Gretel Schumaker said. Gretel and her mother own the candle shop in the Craft Emporium, where they demonstrate the traditional art of dipping and carving folk-art candles. "But I forget what it was for."

Ruby poured mugs of coffee. "Most unique garden, wasn't it?" She grinned. "I guess they couldn't think of anything else. They probably don't have a category for the best poison plants or the most deadly design."

Judith took a coffee mug. "One of the judges told the newspaper that they should give Sybil the garden club's first Hemlock Award. It was probably meant to be a joke."

"Don't be too sure," Sybil said. She was sitting on a stool, separate from the rest of us around the table. It was a voluntary separation, I thought. The others would have been glad to include her, but she held them back with an energy that was almost visible. "They were insulted, I think. Especially Wanda Rathbottom."

"I'll bet you didn't buy any of those poison plants from Wanda," Gretel said. "That's probably what ticked her off." Wanda owns Wanda's Wonderful Acres, Pecan Springs' premier nursery. She only stocks sure sellers, summer and fall annuals, basic perennials, a few standby shrubs and trees—ho-hum plants. Most of the gardens in the contest were planted with Wanda's old reliables.

"What do you plant in a poison garden?" Dottie asked.

"More to the point," Pam asked curiously, "why?"

I knew what Sybil had planted, because I'd helped find some of the plants. I met her a year ago when she came into the shop looking for wolfsbane, a highly toxic member of the aconite family. In earlier times, wolfsbane was stuffed into chunks of meat to poison wolves. Humans sometimes ate the plant by accident—or by somebody else's evil design. The sixteenth-century English herbalist John Gerard suggested an antidote: victims of aconite poisoning might survive if they drank a mixture of olive oil, the juice of laurel berries, and the corpses of several dozen flies that had fed on aconite leaves. Because the flies usually weren't around when the emergency arose, there weren't many survivors who could vouch for Gerard's antidote. Aconite was a poison of choice for centuries, until 1882, when Dr. George Lamson was found guilty of slipping a hefty dose to his eighteen-year-old brother-in-law, Percy John. The trial record makes interesting reading, because the case was the first to rest on toxicological evidence. After Lamson's conviction, the use of aconite became somewhat more risky—from a would-be poisoner's point of view.

Sybil had also acquired several other choice items for her poison garden—oleander, lantana, mountain laurel, mistletoe, castor plants, water hemlock, jimsonweed, foxglove, death camus, delphinium, and belladonna. Attractive as they are, these are plants to be wary of. Children have died after eating lantana's pretty purple berries, which are loaded with a virulent alkaloid. Oleander, which concentrates the natural arsenic in the soil, is so toxic that a hot dog roasted on an oleander twig has been fatal. Another name for belladonna is deadly nightshade, and the death camus, a lilylike plant that grows wild along Texas roadsides, does just what it says it does—it kills.

Usually, of course, people don't give a second thought to these perfectly ordinary plants. I'd bet that members of the garden club own oleanders and mountain laurels and delphinium and don't suspect that they're toxic. But Sybil intentionally collected these deadly plants because they were poisonous. What's more, she had the audacity to enter them in the contest. It was the effrontery of the thing, I suspected, that had provoked the six good and true jurors of the Pecan Springs Garden Club and offended Wanda Rathbottom's respectable soul.

The silence had lengthened. Sybil stared unblinkingly at Pam. "Why poisonous plants?" she repeated.

"Why not?"

"I just meant," Pam said, unruffled, "that it's an unusual kind of collection." Deliberately, she sat down next to Sybil and smiled at her. Sybil didn't smile back.

"Actually, people have been collecting toxic plants for centuries," I said. I cut a wedge of Brie and added it to the apple on my plate. I really wanted a slice of my peach pie, but I felt obligated to leave it for the others. "The monastery gardens of the Middle Ages were full of them, mostly used for medicinal purposes. Digitalis comes from foxglove, for instance. It's a heart stimulant. Wolfsbane is used by Chinese physicians to treat rheumatism and pneumonia."

"Don't tell that to Wanda Rathbottom," Dottie remarked. "Her husband is a doctor. If people go around growing their own heart medicine, what'll happen to him?"

Ruby put out a plate of fruit. "I'm sure she thinks Sybil's about to cast a spell over Wanda's Wonderful Acres."

Everybody laughed, me included. But you can't blame the garden club. They are used to seeing red, white, and blue petunias planted in the shape of the American flag, not a collection of plants with enough poison to dispatch half the population of Pecan Springs.

"Speaking of witches," Mary said, "I'm having a women's Halloween party at my place out in Deadwood on Saturday night. Some of my Wiccan friends from Austin are coming. You're all invited."

"Wiccans?" Gretel asked apprehensively. "You mean, *real* witches?"

"They get lots of bad press," Mary said. "Wicca is a goddess religion that claims to go back to prehistoric time. What Wiccans call witchcraft is their religious liturgy. Their Samhain—that's the Wiccan New Year—coincides with our Halloween, and they celebrate it in a big way. Please wear costumes, the more outrageous the better. Ruby, I was hoping you'd give a few tarot readings for door prizes."

"Sure," Ruby said. "And China can bring some of her famous herbal incense."

Ruby's always volunteering me. But in this case, it sounded okay. I hadn't been to a party for a while, and I was ready. Anyway, I wanted to see what Wiccans were really like.

"I'll bring Samantha," Dottie said. "She loves parties." Samantha is one of Dottie's favorite cats, a stunning black creature with green eyes.

"I'll bring belladonna," Sybil offered with a cool smile. "It was used as an ingredient in witches' flying ointment."

"Hey," Gretel said, "you're really into that stuff, aren't you?"

If Sybil was growing belladonna herself, it would have to be indoors. The plant doesn't fare well in our hot, dry climate. And if she was going to the trouble of growing it indoors, she must really be into the "baneful" herbs. The leaves and root of *Atropa belladonna* contain tropane alkaloids, as do jimsonweed and henbane, deadly nightshades that grow in vacant city lots and along country roads. Belladonna was once used in magical practice to induce visions (its Old English name was dwale, or delusion)— hence its association with the sixteenth-century "flying oint- ments." It's also the herb Juliet's nurse gave her to keep her safe for Romeo, obviously in the wrong dose. Belladonna is a narcot- ic, and some sources suggest that witches condemned in the Inquisition surreptitiously swallowed it to help them doze through the fire. If Sybil was experimenting with the stuff, she'd better be careful. I'd read of dozens of tropane fatalities, includ- ing the mass poisoning of soldiers sent to Jamestown in 1676 to put down Bacon's Rebellion. They ate quantities of jimsonweed (a corruption of "Jamestown weed"), went crazy, and died. Tropane is nasty stuff.

"These witches don't fly," Mary said. "They're white witch- es—you know, good witches. Black witchcraft is the evil kind."

"Oh, yeah?" Pam asked dryly. "Well, *I'm* planning to go, so there'll be at least one black witch there." She looked at Dottie. "Do you rent black cats for the evening?"

"You can *have* one," Dottie said. "In fact, you can have two or three, if you'll give them a good home. I've got plenty of extras."

Ruby served herself a piece of Mary's chocolate cake. "I don't think the good ol' boys who hang out down at the Doughnut Queen can tell the difference between a white witch and a black witch."

"Want to bet?" Pam asked with a snicker.

"You know what I mean." Ruby perched on a stool with her cake and a mug of coffee. "And listen to the good ol' girls at Bobbie Rae's. As far as they're concerned, a witch is a witch is a witch, excuse me, Gertrude Stein."

"That's the mentality that inspired the Salem witch trials," Judith said.

"Salem?" Pam asked. "That was only the tip of the iceberg. Remember the Burning Times? In the fifteen hundreds, there were a couple of German towns where only one woman was left alive. The witch hunters burned all the rest."

"Makes you wonder about the one who was left, doesn't it?" Dottie said. "I'll bet all those witches had cats," she added somberly. "I wonder what they did to—"

"Do you mind if we talk about something else?" Gretel broke in hastily.

"Yeah," Ruby said. "Those days are gone."

Sybil's face was half in shadow. "Are you sure?"

An uncomfortable silence filled the kitchen while we all thought about the grand jury and the Ellis case. Then there was a burst of chatter as everybody started talking about something else. The conversation went on for another fifteen minutes. When the women had said good-bye and left, I helped Ruby wash up the dessert plates and coffee mugs, and we sat down to share the surviving piece of peach pie.

I glanced around the comfortable kitchen, bright with fresh paint and a new sink and countertop. Ruby had even replaced the old fluorescent light that used to make you look like a week-old corpse. The year before—almost exactly a year ago, in fact— she'd bought the house from Meredith Gilbert, whose mother Jo had been our very good friend. Jo had been murdered here, and I often wondered if Ruby was haunted—as I was—by the ghost of Jo's unfinished life. If so, Jo's ghost must have been thrilled. Ruby had papered the walls and stained the woodwork, refin- ished the oak floors, and painted the exterior in shades of gray and soft blue, with coral accents. She'd filled the house with antiques, some of which had been Jo's. Now, she was in the process of petitioning the Pecan Springs Heritage Society to add it to their register of historic homes. I smiled when I thought of New Age Ruby with her cards and crystals and Inner Guide, living in this gracious old house, surrounded by antique furniture. There was something marvelously paradoxical about the idea.

Ruby sat back and her face softened. "China," she said with the air of someone offering a piece of unexpected news, "I'm in love."

I sighed. By my count, Ruby has been in love at least twice a year since her divorce four years ago from Ward. Her last lover ran the computer at CTSU. They'd been going out for about six months when the guy got involved with a twenty-three-year-old blonde who worked for him. The girl was just two years older than Ruby's daughter, Shannon, a junior at the University of Texas this year. Ruby's heart had been shattered, but she was obviously on the mend.

"This time it's real, China," Ruby said. "It's Andrew."

As if I hadn't guessed. Andrew Drake, the photographer.

"He's wonderful," Ruby said. She wore a soft, pensive smile and her eyes were dreamy. "I think I've found my soul mate."

"Ruby," I said crisply, "your last soul mate married the girl in User Services. The one before that went back to his ex-wife, and the one before that—"

"I know, I know," Ruby said. "You don't have to rub it in. I've been working on becoming more aware of my codependency issues. I think I'm finally getting to the point where I can tell whether a relationship is healthy or toxic." She leaned forward. "This one has a lot of potential, astrologically speaking. My Cancer moon is just a few degrees off his Leo sun, in my eighth house."

I don't know enough about the stars to second-guess Ruby's astro-analyzing, but this one didn't sound quite right. "Since when are Cancer and Leo compatible? I thought water and fire didn't mix."

"Sure they do," Ruby said. "How else would you get steam? And the eighth house is all about sexuality, you know. When we're together, it's very volatile."

"It's just that I don't want you to go off the deep end again. I don't want you to get hurt. I'm running short of Kleenex."

I shut up. What gave me the right to give advice, even to my best friend? Where love was concerned, my own record wasn't anything to brag about. Maybe I was jealous of Ruby's ability to *feel* so deeply, to allow herself to be so fully involved with a man.

I'd had a number of scorching affairs, all of which began with wild enthusiasm but eventually perished from lack of proper care and feeding. I couldn't be the world's greatest lawyer and the world's greatest lover at the same time. Actually, I couldn't be a lawyer and anything else at the same time. The year before I quit, I billed fifty-eight hours a week on average, no padding—and that didn't include another twenty hours overhead. I had two sixty-day jury trials, one forty-five-day jury trial, and one bench trial—not to mention innumerable consultations, depositions, and hearings. No wonder I gave up sex. I almost didn't have the energy to go to the bathroom.

But my relational skills haven't noticeably improved since I stopped practicing law. When I moved to Pecan Springs, I promised myself I'd be open to a real relationship, commitment and all. Then McQuaid and I got involved in what seems like a healthy relationship, and while I'm a little less wary and a little more open, I still haven't been able to bring myself to commit. So maybe I don't *really* love him. Or maybe I do and don't know it. Maybe, in fact, I haven't yet figured out what love is. I guess there's no law that says you learn how to love just by getting a little seniority.

That's why I stopped offering Ruby advice on how to manage her affairs, pushed back my chair, and stood up. So did she. "Thanks for tonight's lesson, Ruby. With a little practice, I might even get in touch with my unconscious."

Ruby bent down and enveloped me in a sisterly hug, companionable and loving. I felt once again, as I often do, that maybe *we* are soul mates.

"Maybe there's hope for you yet," she said.

✳ ✳ ✳

I enjoy riding my bike along Pecan Springs streets after dark. Living room lights are on and people don't always draw their drapes, maybe because they want the neighbors to see the new piano or the painting they bought at the last Starving Artists show up in Austin. So I glance inside as I ride to see what the residents do with themselves at night. Most, of course, are watching TV or reading the newspaper or talking on the telephone. Once I saw a man building a ship in a bottle. The scenes are tranquil, pleasant, peaceful—boring, McQuaid would say. Ordinary life in an ordinary small town.

It was peaceful tonight, too. Except that Shorty Ennis, who lives by himself in an unpainted frame house at the corner of Vine and Mayberry, was drinking out of his bottle instead of building a ship in it. From the look of him, it wasn't the first bottle of the day. Three blocks down Mayberry, I surprised two boys smashing a jack-o'-lantern on somebody's front steps, and when I rode past, one heaved a hunk of it at me. At the corner of Mayberry and Crockett, a trio of teenaged ghosts, trick-or-treaters, were spraying pentagrams on car windows with aerosol shaving soap, inspired by witches, no doubt. I yelled at them and they scattered down the dark alley, but I knew they'd be back the minute I'd gone.

Ah, peace. Ah, tranquility. Ordinary life in an ordinary small town.

Thyme and Seasons Herb Company opens for business at nine, when I put the cash tray in the register, get out the herb snacks and tea, and move racks of potted herbs out to the sidewalk. The building that houses the shop is built of square-cut white limestone, with terra-cotta floors, pine ceilings, and massive hand-hewn beams, cut from cypress trees that grew a hundred years ago along the Pecan River. It was remodeled before I bought it by a bright young architect who saved the best and fixed the worst. I live in four comfortable rooms at the back—a large kitchen, a bedroom, a workroom that used to be an office, and a living room, all with stone walls, wide-planked wood floors, and pine ceilings supported by heavy cypress beams. There's a large second-floor loft where I hang drying herbs. Out back by the alley, a remodeled stone stable serves as a guest cottage.

Thyme and Seasons is small, so every square inch has to work. The ceiling is hung with bundles of dried herbs, ropes of red peppers, braids of garlic, and handcrafted wreaths. Wooden shelves along the walls hold glass jars full of bulk herbs and a great variety of herb products—vinegars, jellies, seasonings, soaps, herbal cosmetics, potpourri, incense, oils, teas. The corners are full of baskets filled with statice and baby's breath, multicolored strawflowers, velvety cockscomb, the papery globes of nigella, creamy poppy pods. The front door is always decorated with something seasonal—in honor of Halloween I hung a witch's broom decorated with Indian corn, wheat, miniature pumpkins, and bright orange-red pyracanthus berries. Outside, clay pots overflow with thyme and basil and rosemary, and the front yard is a patchwork of fragrant herb beds. Autumn is a busy time, and sales pick up in mid-October as people start to think about cooking and decorating for the winter season.

By nine thirty on Wednesday morning, I'd waited on a half-dozen customers. People shop here because it reminds them of the good old days before bar codes and shrink wrap. In my opinion, shrink wrap is designed to keep me from seeing that the strawberries on the bottom are rotten. Bar codes are more insidious. By the time I get to the check-out, I've forgotten the price. Something tells me that this is exactly what the Big Thrif-T execs are counting on. That's why I shop at Cavette's Grocery, the third-generation family market at the corner of Guadalupe and Green. Old Mr. Cavette uses a set of antique ink stamps to mark each item. Junior, the youngest Mr. Cavette, heaps all the strawberries in a basket and invites you to pick out the ones you want. The ones nobody wants, he feeds to his chickens.

At ten, Ruby opened the Crystal Cave. Her shop is the same size as mine, with a connecting door. It's stocked with New Age books, tapes, crystals, jewelry, goddess sculptures, star charts, kaleidoscopes—what she calls "tools for expanding consciousness." The air is filled with the fragrance of my best incense and the soothing sound of meditative music. Ruby doesn't have any competition in Pecan Springs, and she usually does a brisk business. This morning, she spent the first hour tending to a flock of customers. As I glanced through the connecting door I caught glimpses of Dottie Riddle buying a tarot deck, a couple of pony-tailed college students (male), and a middle-aged lady in an expensive-looking suit, nervously glancing over her shoulder while she asked sotto voce about astrology books.

One of the nice things about having two stores in the same building is that one person can oversee both, which helps to combat the claustrophobia you feel when you're behind the counter for eight hours at a stretch. Sometimes Ruby takes over for me, sometimes I take over for her. This morning, we both wanted to go to Andrew's grand opening, so we asked Laurel Wiley, a student in my herb classes, to look after both stores. About eleven, we headed next door to the Craft Emporium.

The three-story Victorian that houses the Emporium used to be the opulent home of the owner of the Covenant Trust Savings and Loan, which floated belly-up along with numerous other Texas thrifts. Constance Letterman bought it in a foreclosure sale six years ago and turned the large, high-ceilinged rooms into shop spaces for ten or so tenants. Gretel and her mother have the candle shop on the first floor, in what used to be the best parlor. On the other side of the hall, in the second-best parlor, Clarissa Owens sells vintage clothing—forties and fifties dresses, plastic jewelry, beaded purses. Behind Clarissa is the old dining room where Andrew Drake was opening his new photography studio, Faces. That's where Peter Dudley used to have his Depression glassware shop. A few months ago, Peter reduced his inventory and moved upstairs to the nursery.

A new business is a big deal in Pecan Springs, and people were jammed elbow to elbow in the old dining room, which had been elegantly updated with a gray and mauve color scheme, trendy chrome furniture, and Andrew's artistically spotlighted photographs. I saw Mayor Pauline Perkins talking to Helen Jenson, owner of Jenson's Travels and president of the Chamber of Commerce. Madeline Martin, the manager of the Book Nook, was discussing the drought with Oscar Perkins, owner of the Packsaddle Motel, and Herschel Schwartz, president of Hill Country Fidelity Bank. Jerri Greene, of Jerri's Health and Fitness Spa, was talking hair with Roxanne Spivey of Mane Attraction. (Roxanne trims mine once every two months and keeps pestering me to do something to liven up the brown and cover the wide swathe of gray at my left temple.) The other Emporium tenants were there, and Constance too, wearing a strawberry red tent dress with three or four loops of what looked like gilded dog chain around her neck. She was ladling lemonade punch and doling out cookies at the refreshments table. A little sign in front of the cookie tray said "Cookies by Adele's Sweet Shop." Whoever made the punch must have wanted to remain anonymous.

"You'd never know this used to be a dining room," I told Ruby, as Constance poured my punch and handed me two oatmeal cookies. "Lester Kyle did a nice job with those lights." But Ruby had deserted me. I spotted her standing next to Andrew.

"I'll say this for Andrew Drake," Constance remarked, "his taste isn't all in his mouth. Money doesn't seem to be an object, either." She rolled her eyes in the direction of the former kitchen. "You should see the equipment back there—cameras, lights, the whole works. He must of put ten thousand dollars in that old kitchen." She nodded toward the bank president. "Probably got it at Fidelity, and Herschel came to see what he spent it on."

"Do you think Andrew will make it?" I asked. "It's not exactly an economic boom time." I thought unhappily about my own bottom line.

"He'd better make it," Constance said. "His rent's due the first of ever' month." Constance rides herd on her tenants like a cowboy minding a bunch of irresponsible dogies.

The object of our speculation, Andrew Drake, was making small talk with the mayor, while Ruby looked on adoringly. If she was after good looks she'd found the right man. Andrew was six feet plus, with an engaging smile, a perfect nose, and brown hair cut fashionably long and (I'd bet) sprayed to keep its shape. He wore a pale gray turtleneck, a darker gray sport jacket, and elegantly tailored gray slacks. Among Pecan Springs' males, Andrew's haute couture definitely made him different.

I was studying Andrew and Ruby and wondering whether they were really soul mates or whether Ruby had been misled by a pretty face when Bob Godwin came up beside me. Bob owns Lillie's Place, a bar and grill a couple of blocks up Guadalupe. He's in his late forties, a Vietnam vet with thick reddish hair, eyebrows like two furry red caterpillars, and a tattooed spider on one hefty forearm. He wore Levi's, scuffed cowboy boots, and a disgruntled look on his rugged, pockmarked face. "It wouldn't of been so bad," he said gloomily, "if it wasn't my *favorite* goat." He scowled as he looked for an ashtray. "They didn't need to of kilt him."

"Killed him?" Bob has a habit of starting conversations in *medias res*. I always feel as if I've skipped the first paragraph or two.

"Leroy," he said. He leaned over and drowned his Camel in the half inch of lemonade in the bottom of my plastic glass. "Slit his throat. Hung him up by his heels and let him drip."

"Slit his *throat*?"

Bob shoved both hands into his pockets and rocked back and forth on his heels. "Ask me, it was them damn Mes'can witches. Built a altar in the shed, stuck a buncha white candles and white feathers around, left some quarters and a half dollar on a coupla white plates. Guess they picked Leroy because he was black." He gave a short laugh. "Guess bein' black is unlucky for goats, too."

"I guess," I said. Bob lives about two miles out of town with a golden retriever named Budweiser and twelve goats. Eleven now, I supposed.

"Ol' Bud, he didn't even bark. Guess he's gettin' kinda hard a hearin'. He'll be lonesome. Leroy was his favorite goat. Mine too. Allus hung out at the fence to get his ears rubbed."

"I'm sorry," I said sincerely. I stop at Lillie's Place a couple of times a week, mainly because I like Bob. He's basically a bigot, but if you can get past that, he's a nice enough guy, trying to make an honest buck. I wasn't personally acquainted with Leroy, and his death probably wasn't any more barbaric than the deaths of animals we kill for food. But living alone the way he does, Bob's attached to his animals. His sadness made me sad, and angry.

Constance came up. "Is it true what I hear about your goat, Bob?" She whipped out a small notebook, frowning. "Sounds like Santeria."

"Yeah," Bob agreed morosely. "Damn Mes'can witches."

Constance took out a pencil. "Mrs. Peters found a dead pigeon in the alley behind her toolshed yesterday. It was missin' a head, and there were dimes and quarters scattered around it."

The news about Leroy was disturbing, especially given all the suspicious gossip about witches, but I wasn't surprised to hear that there were Santeros in town. The barrio is on the east side of town, squeezed along the Interstate. Quite a few of the families have been here as long as the town and, for better or worse, have been Anglicized. Tex-Mex. But in recent years, increasing numbers of illegal aliens have slipped across the Rio Grande, fleeing the grinding poverty and political oppression south of the border. A lot of the locals look down on the wetbacks, although they're perfectly willing to exploit them as cheap labor whenever they can get by with it. This is a subject I have strong feelings about. A few years ago, Immigration set up certain conditions under which longtime illegals could apply for resident alien status. Until that amnesty expired, I worked as a volunteer in the program that Sarita Gonzales ran through the Guadalupe Methodist Church, helping longtime undocumenteds qualify for resident status. Sarita's husband Rogelio is the Methodist minister. He ministers to people's souls. Sarita ministers to their lives. Sarita's ministry seems to make a bigger difference.

Sarita told me about Santeria, which in Spanish means "worship of the saints." It's a mixture of Catholic and native ritual involving occult practices that smack of witchcraft. One of these practices is animal sacrifice, so it was probably Santeros who slaughtered Leroy. A few years back, they had done something much worse than that. A pretty blond tourist in a Mexican border town was abducted and ritually murdered by the members of a cult called Palo Mayombe, the dark side of Santeria. They were

narcotics smugglers who believed that their sacrifice would keep
them from getting caught. It didn't. But by that time, the pretty
young blonde was horribly dead, and the rituals surrounding her
murder had made one or two true-crime writers horribly rich.

"I dunno why you wanna put this shit in the paper," Bob
told Constance. "People read it, they figger it'd be a kick to copy
it. I don't aim to lose me another goat."

"But people *have* to be informed," Constance said. "It's your
civic duty, Bob, especially right now, when everybody's in such
an all-fired panic about Leota and the Ellis boy." She leaned forward, her pencil poised. "What color was your goat?"

I was heading for a clean glass and more lemonade when I
was intercepted by Pauline Perkins, who recently announced
that she planned to run for an unprecedented fourth term as
mayor. I usually see Pauline pounding the treadmill at Jerri's
Health and Fitness Spa, where we're both trying to lose weight.
Pauline's more determined than I am. For years, job stress and
never having time to eat kept my weight down. Now, I'm less
stressed, happier, and ten pounds heavier. I'd say it's a fair trade.

Pauline came forward eagerly, swathed in smiles. She had
good news, and I was going to hear it whether I wanted to
or not.

"We've done it, China, we've actually *done* it!" She clamped a
hand on my arm so I couldn't get away and turned to Helen
Jenson, a step behind her. "Haven't we, Helen?"

"Absolutely." Helen agreed, splendid in her royal blue
Chamber of Commerce blazer, the gilt president's patch on her
breast pocket gleaming like an heraldic emblem.

"That's great," I said. "What have we done?"

"Pecan Springs has just been named as a finalist in the City
Square Program!" Pauline said. "The site visit team will be in
town next week."

The City Square Program is one of those state-funded opera-
tions that, under the guise of a competition, doles out large sums
of money for such significant downtown renovations as erecting

a gazebo and building a public potty on the square. Pecan Springs had been turned down twice, much to the personal chagrin of the mayor and City Council. It was my theory that all they had to do was put Pecan Springs on the waiting list and hang out until the powers that be eventually got down to it. Since this was go-around number three, I figured that the town's number was probably due to come up this year, and all the mayor had to do was hold out her hat for the money. But both Pauline and Helen appeared to be taking the competition seriously.

Helen fastened gray eyes on me. "We'd like your help, China. Could you host a Dutch-treat lunch for the team a week from Friday?"

"Sure," I agreed. I wanted to help. With all its quirks and oddities, and setting aside what had happened to Bob's favorite goat (which could have happened anywhere), Pecan Springs is a fine little town.

"Thanks," Helen said, turning to leave. "My assistant will call you to confirm."

Pauline clamped my arm more tightly so I couldn't follow Helen. The woman has incredible strength in her fingers, probably from squeezing voters' hands. "I do hope you realize, China, how terribly important this competition is to Pecan Springs' economic prosperity. The Council and the Chamber have put in simply *untold* hours to make sure that our bid isn't overlooked again. Another defeat would deal an absolutely fatal blow to the town's hopes."

I wanted to tell her that she was dealing an absolutely fatal blow to the circulation in my forearm, but I didn't. I turned up the corners of my mouth and assured her that I would do my utmost to see that Pecan Springs got the attention it deserved from the site visit committee. I stopped short of promising to vote for her, but she let go anyway.

"Thank you, China," Pauline said. There were white marks on my arm from her fingers. "I knew we could count on you.

Oh, RuthAnn," she shrilled, turning from me to her next victim, "have you heard the news?"

Showing better reflexes, RuthAnn Landsdowne stepped back out of Pauline's reach. "I've already agreed to help," she said. "You asked the garden club to furnish the team's motel rooms with fresh flowers. Remember?" RuthAnn is president of the garden club.

"Yes, of course," Pauline said. "Just don't let Sybil Rand help," she added, smiling to signal that she was making a joke. "She might stick something fatal in among the roses. Oh, Howie!" she called, and hurried away to twist somebody else's arm.

"It's Sybil I want to talk to you about, China," RuthAnn said. She glanced around to make sure we weren't overheard. "I suppose somebody's told you about her entry in the garden club contest."

"Actually," I said, "Sybil told me herself."

RuthAnn is a square-faced woman with hefty arms and shoulders. She's usually willing to wade into a fight for a good cause. But this morning she looked as if she'd met her match. "I voted to give her the Most Unique Garden award," she said, "but Wanda Rathbottom felt like Sybil was just thumbing her nose at us. Wanda wants to make a rule that nobody can enter poisonous plants in the contest. You're a plant expert, China. What do you think?"

Just at that moment I spotted Sybil herself, moving through the crowd. She was wearing a flowing black and gold top over skintight black pants, and her slender arm was heavy with gold bracelets. She moved with the purpose and grace of a jaguar. She was headed for Andrew and Ruby.

"I'm an herbalist, not a plant toxicologist," I said, my eye on Sybil, "but I think Wanda's overreacting. A lot of common garden plants will make you sick if you snack on them. Iris bulbs are poisonous, for instance. So is larkspur. So are bluebonnets."

"Bluebonnets!" RuthAnn's eyes got big. The bluebonnet is

the state flower. Telling a Texan that bluebonnets are poisonous is like saying that Christmas trees make you sterile.

"It's the alkaloids that cause the trouble," I said. "I've never heard of a person who died, but livestock can get sick just from eating the seeds." Sybil had reached Andrew. She spoke briefly to Ruby. Then she put her braceleted hand on Andrew's arm, leaned close, and said something in his ear. She moved lazily, but there was an underlying tautness, like muscles rippling under a cat's fur. My instincts jangled. Something was going on here.

"Why, China, I never imagined!" RuthAnn said. "And Wanda just donated twenty pounds of seed so the Lions Club can plant bluebonnets for their Adopt-a-Highway project."

"The seeds won't hurt you if you don't eat them," I said. "But maybe you'd better tell Wanda. Not everything is what it seems."

"Oh, dear," RuthAnn sighed. "Yes, I suppose you're right. I have to tell her. She'll be so upset." Shaking her head, she hurried off in search of Wanda Rathbottom.

I looked back at Sybil and Andrew. They had left Ruby standing alone and were walking together toward the old kitchen, Sybil's black shoulder familiarly brushing the gray sleeve of Andrew's sport coat, an inscrutable smile on her face.

I got my lemonade and went to join Ruby. "Everything okay?" I asked.

"Of course," Ruby said airily, not looking at me. "Sybil and Andrew have some sort of business arrangement. They went to discuss it."

"Oh, I see," I said. If Ruby was worried, she didn't want to talk about it. But then maybe she wasn't. The old saying "Love is blind" definitely applies to Ruby. Roxanne came up to remind me that I was due for a trim, and we got into a discussion of Ruby's last perm, which had turned out exceptionally frizzy, making her look even more like Little Orphan Annie. Then Arlene joined us, of Arlene's Beautiful Nails, and Ruby, Roxanne, and Arlene talked fingernails. I concealed mine, which are short, with ragged cuticles. I spend a lot of time digging in the dirt.

Andrew reappeared, without Sybil, and it was time to start the ceremony. Helen, on behalf of the Chamber, told us how wonderful it was that a new business was bringing jobs and prosperity to Pecan Springs and announced that it was time to cut the ribbon. Constance scurried for her camera, and we went out to the sidewalk in front of the Emporium and lined up behind Andrew, handsomely photogenic and a little bored. The mayor, beaming, handed him a pair of large hedge clippers. Andrew and Helen each took one of the handles. "Say cheese!" Constance cried merrily. We squinted into the sun as Andrew and Helen whacked at the red ribbon with the hedge clippers and Constance clicked the shutter.

Gretel Schumaker nudged me as Constance was taking another photo. "What's that going on in front of your shop, China?"

I looked where Gretel was pointing. Picketers, about a dozen of them, were parading in a tight circle on the sidewalk. But it was Ruby's shop they were picketing. They carried hand-lettered signs that said things like "Witches Do the Devil's Work" and "Tarot Is Black Magic." They were being encouraged by a short, plump, balding man in an immaculate white suit, white tie, white belt, and white shoes. He stood in a shiny white Jeep with white vinyl seats parked at the curb, exhorting the marchers with emphatic arm gestures, like a drum major leading a parade. The bumper sticker read "120,000 Texans Died Last Year. Are YOU Right With the Lord?"

"Who," Ruby asked incredulously, staring at the fat man in the Jeep, "is he?"

"You don't know?" Gretel pursed her lips. "Where've you been for the last year, Ruby? That's the Reverend Billy Lee Harbuck."

"That rat," I said feelingly.

"Yeah," Gretel said. "I hate to say it about a preacher, but that one's a jerk. He was in charge of the bunch that tried to shut down the abortion clinic where my sister works. And he and his pickets closed down poor Mr. Bixby's drugstore. He's out to make a name for himself, I guess. Have you seen his billboard on I-35?"

The billboard featured a flattering likeness of Billy Lee, holding a white Bible against his heart. A large caption demanded "Who Is on the Lord's Side?" Under that was the Reverend's name and his church, the Everlasting Faith Bible Church. I'd also seen him on the Channel 24 six o'clock news, being arrested at the Austin abortion clinic and hauled off, dragging his heels and vowing to fight to the death.

But today, the Reverend Billy Lee Harbuck was very much alive. And from the look of things, Ruby had made it to the top of his hit list.

I am not a fan of *Playboy* and *Hustler*. They reflect our culture's attitude that bodies (and not just women's bodies, either!) are objects to be used. But I am a very big fan of free speech. Last spring, when the pickets lined up in front of Bixby's Drugstore, I offered Mr. Bixby my help. In my mind, the matter was complicated. Under the First Amendment, the demonstrators had a right to express their opinions about the magazines. Under the same law, Mr. Bixby's customers had an equally compelling right to read those magazines. And Mr. Bixby had the right to sell them, especially since he kept them under the counter and didn't peddle them to kids. But Mr. Bixby was seventy-six and getting a little shaky. The whole thing unnerved him so much that he decided to close the drugstore. A month later, his heart quit.

That was one reason why, when I opened the shop at nine on Thursday morning to find a dozen of Billy Lee's followers marching up and down the sidewalk with their signs, I was very ticked off. They were careful to leave ample room for people to pass, but that didn't make me feel any kindlier toward them—especially when I saw the sign that read "Satan Worshippers Kill Goats," under a crude drawing of a black goat hanging by its heels. A couple of pedestrians gazed at it apprehensively, and Vida Plunkett, mowing the little patch of grass in front of her house, gave me a dark look.

I was a member of the tarot class that was being called "Satan worshippers," and I didn't think it was funny. I invited the young man under the sign to tell me on what factual basis he described me as a Satan worshipper and a goat-killer. When he hemmed and hawed, I suggested that he consult with the church's attorney on the difference between free speech and slander. If he didn't, I would, and we'd see about getting an injunction, as fast as you could say "hell and damnation." The sign disappeared.

But the pickets didn't. At nine forty the Reverend pulled up in his white Jeep. In his white suit, his head pink and shiny, he looked like a bald Colonel Sanders. He stood on the front seat to lead a chorus of "Onward Christian Soldiers," while a woman in the backseat played a portable battery-operated keyboard. Unfortunately, they weren't singing loudly enough to disturb the peace.

Ruby came in the back way just as the choir started the last verse. In black silk oriental pajamas with a red sash and red sandals with two-inch heels, she looked more like a geisha than a witch.

"Isn't there anything we can do?" she asked, as they began to sing "Save us from the powers of darkness." "Sue them or have them arrested or something?"

I gave Ruby the same answer I'd given Mr. Bixby. "Our hands are pretty much tied, as long as they don't block the sidewalk or disturb the peace or carry slanderous signs."

"What's a slanderous sign?"

"A sign that says something specifically nasty and that is false or unproven. 'Ruby Wilcox Is a Witch,' for instance. I made them get rid of the worst one."

Ruby gnawed at her lower lip. "Do you think they'll keep customers away?"

"I hope not," I said fervently. "But I guess it depends on the customer." I glanced out the window. "It doesn't look like they've stopped Helen Jenson."

Helen was severe in a tailored navy suit with her Chamber
of Commerce pin on the lapel. "Who are all those screwballs out
front?" she demanded.

"It's Billy Lee Harbuck's bunch," Ruby said. "They're
demonstrating against the tarot class."

"They've got us confused with witches," I said.

"Witches!" Helen gave an disgusted snort. "Don't talk to me
about witches. I was jogging in the park early this morning and I
stumbled across a pile of chickens with no heads. Where's this
going to end, is what I want to know."

"What did you do?" Ruby asked.

"Why, I called the police, of course. Somebody's got to put a
stop to this sort of thing, or the town's going to get a bad name.
Chief Harris said it was Santeros. They'd built an altar out of a
cardboard box, and there were coins scattered around."

"Brace yourself, Ruby," I said. "They'll probably accuse us
of sacrificing chickens."

Ruby did not smile.

Helen turned to me with a back-to-business look. "China, do
you have any more rosemary-tarragon vinegar? And while
you're at it, Mother wants some of that no-salt seasoning blend
you make. She sneaks it on her food when the nurses are looking
the other way." Helen's mother lives in a nursing home in Waco.
If she can't get along without that seasoning, it must be good.

A few minutes after Helen left, Jerri Greene and her sister,
Rita, came up the walk, heading for Ruby's shop. Jerri, who runs
Jerri's Health and Fitness Spa, was wearing a red sweatsuit, her
blond hair snugged into a ponytail. Jerri is dynamic and attractive, proof that a woman can have muscles *and* a great figure.
She aims to make her mark on the world by getting you in
shape. When you've had a workout in one of her classes, you
know you've had a workout. Her younger sister Rita is shy and
plain, with anxious brown eyes behind blue plastic-rimmed
glasses, neat brownish-blond hair, and a strained smile. She fades
into the background when Jerri's around, but there's something

about her that suggests tight control, as if she's clamped down on some part of herself. Maybe it's the part that would like to copy her sister.

"Guess I'd better open up," Ruby said, going to the connecting door. "Jerri and Rita may be the only two customers I'll have all day, considering what's happening out front."

At that moment, the Reverend Billy Lee was telling his rapt flock that Halloween was anything but the harmless holiday it seemed.

"It's a day to worship WITCHCRAFT," he bellowed. "It's an infamous day, the DEVIL'S day, a day the righteous must eschew!" He pointed at the broom hanging on the front door of my shop. "Looka that broom, brethren! It's the symbol of WITCHES! What else do good Bible-fearin' folk need to prove that this is the Devil's very own workshop, right in the middle of our fair city?"

A chorus of fervent amens rose from the picketers. Billy Lee pulled off his white coat. His shirt was soaked. It was a cool day, but he was hot stuff. Uncharitably, I prayed for a stroke.

I turned away from the window. There was no point in wasting time watching the circus. If I didn't have any customers, I could hang the new batch of fall wreaths my wreath lady had delivered. The silvery artemisia was particularly nice this year, and the wreaths were decorated with pink and mauve amaranth, beebalm, yarrow, and soft furry gray leaves of lamb's ears. They filled the shop with their fragrance. I like to make wreaths, but I never have time to make enough for the entire winter season. So I depend on other people—many of them students in my herb classes—to make them for me. They're big sellers, especially between Thanksgiving and Christmas, along with such wonderful wreath books as Carol Taylor's *Herbal Wreaths* and her *Christmas Naturals*, both of which are beautifully illustrated.

I was climbing down the ladder when I noticed that the chanting had died away. I went to the window to see Bubba Harris talking to the Reverend. Then the crowd parted like the Red Sea, and Bubba passed through. He was carrying a plastic bag.

Bubba has been the Pecan Springs chief of police for the better part of a decade. He is a slow-talking, slow-walking, beefy good ol' boy. It's easy to underestimate him because he looks like a B-movie sheriff—cocked Stetson, battered cowboy boots, beer belly, unlit cigar plugged into one side of his face. But Bubba has a reputation for kicking ass and taking names. Not much happens in this town that he doesn't know about.

Me, for instance. Thyme and Seasons had been open a week when Bubba showed up to warn me against making claims about the healing properties of herbs, which in his book amounts to practicing medicine without a license. He went away a little bent out of shape, probably because he wasn't used to going one-on-one with a female who talks law. We tangled again a year ago, when he thought he'd found a killer and I thought he was wrong. Since then, we've struck an uneasy peace. We speak to one another, we even make occasional conversation, but there's a certain armed wariness between us. As far as Bubba is concerned, I'm an uppity ex-lawyer who's too big for her britches. As for me, it used to be my business to challenge the judgment of law enforcement officers. I haven't shed that adversarial point of view. Maybe I never will.

Bubba rolled his soggy cigar to the other side of his jowly face. "That bunch out there causin' you any trouble?" Bubba may not like me much, but he's got a strong sense of social order. Part of his job is the defense of free trade. The pickets out front were challenging my right as a tax-paying merchant to make money. That gets his back up.

"They're not making life any easier," I said. "But much as I hate to admit it, they've got a right. The minute they step over the line, I'll let you know."

"Yeah, I reckon you will." Bubba pulled his black eyebrows together in a bushy V and gave me a narrow-eyed glance. "You know what this is?" He dropped a gallon-sized plastic bag on the counter. In it was stuffed a large wilted plant, roots and all.

I took the plant out of the bag. It had a hairy stem and alternate leaves, divided into three to five coarsely toothed segments, like parsley. It was too late in the year for the characteristic chalk-yellow flowers, but the plant had a single stem of seedheads in a cluster of four erect pods about a half inch long. I opened a pod and spilled the seeds into my hand. They were brown and irregularly shaped, with deep, flangelike wrinkles.

"*Aconitum vulparia*," I said. "Wolfsbane. Where'd you get it?"

"In the park. Beside a pile of dead chickens. The chickens belonged to Miz Bragg, who ain't too pleased that they're dead, especially the rooster. She says that ain't her plant, though."

"It isn't." I hesitated. Mrs. Bubba was vice president of the garden club, and she'd tell him tonight when he got home. I might as well tell him first. "Check with Sybil Rand. The plant might have come from her garden."

"How d'you figger that? I don't see no owner's I.D."

"Wolfsbane isn't exactly a common plant. People usually don't cultivate it, and it doesn't grow wild here. But Sybil Rand has a few plants."

Bubba chewed his cigar. "Oh, yeah. The poison garden. Missus told me about that." He frowned. "This plant, wolfwhatever. It's poisonous?"

"Yes. Very."

Bubba stared at the plant with suspicion. He glanced at me, and I saw the question coming. "Sybil Rand, she practice Santeria?"

"I doubt it. But you'd better ask her." I could guess just how far Bubba would get with Sybil. He'd be called out before he got halfway to first base. It was odd, though. Had some Santero pulled up the wolfsbane to use it in a ritual, or was somebody trying clumsily to implicate Sybil in the slaughter of Mrs. Bragg's chickens? Either way, I was sure that Sybil was home free. Even Bubba couldn't believe that she was the type to hang out with Santeros and dead chickens.

Bubba scooped up the plant and stuffed it back in the bag. "Kinda dumb to grow somethin' that can kill people, 'specially these days, with all this Satanic crap goin' around. 'Less o'course you're plannin' to use it." He gave a narrow-eyed glance at the jars and bottles on the shelves. "Any of this stuff poisonous?"

"Some of it." I shrugged. "But then, so are bluebonnets."

"Bluebonnets?" Bubba was dumbfounded. His mouth dropped open and his cigar clung tenuously to his lower lip. "You gotta be shittin' me."

"No shit," I said. "Don't eat the bluebonnets."

The rest of the morning was uneventful—and miserably unprofitable. The gang outside went for lunch in shifts, the Reverend came back in a fresh white shirt for another round of haranguing and hymn-singing, and when Ruby and I closed up for the day, we had only a few dollars to show for it.

"I never would've thought a few pickets could make such a difference," Ruby said, counting her receipts. She zipped the pittance into her bank bag. "This is peanuts, but I might as well take it to the bank. Want me to make your deposit too?"

"There's not enough to deposit. I guess I'll blow it on dinner. It's my turn to treat McQuaid. Want to join us for an early one?" McQuaid had a meeting at eight. There was a big law enforcement conference at the university next week, and he was in charge. I hadn't seen much of him in the past couple of weeks.

"Okay if I bring Andrew? He's working tonight too, but we planned to take time out to eat together."

"Sure." I couldn't help being curious about Andrew, especially after witnessing the little scene he and Sybil had played. But maybe my curiosity was more like suspicion. I care about Ruby, who is trusting and almost too susceptible, and I hate the thought of another man playing kickball with her heart. "Lillie's Place, six thirty."

"Sounds good," Ruby said. She tucked the money bag into her purse and headed for the door. "See you."

✳ ✳ ✳

Lillie's is less than a block from the shop, but I had an errand to run before dinner so I drove. I parked out front and went in. The crowd was the usual—some tourists, families with kids catching an early dinner, a few quarrelsome university types arguing faculty politics, and a herd of fake cowboys swigging beer at the bar. There aren't many real ones around here because the Hill Country is too rough for cattle ranching, but there are plenty of guys who dress the part—Wranglers, yoked shirts with pearl buttons, boots, George Strait hats. You can tell they're phonies because they wear trophy belt buckles the size of Cadillac hubcaps. (A real rodeo cowboy doesn't wear his hard-won trophy buckles—he hangs them from the rearview mirror in his pickup.) Bob waved at me as I came in, then went to feed more coins into the jukebox, which was wailing some early Flatt and Scruggs. Lillie's is a down-home place.

McQuaid looked up as I sat down. "What's the excitement over at your place?"

"It's Billy Lee Harbuck and his bunch," I said. "From the Everlasting Faith Bible Church. He thinks Ruby and I are witches."

McQuaid grinned. "Maybe he's right." He sat back with his beer and planted his boots on a chair. Lillie's Place is like that. You can put your feet wherever you want. The wooden tables and chairs are scarred and splintered, and some of the initials carved in the tabletops go back twenty years or more. Before the place was called Lillie's, it used to be Bean's Bar and Grill. The owner decided to fancy it up, so she changed the name, tacked posters of Lillie Langtry to the walls, and hung ferns over the bar. When she went to live with her daughter in Del Rio, Bob bought the place. He says he's sick of the posters and he can't remember to water the ferns, and anyway, it's too dark over the bar for anything to grow. He's going to take everything down and go back to Bean's.

"Harbuck's a pain in the butt," I said, reaching for one of Bob's nachos, gooey with Velveeta and ablaze with jalapeños. "A grand total of five people came into the shop today, counting Bubba. And he didn't spend any money, just my time."

I glanced at McQuaid and felt my insides go soft. He was very sexy in Levi's, a white shirt with the sleeves loosely rolled, and polished boots—de rigueur evening wear in Pecan Springs. We've been seeing one another for two-plus years, and you'd think the attraction would have worn off by now. But even in a crowd, there's a powerful energy that makes the space between us crackle. He reached for my hand and I felt charged, as if I were wired to his body circuits and somebody had bumped up the current a notch or two. I may have trouble making an emotional commitment, but I certainly don't have any problems with my physical response. It's instinct. A terrific turn-on.

He squeezed my hand and let it go. McQuaid isn't big on public displays of affection. "You're looking good tonight, China. New dress?"

"Not exactly," I said, "but new to me." I wasn't surprised that he asked, because he's used to seeing me in jeans and tee shirt. But I'd stumbled across this 1950s sundress in Clarissa's Vintage Boutique—blue-and-white checked gingham, with a low-cut square neck and a gathered skirt, with ruffles, yet—and I'd had to have it. "I wore it because I needed a lift, after what happened today. Or what didn't happen," I said morosely, thinking about the empty bank deposit bag. The Reverend might not be able to work any real miracles, but he could turn black ink to red without trying very hard.

"Hang in there," McQuaid said comfortingly. "Harbuck's a publicity hound. I'm sure he'll find bigger fish to fry than a local witch."

"What's this about frying a local witch?" Ruby asked. Andrew pulled out a chair for her and she sat down.

"In a manner of speaking," McQuaid said with a grin. He held out his hand to Andrew. "Mike McQuaid."

"Andrew Drake." They shook hands and Andrew took the chair next to mine, casually splendid in pleated slacks, a cream-colored Dior polo shirt, suede loafers, and that absolutely perfect nose that made McQuaid's look like it had gone fifteen rounds with the world's heavyweight champ. He gave me a smile that aimed to charm.

"Congratulations on your opening," I said. "Is this your first photography studio?"

"Not really," Andrew said, signaling Bob to bring a pitcher of beer.

I waited for him to go on. But he didn't, and Ruby spoke up. "I'm sure Andrew's going be a success," she said. "He's already got one big assignment. Arnold Seidensticker has asked him to shoot his daughter's wedding."

"Shooting a Seidensticker isn't a bad way to get started," I said, and McQuaid snickered. Arnold Seidensticker is not my favorite person. For a while, he tried to get the Austin–San Antonio Regional Airport located near Pecan Springs. That idea went extinct when the U.S. Wildlife Service told him he couldn't destroy the habitat of the golden-cheeked warbler. Now he's backing the high-speed monorail project, which aims to shoot bullet trains every fifteen minutes through one of the most fragile ecosystems in Texas. At the same time, he's supporting a scheme that will moor a flotilla of horse-drawn buggies at the courthouse square, to ferry tourists to the town's attractions. There's no contradiction. Both ideas have one thing in common: money.

"You don't sound like a Texan, Andrew," I said. "Where are you from?"

"You know the old phrase—places too numerous to mention. I've never really settled down." He smiled at Ruby. "Until now."

Ruby flushed. She had traded the oriental pajamas for a simple white shift. With her coppery hair, creamy complexion, and the sprinkle of gingery freckles across her nose, she looked gorgeous—and very much in love. Obviously flustered, she grabbed a menu. "What are you having?" she asked McQuaid.

"Chicken-fried, what else?"

People who live north of the Texas-Oklahoma border think chicken-fried is fried chicken. It isn't. It's smashed cube steak dipped in batter, deep-fried, and smothered with well-peppered cream gravy. Served with chunky fries, thick slabs of toasted and buttered white bread, and a cold beer, it's the national meal of Texas. It's also fat city, so I only eat it twice a month. A doctor I know swears she can tell chicken-fried people just by checking their cholesterol.

While Bob took our orders, I studied Andrew curiously. He'd avoided my questions. Was he hiding something? Or was my concern for Ruby making me too suspicious of a man with a natural reserve about his personal affairs?

Another pitcher of beer arrived, and more nachos. We talked about Billy Lee and the pickets, the sad ending of Leroy the goat, Bubba's odd discovery of wolfsbane, and the cult panic that seemed to be sweeping the town like a prairie fire. Dinner came, and we moved on to larger topics—the economy, the number of women who'd won a seat in the legislature in the last election. But apart from learning that Andrew was left-handed (he bumped my right arm when he picked up his fork), that he had a hint of New Orleans in his speech, and that he held politically correct opinions on just about everything, I wasn't able to satisfy my curiosity about him. By the end of the meal, all I knew for certain was that Andrew Drake was a smooth and charming man with my best friend's heart tucked into the pocket of his expensive designer shirt. And that I had developed an unqualified dislike of him.

After dinner, McQuaid headed to the campus for his meeting

and Andrew drove off in his red Fiat. Ruby and I stood on the sidewalk in front of Lillie's. It was nearly eight, and getting dark.

"Looks like it's just you and me, babe," I said. "Want me to give you a lift home?"

"Sure," Ruby said. We walked to my car and Ruby folded her lanky frame into the passenger seat. My Datsun is seven years and 117,000 miles old, but it's still reliable and cheap to maintain, especially since McQuaid taught me how to change the oil and rotate the tires.

Ruby turned to me as I pulled away from the curb. "So what do you think about Andrew?"

"He's got a beautiful nose. Where's he from?"

There was a silence. "Up north somewhere. Tulsa, I think."

"By way of New Orleans?"

"What?"

"The way he says his r's." I turned the corner onto Pecos. "Has he been married before? Does he have any kids?"

"I don't think so." Ruby turned to me. "What's the matter, China? Don't you like him?"

"Did I say I didn't like him? I asked if he was married."

"It's the way you're asking questions. I'm not a hostile witness."

I sighed. "Don't be defensive, Ruby. Andrew Drake is a charming, elegant man who looks good enough to eat. I'm just wondering how much you know about him, that's all."

"Enough." Ruby leaned forward. "China, what's that fire?"

I glanced in the direction she was pointing. "A bonfire, I guess. Somebody violating the open burning ordinance." I looked again. "Isn't that Judith Cohen's house?"

"It is." Ruby's voice cracked. "And it's not a bonfire, either. Stop, China! It's a *cross*."

I jammed on the brakes and slid the Datsun into the curb, narrowly missing Judith's mailbox. Ruby and I piled out and ran across the yard to the flaming cross, which was billowing thick, sooty smoke. Judith was standing on the front porch, paralyzed, disbelieving. I grabbed the garden hose, reached for the spigot, and turned on the water.

The four-foot burlap-wrapped cross burned as if it were soaked with diesel fuel, and it had a head start. The flames had ignited the dry grass and a nearby bush. It took several minutes with the hose full blast before all the sparks were out. Neighbors came running from both sides and across the street, but there wasn't anything for them to do, so they retreated to their yards where they stared in an embarrassed silence until the fire was out. By that time, Ruby's sandals were a mess and I'd managed to hook my heel in the hem of my skirt. That'll teach me to wear a dress.

Judith stood watching impassively, her face shadowed. "Thanks," she said when the last spark was extinguished.

I coiled the hose. "Who do you suppose did it?"

"Kids," Ruby said. "Looking for kicks." She glanced at Judith. "It could have been anybody's yard."

"But it was mine." Judith's voice was as dead as her face, and her mouth barely moved. "My name's on the mailbox. Cohen."

"But people around here don't give that a thought," Ruby said. "They might have opinions, but I don't think they'd—"

Judith cut her off. "They're boycotting your shop, aren't they?" She went inside.

Fighting the fire had kept me too busy to think about what it all meant. Now that the excitement was over, I was shaken with anger and fear, far out of proportion to the burning of a couple of four-foot sticks of wood. But when sticks of wood are nailed into a cross, they become symbolic, and symbols hook into feelings. Burning a cross is a terrorist act, pure and simple, born out of suspicion or hatred or a sense of racial supremacy. It implicates us all, no matter whose yard it happens in.

The neighbor on the right, a burly middle-aged man in baggy shorts, was sweeping his walk with a great show of attention to detail. I went over.

"Did you see who did this?" I asked.

The man swept some invisible dirt into a crack. "Nope."

"How about a car?"

He stepped on a wooly caterpillar and ground it into the cement. "Nope, no car, no nuthin'."

I heard the same story from the people on the other side and across the street. Monkey see no evil, hear no evil, speak no evil. I understood, but I felt sick inside.

"Why won't they help?" Ruby asked, as we drove off.

"Because they're afraid somebody'll burn a cross in their yard."

"Then maybe we ought to do something. Maybe we should call the police. Burning a cross . . . I mean, it's worse than burning the flag. There's got to be a law."

I gave a short laugh. "There was, but the Supreme Court threw it out. Flag-burning is a form of political expression. It's protected under the First Amendment. Ditto on cross-burning."

Ruby stared at me. "You're kidding."

"Nope. If Bubba caught the guys who burned that cross, he could charge them with violating the open burning ordinance or making a threat. Or they could be charged with a violation of Judith's civil rights. But a community can't pass a law forbidding people to burn crosses or paint swastikas." It was a ruling the defense lawyer in me understood and applauded, while the human part of me wanted to be sick. An utter paradox.

"God." Ruby shook her head. "And to think what a peaceful town this has always been." She hesitated. "That's the way it's *seemed*, anyway."

We drove the two blocks to Ruby's in silence. When we got there, she invited me in for coffee.

"Thanks," I said. I looked down at my dirty hands and muddy feet. I couldn't see my soul, but it felt dirty too. "I guess I'm not in the mood to talk. I think I'll go home and take a bath."

"Sure." Ruby got out and closed the door. "Tomorrow will be better, China."

"Yeah," I said, although I wasn't too sure.

I let myself in through the kitchen door. Khat noisily accused me—inconsiderate and callous fiend that I am—of going out to enjoy my dinner without fixing his. I was guilty under the Texas Penal Code of cruelty to animals (failing unreasonably to provide necessary food for a cat in my custody). A Class-A misdemeanor, punishable by a fine of not more than two thousand dollars or confinement in jail for a term not exceeding one year or both. He planted one paw firmly on my foot while I attended to this oversight, to make sure that I didn't do it again.

When he was eating, I checked the answering machine. There was one message. I played the tape, hoping for something that would redeem the day. A call from the Reverend, maybe, saying that God had told him to pack up his pickets and go home. Or from Publishers Clearinghouse, telling me that I'd won enough not to care whether the pickets stayed or went.

It turned out to be my mother.

"Sorry I missed you, dear," Leatha chirped to the machine. "We haven't talked for weeks and weeks, and I'm dying to hear what's going on in your life. Please call me when you get in."

"No thanks," I muttered, and jabbed the erase button. If Leatha and I hadn't talked for weeks and weeks, there was a reason. I hate pretending that things are okay between us when they're not. The truth is that I hadn't forgiven my mother for being an alcoholic. Talking to her wasn't high on my list of things I wanted to do, tonight or any other night.

But especially tonight.

Friday started off like Thursday. I swept the step and put out the plant racks, but I didn't need to bother. Billy Lee's bunch was parading again, chanting and singing, in well-disciplined lines that left plenty of room for pedestrians. One of the signs read "White Witches, Black Witches, Brown Witches—God Will Strike Down Every One." Another said "Thou Shalt Not Suffer A Witch To Live. Exodus 22:18." Looking at them and thinking about the burning cross made me queasy, so I busied myself with small tasks and tried not to think. But I felt worse and worse by the minute.

Between nine and ten, nobody made it through the line. A few minutes before ten I happened to be standing near the window when I saw Fannie Couch, one of my best customers, talking to the Reverend.

Fannie Couch is seventy-eight years old, with the look of a sweet Southern belle—rosy cheeks and dimples, lavender eyes, and hair like spun silver. She dresses the part, too, in floral-print dresses and the floppy-brimmed, flower-trimmed straw hats that are her trademark. But she has the slim wiriness of somebody who's worked hard for the last six or seven decades and the no-holds-barred candor that characterizes so many Texas women. She and her husband Claude sold their Hill Country ranch and moved to town six years ago. A year later, bored with the garden club and Friends of the Library, she talked the station manager at KPST-FM into giving her a call-in talk show. It's called "Fannie's Back Fence." She's on the air from eleven to two every day, with time out for the news and weather every hour. Her peppery, down-home style invites callers to reminisce and ramble, which they do, but not too long. Fannie manages her callers like a county sale barn auctioneer managing a crowd of bidders.

As I came down the walk toward them, she seemed to be managing the Reverend.

"The Lord abhors witchcraft," he trumpeted. His pink cheeks and bald head shone like the polished granite in the court house foyer.

She looked at him. "How do you know?"

Billy Lee was taken aback. "Why, it says so in the Scriptures. Exodus 22:18. 'Thou shalt not suffer a witch to live.'"

Fannie slipped into the fakey Texas accent she uses on the radio. "Well, don't you go tellin' my better half. Just the other day, Claude and me, we had this fight, and he said to me, 'Why, Fannie, you old witch, you're gettin' meaner ever' day.'"

"Dear lady," the Reverend said soothingly, "that's not exactly the kind of witch the good Lord—"

Fannie's twinkle took some of the sting out of her words. "Bless your sweet heart, Billy Lee, you're tellin' me that you're so holy that you can read the Lord's mind?"

The Reverend pulled himself together. "You'll be doin' His will if you didn't go in those shops, Miz Couch. Miz Bayles here may not be a witch herself, but she rents property to a fortune-teller, and that's ever' bit as bad." He lifted himself to his tiptoes, his voice rising on an ominous quaver. "Eschew the lair of fortune-tellers and the den of evildoers, and you will be saved from the wrath to come."

Fannie lost her twinkle. "Billy Lee, I got to say this, and you got to listen. You are doin' this town a real disservice, carryin' on about the wrath to come. People are scared. They're jumpy as bullfrogs about witches, but they're just as twitchy about witch-hunters. My advice to you is to go home before you start a prairie fire."

The voice of God, in the accents of Molly Ivins. Ignoring the Reverend's protests, she took my arm and we went into the shop, where she bought two bars of herbal soap and some cinnamon sticks.

As I counted out her change, she pursed her mouth. "That man may look like a vanilla ice-cream cone, China, but he's dangerous. Folks around here are pretty laid back most of the time, but this stuff about Leota and the Ellis boy has got them all stirred up. Some woman called in the other day and said she'd seen a bunch of people dancing around a bonfire at the cemetery. Somebody sprayed pentagrams on car windows over on Crockett Street. And there was Bob Godwin's goat and Mrs. Bragg's chickens."

I shut the cash register drawer. "I don't know who built the bonfire or killed the chickens, but trick-or-treaters sprayed the pentagrams. I know, because I saw them."

"A lot of this is just talk. You know this town. People got to have something to talk about." She frowned. "But they've got plenty to talk about, what with the Wurstfest over in New Braunfels." The area was settled by Germans in the 1840s, and the Wurstfest is a traditional German celebration, complete with folk costumes and German music, played by such local notables as Oma and the Oompahs, the Shriner Hobo Band, and the Haygood Family Fiddlers. If you're so inclined, you can also drink yourself under the table with a few pitchers of great German lager.

"It's up to you, Fannie," I said. "You've got to get people off the subject of witches and onto Wurstfest."

Fannie gave me a sharp look. "And you and Ruby got to keep your noses clean, or you could be in trouble. You hear?"

"Tell me about it," I said ruefully. "You're the first customer all morning."

And the last. Mrs. Murray, who runs the Senior Citizens'

Thrift Shop, tried to come in to pick up some hibiscus tea she'd ordered. But she's easily intimidated, and by the time I got out to the sidewalk, the Reverend had already scared her out of her wits.

"Don't pay any attention to this man, Mrs. Murray." I patted her arm. "He doesn't have any right to interfere."

"But what's all this about witches?" Mrs. Murray asked. Her voice trembled. "Does it have anything to do with poor Mrs. Bragg's chickens? Mrs. Bragg is my neighbor on the other side of the alley, you know. That rooster was better than an alarm clock. Went off every morning at five thirty sharp."

"It's too bad about the rooster," I said, moving her toward the shop. "If you'll come in, I'll get you that tea."

Having lost one soul already this morning, the Reverend redoubled his efforts. He raised both arms heavenward. "Lord, defend this dear sister from the UNGODLY ONE!"

That did it. "I b'lieve I'll just go on back to the shop," Mrs. Murray said nervously, pulling her arm away. "I left Hazel by herself and she doesn't like to make change."

"God bless you, ma'am." Billy Lee pressed his Bible to his heart. "The Lord smiles on those who do His biddin' with a glad heart."

Mrs. Murray scurried off, and I turned furiously to Harbuck. "You pull that cute stunt one more time," I said, "and you'll find yourself on the business end of an injunction. You're intimidating my customers and damaging my business, and I'm sick of it!"

The Reverend shook his head sadly. "I understand how you feel, Miz Bayles. 'Course, it's the Lord's business we all need to be doin', not our own." His voice became a caress. "And it's easy, so blessedly easy. All you have to do is kneel down right here on this sidewalk and ask forgiveness." He closed his eyes and raised his soft, pudgy hand. Behind him, there was another soulful "amen."

For a split second, I wanted to tell Billy Lee exactly what I thought. But it wouldn't change his mind or convince him to send the pickets home. I gave it up and went back inside, where I sat on a stool behind the cash register, feeling defeated.

Ruby came through the back door. "Are you all right, China?" she asked anxiously.

"No," I said glumly. "I've had one customer this morning. One." I looked up and gawked. She was wearing a black tunic with a capelike red scarf, black tights, spike-heeled black boots that elevated her to at least six foot three, and Mary Richards' silver goddess pendant. Her orangy-red hair was frizzed all over her head, her eyes were made up to look like Cleopatra, and her long nails were lacquered in blood-red enamel. I almost came unglued.

"Jesus, Ruby, why did you wear that getup today, of all days? All you need is a cloven hoof."

"The worm has turned. We're launching a counterattack." She held up a camera. "Maybe when those sanctimonious turkeys out there see me taking pictures and recording their chants, they'll think twice. Anyway, photos could come in handy if we wind up in court."

It wasn't a bad idea. "Be careful," I said. "It's against the law to threaten pickets."

"What's the penalty? Maybe it's worth it."

"Thirty days and two grand max."

"I'll be meek," Ruby said.

"Ha," I said, looking her up and down.

For the next five minutes, Ruby stalked the line with her camera. She had come back in and was getting ready to open her shop when Bubba Harris pulled up. He lifted himself out of the police car, gave a hitch to his tan polyester pants, and surveyed the scene.

"Maybe he's come to send them off." Ruby sounded hopeful.

"I don't think so," I said.

A minute later, Bubba was standing in the door. "Mornin',

Miz Bayles," he said. "Looks like you still got a problem." He
took out a fresh cigar, peeled it, and stuck it in his mouth.

"Can't you do something about those pickets?" Ruby asked.
"They're ruining our business."

"They start disturbin' the peace, you let me know." Bubba
looked around. "The mayor got here yet?"

"The mayor's coming?" I asked. "What is this, a top-level
strategy session?"

Bubba ignored me. "I got a question for you." He gave
Ruby a hard look. "You know anything about sacrifice? Human
sacrifice?"

Ruby gave the hard look back. "The only human sacrifice I
know about is the seventeen years I was married to Ward
Wilcox."

Bubba frowned. "This ain't no laughin' matter."

"Neither was that seventeen years," Ruby said.

The cigar went up and down. "Got an anonymous call this
mornin'. Some woman said there's gonna be some sorta human
sacrifice 'round here in the next few days. Said people oughtta
be prepared."

I frowned. Human sacrifice?

"And you figured I'd know something about it?" Ruby tow-
ered over Bubba like the Wicked Witch of the West. "Did you
expect me to whistle up my coven and tell them to be good girls,
no human sacrifices this week?"

Bubba took his cigar out of his mouth. "Now, Missus
Wilcox—"

"*Ms.* Wilcox."

"*Miz* Wilcox. I don't know anythin' about whistlin' up any
coven. All I know is, I got this tip, and it's my bid'ness to check
it out." His eyes narrowed at both of us. "An' y'all better not go
tellin' this to the newspaper, hear? I got enough trouble. The
whole damn town's got the willies."

Ruby flung her scarlet cape over her black shoulder. "Well, if
I hear about anybody planning to offer up one of the neighbors,

you'll be the first to know. But I can't promise about the newspaper. How could my coven pass up publicity like that?"

Bubba plugged his cigar back in, looking sorely tried. "I wish you'd climb down off your high horse, Missus—*Miz* Wilcox."

"And I wish you'd think twice before you come in here asking me about a human sacrifice." Ruby wagged a blood-tipped finger in Bubba's face. "You ought to be protecting honest merchants from the kind of ridiculous nonsense that's going on outside right now, instead of coming in here, insulting me, harassing—"

The door opened. I turned to see who had dared to enter the lair of fortune-tellers and the den of evildoers. It was Pauline Perkins, dressed in her mayor's uniform, a gray suit with a pink jewel-necked blouse and pink pearls, a gray bag slung over her shoulder, sensible gray shoes.

"Good morning, Chief Harris," she said coolly.

"Mornin', Mayor," Bubba muttered. Bubba and the mayor don't get along. She treats him as an adjunct of the mayor's office. He'd like to tell her to kiss off, but doesn't dare.

"Ruby," Pauline said, "the Chief and I are here on official business."

"Are you planning to arrange for a sacrifice?" Ruby was still hot.

"A sacrifice?" Pauline looked puzzled. "No, I'm here to negotiate a settlement between you and Reverend Harbuck."

Ruby rolled her eyes. "I knew it," she said, "the minute the Chief started to talk about sacrifice. I can understand why Harbuck's into witch-bashing, Pauline, but why *you*?"

"I am not into witch-bashing," Pauline said with dignity. "There's nothing wrong with you teaching that class, Ruby. It's your timing that's off. While the City Square site visit team is here, it is vital—absolutely *vital*—that we put our best foot forward. This week has been . . . well, we can't exactly call it our best foot." She looked disgusted. "Dead goats, dead chickens, burning crosses, pickets in the streets—"

"Well, I'm glad to hear that you feel strongly about the subject," Ruby said smoothly. "You can be the one to tell Harbuck to call off his dogs."

Pauline licked her lipstick. "What I hoped," she said, "was that you would cancel the class. Then I could approach Reverend Harbuck and ask him to—"

Ruby folded her arms. "Absolutely not."

"Good for you, Ruby," I said.

Pauline's tone became cajoling. "But think what it would *mean*. A favorable report from the site visit team almost guarantees that we'll get the grant. And I've just found out how absolutely critical the money is. City Hall has termites!" At the looks on our faces, she added, "They're all around the baseboards in the city council chambers, and there's not a penny in the budget for spraying. The building's a historic structure, so the grant would—"

"Free speech," Ruby said, pulling herself up to her full height and then some, "is more important than spraying City Hall."

"But it's just a class," the mayor pleaded. "You can always reschedule."

"It's not the class, it's the *principle*." Ruby pulled her gingery eyebrows together. "I am really disappointed in you, Pauline. I know you're counting on this City Square business to win the election for you. But I never thought you'd go to the extent of suppressing legitimate self-expression, just to get a few votes."

"But I—"

"I personally believe that Billy Lee Harbuck is more dangerous than termites. But he's got the same constitutional right to picket my store—as long as he doesn't harass my customers—as I have to teach my class. And you can't make either of us give up that right just to fool the site team into believing that everybody in Pecan Springs is one cozy, happy family." She lifted her chin. "'Tain't so, Magee."

I gave Ruby a respectful glance. She had hit the heart of the matter. And she had zinged the mayor in a very tender spot.

"I am *not* suppressing self-expression." Pauline shifted her weight. "I'm just trying to . . . to smooth things over. To effect a compromise. But if you can't find it in your heart to cooperate, perhaps Reverend Harbuck will."

"I'll compromise," Ruby said. "I won't advertise my class. How's that?"

Pauline beamed. "That's the spirit!"

I looked at Ruby, shaking my head. She hadn't advertised in the first place. The newspaper had turned her down. But I wasn't about to blow it for her. I turned to Pauline. "You'd better have more than that up your sleeve before you talk to Harbuck," I said. "He says God's on his side, and you're going to need some pretty powerful leverage."

Pauline looked coy. "I wouldn't call it leverage, exactly. But it does so happen that my husband has a major interest in KPST-FM. That's the station that carries Reverend Harbuck's gospel message every Sunday morning."

"That's what *I* call leverage," Ruby said, admiringly.

I wanted to plug my ears. Talk about the First Amendment!

Pauline was all business. "Would you come with me, Chief Harris? It's time we had a talk with Reverend Harbuck."

Pauline and Bubba went out on the sidewalk, while Ruby and I watched through the window.

"I can't believe she's using the radio station like that," I said. Pauline took the Reverend off to one side, where his choir couldn't hear what went on.

"I can," Ruby said. "How'd you think she got to be mayor?"

From the look on the Reverend's face, Pauline had him in a tight place. In the end he accepted the inevitable. He returned to his band of followers and raised his hands and his eyes toward heaven.

"The Lord be praised!" he cried. "Our work here is done!"

"Praise the Lord!" the choir echoed, relieved. It must not have been any fun, marching up and down carrying signs all day.

"I wonder how he's going to explain this to his congregation," Ruby said, as Bubba and the mayor climbed into their cars and drove off. "I mean, it's not even close. It's Witches one, Billy Lee zip."

"I'm sure he'll think of something." I frowned. "Demonstrating is at least out in the open. I hope he doesn't decide to try something more devious."

It was Ruby's turn to frown. "There are worse things than demonstrating?"

"I'm sure there are. And the Reverend is perfectly capable of dreaming them up."

Ruby sighed. "I don't want to think about that now. I'm going to go light some incense and do a visualization."

"What are you going to visualize?"

Ruby started toward the door. "What else? A store full of customers and a cash drawer full of money."

❋ ❋ ❋

Whether it was the power of Ruby's visualization or the simple fact that the sidewalk wasn't cluttered with witch-bashers, we both had a decent afternoon. When we closed, we grabbed our gear, climbed into Ruby's red Honda, and drove to Jerri's Health and Fitness Spa, where we take an aikido class from Shirley Kanazawa every Friday evening.

The class is Ruby's idea. She says the martial arts make you less head-oriented and more belly-oriented. As she puts it, belly-people are spontaneous. They come from their "true selves." She decided on aikido because of all the martial arts, it is what she calls the "most ethical." It operates on the basic principle of harmony and balance, and the student in aikido is taught to respect her opponent's body.

Harmony and balance are fine for Ruby, but I go for the exercise. I don't have the discipline to get up at six every day to jog, and aerobic exercises seem stupid, all that flopping up and down. Aikido's not bad, though. We wear white cotton baggies, so the midriff doughnut doesn't show. Shirley is patient, even with me. And I like the slow, deliberate movements, the intuitive evaluating of your opponent's intentions, the subtle and sudden shifts to decisive action. I'm afraid my true self still lives mostly in my brain, not my belly, but it's getting there.

Ruby's much better at aikido than I am, maybe because she also does yoga. Shirley says Ruby is *tsuyoki*, meaning that her *ki*, her inner energy, is strong and one-pointed. She'll soon be ready for a *hakama*—that's the ankle-length black robe that advanced students wear. Me, I'm *yowaki*, meaning weak *ki*, although in my case, Shirley says, the *ki* isn't so much weak as scattered, unfocused. My mind wants to take over my body and my body isn't in harmony in all its parts. I'll probably be in white baggies forever.

Class over, Ruby and I went into the office to pay for next month. Jerri was there, her blond ponytail swinging, talking to her sister Rita. I was struck again by the difference between the two. In a red leotard that revealed absolutely no extra midriff, Jerri glowed with energy and vitality—obviously *tsuyoki*. Rita, wearing no makeup and dressed in a mustard-colored dress that hung limply from slumped shoulders, seemed sallow and listless—terribly *yowaki*. They were talking about Rita's job when we came in. She's an assistant manager at Lake Winds, the upscale resort community where Sybil Rand lived. C. W. Rand, Sybil's husband, was Rita's boss.

"What kind of person is Rand?" I asked, and handed over my check.

"Yeah, I'm curious too," Ruby said, taking my pen. "Is he anything like his wife?"

Rita's mouse brown eyes opened wide behind her blue-rimmed plastic glasses. "Heavens, no. He's not anything like *her*. She's dangerous. C.W.—I mean, Mr. Rand—is very nice. The sweetest person."

Sybil dangerous? I thought. Obviously, her poison garden had made a deep impression.

Jerri shook her head disgustedly. "Swear to God, if I was C.W., I'd divorce that nutty woman. No way would I hang around wondering when she was going to chop up something nasty in my salad."

"I don't want you to think I meant to criticize Mrs. Rand," Rita said in the anxious tone of someone who has spent a lot of years practicing to be a good girl. "I just meant that Mr. Rand is a *very* kind man to work for. In the entire three years he's been at Lake Winds, he's never once yelled at me. It's not easy, managing a big place like that. There's a lot of pressure on a person."

Lake Winds *is* big. There's the real estate development, of course, which involves leasing as well as sales. According to the promotional brochures, there are also two eighteen-hole golf courses, a three-hundred slip marina, a four-thousand-foot paved airstrip, and a world-class tennis center, not to mention horseback riding, swimming, a gym and sauna, and a restaurant. C. W. Rand was probably too busy to worry about what went into his salad.

Jerri put our checks in the drawer. "Be sure and take the posters back to the office," she reminded her sister. "C.W. said to post them on all the bulletin boards. I teach aerobics at Lake Winds and give massages," she told us. "There's a sauna and a gym, and all the equipment anybody'd ever need." She looked around and wrinkled her nose. "It's a helluva lot better than this dump. The air conditioning's on its last legs, the plumbing's shot, and the carpet's a rag. Somebody hand me the money, I'd move in a New York minute." She glanced up at the clock and slammed the drawer. "I'm outta here, guys. I've got a date."

Rita flashed a look at Jerri. "But what about tonight?"

"What about it?"

"It's Mama's birthday. Don't tell me you forgot again, after the huge fuss she made last year."

"No big deal," Jerri said carelessly, "just another birthday. Ma gets one every year. Tell her I'll call her tomorrow." She patted her sister on the shoulder. "You take care of it, Rita. You're good with Ma. A lot better than me."

Rita's shoulders hunched and her face went dark. I couldn't help feeling sorry for her. It looked like a classic case of the plain sister stuck with the demanding mother while the pretty one went dancing. And from the resentment that raked across Rita's face, I'd guess it wasn't the first time, either.

"Are you going out with McQuaid tonight?" Ruby asked as we walked to her car.

"He's still working on that damn conference. Why? Did you have something in mind?"

"All that balance and harmony dehydrates me," Ruby said. "Let's stop by Lillie's."

Lillie's was the usual yup-dudes, marrieds with children, cedar-choppers, and Bob. But the ferns were gone. In their place hung pots of genuine fake philodendrons with plastic bluebonnets stuck in. Even I had to admit that it was an improvement. There'd been no hope for the real ferns. All they did was drop dead leaves onto the bar.

I pulled up a barstool and ordered a Lone Star. Ruby got a Lite and Bob brought us a basket of corn tortilla chips and a cracked white cup filled with Maria Garcia's tomatillo and chile salsa, made with lime juice and plenty of garlic and flecked with cilantro leaves. Maria runs Taco Cocina, over on Zapata Street. Her salsa is even hotter than McQuaid's, which peels the roof off your mouth. Bob was looking gloomy.

"What's the matter?" Ruby asked. "Did you lose another goat?"

Bob shook his head. "Lost the shed," he said glumly, swiping the mahogany bar with a wet rag.

I swigged my beer. "The *shed*? You mean, the one where Leroy was hung?"

"Yeah. This time, though, it wasn't the Santeros. It was the Jesus freaks. Billy Lee Harbuck's bunch."

"Oh, yeah?" Ruby asked, interested. "How do you know?"

Bob dropped the rag and grabbed a flyswatter. Around here, we have flies until the first killing frost, which hadn't happened yet. "'Cause they spray-painted 'Jesus Saves' on a half-dozen trees," he said. "Then they burned down the shed. Guess they figured it needed purifyin'. I don't know anybody else but Billy Lee who'd think of somethin' like that."

Ruby dredged a tortilla in Maria's salsa. "Just like a gang."

Bob swatted a fly. "Yeah. That Harbuck, he's bad news. Has been, ever since he was a kid."

"You know him?" I asked.

Bob's mouth went hard. "You bet I know him. That ol' boy might like people to b'lieve the stork delivered him lily-white and sinless on the church steps, but I know different. He was a coupla years ahead of me in high school, back in Abilene. Real hell-raiser. Not just kids' stuff, neither. Big-time hell."

"Is that right?" Ruby said, with greater interest. She washed down the salsa with beer. "What sort of hell?"

I looked at her. I could see the wheels turning. Ruby has always wanted to be a private investigator but the closest she gets is private-eye novels. She's a charter member of Sisters in Crime, an organization for crime writers and fans. She's also the only adult woman I know who was still reading Nancy Drew when V. I. Warshawski and Kinsey Millhone cracked their first big cases.

Bob scratched his nose with the flyswatter. "Somethin' about a car," he said. "Been so long ago, I cain't rightly remember. But my brother Dickie, he'd know. He was in on the deal some way. The sheriff took 'em both to the pokey. Dickie got to come home, and Ma, she tanned his fanny good, sixteen or not. Ol' Billy, though, he got more'n a hidin'. He got to do time."

Ruby slapped the bar. "There it is, China."

"Where is what?"

"The ammunition we need to scare off the Reverend, in case

we need it. All we have to do is take a look at the records up in Abilene and—"

I shook my head. Ruby's P.I. tendencies worry me. "Ruby, you don't go snooping into people's lives just because you don't like them. It'll get you into trouble. Believe me."

Ruby wasn't listening. "Do you know any lawyers up there who could get the court records for us?"

I tried to be patient. "Number one, the records of youthful offenders are sealed after they're eighteen. Number two, the Reverend's got a loyal following. What'll they do if you start persecuting their hero?"

"I really think we ought to—"

"Anyway, it's the principle of the thing. How'd you like it if somebody dug up something you did when you were sixteen and waved it in your face? How'd you feel if one of your misdeeds came back to haunt you?"

There was a long silence. Ruby turned the Lite between her hands. Finally, she drained the glass and set it down.

"I've got to get home," she said. "Andrew's stopping by in an hour, and Shannon's coming down from Austin to meet him. Want to come over?"

"Thanks anyway," I said. "Ask Shannon if she's going to get us season tickets." Shannon, who is three inches taller than her mother, plays forward on Jodie Conrad's Lady Leghorn basketball team. She looks like Ruby must have looked in her early twenties, all elbows and knees, with the promise of real beauty when things settle down into the right proportions.

Ruby frowned. "I wish you liked Andrew."

"It's not that I don't like him," I said, "it's just that—" I didn't like him. I was instinctively suspicious of him. But I didn't want to hurt Ruby's feelings. "Maybe I'm jealous."

Ruby's eyebrows flew up under her orange fringe. "Jealous? Of Andrew?"

"Of you. That you can care about people the way you do.

That you can be passionate." As the words came out, I realized they were true. I hold back great tracts of myself, post "No Trespassing" signs over entire territories of my psyche. When Ruby falls in love, there are no fences, no walls, no boundaries. She invites total invasion. I envy her ability to open herself this way, and yet I'm afraid for her. To me, vulnerability is more of a curse than a gift.

"You care. About McQuaid, I mean. Don't you?"

"I guess." I stopped. "But that's different. I'm not swept off my feet, the way you are. I'm not a romantic."

"I'll take romance." Ruby looked at her watch. "Cheer up, okay? At least the Reverend's thrown in the towel."

I scowled at my beer. "I'm glad Pauline got the pickets out of our hair, but I don't like the way she did it."

Ruby got halfway to the door before she came back. "Don't forget. Tomorrow's Halloween. We're going to Mary Richards' party."

"Oh, yeah. With the witches."

Ruby shuddered. "Not so loud."

I left Lillie's a few minutes later. At home, I fixed Khat's supper, made a salad, and stuck some leftover chicken-rosemary-parsley casserole into the microwave. I was just sitting down to eat when the phone rang.

"I'm so glad I caught you, China," my mother said, in that sweet southern voice that pours over you like warm honey. Then came the stinger. "I waited and waited last night, but you never returned my call."

"Sorry, Leatha," I said. "I was busy."

She sighed. "You're always so busy, China. I worry that you're working too hard at that dear little shop of yours. Why, we haven't seen one another since Easter, and here it is almost Thanksgiving."

Not quite. I was in Houston in May for a meeting of herbalists, and I stopped in for a short visit. And it wasn't Thanksgiving yet, not by three weeks or so.

"Anyway," she went on with a little pout in her voice, "I've decided to take matters into my own hands. If Mohammed won't come to the mountain, the mountain will just have to come to Mohammed. I want to see you."

"That's nice," I said guardedly. It wasn't, but maybe I could put it off. "I'll have some free time around Thanksgiving. But the holidays are pretty busy, come to think of it. Maybe we should wait until after New Year's."

Leatha is one of the most passive people I know. When she comes up against it, she usually pours herself a scotch. But it was clearly steel-magnolia time.

"I'll be there on Sunday night about eight, China. It's time we had a mother-daughter talk."

Oh, shit

Saturday morning I woke with a huge headache, the kind I usually get when I drink too much red wine. But it wasn't wine. It was everything that had been building all week, with Leatha's phone call topping the whole mess, like the last piece of garbage that won't fit into the trash can.

When I was practicing law, I had neither the time nor the inclination to think about my relationship with Leatha. I've had time since I quit, but still no inclination. Lots of daughters have mother problems—meddling mothers, abusive mothers, pushy mothers, drunk mothers. That was my problem with Leatha. I can remember coming home from elementary school and finding her with her third or fourth scotch, alone in the large house that was done in the stark, monochromatic style my father preferred, filled with the expensive modern art he bought as an investment, so passionless that it chilled the ambient temperature by ten degrees. There was a new white Cadillac in the four-car garage every year, but the house and the car couldn't make up for her husband's nearly total absence—her husband, my father, a lawyer and a man of enormous intellectual strength and compelling physical vitality, whom she loved with an all-absorbed, all-absorbing passion. For Leatha, the scotch compensated, in ways her daughter couldn't, for his absence. I couldn't find anything to compensate for hers.

The headache wasn't going to go away by itself. I got dressed and went out to the herb garden, where I picked a leaf off a feverfew plant and chewed it, making a face at its bitterness. In early summer, feverfew—*Tanacetum parthenium*—is completely covered by white daisylike flowers that some people call bride's buttons. The seventeenth-century herbalist Nicholas Culpeper recommended the leaves for headaches and for "melancholy and heaviness, or sadness of spirits," a perfect prescription for me. Culpeper had the headache part right, anyway. By the time I'd gotten dressed, made the bed, and fixed breakfast, the headache was under control. I couldn't say the same for my melancholy and heaviness.

But the way I felt before I went to the shop didn't begin to compare to the way I felt when I got there. Without a special reason, I don't go into the Crystal Cave unless Ruby is there. This morning, I had a special reason. There was a puddle of something dark seeping under the connecting door. I stared at it for an awful second, my heart thudding in my ears. It had to be blood. But when I touched my finger to it and sniffed, it smelled like the scented oil people put in lamps. Highly flammable stuff.

I unlocked the door and pushed it open. What I saw brought my headache roaring back. Books lay helter-skelter, merchandise was strewn around, shelves were down, crystals and beads were spilled. The side door was open. It didn't take a rocket scientist to see that somebody had jimmied the lock.

I grabbed for the phone. Ruby was there in ten minutes, wearing paint-stained jeans and a rhubarb-pink sweatshirt that should have been in the laundry hamper.

"Happy Halloween," she said. She closed her eyes for a minute as if she were hoping the mess would go away. She opened them again, resigned. "How'd they get in?"

"The side door. The lock was a cheapie. I should have replaced it when you moved in. I'm sorry, Ruby."

"Not your fault. Did they get into your store too?"

"Just yours. I guess we'd better call the cops."

"Yeah, I guess. The insurance won't be good unless we

report it." She looked around disgustedly. "Although I'll bet they didn't take anything. They just wanted to trash up the witch's lair. Sprinkle a little holy water."

I frowned at her implication. "You think Harbuck is behind this?"

Ruby waved her arms. "They harassed us until the mayor ran them off. They purified Bob's shed by burning it down. Of *course* they did this. Who else?"

"I don't know, Ruby." I surveyed the damage. "Harbuck isn't my idea of a righteous man, but I don't think he'd—"

Ruby's face was the color of her sweatshirt. "Don't be obtuse, China. You heard what Bob said. Billy Lee is bad news, a hell-raiser. He's got a record. I tell you, we've got to do something about him!"

"I guess we start by calling the cops," I said, and headed for the phone.

I've got to give it to Bubba, he's quick. He was standing at the door, cigar and all, less than five minutes after I called in the report. But Pecan Springs is a small town. The guys sipping Saturday morning coffee in the Doughnut Queen would probably hear about the break-in within the half hour.

"More trouble, huh?" Bubba asked with a grunt. A burly young policeman with automatic-tint glasses was standing just inside the door with a notebook and a pencil. His glasses were still dark, and I wondered how long it would be before he could actually see.

Ruby was checking the fifty dollars in change she hides in a bank bag in the plastic trash can behind the counter. I tell her it's a bad place to keep money, but she says she's the only one who empties the trash and she won't throw out a bank bag. "What does it look like?" she asked icily. "A Chamber of Commerce picnic?"

"They got in through the side door," I said.

"Figgers," Bubba said. "Harvey, go check that door. I'll be around in a minute." Harvey stuck the pencil behind his ear and left. Bubba turned to Ruby. "Change all there? Anythin' missin'?"

Ruby pulled in her breath as if she were counting to ten. "I haven't had a chance to do inventory, but yes, the change is all here. I doubt if the Right Reverend Harbuck would risk leaving his fingerprints on a vinyl bank bag."

Bubba's cigar tilted toward the ceiling. "You sayin' it's the Reverend?"

"Him or his disciples."

"Y'got proof?"

"That's your job."

Bubba pulled his cigar out. "Miz Wilcox," he said patiently, "it's my job to find out who broke into your store, not to pin it on somebody just 'cause you got it in for 'em. I know you're pissed from hell to breakfast, and I can't say as I blame you. But it don't help for you to go throwin' up accusations like an armadillo diggin' dirt. Now, simmer down and let me handle it. Ya'll go get some coffee and come back in, oh, say, ten-fifteen minutes."

For Bubba, it was a long speech, and it caught Ruby by surprise. I took her arm. "Come on," I said sympathetically. "I'll make tea."

In my kitchen, I evicted Khat from the rocking chair by the window and Ruby sat down. I put on the copper kettle and measured tea into the blue china teapot McQuaid gave me for Christmas last year—lemon balm tea, with a bit of lemon verbena and dried lemon peel. Besides tasting good, lemon balm is supposed to reduce fevers. I thought it might cool Ruby off a little.

When the tea was ready I poured it into two earthenware mugs and put out honey for the tea and a jar of ruby-red jelly for the raisin scones. The recipe for the scones came from Jean and Ron McMillen's *Cooking with Malice Domestic*, a cookbook filled with the favorite recipes of famous mystery writers, as much fun to read as it is to cook from.

Ruby came to the table and sat down. She hadn't said anything for four or five minutes, which is probably a record. But
she drank her tea and ate a scone slathered with jelly, so I
guessed she was all right.

She pointed to the jelly. "What's that?"

"Prickly pear jelly."

"You're kidding. Those green things that look like mittens
covered with thorns?"

"They're good for jelly," I said. "Wonderful, in fact." The
fragrant magenta fruits ripen in September. If you wear leather
gloves, heavy jeans, and snake boots, you can pick enough to
make a tangy jelly that glimmers like rubies and smells like a
field of Texas wildflowers. "I ate the pads in Mazatlán once, but
I think it's an acquired taste."

Ruby devoured another scone. Finally, she sat back. "I *know*
it was Harbuck."

It never helps to argue with Ruby. All I could do was point
out the obvious. "Bubba might turn up a print or two, but unless
they're on file, I'm afraid there's not much chance that—"

Ruby tossed her head. "Oh, I doubt if we'll ever *prove* it, but
I know, just the same. Someday I'll get that holier-than-thou
devil. You just wait and see."

I changed the subject. "Guess who's coming for a visit?"

Ruby closed her eyes for a moment. She opened them.
"Your mom."

I frowned at her. "How'd you do that?"

"It's my Inner Guide," Ruby said. "She's very left-brained."
She gave me a sympathetic look. "When?"

"Sunday night." I sighed heavily. "Maybe I should ask your
Inner Guide how to cope."

We were interrupted by a knock. It was the burly young cop.
"We've got it all wrapped up," he announced. He must have
been working in the shop because his glasses were transparent
again. "Chief Harris said to tell you, when you figure out what's
missing, make a list and bring it to the station."

"Thank you," Ruby said. The cop left. She turned to me. "And thanks for the tea and the comfort, China," she said. "I feel a lot better."

"I didn't do a very good job with the comfort bit."

"Good enough." Ruby smiled. "It's hard to believe that horrible cactus can produce such fabulous jelly, isn't it?"

There was a metaphor in there somewhere. I smiled back.

It was nearly ten when I finally opened the store. Ruby didn't open at all. She spent the day cleaning and sorting and restocking. Between customers, I helped. At noon, I went to the Canton Palace and got take-out specials for two—chicken with cashew nuts for me and beef with garlic sauce for Ruby, who likes it hot. Her fortune cookie said, "A surprise is in the cards." My fortune cookie was empty. At two, Sybil Rand phoned to ask if she could ride to the party with us, since we knew the way. She also asked if we'd mind stopping by a few minutes early, so she could show us something. Her call reminded me that I'd planned to take some herbal incense. I found it and put it in a bag.

About four, looking disheveled and dusty, Ruby came through the connecting door.

"Well, I guess that's it," she said.

"Anything missing?"

She scowled. "My knife."

"The ritual knife you showed us at the class Tuesday night?"

"Uh-huh. At least, I think it's missing. I brought my box of tarot cards and ritual pieces to the store, and left it on the counter so I'd remember to take it to the party tonight. I thought the knife was in the box, but maybe it wasn't. Maybe it's at home."

"When you find out, better let Bubba know."

"I will," Ruby said wearily. "But right now, I'm going home and wash off this crud. I tried to call Andrew, but I guess he's already gone to San Antonio. He was planning to see a friend down there—some guy he used to work with."

"We don't *have* to go to the party tonight," I said. "If you're too tired, we can skip it." If we skipped it, I could call McQuaid and see if we could connect for the evening. It was a tempting thought, given how little I'd seen of him lately.

Ruby shook her head. "I promised to do tarot readings. I guess I'll have to dig up something exotic to wear. What time are you picking me up?"

"About six thirty. Sybil wants a ride, and she's asked us to stop by a few minutes early."

Ruby stretched. "What a day. What a week. Are we having fun yet?"

"Without a doubt. And there's more coming, according to your fortune cookie."

"Yeah. A surprise is in the cards. I wonder what the universe has cooked up for us now."

"Cooked up for you," I said. "My fortune cookie was empty, remember?"

❋ ❋ ❋

Ruby came out to the car dressed like a belly dancer in gauzy red harem pants slung low over her hips and a matching red bolero that left no reasonable doubt about anything. She was wearing three-inch gold hoop earrings, bangle bracelets, a gold chain-link belt, and gold sandals. Her eyelids sparkled with gold eyeshadow, and there was gold dust in her hair and on her shoulders. She was carrying a tambourine.

"Wow," I said respectfully.

"Thank you." She glanced at me. "Batwoman, I presume?"

"Close enough." I was wearing the only exotic thing I own, a black nylon jumpsuit with a neckline that dove all the way to my navel. I bought it at a yard sale for a dollar and a quarter. I was also wearing the black Batman hood that McQuaid's son Brian had left under the sofa cushion the last time he was over. "Find your knife?"

Ruby shook her head. "I guess they wanted a trophy with my name on it."

"Maybe we should go by the police station and let Bubba know."

"In these outfits? He'd arrest me for indecent exposure and have you tested for rabies." She rattled her tambourine. "Rev up this Batmobile, chum. I'm ready to party!"

Lake Winds sprawls over several hundred parklike acres on the east side of Canyon Lake. The Rands' house was the largest on a street of homes with six-figure price tags, within shouting distance of the eighteenth tee and a stone's throw from the lake. From the street, it looked like a fort with carved double doors wide and high enough to take a delivery van. From the rear, when Sybil led us into the backyard, it was a glass box with a wraparound deck, a garage big enough to house the Pecan Springs fire department, and a landscaped swimming pool shaped like the state of Texas. The grand tour began in Sybil's poison garden, which occupied a lovely green corner north of the pool's Panhandle.

"That's where they pulled up the wolfsbane," Sybil said, pointing to a hole in the ground. Behind it was a lush oleander and a spreading wild cherry tree. Since 1820, *U.S. Pharmacopoeia* has listed wild cherry as an expectorant and mild sedative, but the bark, leaves, and pits contain a fatal cyanidelike chemical. At the foot of the tree was a thriving clump of monkshood, close cousin to wolfsbane and just as deadly. The brick path was bordered with pennyroyal, the oil of which is used in pet flea collars. One woman died after swallowing two teaspoons of it, and as little as a half teaspoon can produce convulsions.

As I looked at Sybil's plants, I thought again of the fascinating paradox they posed. Each one was well-tended, green, and innocently lovely—but not one was what it seemed. And what of Sybil, who had brought these odd and threatening plants together? I could dismiss the question lightly—after all, some people raise piranhas, others wrestle rattlers. But standing here, up to my ankles in virulent plant poisons, the question held greater energy. Who *was* Sybil Rand, that she found pleasure in creating such a dangerous collection? Why did she do it?

"Whoever stole your plant must have known what they were looking for," Ruby said.

"I understand that some traditional cultures use wolfsbane to ward off witches," Sybil said. She looked like a witch herself in a high-necked black robe with long flowing sleeves and a heavy neckpiece of polished wood beads and carved ivory that might have belonged to an African shaman. Her hooded eyes were dramatically made up and her long nails were painted a red so dark it was almost black.

"Really?" It was a bit of herb lore I hadn't heard, but I could see the logic.

Sybil smiled, not pleasantly. "My husband says the garden is a neighborhood nuisance. He told me not to plant it, and this week, he threatened to have it destroyed." She paused. "He's not entirely supportive of my esoteric interests, you see—the garden, tarot, astrology. He's afraid of them."

There was an uncomfortable pause. A black-masked butcherbird chirped once from the wild cherry tree, then flew away.

"I don't think I've met your husband," Ruby said.

"I'd introduce you, but he went to Atlanta yesterday to handle some family business." Sybil gave Ruby's belly dancer costume a glance. "I'm sure he'd be very glad to meet *you*." She turned back toward the house. "But I didn't ask you here just to see the garden. There's something else—not important really, but Angela insisted that I show you."

She led the way across the wooden deck and into a kitchen that could easily have handled the Mayor's Prayer Breakfast. A young Hispanic woman in jeans and an oversized checked apron was putting dishes away. She smiled when she saw Batwoman and a belly dancer coming through the door.

I smiled back. "Hello, Angela," I said. Angela Sanchez is in her early twenties. She has regular features and dark hair in a heavy braid halfway to her waist. I met her when Sarita Gonzales and I helped her brother and cousin get their citizenship papers. To say thanks, she invited us to her sister Eusebia's *Quincenera*, the traditional Mexican fifteenth-birthday celebration. After mass, there was a dinner and a dance at the Centro Mutualista Cuauhtemoc, with Eusebia in a white dress, surrounded by a court of honor numbering in the dozens. At midnight, everybody stopped drinking and sat down to hot, aromatic bowls of menudo, made of tripe, hominy, and chile poblano stewed with onion, garlic, and peppercorns, and served with hot tortillas and small dishes of chopped chile serranos, chopped onion, and wedges of lime. I don't know whether it was the fellowship or the menudo (which is said to be a cure for hangovers), but I went home feeling good and woke up feeling better.

"Hello, China," Angela said. "Hi, Ruby." She gave Sybil a close look. "Are you going to show them, Mrs. Rand?"

Angela Sanchez is not a woman who sits back and waits for somebody else to take command. She's a graduate student in the anthropology program at CTSU. She plans to get her doctorate and teach. For now, she supports herself by working in the homes of women who can afford to hire other women. She's a good worker, the best, and she doesn't work for minimum wage.

Reluctantly, Sybil went to a desk. On it was a typewriter with a sheet of paper rolled into it, a list of Latin plant names, probably an inventory. She opened the desk drawer and pulled out a curious doll-like object dressed in black. It had black yarn for hair and a bit of shiny copper wire twisted around its neck. Sybil put it on the counter, smiling tightly. "A passable imitation, don't you think?"

"A *voodoo* doll?" Ruby asked.

"Yes," Angela said. "Santeria."

"I found it on the deck this morning," Sybil said, "with this."

She held up a tarot card. It pictured a grim skeleton holding a scythe.

Ruby's face became still. "Death. Who sent this, Sybil?"

"If I knew," Sybil said shortly, "I would have sent it back." She tossed the card on the counter beside the doll. "Anyway, it's nothing to get excited about. It's just some friend's idea of a joke. I wouldn't have told you, but Angela insisted."

I picked up the card and studied it. I hadn't gotten my own tarot deck yet, but I'd looked at Ruby's, and I remembered this card, sinister and threatening, a symbol that evoked an ancient fear. "Your friends like to play jokes like this?"

Angela took off her apron. "This is no joke," she said firmly. "When I was a child, my cousin Juanita's husband, an Anglo named Carl, decided he wanted a divorce. Juanita said no, because she was Catholic. Carl got this old *bruja*—a Mexican witch—to make a doll and put pins in the throat. When Juanita found the doll at her door, she nearly went crazy. The next morning, when she woke up, she couldn't talk. For two or three days, she couldn't talk. She went to the doctor, but there was nothing wrong with her, not physically, anyway. She went to the priest, but he couldn't help, either. Finally, after a couple of weeks of this, Carl brought over this paper saying that Juanita would give him a divorce. The minute she signed, her voice came back." She opened the pantry and hung up her apron. "A *bruja* made this doll, too. The death card makes the magic more potent. Somebody's got it in for Mrs. Rand."

Sybil folded her arms. "If you're finished with the kitchen, Angela, you can go."

Angela refused to be dismissed. "I don't think you're taking this seriously enough, Mrs. Rand. It's witchcraft. Santeria. It's dangerous. Ruby can tell you—she knows about such things."

I was surprised that Angela, with her education, was still trapped in the old superstitions. "Your cousin got sick because she believed in the power of the doll," I said.

"Yes," Ruby agreed. "It was her fear that kept her from speaking, not the doll itself. That's the way magic works. It has a great deal of power, but only over those who believe in the power."

Angela's dark eyes flashed scornfully. "You're all missing the point. What Mrs. Rand believes or doesn't believe doesn't matter. What matters is the sender's *motives*. If this threat doesn't accomplish the purpose, whatever it is, that person is likely to try something more direct."

I felt like a rebuked kid who'd been set straight. "You're right, Angela. Would you mind keeping an ear to the ground? Maybe you'll run across the *bruja* who made the doll."

That piqued Ruby's P.I. curiosity. "Sure. If we can find the witch, we can get her to tell us who she's working for. I'll bet there are fingerprints on the card, too."

"Yes," I said. "Sybil's and mine."

Ruby made a face at me and I had to smile. Batwoman and a six-foot belly dancer poised to jump into an investigation of Mexican witchcraft. What a team.

Sybil tossed her head. "This is all totally ridiculous," she said lightly. "The doll's a joke, not a threat. I can't believe you're taking it seriously."

I looked at her. Her tense, synthetic smile and the uneasiness in her eyes contradicted her words. Who was she afraid of? Who had sent the doll?

Angela went to the back door. "I'll ask around," she told me. "Maybe I'll hear something." She looked at Mrs. Rand. "Lock up, okay?"

When Angela had gone, Sybil turned to Ruby and me. "Just before you came I got a call from a friend who'll be dropping by later. I'll need to leave the party about ten thirty. If that's a problem, I can follow you in my car, instead of riding with you."

"It's fine with me," I said, wondering what sort of friend came calling so late at night.

"No problem for me either," Ruby said. "There's been some pretty nasty *brujería* in my life lately. By ten thirty, this belly dancer will be ready to hang up her tambourine."

✳ ✳ ✳

Deadwood is a crossroads town made up of one store, a volunteer fire station, and a couple of dozen houses loosely strung out along gravel lanes. Mary's is a cedar-shingled geodesic dome with a wooden deck that overlooks an expansive lawn bordered by flower and herb beds and shaded by huge pecan trees. Beside the large dome is a smaller one, Mary's studio, which she had prudently closed for the party. I made a mental note to ask her if I could come back some day and see where she works.

The lawn was crowded. Fifty-plus goblins, fairies, goddesses, Indians, countesses, fortune-tellers, and assorted revelers had showed up, including one Lieutenant Uhura, two Hillary Clintons, and three belly dancers. Gretel was there, a fraulein, and I caught a glimpse of Judith wearing a brown hooded robe and carrying a shaman's staff. Mary's Wiccan friends weren't nearly as witchy-looking as Sybil. They wore long white garments with coronets of daisies and fern. Dottie had brought her black cat, somebody had a pink plastic flamingo, and somebody else wore a live boa constrictor named Balboa draped over her shoulder.

After we'd been partying for a while, it was time to sit in a circle for the Samhain celebration. Mary sat next to me and provided whispered explanations of the ritual. Three women dressed as the Fates came forward, chanting blessings. They were followed by eight Wiccans costumed to represent the festivals of the pagan year—Winter Solstice, Candlemas, Spring Equinox, May Eve, Midsummer, Lammas, Autumn Equinox, and Samhain. Each one danced and chanted and offered up wine, bread, and flowers symbolizing the seasons.

Because Samhain marks the year's end and the passing of

life, the eighth priestess was a crone, dressed in a sooty robe and crowned with a circlet of bones. "I am the mother of the dead," she cried. "This is the night to commemorate our sisters who have died."

One by one, women, often weeping, spoke the names of the dead—mothers, sisters, cousins, friends, women they had read of—and told how they died. I was struck by the number who had been victims of violence, and enveloped by the terrible sense that in our society the law protects the powerful and leaves the powerless undefended. Ruby reached for my hand, and we called out our friend Jo's name, sadly remembering how she died the year before. I've never been big on ceremonies, but this one was different. The saying of the names was testimony to our common grief and love for our lost ones, yet at the same time, it lifted us out of sorrow and into an acceptance of our own mortality.

Then the crone raised her wooden staff and invited us all to offer up the things in our lives whose time had come to die. "My fear," one woman cried. "My addiction," someone else said. "My impulsiveness," Ruby muttered beside me. I hesitated, then heard myself whispering, "Denial." Denial of what? I wasn't sure, for the word had come without my thinking it.

When all the gifts had been given, the crone invoked the names of the Goddess. "Hecate, Cerridwen, Dark Mother, we have reached the cusp of the ancient New Year. Let those who are gone teach us to live our own lives more fully, keeping our hearts in courage and grounding our courage in justice."

It wasn't a ritual I would have designed, and part of me felt uncomfortable about participating in the hocus-pocus of costumes and unfamiliar names. But I couldn't help being deeply moved by its simplicity and sincerity, and I found my face wet with tears. As I looked around the circle, I saw tears in other eyes, too.

"No more weeping!" the crone cried. "This is the time for celebration!" She planted her staff in the middle of the circle and lit it, and it became a flaming torch. As I watched the sparks spiraling into the velvety blackness of the night sky, I thought of the burning cross in Judith's yard. I was glad to let that image go and replace it with this. We stood up, joined hands, and began to dance. Led by the crone and the Wiccans, we chanted and danced, louder and louder, faster and faster.

That was when the party *really* got interesting. Out front, a siren wailed. Ruby looked at me, startled. "The cops?"

Two men in tan uniforms, boots, and Stetsons—county mounties, they're called around here—marched into the yard carrying foot-long flashlights. "Who's in charge here?" one of them demanded raspily, shining his light in our eyes.

"I am." Mary stepped forward, shielding her eyes from the brightness. "Who are you? Is there some problem?"

"Sheriff Blackwell, Adams County Sheriff's Department," the raspy-voiced man said. He was thick-shouldered and stocky, with sandy hair cut short military style, a square jaw, broad square chin. "Somebody phoned in a report about a Klan meeting." He flicked his light around the circle, picking out the white-robed priestesses. "You got a permit?"

Mary let out a peal of laughter, and the circle caught it up, laughing helplessly. "The Klan?" she managed at last. "You think *we* are the Ku Klux Klan?"

I was laughing too. What Sheriff Blackwell was looking at was probably the biggest assortment of witches, pagans, fortune-tellers, belly dancers, and other radical females ever gathered in Adams County—and he thought we were the Klan!

Mary finally got control of herself. "I'm sorry to disappoint you," she gasped, "but we're not the Klan. We may look a little weird, but we're perfectly harmless. We're having a Halloween party."

I stepped forward. "Can I help sort this out, Sheriff?" He squinted at me. "Oops," I said, and jerked off my Bat hood.

He goggled. "China Bayles?"

McQuaid had introduced us at a party for town and county

law-enforcement officers. Blackwell and McQuaid, as it turned out, had been undergraduates together in the criminal justice program at Sam Houston State. There's nothing more fraternal than two cops, even when one of them leaves the brotherhood.

"I don't believe a permit is required for a party on private property," I said in my best lawyerly tone. "I trust we're not disturbing the peace."

"Not yet, anyway," Blackwell said gruffly. "Just be careful of that torch. Everything's tinder-dry." He might have pressed the issue, but seen up close, the white robes obviously weren't Klan robes, the burning staff clearly wasn't a burning cross, and the twenty-five overtime hours it would take to book the lot of us would probably sink his budget. He eyed the six-foot belly dancer standing next to me with her bolero gaping open, and his mouth quirked at the corners. Then he turned away and he and his deputy disappeared around the house.

I laughed again, remembering what Ruby had said Tuesday night. You can get away with murder as long as you don't tell people exactly what you're doing.

The sheriff's raid was the high point of the party. After that, we ate some more and drank some more. Ruby set up her table and gave a few short tarot readings while the rest of us talked and sang. Then we wished everybody a merry Samhain, and Ruby and Sybil and I got in the car and started home. It was eleven when we left Sybil in front of her fortresslike house.

Ruby had said very little. She broke her silence the minute Sybil was out of the car.

"China," she said urgently, "that was my card."

I shifted gears. "Come again?"

"The Death card Sybil got, with the voodoo doll. It was mine, out of my deck."

"How do you know? Are your cards marked?"

"Well, no." She hesitated. "But mine's gone. I missed it when I was laying out the Trumps tonight, before I started reading. I always do that, just to get in touch with the cards."

"Maybe it's a coincidence," I said, although it seemed much too coincidental.

Ruby shook her head wordlessly.

"So somebody stole your card and your knife, and gave the card to Sybil." We stopped at the corner. A car went by, and in the flash of its lights I saw that Ruby was pushing her lips in and out, something she does when she's very bothered. "I wonder what happened to your knife."

✳ ✳ ✳

It was after nine the next morning when I found out. The phone rang on the table beside the bed. Khat stirred next to me and began to wash his charcoal face with one charcoal paw. Getting tidy is always his first serious business of the morning. I groped for the phone.

"Hello," I grunted. Nothing came out. Even for Batwoman, the week had been a dilly, and I had slept the sleep of the dead. I cleared my throat and tried again. "Hello."

Ruby's voice was fragile and faraway, as if she were phoning from the North Pole. "She's dead, China."

I sat up, jostling Khat, who stopped in midswipe and glared at me. "Who's dead?"

"Sybil Rand. Somebody stabbed her last night. With *my* knife."

Khat went back to his face-washing.

I pulled on my jeans and an orange-and-white U.T. sweat-shirt and drove over to Ruby's. She was pacing the sidewalk. She jumped into the car and I pulled away from the curb as she slammed the door.

"How'd you find out?" I asked.

"Judith called. She found the body when she went over this morning to pick Sybil up. They were going to San Antonio today." Ruby covered her face with her hands. Her muffled voice was shaking. "She said she saw my knife on the floor, and she thought I'd better know."

"She called the cops, I assume."

"She called Bubba's office first, but Lake Winds isn't in his jurisdiction. It's Adams County."

"Blackie," I said.

Ruby looked up. "What?"

"Blackie Blackwell, the county sheriff who raided the party last night."

"Rats," Ruby said. "Do you think he'll remember us?"

I recalled the way Blackie had looked at her belly-dancer cos-tume. "He'll remember."

There were three brown-and-white county cars, a green Oldsmobile, and a blue Toyota in front of the stone fortress. "The Toyota belongs to Judith," Ruby said.

The Oldsmobile belonged to Maude Porterfield, Justice of

the Peace. Texas law requires a J.P. to rule on all suspicious deaths, an archaic provision that occasionally creates disharmony at the crime scene. When we reached the open door guarded by a uniformed deputy, I saw Miss Porterfield standing in the foyer, talking to the sheriff. She is seventy-four years old and has been a justice for forty-one years. She was dressed for church in a navy-blue dress with a white lace collar, gray hair strategically arranged to cover thin spots and fastened with plastic combs. A hearing aid was tucked into her right ear, and the sheriff was standing close to her, talking loudly and distinctly.

"I think you've done about all you can do here, Miss Porterfield. You want to look at anything else?"

Miss Porterfield shook her head. "I've seen enough blood for one morning. Shall I put my report in the mail?"

"One of my men will pick it up," Blackwell said, and ushered her to the door where we were standing.

She eyed Ruby. "That your knife in there, Mrs. Wilcox?"

Ruby looked pale. "I haven't seen it since somebody broke into my store and stole it. And I'm not Mrs. Wilcox anymore." She turned to me. "Miss Porterfield married Ward and me."

"Shame you had to get mixed up in this," Miss Porterfield said, shaking her head. "It's a bloody mess. How's Ward?"

Ruby raised her voice. "I don't see much of him lately. We're divorced. He married again."

"Is that right?" Miss Porterfield asked, eyes bright with curiosity. "Who'd he marry? Was it that young—"

"Thanks for coming," the sheriff shouted, and signaled the deputy to take Miss Porterfield's elbow and help her down the stairs. "It'd be good if we could have that report this afternoon." He didn't say "whew" and wipe his brow when she had gone, but he looked plenty relieved.

"I'm Ruby Wilcox," Ruby said in a small voice. "Judith Cohen said it was my knife that—"

"I know." The sheriff looked at her. "Weren't you at the Halloween party last night? In the, er, ah . . ." He stopped, looking at her shirt. She was completely covered this morning, in black sweats with—I did a double take. Across the front of her black sweatshirt was blazoned, in big red letters, "Sisters in Crime." Beside the words was a dagger dripping blood.

"Yes, I was there," Ruby said. "Sybil was with us. We brought her home about eleven."

"We'll get to that." He turned to me. His eyes were pale blue and steady under sandy eyebrows. "What's your business here, China?"

I pulled my eyes away from the bloody dagger on Ruby's shirt. "I'm Ms. Wilcox's legal counsel," I said. Ruby glanced at me, startled.

"Do you think she needs one?"

"I guess that's up to you. Ms. Wilcox wants to cooperate with your investigation."

The sheriff turned. "Den's this way."

We followed him through the opulent living room and down a hallway to a large, open room with an ivory cut-velvet carpet. Two walls were cedar-paneled, one wall was floor-to-ceiling glass with a view of the pool, and the remaining wall was lined with bookshelves on either side of a massive limestone fireplace. A fingerprint team was at work by the door, a cop with a notebook was talking to Judith on one of the two white sofas, and a photographer was taking pictures. There was a body on the floor.

Ruby gasped.

Sybil appeared to have been killed when she was sitting on the floor in a cross-legged position in front of the fireplace. Still clothed in the black robe she had worn to the party, she had fallen facedown and slightly to the right. In a ragged circle around and under her, the carpet was no longer ivory. It was soaked with what looked like reddish-black tar.

I suddenly felt sick. Last night, at the Samhain ritual, we had called out the names of the dead. This morning, the first day of the ancient New Year, Sybil was one of them. Next Samhain, if we celebrated the ritual again, Judith or Ruby or I would call out her name. Why had this happened? Was her death a stranger's random violence, or did she know her killer? I thought of Sybil's often offensive manner and the doll and Death card someone had sent. Had she herself invoked the dark god who dragged her across the bloody threshold?

But the questions all spun together into one final question. Who? That was the question Blackie was charged by law to answer. I hoped he'd do it quickly, for all our sakes.

I leaned forward for a closer look. Bloody footprints led from the body to a telephone on a table, then to the sofa where Judith was sitting with the cop. A knife—bone-handled, the word "Ruby" etched on its blood-stained blade—lay on the carpet behind the body and slightly to the left. In front of the body, there was a black dish filled with coins, a wooden wand tipped with a crystal, and a wine goblet. The goblet lay on its side. The wine, redder than Sybil's blood, had soaked into the rug. Under the body, I could see a circle of tarot cards.

"God," Ruby whispered, "how *awful!* She was stabbed while she was doing a spread." She looked at me. "The Death card," she said. "*My* card. Where is it?"

"A spread?" Blackie asked. "The Death card?" A strobe flashed, and the photographer repositioned herself to take another shot.

"A spread is a layout," Ruby said. "With the tarot cards. She was in the middle of a ritual."

Blackie's eyes narrowed, wary, suspicious. "Fortune-telling cards?"

"Some people tell fortunes with them, but that's not what Sybil was doing. I teach my students to use them to ask for guidance."

"Guidance? Guidance for what?"

"I don't know," Ruby replied testily. "I don't pry into what they're seeking. That's up to them." She pointed with the toe of her sneaker. "These other things—the coins, the wand—they're part of the ritual, too. They're symbols of the elemental energies that the cards represent. The coins are earth, the goblet water, and the wand fire. The knife represents air."

I felt sorry for Blackie. This was probably his first encounter with the New Age. "She was your student, huh? Is that how your knife got here? And what's this about a Death card?"

"The knife was stolen from my store on Friday night. So was the thirteenth trump—the Death card. It's got a picture of a skeleton on it. Somebody broke in and trashed out the place. I reported the break-in and Bubba, Chief Harris, I mean, came and investigated. I didn't get around to reporting the knife, though. I didn't miss it until late yesterday afternoon. I didn't find out that the card was missing until last night."

Blackie bent and lifted Sybil's hip slightly. "This the card?" Under her body was the thirteenth trump. The grim reaper with its malevolent scythe, harvesting Sybil's blood.

Ruby pulled in her breath sharply. "That's it."

"Could Mrs. Rand have stolen the knife and the card?"

"Of course not." Ruby gestured at the luxurious room. "Why would she break into my store and trash it when she's got all this? Anyway, somebody sent her the card. With a voodoo doll."

"This thing?" Blackie pointed with his boot to something half hidden under Sybil's hand.

I bent over. The black-haired thing stared up malevolently, the copper wire tight around its neck. "That's it. It came with the tarot card, according to Sybil. The last time Ruby and I saw either one was when she put them on the kitchen counter, just before we left for the party. She was showing them to us."

Blackie looked at me. "So whoever sent her the doll sent the card, too? How'd she seem about it?"

"She seemed . . . " Ruby paused. "She acted as if she didn't want us to know how much it frightened her. The Rands' maid was here, Angela Sanchez. Angela insisted that the doll was sent by someone who had a grudge. Sybil tried to treat it as a joke, but I thought she seemed scared."

While Ruby and the sheriff were talking I had stepped to the bookshelves. Sybil had collected as odd and interesting an assortment of books as she had plants. *A Witch's Guide to Gardening* was there, along with all eight volumes of Thorndike's *A History of Magic and Experimental Science* and a book called *Cauldron Cookery*. She also had the 1985 AMA *Handbook of Poisonous and Injurious Plants* and reprints of several old English herbals I itched to get my fingers on. On the shelf below I saw several books on tarot, including an intriguing one called *The Qabalistic Tarot*, as well as half a dozen astrological texts. There was more, but I needed to get back to the conversation.

The sheriff was zeroing in on the weapon. "This knife—is there some special significance to it? That why it's got your name on it?"

Ruby lifted her chin. "It's my personal ritual knife. I use it in my own tarot ceremonies and when I teach the cards. In tarot, the knife—it's called the *athame*—symbolizes the power to discriminate intelligently, to draw lines, to make choices. It represents the cutting edge of moral courage, knowing the difference between right and wrong. It's not meant to actually cut anything. That's why it's so dull."

Blackie gave a gritty laugh. He picked up the knife carefully and held it out on the flat of his hand. "Oh, yeah? If it was so dull, why did it slit Mrs. Rand's throat easy as bleeding a deer?"

Ruby put her hand to her mouth. "Slit . . . her throat? I thought she was stabbed."

I felt a chill, and the room suddenly felt like a great white-floored cave, empty and echoing. Somehow, the idea of Sybil's throat being cut was much harder to handle than the idea of Sybil being stabbed. I pulled in my breath, remembering why I was there. "Judith Cohen phoned Ruby after she found the body this morning. According to her, Sybil was stabbed."

"You can bag this, Malory," Blackie said, handing the knife to one of the print team. "Ms. Cohen didn't want to look too close," he said to Ruby. "No question about it. The lady's throat was slit. Very neat, very clean, very fatal. Kind of makes me wonder."

It made me wonder, too. It looked as if the killer had come upon Sybil from behind so stealthily that she didn't know he was there. He? In this case, likely. Throat-slitting isn't a means of murder often chosen by women. I knew about it in only two contexts, professional murders and ritual killings. If I had to make a snap judgment, I'd go with the ritual killing. What's more, I'd bet that most of the elements of this crime appeared on the cult indicator list the Department of Public Safety had sent to Bubba.

"If it was my knife that did this," Ruby said, "the blade had to have been sharpened."

"You're saying you didn't sharpen it?"

"No. I don't know how."

I could see where Blackie was going. Premeditation. You usually don't go to the trouble of sharpening a knife unless you intend to use it.

"If you ask me, this thing is connected with Sybil's poison garden," Ruby said. "First somebody steals her wolfsbane, then somebody makes a voodoo doll, then . . . this. It might even be connected with Bob Godwin's goat. There was that business about the human sacrifice, too." She snapped her fingers. "And the picketing."

I frowned at her. The Reverend couldn't have anything to do with this, unless she thought . . . I didn't want to think about what she thought.

"I know about Godwin's goat," Blackie said, "but what's this about a poison garden? And a human sacrifice?"

It took a minute to fill Blackie in on the things that had been going on in Pecan Springs, including Sybil's award for Most Unique Garden, her stolen wolfsbane, Mrs. Bragg's chickens, and the tip Bubba had gotten about a human sacrifice.

Blackie went for the garden first. "Why would Mrs. Rand cultivate a bunch of poisonous plants? Do you think she was planning to use them?"

"I don't know," I said. "She seems to have had quite a wide-ranging intellectual interest in the occult." I gestured at the bookshelves. "Magical herbalism, astrology, the tarot."

The sheriff glanced at the books, stepped closer, took down a volume of Thorndike and thumbed it. "You know of any cult she belonged to?" He put it back again and turned around.

"She was a loner," Ruby said, "a solitary. She was too independent to belong to a ritual group."

"What about the sacrifice?"

"That was some sort of anonymous tip," I said. "You'll have to ask Chief Harris about it."

"And the picketing?"

Sharp, I thought. He didn't miss a thing. "The picketing has nothing to do with this." I avoided looking at Ruby. "We've had a little trouble at the stores, but the mayor got them to move on. It's all settled."

"They thought we were witches," Ruby added helpfully.

"I wonder why," Blackie said.

Judith got up from the sofa, gave us a small, tight-lipped nod, and left. Blackie turned to the cop who had been questioning her. "If you're all through, Knight, get on the horn to the hospital and see what's keeping the transport. You can use the phone in the kitchen if the print team's finished in there."

"Do you have a time of death?" I asked, as the cop headed for the phone.

Blackie countered with another question. "You say you left her here at eleven?"

"Yes." I remembered something. "She was expecting company." Was it her killer she had expected?

"That's right," Ruby said excitedly. "She got a call from a friend who wanted to come over, so she had to get home."

"Kind of late for a visitor," Blackie said. "Did she say

whether this friend was a man or a woman?"

Ruby and I traded looks. We shook our heads. She hadn't said.

"Who were her friends?"

"Judith, for one," Ruby said. She paused, considering the question. "You know, I can't think of any others. China and I, I suppose. But we really didn't know her." She looked down at the body. "She wasn't an easy woman to know. There was something . . . private about her. Something remote. I don't think she liked most people."

"She and her husband on good terms?"

"I don't know," I said. "I don't know him."

The cop came back from using the phone. "The ambulance is on the way."

Blackie nodded. "I understand that Lake Winds has some kind of full-time security. See if you can track down whoever was on duty last night." He turned back to us. "One more thing. After you left Mrs. Rand here, what did you do?"

"China dropped me off at eleven fifteen," Ruby said. "I read for a while—the latest Linda Grant mystery—then I went to sleep."

"Witnesses?"

Ruby sighed. "I wish."

Blackie turned to me. "How about you?"

It would have been convenient if McQuaid had come over to give me an alibi, but he hadn't. "I got home at eleven thirty, roughly, and went to bed." I smiled. "With my cat."

Blackie didn't smile. "You two can go now. But I may have other questions, so let me know before you leave town."

Ruby looked uneasy. "You don't suspect either of us, do you?"

Blackie shrugged. "I'm a suspicious person. I suspect everybody."

8

The mayor's truce held. Of course, there might not have been any pickets anyway, since it was Sunday afternoon and they'd presumably honor the Sabbath. On Sundays, Ruby and I are open from noon to four, just to catch the tourists.

Since Maggie's Magnolia Kitchen opened up across the street, the Sunday tourist traffic has improved. Maggie Garrett, the trim, lively ex-nun who bought the old restaurant last June, also bought the vacant lot next door. She created an open-air dining area under the pecan and live oak trees and I landscaped the rest with perennial herbs such as Russian sage and Mexican oregano (*Poliomintha longiflora*, a shrub that bears lavender flowers on glossy leaves and has the same scent as Greek and Turkish oregano) and Texas wildflowers—coreopsis, eryngo, gayfeather, beebalm, and several asclepias for the butterflies. Maggie, who used to be called Sister Margaret Mary, managed the Benedictine Sisters' kitchen at St. Theresa's Convent outside of town for ten years. She left the order last year and brought her culinary talents—speciality omelets, fine pastas, and wonderfully fragrant breads—to the old Magnolia Kitchen, which closed when its owner died. Maggie's has become a Sunday lunch tradition for people from Austin out for a leisurely drive through the Hill Country, and a lot of people wander across the street to Thyme and Seasons.

I was glad to be busy. The work kept my mind off the corpse

on the bloody carpet. But whenever I had a breather, the questions elbowed their way front and center. Who killed Sybil? Why? Was it some sort of ritual killing, as everything seemed to indicate? Or had someone had a reason to hate her—a hate compelling enough to lead to murder?

The questions filled me with a heavy sense of déjà vu, as I thought of what lay ahead. Blackie had already started analyzing information and developing a theory. Before long, if he got a few breaks, he'd have a case. There'd be an arrest, an arraignment, an indictment, and, if the D.A. did his work, the grand jury's true bill. Then discovery motions and a pretrial hearing, while the prosecution and the defense worked their asses off to develop both sides of the story. Finally, jury selection and trial, drawn out as long as possible by the defense until there was, inevitably, a verdict. If the defendant was found innocent, that was the end of the road—as my senior partner used to say, it's pretty damned tough to try two different people for the same murder. Guilty, and the appeals could go all the way to the Supreme Court. Five years, ten years, twelve years from now, when time and luck and appeals ran out, we the people would exact a life for Sybil's life: strapped to a gurney in the Huntsville death row, the murderer would die by lethal injection. The road to what we call justice is a hell of a lot longer than the road to murder. The thought was almost as depressing as the violence of Sybil's death.

News travels fast in law-enforcement circles. McQuaid called at two to tell me he'd heard. "How about having dinner with Brian and me this evening?" he asked. "You can fill me in on the gory details then."

"Leatha's coming at eight," I said without enthusiasm.

"No sweat. We can eat at six. It doesn't take long to get around a plate of ribs and sausage. The mesquite's already fired up and the sauce is on the stove, along with the beans." In addition to his other talents, McQuaid cooks.

"Super," I said. "Listen, before you put the ribs on, would you do me a favor? Drop by the Rand house out in Lake Winds and see what kind of a line you can get on the case." I gave him the address.

There was a moment of silence. I suspected that McQuaid was deciding whether Blackie would want his old buddy to trespass on his turf. Fraternity or not, cops don't like other cops nosing around. "Yeah," he said finally, "I guess I can do that. I'm kind of curious myself. See you at four thirty for margaritas, huh?" Margaritas don't exactly go with ribs and sausage, but McQuaid makes good margaritas, too. Anyway, there's no Emily Post when it comes to barbecue.

"Okay," I said. "I'll bring salsa." It was only fair.

❋ ❋ ❋

McQuaid lives about six blocks from the university, in a three-bedroom fifties' bungalow he rents from Mr. McCreary, who lives across the street. When I locked my bike to the gate, I saw that the front yard needed mowing and that Howard Cosell, Brian's ancient basset hound, had dug another hole under the forsythia, next to the hole he'd dug last week. He was lying in it, asleep. There was a basketball in the gutter, a scarred skateboard in the middle of the walk, and two bikes chained to the porch rail. When I opened the door and went in, the family Mac sat on the coffee table, where Brian had been playing Dungeons and Dragons. Little blue blips were chasing little red blips across the screen.

"Anybody home?" I called. I could hear the tinny, twangy sounds of Bob Wills. McQuaid listens exclusively to cowboy music. According to him, everything else is for weenies.

"I'm back here," McQuaid replied, from the distant reaches. "In the armory."

McQuaid's armory is in what used to be the third bedroom, at the end of a hall. There's a long homemade pine worktable across one wall, with tools neatly hung above it on pegboard and stashed on shelves. Bolted to one corner is a heavy reloading press with a hand-operated lever. Reloading ammunition is something serious gun nuts do to save money and produce special loads—combinations of different types and weights of bullets and powder that aren't commonly available. Under the worktable are stacks of olive-drab Army ammunition cans filled with bullets. He keeps the powder separate, in a larger can filled with silica gel to eliminate moisture. A six-foot high, glass-fronted gun cabinet stands in one corner, filled with a half-dozen rifles and shotguns and several pistols in their holsters. The room is an arsenal, pure and simple.

McQuaid and I have oppposite views on guns. To me, they're deadly weapons. To him, they're precision instruments whose performance is infinitely perfectible. We don't discuss this topic very often, because it might lead to open warfare. Also, I'm uncomfortable with the idea of an arsenal in the same house with a curious young boy. But McQuaid's security procedures are highly professional, and his standards of training and discipline are exactly what you'd expect from an Eagle Scout. Brian has his own rifle, which is locked up with his father's. As for my concern about the hazards of storing powder indoors, McQuaid maintains that it's less flammable than the lawnmower gas stored in the garage or some of the cleaning solvents under the kitchen sink.

Right now, he was pouring powder into a reservoir on top of the press. A disassembled .44 Magnum lay on the worktable.

"What are you doing?" I asked, and was immediately sorry. If you ask McQuaid a question about guns, you get an answer. A detailed answer, complete with footnotes and bibliography.

McQuaid looked up and grinned. "I'm reloading a batch of forty-fours." He handed me a shiny cartridge an inch and a half long. It filled the palm of my hand and felt like it weighed a half pound.

"What are you shooting with this? Rhinos?"

"Nope, can't. They're endangered. Actually, I have to lighten up a bit," he added, not seeing my grin. "The last batch, I had some failures." He held up an empty brass casing, a hairline fracture running a third of its length. "I've been experimenting with these two-hundred-forty-grain jacketed hollow-points. The loading table calls for eight point nine grains of powder. I've been using Hi-Skor 700-X, which should give me twelve hundred twenty feet per second and a chamber pressure of thirty-nine thousand pounds. Of course, the tables are conservative, so I upped the charge a bit." He nonchalantly tossed the casing to me. "Maybe a bit too much. The chamber pressure might have gotten as high as forty-two thousand p.s.i."

"In other words, the gun almost blew up in your face."

"Nah. A forty-four will take a lot more than that, unless it's an antique. I've got one in the cabinet, an old Smith and Wesson that goes back to the turn of the century. If you put more than fifteen thousand p.s.i on the chamber you're headed for Boot Hill. Back in those days, they relied on bullet weight for knockdowns, not velocity. You could almost see the bullet coming. You're talking seven hundred fifty feet per second, versus twice that for the Magnum. Gives you a real kick in the ribs. That's something you need to think about with that little nine millimeter of yours. You've got eleven hundred feet per second but you're only looking at a hundred-twenty-grain bullet, so you'd better hit something vital or—"

If I didn't stop him now, we'd never eat. "Speaking of ribs, how're they doing?"

McQuaid looked at me blankly. "How're they doing what?"

"You know, as in cooking. You did say we were having—"

"Omigod," McQuaid said, and dashed out the door and down the hall. I followed in a more leisurely fashion.

The barbecue was blazing merrily. While McQuaid doused the flames, I went over to watch Brian pitch horseshoes. At nine, coached by Mr. McCreary, he became the junior champion horseshoe pitcher of the Pecan Springs Parks Department, a title he has successfully defended against all comers for the past two summers. Brian looks a lot like his dad—dark hair, pale blue

eyes, quirky grin. Today he was wearing Mr. Spock ears, a
"Beam Me Up, Scotty, This Place Sucks" shirt, baggy black
pants two sizes too large, and unlaced Reeboks that would fit
Magic Johnson. He dropped a horseshoe neatly around the pin.

"Not bad," I said approvingly.

Brian looked up and gave me the Vulcan blessing. "Dad says
you discovered a dead body."

I returned the Vulcan blessing and followed it with a two-
second hug, which is about as much as either Brian or I are good
for. He is in an outspoken antigirls phase, but I don't qualify as a
girl. I am not partial to children, having had what Ruby calls a
toxic childhood, but I make an exception with Brian.

"I didn't discover it," I said. Over his head, to McQuaid, I
mouthed, *What did you tell him?*

"I told him who got killed and how." McQuaid was wreathed
in a cloud of pungent, mesquite-flavored smoke.

Brian headed for the patio door. "He told me she was a
witch. Is there any lemonade?"

"Don't spill it," McQuaid told him. "I just mopped the
kitchen floor. It reminded me of the La Brea Tar Pits."

"She wasn't a witch," I said firmly. "That's a lie." I turned to
McQuaid. "What else did you tell him?"

"I didn't say she was a witch." McQuaid brushed the ribs
with a paintbrush dipped in his secret sauce. He gave me the
recipe for my birthday, which was also the second anniversary of
our first date. That's how secret it is. "I said that people might
think she was a witch."

Inside the house the phone rang and Brian yelled, "It's for
me!" It almost always was, and I was glad. I didn't want to talk
about Sybil's murder in front of an eleven-year-old. There are
other things I don't like to do when Brian is around, such as
make love with his father. McQuaid doesn't seem to mind that
his son is asleep, or supposed to be asleep, on the other side of a
thin wall, but I find the knowledge inhibiting. Brian is one of the
reasons I can't make a commitment. Agreeing to move in togeth-

er would mean a major reorganization. If I tried to fit McQuaid into my life, plus a noisy, untidy (albeit very likable) Vulcan child and a grouchy basset, accommodations would have to be made, most of them major. I dislike dogs, especially bassets that dig holes in herb beds. Howard Cosell hates cats. Khat hates dogs and children in that order.

"Blackie doesn't think she was a witch, does he?" I asked.

McQuaid turned the ribs. "I stashed a pitcher of margaritas and a couple of glasses in the refrigerator. Mind getting one for me when you get yours?"

I found the pitcher, salted the rims of the two cold glasses, and poured the glasses full. While I was at it, I filled a bowl with tortilla chips and opened the jar of salsa verde I'd brought. It's made with green chiles.

"Cheers," I said, presenting McQuaid with his margarita. "Does he?"

McQuaid put down the barbecue fork, took his glass, and tipped it against mine. "That's the theory he's going on now," he said. "Well, maybe not a *witch* witch. Maybe more like somebody who got interested in it intellectually, started playing around, and made the mistake of falling in with people who take their magic seriously. Like the Palo Mayomberos who murdered that tourist in Mexico a few years back."

"So he's pursuing the cult angle?"

He licked his finger and rubbed at a spot of barbecue sauce on his yellow Father's Day polo shirt. I took Brian to Wal-Mart to shop for it and ended up buying not only the shirt but a basketball. "Yeah," he said, "in the absence of anything else. The door between the den and the patio was unlocked, but there wasn't any sign of breaking and entering. No sign of a burglary, either. And no indication that she actually entertained the visitor she mentioned to you. There are prints. He's going through the elimination process now. He'll probably get yours and Ruby's tomorrow." He squinted at the spot. "Think I ought to bleach this?"

"Definitely not. Got any sorrel leaves? They'll take it out."
At the look on his face I sighed. "Try soda water. What about the
husband?—C.W., isn't that his name?"

"Kind of hard to make him out the throat-slitter, if that's
what you're asking," McQuaid said reflectively. "First thing he
knew about it was when he got home from Atlanta this afternoon and found a strip of yellow crime-scene tape across his
front yard." He unfolded two lawn chairs and put them on the
upwind side of the grill.

I sat down gingerly. My chair was the one with the webbing
coming loose. "C.W. really *was* in Atlanta, then."

"Apparently so. He had an Atlanta boarding pass and a ticket
stub. I was there when he showed them to Blackie."

"What's he like?"

McQuaid licked the salted rim of the glass. "Affable, styled
hair, Cozumel tan. Good-looking, big, bit on the heavy side.
Four-hundred-dollar Tony Llama eelskin boots, three-hundred-
dollar Hi-roller hat, first-class tailor. Drives a brand-new Le
Baron. He seemed pretty upset when he found out what happened. I'm sure Blackie'll check him out, see if he's for real."

"What kind of guy is Blackie?" I had my own ideas, but I
wanted to hear McQuaid's.

"One of the smart ones," McQuaid said without hesitation.
"Grew up here in the county, where his old man was sheriff for a
long stretch. Went to Sam Houston same time I did, spent a couple of years on the streets in Dallas, then went to the sheriff's
office up in Taylor County, around Abilene. He moved back
here when his dad died. It was easy for him to get elected—folks
remembered his dad. He's well-trained and systematic, and he's
not in bed with any of the county politicos. He's straight."

"Sounds too good to be true." I sipped my margarita.
McQuaid may be an ex, but when it comes to his cop friends, it's
still one big lovefest. It reminds me of MacArthur's final speech
at West Point. The Corps, the Corps, and always the Corps.

McQuaid sniffed the air. "Better stir those beans or we'll be scraping them off the bottom of the pot." He hoisted himself out of the chair and went inside.

I sat looking into my glass, eating tortillas and salsa verde, and remembering the Boy Scout laws I had helped Brian memorize. They had reminded me of his father. A good scout is trustworthy, loyal, helpful, friendly, courteous, kind, obedient, cheerful, thrifty, brave, and reverent. I wasn't sure about obedient and reverent—McQuaid is mostly irreverent and the more stupid the rule, the more he enjoys breaking it. But everything else pretty much fits. Plus sexy and good-looking, attributes which don't have anything to do with scouting but which are nice to have in a lover. And he cares, perversely, about me. Good lord, what more do I want?

At that moment, Howard Cosell dragged himself around the corner of the house, went to the barbecue grill to inquire briefly about the progress of dinner, and then settled under McQuaid's chair with an exhausted sigh, as if the inquiry had been too much for him and he could only be restored by a nap. I doubted that, since this nap was the continuation of the one he'd been having in his hole under the forsythia. A moment later, Brian and his friend Creep wheeled around the corner. Creep was carrying his pet iguana, Einstein.

"Dad, can I—" Brian began. He saw the empty lawn chair and raised his voice. "Dad, where are you?"

"He's stirring the beans," I said.

Without moving, Brian raised his voice another notch. "Dad, can I go to Creep's house?" Howard Cosell wearily opened one eye and rolled it. I wondered if he'd come around the back to get away from Brian.

"We're eating at six," McQuaid yelled back from inside the kitchen.

"Okay. Can Creep and Einstein eat with us?"

"Not tonight, okay? China's here."

Brian screwed up his face. "Aw, Dad."

Creep came over to my chair. He is thin, with wire-rimmed

glasses and rabbity front teeth. His tee shirt said "Thank You for Not Barfing," and he wore a red cap turned backward, the bill hanging down in back. He dropped Einstein on the table beside the tortilla chips. "D'ja really find a dead witch?"

"No," I said. Einstein flicked his tongue in the direction of the salsa verde.

"You putrid liar," Creep said to Brian.

Brian opened his mouth to yell again, but I stopped him. "If you want to talk to your dad, why don't you go in the house? That way you won't have to yell."

"That's okay," Brian said, "I don't mind yelling." He cranked it up a couple of glass-shattering decibels. "Hey, Dad, can I eat at Creep's house?"

Howard Cosell opened the other eye. Einstein began to crawl in the direction of the salsa, his tongue flicking.

"Yeah," McQuaid said.

Brian, Creep, and Einstein raced back around the house. I breathed a relieved sigh. Howard Cosell closed both eyes and began to work seriously on his nap. McQuaid came out of the house and stepped up behind me. He leaned over, put his arms around my shoulders, and kissed my ear.

"The kid's gone," he said, nuzzling my throat. "How about a roll in the hay?"

"In the middle of the afternoon?"

McQuaid chuckled. He pulled up my blouse and cupped both breasts. "I can't think of anything better to do, can you?"

I couldn't.

A little while later, lying beside McQuaid with his arm under my head and the smell of mesquite smoke drifting through the open window, I thought again of my question. What more did I want? I was beginning to think that I might very well want McQuaid on a long-term if not permanent basis, although the thought of moving to the city when McQuaid found a new teaching job was totally unthinkable. And even if I got past that part of it, there was Brian. I doubted very seriously whether I could take McQuaid's son, the son's dog, and assorted friends and iguanas into the bargain.

Fifteen minutes later, I had shelved the question. The ribs were crisp and brown outside and juicy inside, the beans agreeably spicy, McQuaid's jalapeño hushpuppies soul-searing, and the strawberries ripely cool. While we ate at the picnic table on the patio, I gave McQuaid my side of this morning's story and answered his cop-type questions, which were pretty much the same questions Blackie had asked. When I told him about Sybil's visitor, I added, "It crossed my mind that it might have been Ruby's Andrew. I saw him with Sybil at his grand opening. They looked . . . intimate, I guess you could say."

McQuaid raised his eyebrows. "I noticed that he didn't volunteer his life history the other night at Lillie's. Did you mention him to Blackie?"

I shook my head. "Ruby was there. If I dragged Andrew into this, she'd never forgive me. Anyway, I could be wrong."

"Maybe. But Ruby doesn't want to be mixed up with a guy who's mixed up with a married woman." It's the Eagle Scout in him. Totally out of touch with the way people carry on their affairs, but I rather like it.

"Actually, she's pretty interested," I said. "She might be willing to overlook a few small details." Ruby is no Eagle Scout.

While we washed the dishes, McQuaid recounted the latest episode in his long-running feud with his department chairman, a man named Patterson. McQuaid has already published more articles and given more conference papers than anybody else in the department, a fact that Patterson regularly overlooks when it comes to recommending merit increases.

"He'd better put me in for a big raise in the next budget." McQuaid attacked the bean pot as if it were Patterson. "Or I'm going to get my résumé together. I've got another article coming out next month, and I'm giving a paper at the conference next week, as well as handling most of the shitwork. I do it because I like it, but it ought to be worth a little extra in the pay envelope."

I didn't say anything. I usually don't, when McQuaid talks about updating his résumé. I'm afraid he'll ask me to go with him, and I don't want to have to say no. But I can't say yes, either, which leaves me with nothing to say.

I hung up the dishtowel. "I have to get home," I said. "Leatha will be here in an hour."

McQuaid put sudsy hands on my shoulders and kissed me. "Are Brian and I going to get to meet your mother at last?"

"Depends on how long she stays." So far, I'd managed to avoid introducing McQuaid and Leatha, which seemed to me to smack of permanency. With any luck at all, she'd get bored and go back to Houston the middle of the week. "Anyway, you'll be busy with the conference."

"Call me," McQuaid instructed. "We'll work something out."

The front door slammed and the dishes rattled in the cupboards. Brian came into the kitchen, Howard Cosell shuffling after him, dragging his ears. "What's for dessert?"

"Strawberries," McQuaid said.

Brian clutched his throat, gagging, and staggered to the refrigerator. "Barf-o. Good thing I wasn't here. Got'ny ice cream? Howard wants some."

"See you later, guys," I said, and fled.

✳ ✳ ✳

I got home with forty-five minutes to spare, but I still had to find fresh towels, make the bed in the guest cottage, and sweep. I'd been drying herbs in the cottage, and the floor was littered with leaves and seeds.

I was heading out the door with a stack of fresh sheets and towels when the phone rang. It was Ruby.

"Andrew just left," she said. Her voice was brittle. "He saw a story about Sybil on the TV news."

"Oh, yeah?" I tucked the phone under my chin and reached for the lemon oil and a dusting rag.

Ruby paused. "He didn't know I'd already talked to the sheriff. He asked me to . . . to say he was here last night. All night."

My attention was suddenly riveted. "What did you tell him?"

"That I'd already told the police I was alone last night."

"Did he say why he needed an alibi?"

"I got the impression that he and Sybil had some sort of business arrangement, and he was afraid that the sheriff might . . . well, you know. Find a way to connect him to the crime."

"Ruby," I said quietly, "the sheriff can't connect Andrew to Sybil's death unless he *is* connected."

When Ruby finally spoke, the words were chipped out of ice. "I know you don't like him, China, but that's no reason to think he killed Sybil."

I softened my tone. "It's not a matter of liking or not liking, Ruby. We're talking about facts. Blackie won't go looking for Andrew unless he's got some reason to suspect him. Fingerprints, a witness, something concrete."

"Facts don't always tell the truth," Ruby said stubbornly. "You know yourself, the fact can be right but people interpret it wrong. You can't trust facts."

I tried again. "Did Andrew say where he was last night?"

"He went to San Antonio, but he got back pretty early."

"How early?"

"Around ten."

"Well, if Andrew were my friend, I'd tell him to let Blackie know about his arrangement with Sybil, whatever it was. I'm sure Blackie would appreciate it all to hell. He might even look kindly on Andrew for helping with the investigation."

Ruby hesitated. "I can tell him, but I don't think he'll listen. He doesn't want to get involved."

People who don't want to get involved are usually already in it up to their eyebrows. "Well, then, if I were you, I'd consider talking to the sheriff myself."

"But Andrew would think I betrayed him!"

I spoke slowly, giving the words extra weight. "Wouldn't it be better to run that risk than to be an accessory after the fact?"

Ruby's voice was a crescendo of injury. "So now *I'm* guilty!"

There wasn't any point in reminding Ruby that her knife had killed Sybil and that she had no alibi either. I excused myself, went out to the guest cottage, and began to make the bed, wishing that Leatha had stayed in Houston. But the tension at the back of my neck wasn't due to my mother's visit. People don't go around asking other people for a fake alibi just for the hell of it. Andrew must have felt pretty desperate, or he wouldn't have asked Ruby to cover up for him. Cover up what? What was the connection between Andrew and Sybil? Had they been business associates? Friends? Lovers?

For a moment, I toyed with the idea of telling McQuaid that Andrew was alibi-hunting, counting on him to get the word to Blackie. But that kind of back-channel communication was pretty underhanded. If I felt this was something Blackie should know, why didn't I call him myself? I knew the answer to that. If I told the sheriff, I'd feel like a traitor to Ruby. Damn.

I put out the towels, turned on the hot water heater, and checked for scorpions in the shower, then started on the living room. Once upon a time, the cottage had been a stone stable. The architect who remodeled the house did the stable, too, rather nicely. The walls are rough plastered and painted white, the floors are red clay tiles, and a stone fireplace with a heavy oak mantel dominates the living room. The kitchen is compact and tidy, and French doors in the bedroom open out onto a thyme-bordered patio. I've been thinking of renting it and I just might, if the financial situation gets any shakier. This year, I've used it to dry herbs, and the whole place smells like a meadow under a hot July sun. I swept the tile floor, trying to remember if Leatha was allergic to anything hanging from the beams.

I checked the refrigerator and turned it on, found a bottle of scotch and a half bottle of gin on the shelf, and carried them with me back to my place. It took just one drink to get Leatha loaded. The trouble was, as George Burns once remarked, you couldn't be sure whether that drink would be the thirteenth or the fourteenth. Leatha could bring her own poison.

Eight o'clock came and went, then eight twenty. I wasn't surprised. Leatha has spent years cultivating the critical social skill of correctly calculating just how late everybody else will be. Nevertheless, she's an alcoholic with a driver's license. I was almost glad to see her when she finally knocked on the kitchen door at eight thirty, a basket in her hand.

"China, *darlin'*," she said in the rich slow drawl that always reminds me of magnolias and N'Awlins café au lait, "how absolutely *mar*velous to see you! I'm awfully sorry to be late, honey, but I had a visitor this afternoon, an' the time just flew away."

We exchanged obligatory hugs, and then I stepped back, surprised. Leatha had gained ten, maybe fifteen pounds since I'd seen her in May. Scotch and cigarettes kept her weight down, and she'd always been wiry and taut. I remembered having a distinct preference for Aunt Hettie Greenfield's bosom over my mother's. Aunt Hettie was the black woman who came in to cook around the time I was four and stayed until I went to middle school. Under her starched white dress and apron, she possessed a motherly bosom on which I pillowed my head while she held me and read Grimm's fairy tales. My mother didn't have a motherly bosom. She didn't read fairy tales to me, or anything else for that matter.

When I got over the shock, the extra weight actually looked good. She was impeccably dressed in a Lord & Taylor silky gray shirtwaist with a two-strand rope of pearls, and she was elegant. There was something different about her hair, though. It was the same artful bouffant, a shade lighter than champagne, but I could see silver in it, and the roots were definitely silver. Only her hairdresser knew for sure, but I had my suspicions.

I must have looked surprised, because Leatha laughed. Her hair might be going natural, but her laugh was the same lightly artificial tinkle, like harp strings sounding up and down the scale, that used to infuriate my father. Her laugh annoys me, too, even though I know she shares the affectation with other southern women. For her, laughter is like a conductor's baton. It's an instrument for bringing everybody into tune, for harmonizing the social exchange.

My grandmother died when Leatha was born, and she was raised by her daddy and his sister Tullie in a plantation house near Greenville, Mississippi. One wall in her bedroom is hung with framed photos of herself as a deb, smiling, radiant, a vision in white tulle. After that her proud daddy sent her, accompanied by Aunt Tullie, to Sophie Newcomb College for Women, next door to Tulane University in uptown New Orleans. Leatha moved into Josephine Louise Residence Hall and Aunt Tullie moved into a small apartment across Broadway. Leatha took art, music, and literature, became a Kappa, and dined every evening with Aunt Tullie and several times a month with her daddy, who regularly came to the city to see that she was behaving.

In her sophomore year she met my father, Robert E. Bayles, back from three years in the Pacific, a student at Tulane Law and editor of the Law Review. The Bayleses were true Brahmins, with a huge pillared house behind a wrought-iron fence just off St. Charles, uptown. Grandfather Baxter Bayles was Tulane, Boston Club, and Rex, Comus, and King of Carnival. Grandmother China Bayles was president of the Newcomb alums, organized charity bazaars, and worked in her extravagant gardens. It was Gram who gave me my name and my love of plants.

The oil portrait that commemorates my parents' wedding at the end of my mother's junior (and last) year at Newcomb, hangs over the fireplace in her living room. She's sitting in a chair gazing up at my father, the antique lace train of her elaborate satin gown carefully arranged in folds that exhibit its opulence. He's standing beside her, strong and powerful, eyes forward. His hand rests firmly on her shoulder, as if to keep her from rising. The pose mirrored their marriage. After the wedding, they moved to Houston, where my father joined a large corporate law firm and my mother vanished into the big house in University Hills. Even in those days, Houston was a far cry from either Greenville or N'Awlins, and Leatha was totally overwhelmed by it. Lacking light of her own, she became my father's satellite, his dark moon, always in his orbital shadow. After a while, having nothing else to do, she learned to drink. As time went on, she drank to forget that my father hated her because she drank.

Leatha laughed her harplike laugh again, and touched her hair. "Don't you think it's time I let myself have a few gray hairs? After all, I'm old enough to be a grandmother."

I didn't know what to say, especially to that dig. I'm not likely to give her any grandbabies. But then, I hardly ever have anything to say. My mother and I never developed the ability to talk to one another.

I fell back on the social graces. "I'm sure you're tired. It's a long drive. Let me show you to the guest cottage."

"It's only four hours, honey," Leatha said. "I'm not that tired." She put the basket on the table. It was garnished with a cleverly tied bow and filled with little boxes of gourmet teas. Coals to Newcastle. There was enough tea in the shop to float the *Titanic*. "I thought we might have a cup of this nice tea an' a good little talk."

I cleared my throat. "I guess I'm the one who's tired. Someone I know died last night, and I spent the morning with the sheriff."

Her "Oh?" lacked curiosity.

"It was a murder," I said. Perhaps I wanted to shock her into interest. "It's been a *very* difficult day," I added, exaggerating. "Extremely tiring."

She was sweet. "Well, then, we'll just put off our little talk until you're rested. I wouldn't dream of makin' your day a minute longer than it needs to be." Aunt Tullie had taught

Leatha to yield to the wishes of others and never, *never* show impatience or anger. My father knew exactly how to take advantage of this discipline of concealment. I was taking advantage of it now.

But I *was* tired, I realized, as I helped Leatha carry her bags from her powder-blue Chrysler into the guest cottage. She had stayed there several times before, for a day or two, but judging from her stack of luggage, this time she planned to stay longer.

She put her purse on the coffee table and looked around. "I thought I'd just settle in for a week or maybe two. I have some serious thinkin' to do. I find lately that it's easier to think away from that big, empty house." The tinkling laugh again, up the scale and down. It was already grating on my nerves, which was a bad sign. There was at least a week to go, maybe more. "And I *do* want us to have that talk, dear. We haven't had a really good conversation in years."

Let's just leave it that way, I wanted to say. But I simply showed her where the extra towels were, said I'd see her in the morning, and wished her a good night. When I left, she was carrying a brown paper bag from the Chrysler to the cottage. It didn't take a detective to know what was in it.

As it turned out, however, the bag held breakfast fixings. At seven, while I was still in bed, Leatha came into my kitchen and began to stir pancake batter, cook eggs, and broil bacon.

"What are you *doing*?" I asked groggily from the doorway. I always sleep a little later on Mondays. I was still wearing my favorite ragged nightshirt, and my hair was tousled. Leatha was wearing a lavender running suit and my green-checked apron and her hair and makeup were perfect.

"I'm cookin' breakfast for you, dear," she said, breaking an egg into the pancake batter. "You look like you could use a good meal."

I gave a helpless laugh. "I *had* a good meal, just last night. I eat very well. Better than you, actually," I added tackily. Leatha doesn't eat. She just picks at her food. And she's never cooked breakfast for me. Well, maybe not never. But almost. We'd had a string of cooks—Aunt Hettie of the generous bosom was only the first I could remember. My father insisted on the arrangement, partly because he liked to entertain, partly because Leatha didn't cook.

"I've turned over a new leaf," she said, testing the griddle. "I'm eatin' a lot better." She poured out a pancake, then two more. "Can't you tell?"

"Well, I did notice an extra pound or two." I put on the kettle for tea and struck a match.

"That's probably because I'm not drinkin'," she said casually, ladling a fourth pancake onto the griddle. "Bein' sober does tend to put on the weight."

I stared at her. The match burned my fingers and I shook it out.

"Your father'd be surprised," she said, watching the pancakes begin to bubble at the edges. "He swore I *couldn't* stop, it was in the blood, 'cause Daddy was a drinker. He probably wouldn't like it that I've been goin' to a group. He always said he didn't want me barin' my soul to a bunch of drunks."

The second match broke. "*You're* going to AA?"

She picked up the pancake turner. "What a *horrible*-soundin' name. AA. Like it was an automobile company or something. But yes, I go to a meetin' every day, and once a week I go to see this sweet lady named Marietta, who grew up in Gulfport and lets me talk about anything that comes into my head, no matter how silly it is. And Marietta's got a ladies' circle that meets once a week, and we read books and talk about . . . oh, women things." She did a credible job of flipping the pancake. "It was *very* hard in the beginnin', I'm here to tell you, an' it's not much better now. I have to say I miss the liquor, guess I'll *always* miss it. At least that's what ever'body in AA says, you never get over missin' it. But Marietta says I'm gettin' better, an' it's true I'm eatin' better, an' feelin' better. Even lookin' better, which of course wasn't hard, I did look so pitiful an' thin. A good Gulf breeze could've blown me away. I've stopped smokin' too," she added as an afterthought.

I tried again with a third match, and this time got the burner lit. I sat down at the table. "What prompted all these remarkable changes?" I asked, and immediately regretted the sarcasm. But I couldn't take it back, and I was glad when Leatha pretended she didn't hear it. Selective deafness was another thing Aunt Tullie had taught her, which I both hated and used—and hated myself for using.

"Decided it was time I had a life of my own. My daddy an'

your daddy have both been dead a while now, and all that old stuff ought to be over and done with, wouldn't you think?" She flipped another pancake. "It was hard enough livin' with those two old roosters when they were alive. There's no point in me carryin' 'em to my grave, the way Aunt Tullie did."

I stared at her. My father and her father had always been her sacred icons. What had this "ladies' group" done to my mother's *head*?

She went on, chatty and conversational. "It's a shame you never knew your Great-aunt Tullie, China. She would've liked it that you went an' got your law degree. She'd like it more that you've got your own business, instead of workin' for a bunch of men. That's the way she would've done it, if she could've. She was in school when my mama died, you know. My daddy made her come back to Greenville to take care of me because she was his only sister an' not married. But of course he wasn't doin' anything out of the ordin'ry. It's always been like that, men expectin' women to do certain things." She put two pancakes on a plate, added two boiled eggs, and some bacon. "There," she said, with obvious satisfaction. "That'll help you face the day. That's what Aunt Tullie always said. Get yourself a good breakfast, Leatha, an' start the day right." She put the plate in front of me.

I usually eat homemade no-fat granola. All this made me very uncomfortable—my mother dishing out family history with the bacon and eggs and pancakes, not to mention her joining AA, finding a shrink, and attending a "ladies' circle" that sounded suspiciously like a women's consciousness-raising group. None of it fit my image of her—the daddy's deb swathed in white tulle, the adoring bride in white satin, the helpless mother adrift in her own boozy fog. Those were the pictures that had silently fueled my drive to make a place for myself in a man's world. My anger at my mother and what had created her might not be rational and it might not be healthy, but it was *mine*, the only functional thing inherited from a dysfunctional family. It was what had kept me separate from her, kept me moving toward my own goals while she drifted aimlessly in an amber-colored sea.

Leatha sat down across from me. "One of the things Marietta's been after me to do is to have a talk with you." She poured maple syrup over her pancakes.

"Isn't that what we're having?"

She leaned forward and poured syrup on my pancakes. "A talk about us."

I scraped the syrup off. "Why?"

Leatha's eyes are gray, like mine. They were uncomfortably direct. "You don't think it's a good idea for us to get reacquainted?"

I hedged. "I'm glad you're getting your life straightened out, but I don't know what that has to do with me." The kettle boiled, and I got up to measure mint tea into the teapot.

"That almond tea I brought is nice."

"I'll try it later," I said.

Leatha pushed her pancake around on her plate. "You're a lot like your father."

"Probably." Certainly, and not by accident. All the years of my growing up, I'd consciously tried to model myself after him. When he was around, it was clear that the power, the authority, the will to act belonged to him. When he wasn't around, which was most of the time, I could imagine his power and authority out there in the real world where wrongs were righted and fortunes made at the snap of his finger. If I grew up to be like him, I'd never be like her. If I grew up to be like her, I'd never be anybody at all. It was as simple as that.

She picked up her orange juice glass. "You're very hard to talk to, dear."

I sat down and went back to work on my pancakes. "I don't mean to be," I said, not truthfully, "I just don't have a lot to say, especially at breakfast. Look, Leatha—"

She put down her glass without drinking. "Do you think there's any way you could bring yourself to call me mama?"

I've been calling her Leatha since I was eleven and got my first period. "Why?"

She spaced her words, saying them slowly, as if each sentence represented a month's thought. "Marietta says that one of the things that will help me . . . stay away from drinkin' is for us to have a better relationship. An' one of the steps in the . . . program is to make amends. I'd like to do somethin', I don't know what, to . . . make up. For what we missed. All the lost years."

I looked down at my plate. If I said no, it was probably the same thing as saying I didn't care whether she stayed sober or not. If I said yes, I opened the door once again to her shame, her depressions, her suppressed angers. I took the coward's way.

"Let's do it later." I pushed my plate away and stood up, managing to smile. "This morning's kind of full. I'd better get started."

She pouted. At least that old trick hadn't changed. I was almost glad to see it. "But you haven't had your tea. And I thought you were closed on Monday."

"I am. But I need to finish landscaping the fountain McQuaid put in last week. I have to get the plants in the ground before we get a frost." It was an evasion, and both of us knew it. I headed for the bedroom to dress. "I'll have a cup of tea later," I said over my shoulder. "Oh, and thanks for the breakfast."

She picked up her fork. "Before you go, do you happen to know somebody named Pam Neely?"

I stopped, my hand on the knob. "Yes. What about her?"

"Marietta gave me her name an' said I should see her while I'm here, if I felt like talkin'."

I heard the implicit threat—talk to me or I talk to a psychologist. I decided to call her hand. The social circles she moves in do not include blacks. "She's good, I hear," I said.

Leatha bit her lip. "Do you suppose you could at least manage lunch?"

"Yes," I said, "I suppose I could." I went into the bedroom and shut the door.

✳ ✳ ✳

The weather was changing. The temperature was dropping from the seventies we'd enjoyed the week before, and the breeze was blowing a gray overcast out of the north. I pulled on a sweater, chose the plants and seeds I wanted, and went to work, trying not to think about Leatha. I was planting a border that would produce edible flowers next spring—borage, chives, anise hyssop, nasturtiums. I planned to teach a class on cooking with flowers.

I'd been working about fifteen minutes, seeding some Double Dwarf Jewel nasturtiums, when the sheriff's car pulled up out front. Blackie got out and came to where I was working.

"Mornin', Ms. Bayles," he said. His short sandy hair was even shorter than it had been the day before, and there was a pale strip over his ears and around the back of his neck. He'd probably just been to the barbershop.

"Good morning, Sheriff," I said. He didn't call me China, so I didn't call him Blackie. "You're out early." It wasn't even nine o'clock.

"Thought maybe you could give me a hand with a few names."

"Whose names?"

He pulled out a white index card and a stubby pencil. "I understand that Mrs. Rand was taking a fortune-telling class, and that you were in it. I'd like to have the names of the other students."

I straightened up. "It isn't a fortune-telling class. We're studying tarot."

To Blackie, it was a distinction without a difference. "How about the names?"

I ticked them off on my fingers. Gretel Schumaker, Judith Cohen, Pam Neely, Dot Riddle, Mary Richards, me, Ruby. Only six warm bodies left, now that Sybil was dead. Maybe Ruby would decide to postpone the class for a while, under the circumstances.

"Any of these people friends of Mrs. Rand?"

"Just Judith Cohen, I think. None of the others seemed to know her."

"This Mary Richards—she the one who had the Halloween party Saturday night?"

"That's right."

"I understand that the people in the white robes were witches, and that there was some kind of ceremony where a witch wearing bones made everybody chant the names of dead women. You know anything about that?"

I grinned. "Somebody must have been looking over the fence." Probably the same person who reported the KKK meeting.

He repeated his question, deadpan. "You know anything about it?"

"Yes, but it didn't happen the way you heard it. Nobody made anybody do anything. It was simply a commemoration of people who have died, to celebrate the beginning of a new year. It was very moving."

Blackie frowned. "Saturday was Halloween, not New Year's."

"Halloween is the Wiccan New Year. The people in the white robes were Wiccans, which is a sort of nature religion." Sort of. I felt as if I were condensing a graduate course in comparative religion into a ten-second sound bite.

"These Wiccans, they witches?"

"Well, yes, but I don't think they're the kind of witches you have in mind. Witches are like Baptists—they come in different varieties."

He didn't laugh. "So how do *you* know what kind of witches I have in mind?"

"I can hazard a guess. Anyway, if you want to know about the women who were at the party, ask Mary Richards. She can give you their names and explain their religious practices. Really, Sheriff Blackwell, you're barking up the wrong tree if you think—"

"Ms. Bayles," he said patiently, "I have to bark up *every* tree. Ninety-nine out of a hundred are the wrong trees. It's that one tree I have to watch out for." He turned the card over. "I wonder if you might've happened to remember the names of any other friends of Sybil Rand."

Andrew, I thought. Out loud I said, "I doubt that she had many friends."

The sheriff jerked his head in the direction of Ruby's store. "On the subject of friends, this Ruby Wilcox who runs the store there. I hear she's a friend of Andrew Drake. That so?"

My seed packet started to blow away and I bent over to retrieve it. When I straightened up, I'd gotten control over my face.

"Yes," I said. At least I hadn't been the one who had told him first. "As a matter of fact, the two of them had dinner with Mike McQuaid and me last week. Why? Is Andrew involved in this?"

"Hard to say," the sheriff said, and pocketed the card. He looked down at the seed packet in my hand. "Nasturtiums, huh? My wife plants a lot of 'em, out by the garage. She's always try-ing to get me to *eat* 'em—flowers, leaves, especially the seeds. She pickles the seeds in vinegar and throws 'em in my salad." He shook his head. "Crazy, huh?"

"Not really," I said. "But a scientist just discovered that the seeds are full of oxalic acid. Tell your wife that a few won't hurt, but you shouldn't eat them by the pound."

Blackie's face lit up. "No kidding? Hey, I'll get her to come by and talk to you."

"Anytime." I knelt down again. "Good luck with your witch hunt."

"Yeah," he said, and headed for the car.

❋ ❋ ❋

By eleven thirty, I had finished planting the flower bed, transplanted a half dozen gray wooly pillows of lamb's ears into various empty spaces, and broken apart several clumps of thyme, replanting them along the path with the creeping phlox and sweet allysum, where they could spill over onto the gravel. I was wondering if I had enough time to attack the tansy, when Leatha came across the street from the Magnolia Kitchen, carrying two take-out boxes.

"Lunchtime," she warbled. "I've brought somethin' simply *delightful* from that charmin' little place across the street."

I followed her into the house. She had brought a carton of thick tomato soup, Maggie's broccoli salad (she makes it Greek style, with feta cheese and olives and gives you a separate container of olive-oil dressing), and two cinnamon-basil cupcakes studded with walnut pieces. While I washed my hands and dug most of the dirt from under my nails, Leatha spread lunch on the kitchen table, picnic style. I found two bottles of homemade root beer in the refrigerator, left over from a batch Brian and I had brewed, and we settled down.

"I heard somethin' odd while I was waitin' for the food," Leatha said. "People were sayin' there's some sort of cult in town. They held a ceremony in the cemetery last night an' sacrificed a lamb. Cut its heart right out."

"Just what we need," I said. "More spook stories. That should keep things stirred up." I spooned dressing onto my salad. "Did you talk to Pam this morning?"

Leatha frowned just slightly. "Yes." She dipped her spoon into her tomato soup, not looking up. "You didn't tell me she was . . . colored."

"Does that make a difference?" I wondered how my mother had handled it, but I wouldn't know unless she told me. The relationship between a therapist and a client is as privileged as the one between a lawyer and a client.

"I suppose it doesn't," Leatha said, slowly. "She seems to be every bit as intelligent as—" She paused. "What I mean to say is that she seems just as—" She stopped. "She's not one to pussy-foot around, is she?" She put down her spoon with the look of a woman who has just made up her mind. "She gave me some good advice. She said I should just come right out and tell you."

"Tell me what?"

The phone rang. "Go on an' answer that, honey," she said. "I can tell you later."

I reached for the phone and took it at the table. It was McQuaid. "I'm not interrupting anything important, am I?" he asked.

"Leatha and I are just having lunch. What's up?"

His voice was flat, no inflection, coplike. "I've just come from the sheriff's office. Blackie's identified a thumbprint taken from the front door of the Rand house, and fingerprints from the doorjamb in the room where Sybil was killed. They belong to Andrew Drake."

I spilled my root beer.

"I'll take care of it," Leatha said. "You go on chattin' with your nice young man." She jumped up and went for a towel.

"There's more," McQuaid said. "Blackie identified the prints by sending them to the feds. Drake's in the FBI file. He was arrested in New Orleans three years ago for fraud."

"Oh, *shit*," I said. "God, poor Ruby."

Leatha came at me with the towel. "Lift your elbow, dear, and let me get this before it drips on the floor."

"That's not all," McQuaid said. "Blackie located the security guard who was on duty at Lake Winds Saturday night. Floyd, his name is. Every couple of hours Floyd cruises around the area, checking. He was turning into the Rands' street about midnight when he saw a car pulling away from the curb. Said he maybe wouldn't have paid any attention, but it had one taillight out."

"Don't tell me," I said. "A red Fiat."

"Right. Floyd whipped out after it, thinking he'd let the driver know about the burned-out taillight. But he ran into a bunch of teenagers around the corner—at least, that's what he thought they were. It was dark, and he couldn't be sure. Most of them were wearing sheets and masks. They said they'd been to a Halloween party."

"Did he question them?" Halloween costumes are the perfect cover for almost anything.

McQuaid gave a short laugh. "It was the end of his shift. He told them to go home. He was meeting a buddy for some night fishing under the I-35 bridge, and he didn't want to keep the catfish waiting."

"So we don't know if they were teens or Santeros."

"Or some other cult." McQuaid's chuckle was dry. "Wiccans, maybe. Blackie said he ran into a gang of them earlier in the evening. They had on white sheets too."

I made an impolite noise.

"Don't be vulgar," McQuaid said. "Anyway, there's something else."

Leatha came back from the sink with a clean towel. "Lift your arms so I can dry the table, China."

"Do you *mind*?" I snapped. "This is *important*."

"I'm sorry." Leatha sat down, not looking at me.

"What?" McQuaid asked.

"That wasn't for you."

"Well, I hope it wasn't for your mother," McQuaid said. "I couldn't snap at my mother that way. She'd box my ears."

"I wasn't snapping. What's the something else?"

"Blackie sent a deputy around to Andrew's apartment complex to ask questions. He turned up a woman who was walking her dog at eleven forty or thereabouts, when Andrew drove up.

He went into his apartment, then came right back out and left again, which she thought was odd, because it was so late. About twenty after twelve, after she'd gone to bed, she saw lights on her drapes. She looked out. It was Andrew, coming back."

"Good thing Ruby said no to the phony alibi."

"What phony alibi?"

I told him. "Looks pretty bad for Drake, doesn't it?"

"Blackie sure thinks he's onto something. Are you going to tell Ruby about this?"

"I have to," I said. "None of this stuff is confidential, is it? Did Blackie know you were going to tell me?"

"He didn't say it was off the record. Anyway, he was bringing Andrew in for questioning when I left, so he's moving pretty fast."

"Sounds like he's got something to move on," I said. "Keep me posted, McQuaid."

"Yeah," McQuaid said. He paused. "Hey, cut your mother a little slack, okay? She can't be that bad."

"How do you know?" I countered testily. "See you." I hung up. "Okay," I said to Leatha, pointedly raising my arms. "You can dry off the table now."

"It's just that root beer is so sticky," Leatha said, getting up again. When she finished, she hung up the towel. "That was Mike, wasn't it?"

"Yes," I said. I was wondering whether it was going to be difficult to run Ruby down. I didn't want her finding out from the grapevine about Andrew being taken in for questioning. And that's just what would happen if I didn't catch her quick. I reached for the phone.

"You know," Leatha said thoughtfully, "I've always wondered why you don't call him by his Christian name. Your young man, I mean. McQuaid sounds so . . . well, so *cold*. As if you don't care."

"I've always called him McQuaid," I said, trying not to snap.

"I called him that when I met him. He was a cop. I was a lawyer. We were on the same case, opposite sides. It seemed natural."

Leatha wrinkled her forehead. "Yes, but that was business. Now it's personal. And you're on the same side. Aren't you?"

"Excuse me," I said. "I have to make a phone call."

10

I tried Ruby's house, I tried the Cave, and I tried Mane Attraction, where she sometimes goes on Monday afternoons. The answering machine at the house said nobody was there, the answering machine at the Cave said she'd be in tomorrow, and Roxanne Spivey at Mane Attraction said I'd just missed her.

"You won't know her when you see her," she added. "We got that extra curl ironed out."

I left messages and gave up trying to track Ruby down. Leatha went back to the cottage to read a book, and I went out to the garden to cut the last of the Silver King artemisia for wreaths. The wind had gotten colder and it was spitting rain, and I didn't want to lose what little was left standing, even if it did look a bit tattered. It would make good wreath filler. I was almost finished when Constance came bouncing up the walk. She had on a dumpling-yellow pants suit and a clear plastic rain scarf.

"I've just come from the sheriff's office." She stopped to breathe heavily. "Andrew Drake's in trouble. Big trouble."

"He is?" I finished tying the last bundle and stuck it into my basket. "How do you know?" If Constance knew I could stop trying to get to Ruby first.

"Maureen McKenny had her appendix out on Friday, so Arnold asked me to take her courthouse beat." Constance dropped onto the bench at the end of the mint bed. "I was in the sheriff's office talkin' to Blossom Rheinlander. She's the one who gives Maureen the news for the Sheriff's Rap Sheet column. Thangs like the flag that got stolen from the high school and the kids that were jumpin' off the highway bridge into the river, thangs like that. Blossom's worked there since the Flood and knows just about—"

"Constance," I said, "just tell me about Andrew."

"He was in the back, in the jail, and he came in with all these papers and threw 'em down on Blossom's desk—"

"Andrew?"

She opened her yellow tote, pulled out a white hanky, and blew her nose. "The sheriff. He was really ticked off. He told Blossom to get to typin', but the statement part would have to wait because Drake wasn't goin' to say anythang for the record until he got himself a lawyer. Then he left, the sheriff, I mean. Since Blossom had already given me the stuff for the Rap Sheet, I left too. That's when I saw Andrew bein' hustled down the hall by a couple of deputies."

At that moment, Ruby's red Honda pulled up out front, and Ruby came flying up the walk. "China! You've got to come with me," she cried.

I picked up the basket of artemisia. "Where are we going?"

"The sheriff's office. I ran into Blossom on the square. The sheriff wants to fingerprint me and get a statement."

Constance's eyes were as big as walnuts. "Is he goin' to arrest you *too*?"

"What do you mean, me too?" Ruby looked at me. "What's she talking about?"

"I called around to find you, Ruby," I said. "The sheriff has taken Andrew in for questioning." It was more than that, but I thought we'd start there.

Ruby's face went white. She sank down on the bench beside Constance. "Andrew? *Why?*"

"I don't understand it, either," Constance muttered, shaking her head. "He's such a *nice* man. He's a person you can trust. He's paid three whole months ahead on his rent."

Ruby's voice was urgent. "What can the sheriff possibly have on him?"

I shot a glance at Constance. If I told Ruby what I knew in front of Constance, half the town would know it before Ruby was fingerprinted. "I'll put this stuff in my kitchen and be right with you," I said, hefting the basket of artemisia.

We said good-bye to Constance, left the basket in the shop, and climbed into Ruby's Honda. "So tell me," Ruby commanded between clenched teeth. "They can't possibly have anything on him." She started the car. It died. She started it again. "What do they *think* they've got?"

"Andrew's neighbor was out walking her dog at eleven forty on Saturday night. Andrew drove up, then left again. He came back at twelve twenty."

She pulled jerkily away from the curb. "That doesn't prove anything. He could have gone out for beer."

I tried to be gentle. "If he did, he got it on his way to Sybil's. The Lake Winds security guard puts him there at midnight. That's when he saw Andrew's Fiat leaving the Rand house."

That one was harder to explain, but she tried. "Maybe he just went there. Maybe he didn't get out of the car. I *know* it wasn't him, China."

She already sounded so desperate, I hated to tell her the rest. But she'd better have it from me than the sheriff. "He got at least as far as the door to the room where Sybil was killed, I'm afraid. They found his fingerprints on the doorjamb. They also found a thumbprint on the front door." I hesitated, feeling like a jury foreperson bringing in a guilty verdict. "According to McQuaid, Blackie identified the prints through the FBI. They've been on file since he was arrested on a fraud charge in New Orleans three years ago." I put my hand on hers and squeezed. "I'm really sorry, Ruby."

There was a long silence while we negotiated the backed-up stoplight at Guadalupe and MLK. When Ruby spoke, her voice was choked. "At least you didn't say I told you so."

"Just because somebody's questioned, it doesn't mean he's guilty. Not even if he's charged, Ruby. People get arrested all the time, but it doesn't always stick." On this count, I could speak with authority. I hoped it was comforting.

Apparently not. She was gnawing her lower lip. "It sounds pretty bad."

"He needs a good lawyer. The sooner the better. His lawyer needs to get into the investigation before the D.A. brings an indictment to the grand jury. There's always the possibility of digging up something the cops overlooked and getting the prosecutor to back off." I was getting ahead of the game, but I wanted to put the best spin on it.

She shot me a glance, her meaning plain as day. I shook my head. "Nope. I'm out of the business. I don't have a staff or an office. I don't want to take a case to trial."

"But you already know Andrew," she said plaintively. "You know the sheriff. You saw the body. You're perfect."

I was firm. "I'll go with you this afternoon, but Andrew has to get his own lawyer. He needs somebody who's set up to go to court."

"Maybe you'll change your mind."

"Sorry," I said. "By the way, what's happened to the tarot class? Is it still on?"

Ruby shook her head. "I called everybody else and postponed. I left a message on your machine."

She pulled up at one of the one-hour meters in front of the sheriff's office, which is in the old library building on one corner of the square. The meters were unpopular when they were installed a couple of years ago and got even more so when the hourly rent went from a dime to a quarter. "Why does the sheriff want my fingerprints?"

"He's eliminating people. He's interested in yours because it was your knife and you were there on Saturday. He'll ask for mine too. He's probably already got Judith's and Angela's and the husband's."

She fished in her purse for a quarter. "When he starts asking questions, what should I tell him?"

"The truth," I said simply. We got out of the car. I looked at her. "I like your hair," I said.

"Thanks," she said. She tossed her head. "At least I'll look good for the mug shot."

❋ ❋ ❋

Blossom Rheinlander is in her sixties, a friendly, capable woman with short-cropped gray hair, a leathery face that has seen plenty of Texas sun and needs no makeup. She was pleased when I remembered that her granddaughter Julie Ann was last year's Quarterhorse Queen at the Adams County rodeo and rode a mean barrel race. She showed us into a small cubicle, told us the sheriff would be along directly, and pointed out the hot plate and coffeepot. The walls of the room were painted green, the floor tile was also green, and a photograph of the governor hung by the window. I skipped coffee, having gone to the effort of flushing most of the caffeine out of my system a couple of years ago. Ruby helped herself.

Sheriff Blackwell came in and sat down, rubbing his square jaw. His eyes flicked to me, back to Ruby. "Afraid you might say something incriminating?" he asked her with what could have been a smile.

"I thought it was a good idea to ask her to come," Ruby said. She drained her cup and set it aside. "What do you want to know?"

He took a white card out of his pocket, wrote Ruby's name on it in a minuscule, cypherlike script, and jotted the number one in a corner. "Let's start with Sybil Rand." He had the voice of a tax auditor. "How long have you known her?"

"About a year. She comes—" She swallowed. "She came into the shop every once in a while. She bought books, crystals, incense, things like that. Mostly books, I guess. She asked me to order titles for her. Esoteric stuff."

"Books on magic?"

"Magical herbalism, astrology, tarot. Some of what she wanted was out of print. I had to get it from a book search company."

"Do you know her husband?"

"No."

"Do you know her maid?"

"I've met Angela once or twice. I talked to her on Saturday."

"Do you know she loaned twenty-five thousand dollars to Andrew Drake?" The question was asked in the same even, emotionless tone.

Ruby's head snapped up. "No!"

"Do you know whether he paid any of the money back?"

I was proud of her. "How could I, if I didn't know she loaned it to him in the first place? What was it for? The business?"

"How well did Drake know Sybil Rand?"

Ruby dropped her eyes. "As far as I know, they were just acquaintances."

The sheriff made a note. He knew his stuff. "Just acquaintances? Not lovers?"

"Not as far as I know." Her shoulders were hunched.

"Judith Cohen says they were sleeping together."

Ruby's lips thinned. A red stain seeped up from the neck of her open shirt. "Maybe Judith knows something I don't."

"How well do you know Drake?"

"It depends on what you mean," Ruby said. The red crept swiftly from her neck to her lower jaw. "We've been . . . going out together quite a bit, lately. The last few months, I mean. Since he's been in Pecan Springs."

He made another note. "Are you lovers?"

Ruby's face matched her hair. "We've been to bed together, if that's what you mean. What does that have to do with anything?"

"How much do you know about him?"

"About his past, not much. It wasn't important."

"Do you know about a fraud case in New Orleans he was mixed up in?"

Ruby shot a glance at me. "No," she said. "I mean, well . . ."

I leaned forward. "I gave Ruby the information you gave to McQuaid this morning."

"Figures," the sheriff said without surprise. "Let me rephrase the question. Before today, did you know that Drake was arrested for defrauding a wealthy New Orleans woman?"

"A wealthy . . . ?" Ruby closed her eyes. "No. I didn't know."

The sheriff got up and left the room.

Ruby spoke in a whisper. "Why is he asking me about—"

I put my finger to my lips. Ruby got up and refilled her Styrofoam cup with coffee and sat down again, sipping it. She grimaced at the taste. The sheriff came back with a cardboard box. He put it on the table in front of Ruby and sat down.

"Understand you're something of an expert in the occult," he said. "I'd like your professional opinion about these two things." He opened the box and took out a black leather-bound book bearing an embossed gold pentangle. Beside it, he spread out a deck of tarot cards. But the cards weren't at all like the ones we used in Ruby's class. The images on these cards were dark and ominous, almost frightening, filled with an angry energy.

Ruby opened the book and looked at the flyleaf, then flipped through the pages. She closed the book and pushed it away from her. "It's exactly what it says it is," she said. "*The Satanic Bible.* It was written by Anton LaVey. It's the operating manual for his Church of Satan." She glanced at the cards. "That's a deck of tarot cards called the Thoth Tarot, designed by Aleister Crowley. Where did you get these things?"

"They aren't yours?"

"Of course not," Ruby flared, indignant. "I've never even had a copy of LaVey's book in the store."

"Why not?"

"I don't go in for that stuff. It's dangerous. Were these Sybil's?"

I looked at the book. I didn't remember seeing it on the shelf in the room where Sybil was killed, but that didn't mean anything. It could have been anywhere in the house. I'd never seen the cards before, either. They certainly weren't the ones Sybil was using when she died.

"Are the cards Satanic too?"

"Not exactly." Ruby paused. "Crowley had a reputation as a Satanist, but his brand of magic was mostly renegade Masonry, decorated with a lot of Latin mumbo jumbo. But it's the energy in the cards I don't like. Some of the images are very harsh, violent. It's not a deck I recommend to most people."

The sheriff opened the book and pointed to something written on the flyleaf. "The Order of the Trapezoid—what's that all about?"

"It has something to do with German mysticism and the Church of Satan." She looked at him. "Where did you say you got this book?"

"Does it have anything to do with Nazism?"

The burning cross in Judith's yard flared in my mind. Was it connected with Sybil's death?

"Maybe," Ruby said. "I really don't know. It's not my thing." She grinned crookedly. "If you want to know, I have a book at the shop that has some stuff in it about LaVey. It's quite respectable, really. Written by a professor of sociology."

The sheriff was not only sharp, but persistent. "Would you say that whoever owned this book was a Satanist?"

Ruby looked uncomfortable. "I guess they wouldn't have had it if they weren't interested in magic. But I own books I haven't read. Having a book on a subject doesn't make you a believer."

The sheriff put the lid on the box. "Why do you say that Satanism is dangerous?"

"Because Satanists believe that just because they want to do something, it's okay," Ruby replied. "Satanists are on a perpetual power trip. They're out to control other people. They manipulate."

The sheriff made notes on the card. "Was Sybil Rand a Satanist?"

"No." Ruby frowned. "At least, I don't think so. I never saw any indication that she was."

Blackie turned to me. "How about you? I understand that you know all about those poison plants of hers. Did she use them in Satanist rituals?"

"She could have, I suppose," I conceded. "They've been used in so-called black magic in the past. Belladonna, henbane, monkshood, jimsonweed—"

"Those are plants she had?"

"Yes, some of them. She also had others."

"You can identify the black magic plants for me?"

"I can identify those that have a history of magical use, yes."

"Yesterday, I asked you whether the lady was into Santeria, and you said you didn't think so. Now I'm asking you about Satanism. Ever see anything that made you think she was a Satanist?"

I thought of the tarot, the plants, the books on Sybil's shelf, about her black clothing, her jewelry. I could see why Blackie, putting two and two together, would come up with four. But while I couldn't quarrel with his arithmetic, I still thought he was wrong. Sybil wasn't the most conventional person in the world. She may even have been on a power trip of some kind. But that didn't make her a Satanist.

"No," I said.

Without missing a beat, Blackie turned back to Ruby. "What about your friend Drake? He a Satanist?"

"Andrew?" Ruby was incredulous. "You're kidding."

"Do I take it that's a no?"

"Yes, definitely." She frowned. "I mean, no. No, he's not a Satanist."

The sheriff jotted a microscopic note. At the rate he was going, he could put Ruby's life history on card number one. He wouldn't need card number two. "What about this Order of the Trapezoid? Did he belong?"

Ruby was getting angry. "I just said no, didn't I? If he'd been a Satanist, I would have picked it up somehow."

The sheriff pocketed the card, picked up the box, and stood up. "Well, if he's not a Satanist, how come we found this Satanist bible in his apartment?" His look bore no trace of humor. "Was he studying up on how to turn people into frogs?"

I don't think he meant for us to laugh. We didn't.

✳ ✳ ✳

When we got back to the Honda after leaving our inky fingerprints with the appropriate deputy, the meter was ticking out its expiring minute. Agnes Rhodes, Pecan Springs' parking cop, was poised beside it, her ticket book in her hand. She grinned when she saw Ruby. "Thought I was going to get you. Another thirty seconds, and I would've." To break the boredom of her route, Agnes makes a game out of it.

Ruby wasn't playing. Agnes, seeing that nobody was in the mood for fun, stuck her ticket book in her back pocket. "Well, have a good one, what's left of it," she said, and walked away.

Ruby turned on the ignition. "Let's get a beer. I need to wash the taste out of my mouth."

It was early, and Lillie's was almost empty. We sat down at the bar and Bob pulled us a Lite and a Lone Star and brought a basket of chips. "Maria hasn't come in with the salsa yet today," he said. He squinted at Ruby. "You read the latest?"

Ruby threw a despairing look at the ceiling. "Don't tell me Constance's got it in print already!"

"Got what?" Bob asked. "I'm talkin' about Billy Lee's newspaper. I'll go see if I can find it." He went into the back.

Ruby turned to me. "It was awful, wasn't it?" she asked. "The questioning, I mean."

"Actually," I said, "Blackie was pretty cool." Pretty good, too. He'd played the rhythm of his questioning like an expert bass player, signaling the shifts in melody without giving anything away. "You did fine, Ruby."

"I didn't feel fine. I felt like he'd already made up his mind about Andrew. I was just there to confirm." Ruby took a long swallow of her beer. "It sounds like Blackwell's been digging up all the dirt he can get his grubby hands on. What do you suppose this New Orleans thing is all about?"

"I wonder. Blackie said Andrew had been arrested, but didn't mention a conviction. Maybe they couldn't make it stick."

Ruby put her beer down. "Maybe it was one of those false-arrest things."

"Tell you what," I said. "I know an assistant D.A. in New Orleans. I'll call first thing tomorrow and ask her to nose around for us."

"Are they going to let him out on bail?"

"Wait," I said. "We don't know he's been arrested."

"But if he has?" Her heart was in the question.

"Bail's iffy in a murder case, especially with a prior arrest. The judge has a lot of discretion. It's likely to be in the neighborhood of a hundred thousand dollars."

Ruby paled. "A hundred thousand!"

"Maybe more. Andrew's new in town. That makes a difference."

Ruby's freckles stood out on her face but her eyes were steady on mine. "China, I know you're not crazy about Andrew, and maybe he's done a few things that weren't too smart. Maybe he borrowed money from Sybil. Maybe they were sleeping together. But I *know* he didn't slit her throat. And I'm not saying that just because I care about him. I'm saying it because I have this gut feeling."

I've known Ruby long enough to respect her gut feelings, but I couldn't help thinking that she was being deceived by her attraction to Andrew. If love makes you blind, sex can make you deaf and dumb. "I hear you, Ruby," I said. "But you've got to see it from Blackie's angle, too. He's developing a cult theory that's pretty plausible, given what he found at the crime scene and in Andrew's apartment."

Ruby shook her head, adamant. "There's a difference between what's plausible and what's probable. Andrew may have been mixed up with her, but somebody else killed her. And if you want to talk cult, there's plenty going around. Sybil's murder isn't the only weird thing that's happened lately."

Bob emerged from the back. "Here it is." He shoved a folded newspaper across the bar. "Took me a minute to find it. It'd already gone into the garbage. Where it belongs."

The newspaper was stained with coffee grounds and catsup, but it was still legible. The front-page banner proclaimed itself *The Community Conscience*, published monthly by the Everlasting Faith Bible Church, Pecan Springs, Texas. Under the banner was the headline, "The Church Takes On the Devil." Under that was a story about the picketing—what the newspaper, with a rhetorical flourish, called the "divinely blessed campaign of righteousness against the evil rampaging in our midst." There was another article about the church's stand on divorce, which apparently ranked right up there with devil worship. And there was a picture of the Reverend in his white suit, his arm around a woman with a Tammy Faye face and a Dolly Parton profile. According to the caption, her name was Barbie. It figured.

"Yuck," Ruby said distastefully. "Look at those boobs."

"Look at *this*," I said, and pointed to an article under the picture. It was headlined "This Month's Business Boycott," and the first sentence read, "In the opinion of the editorial board, the following businesses support unholy practices and should be considered anathema." The list was short. It consisted of the Crystal Cave and Thyme and Seasons Herb Company.

"Damn and blast," Ruby said.

"Yeah," Bob said. "Makes you want to puke, don't it?"

Ruby crumpled up the paper and slam-dunked it into the plastic trash bucket behind the bar. "I thought Pauline told Harbuck to can this stuff."

"She told him to stop *picketing*," I reminded her. "She didn't want the site visit team to see us squabbling. The team will probably never read *The Community Conscience*."

"But it'll *kill* business," Ruby wailed.

"That's what Billy Lee's after, don't you reckon?" Bob pulled another couple of beers. "On the house."

"Thanks, Bob. You're a peach." Ruby licked the foam off the top of her beer and turned to me. "Can we sue?"

"We'd have to prove malice," I said. "Anyway, I don't think we do much business with the Reverend's congregation. So what if they boycott?"

Ruby hunched her shoulders. "It's the principle of the thing."

Bob began to slice margarita limes into a bowl shaped like a catcher's mitt. "Ask me, the guy's a jerk. It's goin' to cost a coupla hunderd to build a new shed."

"He's worse than a jerk," Ruby said grimly. "He may even be behind Sybil's murder."

"Watch it," I said.

Ruby was defiant. "Well, I mean it."

"You're prob'ly right 'bout that, too," Bob said, putting the catcher's mitt on the back of the bar. "Nothin' but a jerk. Even as a kid. Wasn't just a car he stole, neither. I asked my brother Dickie this weekend. He said before the car, they ripped off a coupla fillin' stations. Never got much, just some soda pop money and candy bars and a few cases of beer." He poured a plate full of salt and put it beside the catcher's mitt. "Good thing Ma never found out, or Dickie woulda got worse'n a hidin'. He'da got creamed. Dickie says there was a girl, too."

"A girl?" Ruby asked.

"Yeah. Dickie says Billy Lee knocked her up, just before he

got sent up to do time for the car." He fished the crumpled Tammy Faye/Dolly Parton look-alike out of the trash and grinned at it. "Wonder what ol' Billy Lee's new wife'd say if she knew about the girl her ol' man knocked up back in Abilene."

Ruby made wet rings on the bar with her beer mug. "China," she said slowly, "do you think—"

"No, Ruby," I said. "I don't."

She swiveled around to face me. "Well, *I* do. It's just too coincidental. The Reverend is out to get witches, so he pickets us. Somebody breaks into my shop—"

"And somebody burns down my shed," Bob put in helpfully. "And didn't I hear something about a cross?"

"Right," Ruby said, "and then somebody kills Sybil." She banged her glass on the bar. "I'm not saying the Reverend actually did the dirty work himself. I'm just saying maybe he psyched up his disciples for a witch-hunt and they got carried away." She frowned, with that slightly out-of-focus look she always gets halfway through her second beer. "And now here's the sheriff, putting an innocent man in jail, while the guilty party, excuse me, the *possibly* guilty party, goes around printing up newspapers and telling people to boycott our stores because we're witches." She burped.

Bob looked up from the maraschino cherries he was dishing out. "Who'd he put in jail?"

"You mean you haven't heard?" Ruby was mournful. "Andrew Drake." Tears began to trickle down her cheeks.

"Nooo," Bob said sympathetically. He held her empty glass under the beer tap. "Have another, Ruby. You'll feel better."

"Thanks," I said hastily, standing up. "We've got to go. I forgot something I'm supposed to do. Come on, Ruby, I'll drive you home."

"It's all right," Ruby told Bob. She made a belligerent fist. "I'll get the sonofabitch. Just wait 'n' see."

"Sure, you will," Bob said reassuringly. He leaned both elbows on the bar. "Listen, Ruby, you lemme know if I c'n help, okay? I got connections back in Abilene."

11

The something I had forgotten was Leatha. I had left for the sheriff's office early in the afternoon without telling her where I was going, and it was now nearly six. I wouldn't have been a bit surprised if she'd fallen off the wagon while she was waiting.

She hadn't. She was sitting on the batik-print loveseat in the cottage, reading a book and drinking Perrier in a champagne glass. She'd changed into a pale pink sweater and matching pink slacks. Still dressed in the sweats I'd worn all day, I felt heavy and grubby. But I always felt that way around her. Even blitzed out of her mind, my mother managed to be beautiful. I suppose it was another reason for resenting her.

"Sorry I'm late," I said. "The sheriff is questioning Ruby's boyfriend about the murder of Sybil Rand. He questioned Ruby too. She asked me to go with her."

She looked up, startled. "How *awful* for her. But she's lucky she has you to turn to. Are you going to represent her friend?"

"No," I said emphatically. "Listen, do you mind if we just go across the street to eat? I have to see someone at seven thirty, and I don't want to take the time to cook."

Walking back from Ruby's in the chill early twilight, I'd decided to drop in on Judith this evening. I was especially curious about what she'd told the sheriff. I'd called her when I got home. She had agreed to see me, although she hadn't sounded too thrilled about it.

A disappointed look crossed Leatha's face, and I remembered how short I'd cut breakfast and lunch. "I won't be out more than an hour. We can get together after I get back."

"That's fine," Leatha said. "In the meantime, I have a book to occupy me." She held it up. It was a book for children of alcoholic parents. "Have you read this? It's very good."

I shook my head. Ruby had suggested a couple of similar books, but I'd resisted. It was a subject I knew by heart. Why did I need a book?

Leatha stood up. "I'll give it to you when I'm finished."

"I really don't think I—"

"I know," she said compassionately. "It's awfully hard to talk about, isn't it? Until Marietta made me, I simply *refused* to let myself think about how my daddy's drinkin' tore me up. You must feel the same way about me, China."

"Actually, I haven't given it a lot of thought." *Liar*. It had been on my mind for years. Why did it embarrass me to hear her say it?

Leatha smiled. "Well, you're not the only one in denial, honey. Everybody's simply smothered under it, tons and tons of it. Marietta says it's the first thing we've got to flush out of our systems."

We set out for dinner.

Maggie's Magnolia Kitchen is a long room with white walls and strategically placed panels of green and white lattice, draped with climbing vines—real ones—and hung with pots of cheerful red geraniums. The ceiling is the original pressed tin, probably worth more on the antique market than the rest of the restaurant. It's painted forest green to match the painted wood floor. The tables are white, the chairs are green. On each table there is a clay pot of herb plants, thyme and marjoram and different varieties of basil. If you watch, you'll catch people surreptitiously rubbing and sniffing. I have a theory that herbs love to be rubbed as much as people love to rub, as long as they don't pinch.

It was Monday night, early, and business was slow. The

room was mostly empty, except for a half-dozen women gathered around the round table in the back. They had the look of nuns—dark skirts, white blouses, short hair, sensible shoes. Maggie, sitting with them, gave us a wave and stood up. As I waved back, I wondered if they missed her cooking at the convent.

Leatha and I took a table near the front. Maggie, menus under her arm and glasses of water in her hands, came to greet us. She'd met Leatha at lunchtime, and she sat down a minute to talk. Maggie is short and stocky, with farm-worker hands and arms. Her graying hair is razored short over her ears, her square face is beautifully plain, and there's not an inch of artifice in her. With Maggie, what you see is what you get, a woman who knows herself and invites you to know her too. She was wearing a plain gray shirtwaist, a white bib apron handpainted in green with her logo and a larger-than-life magnolia, and black crepe-soled oxfords.

"How's it going?" she asked me.

I made a noncommittal sound. It's hard to trade polite social lies with Maggie. Her eyes challenge you to tell the truth, and I wasn't up to it.

"China's involved in a murder," Leatha volunteered.

I rolled my eyes.

"Sybil Rand?" Maggie asked, then answered her own question. "Has to be. It's the only murder in town." She sighed. "A sad business."

"Actually, I'm not involved," I said. "The sheriff is questioning a friend of Ruby's."

"I heard." Maggie shook her head. "I don't know which is worse, to think she was killed by a cult, or by somebody who hated her." Her gray eyes showed genuine concern. "How's Ruby?"

"Bearing up." I picked up the menu. "What are you cooking tonight?"

Maggie understood, bless her. "The quiche just came out of

the oven," she said briskly, and stood up. For Leatha's benefit, she added, "It's sage and onion. China and I planted the sage, out on the patio."

We ordered spinach salad and the quiche. I was ready for a glass of wine, but I wasn't sure about the etiquette of it. Or the morality. Are you supposed to drink in front of a recovering alcoholic?

"Get wine if you like," Leatha said, taking the decision out of my hands. "I'll have coffee," she told Maggie.

Maggie gathered our menus. "Tell Ruby I'll pray for her," she said. "And for her friend."

I smiled. When Maggie says she'll pray, she means it. "Thanks. Ruby will be grateful." It wasn't a social lie.

We started on the homemade bread, which came on a round wooden breadboard. Leatha sliced two pieces. It was hot and fragrant with flecks of garden herbs.

"Can I finish what I started to tell you at lunch?" Leatha asked.

"Fine," I said absently. My mind was on Ruby. I'd left her at home, pacing up and down the living room, frantic about a man who, if I believed Blackie's theory, could be a murderer. Did I believe it? I did and I didn't. There were Andrew's fingerprints and the Satanist bible—hard evidence. The eyewitness testimony of the neighbor and the security guard. The prior arrest. I could see where Blackie was coming from. If I were a cop looking for a killer, Andrew would have to be high on the list.

But Blackie's wasn't the only interpretation that could be drawn from the evidence. I didn't like Andrew and I didn't trust him. I hated to see Ruby hand over her heart to somebody who might hurt her. But Andrew could be a two-timing louse without being a murderer. He could be—

"I've decided to get married," Leatha said.

"Wonderful," I said, reaching for the butter. I froze. "You *what?*"

Leatha shifted in her chair. "There was just no easy way to

tell you, honey. Both Marietta and Dr. Neely thought I just ought to say it straight out, without tryin' to prepare you."

"Get married?" I asked blankly. "Who to?"

"Sam Conners. He owns a ranch near Kerrville."

"But . . . but . . . How long have you known him?"

"Just a few months," Leatha said. Her cheeks were pink and she actually giggled. "But it feels like forever."

The wine came and I reached for it. I guess I hadn't considered the possibility of her marrying again. She'd been married to her liquor. And of course, she wasn't hurting for money. Dad had left her with plenty. But maybe I should have considered it. Maybe I should have worried. She was certainly an attractive target for some fortune-hunter.

Leatha leaned forward and lowered her voice, serious now. "Your daddy's been dead ten years, China. We never were happy together, except maybe for the first little bit, before Robert got so involved with his practice. Life was pure and simple hell while you were growin' up. I wanted us to be a family. But he was never home, an' when he was, he was cold, like an iceberg. Like my daddy." She twisted off another slice of bread, not looking at me. "I'm still workin' on that old stuff. There's a lot about my daddy I don't want to remember. Marietta says I need to, though, so I'm tryin'. But it hurts."

I stared at her. In all the years I had known Leatha, she had never shown negative feelings. She'd always been perfectly compliant, perfectly agreeable, perfectly perfect. Even when she drank, she drank quietly until she passed out. I couldn't remember a single argument, a single critical word from her against my father. Not that he didn't deserve it. I had watched him practice cruelties, large and small, always calculating exactly how much he could hurt her. I had seen her turn to the only comfort she knew and hated her for not being strong enough to stand up to him, to defend herself. And what was this about *her* father? I remembered the photograph of Leatha as a deb, her eyes shining into her father's eyes, his arm protectively around her, his smile proud as a young bridegroom's. I shivered. What was it she didn't want to remember?

Leatha's mouth was set in an expression I'd never seen. "Maybe you don't think I should say things about your daddy and him not here to defend himself. But Marietta says I have to stop sweepin' all the old bad stuff under the rug. I have to face it. Your daddy was abusive—words, mostly, but his condescension and sarcasm hurt just as much as if it was the other kind. I just wish I'd've had the strength to stand up to him. I should have left him. For your sake, if not for my own."

I was still staring, feeling a sharp, clear pain as I realized that for all these years I had hated my mother for not doing something she couldn't possibly have done. Where he was concerned, "yes" was the only word she knew. It was a word she had been taught by her father, by her aunt, by her whole world. How could I have hated her for *that*?

Maggie came with the quiche. Plates were set down, silver rearranged, water glasses refilled. I tried to cope with my enlightenment. Finally, I asked, "Who is he? This man, I mean."

"Sam's a widower. He has an apartment in Houston, because he comes for business. But mostly he lives at the ranch. That's where we're going to live."

"A . . . *ranch*?" To my knowledge, the closest Leatha had come to animals was organizing charity affairs for the zoo.

She laughed her trilling laugh. "Isn't it just too funny for words? Me, on a ranch? But it's not a regular ranch. Sam keeps exotic game. You know, deer and antelope from Africa, weird things from Asia, from China." She picked up her fork. "He'll explain it to you, dear. It'll be a while before I know what I'm talking about. But of course, he'll teach me, and his children are around to help."

I was way out of my depth. "Children?"

"Sam Junior's the eldest. He manages the ranch and his wife Becky Sue does the bookkeepin'. They live in the big house with Sam. They have two children, Jack and Allie, just the *sweetest* little things. It's not goin' to be a bit hard to be a grandmother. Then there're the twins, Steve and Sara. Steve is a doctor in San Antonio and Sara is the president of a bank in Houston. Sara is awfully nice. We go to lunch every week. She's sort of adopted me." She began on her quiche with gusto. "I think she misses her mother. Neither she nor Steve are married. Brenda Lee—she's the baby—got married this summer, right after she finished nursin' school."

"Have you, uh, set a date yet?" I asked, when I could find my voice.

"Sam wants to meet you, of course, and have you out to the ranch for a long weekend before we announce anything. And he's tryin' to wrap up this big business deal before we get married, so we can have a real honeymoon, maybe a cruise. Then there's the problem of gettin' the children all together. Maybe summer." She put down her fork and leaned forward, dropping her voice confidentially. "I can't tell you how glad I am that you're taking it this way, China. I was worried that maybe you'd be . . . well, difficult."

Maggie's quiche was perfect, as usual, but I had lost my appetite. I was trying to make conversation with a mother I didn't know, a mother newly sober, newly shrunk and self-actualized, newly feminized, and newly engaged. Having gone to a fair amount of effort to maintain my own simple, uncluttered life, free of emotional obligations and responsibilities, I was now about to become a member of a very extended family: a step-father plus (if I counted right) four step-brothers and sisters and various spouses, in addition to a step-niece and step-nephew. A cast of thousands.

I hoped Leatha could handle it. I wasn't sure I could.

Judith had raked out the spot on the lawn where the cross had burned, but I could still see the charred grass. She came to the door barefooted, in black stirrup pants and a cranberry-red sweater, hair piled loosely on top of her head. She led me to the living room at the back of her house. The room was as spare and ascetic as Judith, with bare floors, a minimum of furniture, a few oriental drawings, and a waist-high sitting Buddha, eyes cast down, mouth eternally fixed in an inscrutable smile. The room overlooked the ravine at the back of the house. I could see the angular shapes of bony trees, backlit by the streetlight on the next street. The drapes were pulled back and there was nothing to prevent someone on the other side of the ravine from looking in. I wondered what a Peeping Tom might make of Judith's Buddha, and whether that had anything to do with the cross-burning.

I sat down on a small black leather sofa. "The sheriff questioned Ruby this afternoon," I said without preamble. "He said you think Sybil and Andrew were having an affair."

Judith sat on a small blue rug in front of the window and tucked herself easily into a full lotus, Buddha-like. There was only one light on, and the planes of her angular cheekbones were shadowed. "She never actually told me so." Her voice was cool, a little distant, and I realized that I didn't know her very well. She was closer to Ruby than to me. "It was something I just picked up on. Why are you asking?"

"Because Andrew Drake is involved, which means that Ruby is involved. She doesn't think Andrew did it."

"You're trying to get Andrew off?"

I tried not to feel defensive. "I'm helping Ruby figure out what happened, and it's hard because Sybil's such a mystery. Do you mind talking about her?"

She tilted her head and rotated it as if she were exercising her neck. "I'm not sure how much I can help. Sybil was a very private person."

"How long did you know her?"

"She and C.W. moved here from Dallas about three years

ago, when C.W. took over as managing partner at the resort. She heard about my yoga class and enrolled. She was a good student, very disciplined, very serious about her practice. We've been friends ever since, as much as Sybil would allow. We weren't close."

"What about her husband? What's he like?"

Judith looked past me at the Buddha. "C.W.? He likes to impress. His business was real-estate development—until the bottom dropped out. But from things Sybil said, I gathered the bust was just a trigger for a trap of his own design." Her eyes came back to me, her voice almost amused. "Sybil didn't have a very high opinion of C.W.'s business abilities. She said once that he was a little shark who kept on swimming with the big sharks even after they chewed his tail off."

It sounded like something Sybil might say. "If he was in trouble, how'd he get into Lake Winds? Buying into the partnership must have cost plenty, not to mention the quarter of a million or so they spent on that house."

"It was *Sybil*'s house, and her money that bought into the partnership. Oil money. She inherited it from an aunt before she and C.W. were married. It was her separate property, and she kept it very well shielded from C.W.'s creditors, and from C.W. himself. Every now and then she'd make him a loan or an outright gift that would keep him going." Judith straightened her legs and opened them wide, clasping her right leg at the calf and bringing her forehead to her knee. Her spine was straight, her arms gracefully curved. I couldn't see her face. "But she was tired of bailing him out," she said to her knee. "*She* was bailing out."

"How so?"

Judith straightened, clasped her left leg, and brought her forehead to her left knee, holding it for a moment before she answered. "She was planning to file for divorce."

I was startled. "Divorce?"

She released the stretch and resumed the lotus looking full at me. "Yes. She didn't talk about it much. But I know she went to see Charlie Lipman about some legal papers last week."

I remembered the proprietary way Sybil had claimed Andrew the day of the grand opening. "Was the divorce because of Andrew, do you think?"

"It's possible, but I don't know. She never talked directly about Andrew, except to say she'd made him a loan to help him start his business."

"Did she say how much?"

"No."

"Do you know of any other reason for the divorce?"

"C.W. was having an affair. Sybil wasn't happy about it."

"But if she was sleeping with Andrew—"

She looked at me. "*If,*" she said. "I could be wrong. Anyway, it was more complicated than that. C.W. had problems with women. One husband threatened to name him as a corespondent in a divorce case. Another time, there was an expensive paternity suit. Expensive for Sybil, that is. She made C.W. promise that there wouldn't be any more extracurricular activities."

"So this affair made her angry?"

"I don't know that it was anger, so much. And it certainly wasn't jealousy." Judith frowned. "I think she was just tired of C.W.'s foolishness. I'm guessing about Andrew," she added, "but not about the divorce. Charlie Lipman had already started the paperwork."

"Did Sybil tell you who C.W. was involved with?"

"Jerri Greene. She teaches aerobics out at Lake Winds."

It made sense. Jerri was a sexy, attractive woman. There was a certain sharky quality about her, too, that might appeal to a man like C.W. Jerri knew what she wanted and she'd get it, regardless of whose tail she had to chew.

"One more thing," I said. "Sheriff Blackwell seems to be working on the theory that Sybil and Andrew were involved in some sort of cult. Do you think Sybil was a Satanist?"

"No!" Judith spoke sharply. "The idea's ridiculous."

"Then why *did* she grow those plants?"

She shrugged. "For the same reason anybody does anything different. To be noticed. To stand out from the crowd. Or maybe just to make C.W. mad. He hated her plants. He thought she was planning to poison him."

"Seriously?"

"That's what Sybil told me, anyway. C.W. was scared to death of the plants. She seemed to think it was a good joke."

As I biked home through the chill November dark, I thought to myself that for somebody who claimed not to know very much about Sybil, Judith knew an awful lot. The conversation had been productive. When I was preparing a case for trial, there had always been a point at which it came to life. It stopped being just a paper chorus of he saids and she saids, claims and counter-claims, and became a drama in which real people, compelled by powerful motives, acted in predictable and unpredictable ways. This wasn't my case, but it was coming to life.

What *was* the powerful motive that drove someone to kill Sybil? If I discounted Blackie's cult theory, I couldn't see that Andrew Drake had a motive. What would he gain? The money she had loaned him? Maybe, but it didn't seem like sufficient incentive. On the other hand, he'd been spotted leaving the scene of the crime. And who knows what had gone on between him and Sybil. Maybe there was more than money involved. Maybe she knew something about him that he couldn't afford to have known, and was holding it over his head. Maybe—

But while I was groping in the dark for Andrew's motive, C.W.'s motive sang out loud and clear. Sybil's widower stood to gain much more from her death than Sybil's ex-husband might have gained in a divorce. The fact that he'd been in Atlanta when she was murdered was almost irrelevant, given the fact that murder, like anything else, can be bought and sold. And Sybil's killing certainly had all the earmarks of a professional job. Your average murderer stabs his victim. A professional killer can easily slit a throat.

Yes, it had been a very productive conversation. But as I wheeled my bike into the ramshackle garage I rent from Constance Letterman, I was left with one big question.

If I could see C.W.'s motive so clearly, why didn't Blackie see it too?

✳ ✳ ✳

I'd been back five minutes when McQuaid and Brian knocked on the kitchen door, on their way home from a Scout meeting. McQuaid is the only man I know who manages to look sexy in a Scoutmaster's uniform.

"Hi," McQuaid said. "Too late for company?"

Brian gave me the Vulcan blessing. "Found any more dead witches?"

"She wasn't a witch," I said, letting them in. McQuaid kissed me on the cheek. "How about some hot chocolate?"

"Cool," Brian said. "Put a marshmallow on it, okay? Can I watch the last half hour of 'Star Trek'? They're rerunning Mr. Spock's brain."

"Keep the volume down," his father said, and Brian vanished into the living room.

McQuaid sat in the rocking chair, pulled off his shoes, and put his stockinged feet on the windowsill. "I stopped at the sheriff's office this afternoon, late. Blackie seems to think Ruby's off the hook."

"Great," I said dryly. I got out the pan for the hot chocolate. "Did he expect her to confess to being Andrew's accomplice in a Satanic spell designed to change everybody in Pecan Springs into toads?"

"It *was* her knife."

"Stolen from her shop." I put the pan on the stove. "That's another thing. Why would Andrew trash Ruby's place and steal her knife? And why would he want to incriminate her? After all, they were sleeping together." Even if he was sleeping with Sybil too. It was almost enough to make me want to be celibate. I sneaked a glance at McQuaid. Nope, not quite.

"Have you pointed all this out to Blackie?" he asked.

"Not yet. I just thought of it. Are there any cookies in that jar?"

McQuaid got up and took the lid off the cookie jar. "Yeah," he said. "A few." He put one in his mouth. "This one seems to be oatmeal raisin." He took two others.

I handed him a plate. "What else?"

He looked at the cookies in his hand. "This kind's chocolate chip. But the other kind's got little bits of burned twiggy stuff all over it."

"Coconut. If you don't like it, don't eat it. Anyway, that isn't what I was asking. What else did you find out about Andrew?"

McQuaid emptied the cookie jar onto the plate. "That he was never indicted on that fraud count in New Orleans."

I stood still with the can of cocoa in my hand. "Oh, yeah? How did that come about?"

He put the plate on the table and sat back down in the rocking chair. "The plaintiff died before the D.A. could take the case to the grand jury."

"*Died?* How?"

"Blackie hasn't dug that far yet. But without her testimony, the D.A. couldn't make it stick." He folded his hands behind his head and rocked. "Very convenient, huh?"

"Convenient for Andrew." I measured cocoa and sugar into a pan and added hot water from the kettle on the back of the stove. "Not so convenient for the plaintiff. Or the D.A." I frowned, not liking the parallels. Andrew, money, and two dead women. The list of Andrew's possible motives had suddenly grown longer. Maybe Sybil had found out about the trouble in New Orleans and he'd killed her to keep her from spilling it. Score one for Blackie. A *big* one.

"Andrew still hasn't given a signed statement," McQuaid said. He munched on a cookie. "But Blackie's probably already got everything he's going to get. Andrew admits that he went to the Rand house on Saturday night. According to him, he had an eleven o'clock date with her."

"So *he* was the one she was supposed to meet."

"Yeah. He says he was going to write her a check for fifteen thousand dollars in partial payment of the loan. But he went to San Antonio to see a friend and didn't get back until eleven fifteen. He stopped at his place and called her, to ask if it was too late for him to come over. She said come ahead. He went to her house. He knocked at the front door and didn't get an answer. He went to the back of the house—apparently, he'd been there before—and found her dead. He panicked and decided to get the hell out of there. He was just pulling away when the security guard came around the corner."

I stirred a few drops of mint flavoring into the chocolate syrup and added milk. "I suppose Blackie'll take a look at Andrew's bank account to see whether he actually had the money."

"No doubt," McQuaid said. "But it doesn't change Blackie's mind. He still thinks Andrew killed her."

"But there's a problem," I said. "Andrew's prints were on the front door and the patio doorjamb, but they weren't on the knife. Why not? Did he wipe the knife and forget the doors? Did he put gloves on after he got in the room? Pretty clumsy, for an intelligent man."

"Yeah." McQuaid rocked back in his chair. "I'll bet Blackie'll stay up half the night trying to come up with an answer."

"Did he find any bloodstained clothes?" The attack had come from behind. The killer would have ended up with blood somewhere, probably on his arms, certainly on his shoes.

"Nothing's turned up yet. Blackie's asked Bubba to check all the dumpsters in the neighborhood. Bubba's got more available manpower." He looked at me. "Personpower."

"What about the Satanist bible? What did Andrew say about that?"

"That it belonged to a roommate he'd had back in New Orleans. The guy was a member of some squirrelly outfit called the Order of the Trapezoid. But Blackie's sticking with the cult angle."

"It's the wrong angle, if you ask me." I poured hot chocolate into two mugs. "The bereaved husband has a much more powerful motive."

McQuaid whistled when I finished telling him about the divorce. "Did Judith tell all that to Blackie?"

"I'm sure she did. And that has me puzzled. Why isn't Blackie going after C.W. as a possible suspect?"

"Maybe he knows something we don't." McQuaid reached for a mug. "There's no law says he has to give me *all* the pieces of his case." He frowned. "Come to think of it, I wonder why he's giving me any at all."

"Maybe he just wants your opinion."

He grinned. "Or yours. He knows about that little problem you solved for Bubba last year. Maybe I'm just a pipeline to you. How much do you charge for consulting?"

I found the marshmallows I keep for Brian, added a couple to the Star Trek mug he gave me for Christmas, and poured it full of hot chocolate. It's one of those trick mugs. The Klingon spaceship began to vanish. "Tell Brian his chocolate's ready."

McQuaid raised his voice. "Beam yourself in here, Trekkie. Time to refuel."

Brian bounded into the room. "Mr. Spock got his brain back!"

"Was there ever any doubt?" a light voice asked from the kitchen door.

I'd forgotten about Leatha.

The next few minutes were filled with introductions, small talk, smiles, and general bonhomie, while I made more hot chocolate. When the cookies ran out, which happened almost immediately, I popped some popcorn. McQuaid, charming in his Scoutsuit, behaved in a terribly civilized way and Brian was utterly captivating. *I* was the churlish one, partly because I was still thinking about Andrew and Sybil and Ruby and partly because I felt guilty at having forgotten my mother. But mostly, I'm ashamed to admit, because I was pissed off at McQuaid for being so nicey-nice and at Brian for being such an angel that I almost felt like measuring him for a halo. Leatha was obviously smitten. I was glad when McQuaid remembered that it was a school night and took Brian home.

"Well," Leatha said, arching her eyebrows, "it looks like I'm not the only one with a little romance in her life. Why haven't you *told* me, honey?"

"I don't know what you mean," I said, rinsing out the cups. I wiped Brian's Trekkie mug and put it on the shelf where he could find it the next time he came.

The laugh. "Why, of course you do. Mike's crazy about you. And Brian—what a *delightful* child. Really, China, I don't understand why you're holding back. Marriage would be so *good* for you, dear."

I didn't answer. Marriage would be good for me, would it? After she had admitted how awful her own marriage had been? When I knew that if McQuaid and I were married, one of us would have to give up something very important and would probably end up resenting the hell out of the other?

Not my idea of fun.

12

Right after I opened the store the next morning, I called
Joyce Moyers, the assistant D.A. in New Orleans. She wasn't in
so I left a message, describing what I needed.

Leatha was exploring the shop, examining the herb shelves,
leafing through recipe books. I looked at her thoughtfully. I had
errands to run. If she was going to hang around, she might as
well be useful.

"How would you like to take over the store this morning?" I
asked.

"Could I?" she asked eagerly. Then her face clouded and she
gave me her predictable answer. "But I really don't know the
first thing. I'd just mess up."

I looked at her. "Would Marietta let you get by with that?"

She digested the question for a moment. "What do I have to
do?" she asked.

It took about ten minutes to explain my system for handling
cash and giving receipts and deciphering the price tags and
labels. "Ruby will be opening up at ten, if you need help."

She settled herself on the stool behind the cash register,
ready for customers. "Where are you goin'?"

"Down the street to Charlie Lipman's." I looked up the
phone number and gave it to her. "You can call me there if you
run up against something Ruby can't handle."

Charlie Lipman's office is a gentrified frame cottage painted gray with green trim and landscaped with native plants—sage, yucca, sedums. Charlie had been Ruby's lawyer when she split from Ward. If Judith was right, he was Sybil's lawyer, too.

The receptionist looked up from her typewriter when I came in. I had put on a khaki camp shirt and denim wrap skirt that morning, even—in honor of Charlie—a touch of lipstick. But I wasn't any match for the receptionist. A fresh-cheeked Texas beauty with honey-colored hair, she was wearing a short, tight red skirt and a sleeveless white turtleneck glued to perky breasts. Her mouth was right out of an Estée Lauder advertisement. I had to question Charlie's choice. Me, I'd have hired an older woman who'd make my female clients feel a little less like Grandma Moses and save my male clients from making fools of themselves.

"Is Charlie in?" I asked.

"Your name, please?" Miss Texas asked brightly.

"China Bayles."

"Do you have an appointment?"

"Do I need one?"

"Yes," she said, showing what she was made of. She pulled a schedule book toward her. "Next week, at the earliest."

Charlie appeared in the door. "China! Hey, great to see you! Come right on in, gal. Where ya been keepin' yourself?"

Charlie Lipman is turning soft, with the beginnings of a belly sagging over his belt and a fast-receding hairline. He was in shirt sleeves, open collar, loose tie. With a smile and a wink at Miss Texas to show her that she'd done her job, he ushered me into his office and closed the door.

"So," he said, lowering himself into a leather chair behind a glass-topped walnut desk, "whut can I do for you?" He chuckled. "It cain't be a divorce, since last I heard you and McQuaid hadn't tied the knot." Charlie grew up in the wealthy Highland Park area of Dallas. He is not a country boy. But in his business it pays to talk like one. Charlie is as bilingual as your average politician.

"It's a divorce," I said. "But not mine. Sybil Rand's."

Charlie's brow furrowed heavily. "Now, China, you know I ain't supposed to—"

"She's dead, Charlie."

"I know, but—" He frowned. "Ruby talk you into representin' Drake?" Charlie and Ruby had dated for a while after her divorce. They were still friends.

I held out my hand and waggled it from side to side in a maybe-yes, maybe-no gesture. It wasn't quite a lie.

Charlie snorted. "I figgered you couldn't stay out of the courtroom forever. Just got to missin' that action, dint you? Well, Drake could do worse." He paused. "So whut d'you wanna know?"

"I understand that Sybil was getting ready to file a divorce action. What kind of settlement did she propose?"

Charlie picked up a pencil and tapped the desk. "Half the community property, whatever that amounted to, plus a quarter of a million from her funds. Hell of a lot better'n she had to. Their prenups tied him up like a roped calf. She wouldn't've had to give him diddly if she wadn't feeling generous. Specially with that track record of his."

"Why was she so generous?"

"Dunno. Maybe she was gettin' some herself on the side and she felt guilty. She had it all worked out when she came in. Had the numbers down on paper."

"Had she told C.W. what she planned to do?"

Charlie picked up a gold pencil and balanced it on his finger. "Not yet. Said she was fixin' to, before he went out of town. Wanted to give him plenty of time to think about it."

"So," I said, "if C.W. knew that Sybil was planning to—"

Charlie's quick. "Are you thinkin' maybe he fixed her wagon before she could get around to divorcin' him?"

"It's a possibility."

He shook his head. "Not unless that ol' boy was at the end of the line when the good Lord passed out brains. Along with set-tin' up the divorce, the lady also added a codicil to her will. She cut him out. The whole estate goes to some cousin up in the Panhandle, with the exception of a few small personal bequests—the maid, Judith Cohen, a couple others. O'course, the husband will get his split of the community property, although from what she said I'm bettin' there ain't a lot left."

I leaned forward. "C.W. *doesn't* inherit her estate?"

"Ain't that whut I said?" He grinned. "Tell me, counselor, whut kind of angle you figger to work on this case? Looks like a tough defense to me. If I was you, I'd—"

The price I had to pay for my information was ten minutes of Charlie's learned views of how Andrew's defense ought to be structured. I'd gotten a bargain. It could have been twenty.

Miss Texas was making over her lips when we came out of the office. She dropped her equipment into a drawer and bent over the typewriter again. Oh, the drudgery of it all.

Back at the shop, Leatha was ringing up a sale. "How's it going?" I asked when the customer left.

Leatha was radiant. "Oh, China, this is such *fun!* I've met the most interestin' people. And I've sold"—she consulted her receipts—"fifteen dollars and twenty cents worth! How about that?"

"Fantastic," I said sincerely. "Did Joyce Moyers call from New Orleans?"

"No. But a woman named Dottie called to ask about some herb. It sounded like a specialty item. She said it was for her cats." She consulted a note. "It's called Paw de Ark."

I smiled. "That was Dottie Riddle, the cat lady. She collects every stray in town. The herb is pau d'arco." I spelled it for her and pointed it out. "She'll also want echinacea root. Tell her I'm out of red clover, but I've reordered." I looked at her. "I have a few more errands. Do you want to stay, or shall I call Laurel to come in?"

Leatha settled herself behind the cash register. "Call Laurel? Don't be ridiculous! Of course I'll stay."

I checked the mail, then went next door to find Ruby unpacking a box of merchandise. She was wearing turquoise blue leggings and a matching batwing top, her hair a gingery halo. She gave me a large hug. "I really appreciate your talking to Judith last night. Andrew will appreciate it too."

That's a small town for you. You can't go to the bathroom without somebody knowing about it. I gave her a close look. "Are you going to see him this morning?"

"Yes. And when I tell him you're interested in his case, it'll cheer him up. He has a lot of respect for you, China."

I stepped back. "Hang on, Ruby. Just because I asked Judith a few questions doesn't mean—"

"What did you find out from Charlie? Anything that could clear Andrew?"

I sighed. There is no such thing as a confidential investigation. "No, Ruby. If anything, Charlie's information puts Andrew in deeper. C.W.'s no longer a probable suspect. Charlie says that Sybil planned to tell her husband that she was divorcing him. What's more, she made a new will and cut him out, which totally blasts his motive. And I've already told you, I'm not taking the case. It's out of the question."

Ruby has a way of getting to the heart of things. "Then why are you investigating?"

"I'm not investigating," I said evasively. "I'm just following up on a couple of open questions, that's all."

"Oh," Ruby said. She reached into the box and took out a crystal pyramid. "Well, you're the only one in town who doesn't have all the answers," she said, holding it up. It refracted the light like a prism, casting a rainbow against the wall. "Everybody else thinks Andrew's guilty as hell."

"He's not guilty until the jury says he is."

"Maybe." Ruby polished the pyramid with her sleeve and put it carefully on the shelf between a Chilean cactus rain stick and a deck of Karma Cards. "But in this case, the jury's already brought in the verdict. They're having coffee at the Doughnut

Queen, talking about how Andrew didn't just kill Sybil, but that other woman too. The one in New Orleans."

I stared at her. "How'd they find out about *her* already?"

"One of the deputies told his sister, who works the night shift at the Exxon station." Ruby chewed her lower lip, forehead furrowed. "You know this town, China. By the time the sheriff figures out who really killed Sybil, it'll be too late. In fact, it's probably already too late. Andrew might as well sell his studio and go someplace else."

I hated to admit it, but Ruby was right. In a small town, the stain of murder is like the blood on Lady Macbeth's hands. You can't wash it out, you can't bleach it out, it'd be there even if you cut off both hands. If Andrew was innocent, the real killer had better turn up in a hurry or there'd be two tragedies. Sybil's and Andrew's. *If* Andrew was innocent. With C.W. out of the picture, Blackie's theory had gained merit.

Ruby took a buckskin medicine bag out of the box and spilled a half-dozen polished stones on the counter. "I guess I'm just going to have to get involved," she said, counting them. "I know Andrew didn't do it, which means somebody else did."

"Get involved?" I asked. "Aren't you involved enough already?"

She picked up a shiny green stone flecked with red and rubbed it against her cheek. Then she put it in her pocket, and put the other stones in the bag. "The answer's got to be right in front of us, China. Don't forget that the murder weapon was stolen from *this* store. If I knew who broke in and took that knife, I'd know who killed Sybil." She paused. I could see the wheels turning. The next question was entirely predictable. "Do you think your mom could watch both shops, China? I've got a few things I want to do."

"Better call Laurel Wiley," I said. "Leatha's probably got her hands full." I looked at her. "What was that stone you put in your pocket?"

Ruby put the medicine bag on the shelf beside the pyramid. "It's a bloodstone. It symbolizes the planet Mars."

"I'm afraid the significance escapes me."

She picked up the box. "It stands for strength." Her eyes narrowed. "Strength and resolve."

It figured.

※ ※ ※

Blossom was leaning over her typewriter, dabbing correction fluid on a typed form. "Don't know what I did before they invented this stuff," she said. "I go through a bottle a week, between using it up and letting it sit around with the top off. Anybody gets arrested, there's five pounds of paperwork."

I propped my elbows on the counter. "I read that a woman cooked it up in her kitchen. Made her rich."

Blossom arched both eyebrows. "No kidding? Stands to reason. Man makes a typo, he just exes it out, doesn't worry about it looking neat. What we need is a computer. Sheriff's putting it in the budget. You want to see him?"

"If he's not busy. Tell him I've got just one question."

The sheriff was penciling numbers onto a time sheet. I looked at it. "More paperwork?"

He flung his pencil down. "Want to know how many man-hours we've put into this investigation so far?" He waved the question away. "No, you probably don't, China. You're not a county commissioner with an axe to grind."

It wasn't lost on me that we were back to first names, so I responded in a friendly way. "They're after you about efficiency, huh?" I'd read in the *Enterprise* that Blackie had asked for an eighty-thousand-dollar budget increase, including salaries for two more deputies. The commissioners gave him half and told him he could have the other when he justified the two new positions. I wondered if Sybil's murder would do it.

"Is that your one question?"

I sat down in the chair beside the desk. "It's about C.W. Rand."

"What about him?"

"I want to know when he found out about his wife's new will and the proposed divorce settlement."

Blackie tilted his chair back and took a toothpick from a square wooden holder painted with a Texas flag. "Word gets around. Are you representing Drake?"

I'd already lied once that morning. I might as well do it again. "I'm thinking about it."

"Well, it's about time he got somebody. The preliminary hearing is this afternoon, lawyer or no lawyer. If he doesn't have one, the judge'll see that he gets one."

"What about C.W.?"

Toothpick in mouth, Blackie debated between being cooperative and dragging his feet. He decided on cooperation, more or less. "Don't see why not. We're all friends here. Anyway, you'll get it quick enough, you sign on with Drake. Yeah, Rand knew about the divorce. He and Mrs. Rand talked about it after she got back from seeing Charlie. She even typed up a note describing what she planned to do, date at the top, name at the bottom, whole nine yards. Kinda blows his motive, if that's what you were thinking."

I got up. "Thanks."

"Yeah, sure." He stood up too, and spoke around his toothpick. "You ought to take Drake's case, China. Way I get it from McQuaid, your talents are being wasted on flowers. And this one could be pretty interesting." He grinned. "Kind of like sacking rattlesnakes."

I'd settle with McQuaid later for the crack about talents. "Rattlesnakes? You got something I don't know about?"

He cocked an eyebrow. "Hey, you said one question."

I went back to the car and sat staring out the windshield. Rattlesnakes was right. Lucky for Rand that Sybil had told him about the will and the settlement. Even luckier that she'd decided to write it down. I frowned, thinking I'd heard something like that before. Evidence in an old case, maybe. My brain used to be cluttered with stuff like that. But I'd put a lot of effort into flushing it, and whatever the thought was, I couldn't pull it up.

I turned on the ignition. Yeah, rattlesnakes. But now I was curious. Maybe it was time I met the merry widower.

✳ ✳ ✳

C.W.'s office was in the central Lake Winds Resort complex, a cluster of buildings housing a gym, indoor tennis courts, a restaurant, and several shops. All the buildings were upscale rustic, native limestone, with lush landscaping and mass autumn plantings of yellow and rust chrysanthemums and pansies.

As I parked the car and got out, I saw the aerobics teacher, Jerri Greene, coming down the walk, wearing a cowboy shirt, calf-length denim skirt, slim and split to the thigh, and high-heeled cowboy boots. She smiled and waved in my direction and got into her red Mustang convertible, looking pleased with herself. She backed out with a spray of gravel.

I stood for a minute, watching Jerri drive away and wondering whether she had been visiting her sister or C.W. Then I went inside. The office was plushly carpeted, paneled in red cedar, and decorated with photographs of Lake Winds properties and the notables who had entertained or been entertained there—Arnold Palmer, Ronald Reagan, the Dallas Cowboy cheerleaders. Against a wall was a brown cowhide sofa, flanked by two chrome chairs and an inlaid wood coffee table on which was displayed a spikey cactus and a bleached cow's skull, together with several copies of the University of Texas alumni journal and other Texas magazines. There were two desks. One, a receptionist's desk, was empty. I walked toward the other, where Rita, Jerri's sister, was sitting. She was holding her head in her hands. She hadn't heard me come in.

I cleared my throat. Rita looked up. Her mascara was smeared under her eyes and her eyelashes were gummed together in little clumps. Papers littered the floor, as if they'd been swept off the desk, and a cup of pencils had been overturned. It was a safe bet that Rita and her sister had had words.

"Uh, hello." She gave me a half-hearted smile and turned away to dab at her eyes. "Is there something I can do for you?" She spotted the papers and got up to retrieve them. In her pink-and-blue floral ruffled print dress and matching hair ribbon, she had the look of a homely high-school girl who'd tried to make herself pretty for her first date and hadn't quite got it right. There was something almost pathetic about her, and I thought again of the contrast between her and Jerri—according to Judith, the Other Woman in Sybil Rand's marriage.

I gestured toward a door that bore a gold plaque with the words "C. W. Rand." "I wonder if Mr. Rand is in. I know this is a very difficult time, so I won't keep him long."

"He should be back within the next few minutes." She went on picking up papers, trying to pretend that nothing was wrong. "It's a terrible thing to've happened. Mrs. Rand, I mean."

"It is," I agreed sympathetically. "While I'm waiting, Rita, I wonder if you could answer a question for me."

She clambered to her feet, arms full. "I'll try. What do you want to know?"

Sometimes, when you're questioning witnesses, you've got a good idea what you're looking for and you go for it. Other times, you go fishing. I hadn't planned to ask Rita about Jerri and C.W., but it suddenly felt right. "I've been told by one of Sybil's friends that her husband and your sister have been having an affair. Is that true?"

Rita's face turned ashen. "No, it isn't. Where did you hear that?"

"I can't tell you," I said. "But the person who made the statement felt sure it was true."

"Well, it's a lie." Rita's voice sounded frayed with the effort of maintaining control. "Mr. Rand isn't that kind of . . . he wouldn't do a thing like—" Her chin trembled and she turned away.

"I see," I said to her back. "Well, I'm sure you know him better than the person who told me. And you know Jerri, too. If she were involved in something like that—"

She turned around again, clutching the papers as if they were a life vest. "Well, she's not!" The color was crawling back into her face, spreading upward in a dull red flush.

"Thanks," I said. "I'm really grateful to you for clearing this up, Rita. You know how rumors are—if they're not stopped in the beginning, they just go on and on." I gave her a sympathetic look. "How are *you*? Mrs. Rand's murder must have come as a terrible shock to you."

"Yes," she said. "It was just *awful*. And that poor Mr. Drake—" She stopped, searching for the rest of the sentence.

"You don't think he did it?"

She shook her head mutely.

"Then who did?"

The question momentarily stumped her. Then her eyes fired, and her voice caught the passion. "Those horrible Santeros, the ones who've been killing all the animals. It was Halloween. And there was that tip Chief Harris got—I mean, it *has* to have been them." Her voice rose, shaking. "They could kill anybody. Any one of us. Even you. Even me."

The *Enterprise*'s coverage of Sybil's murder hadn't spared the details. I was willing to bet that half the citizens in Pecan Springs were going to bed with a poker handy. "Really, Rita, there's no danger. I'm sure that the police—"

She wasn't finished. "And she . . . she could even have been part of it, too. With all those poisonous plants, and those spooky books, and the fortune-telling cards—"

"Rita, honey, you shouldn't be talkin' like that. Sybil had nothin' whatsoever to do with a cult. Not on purpose, anyway."

Rita's papers fluttered to the floor again. I turned.

The man who spoke had a rich voice and an appearance to match. Prematurely gray hair carefully styled, hazel eyes, teeth so brilliant they had to have been whitened, full lips, fleshy jaw. He could have just walked off the set of a TV soap. He wore a gray silk shirt with a western-style yoke and pearl buttons, red string necktie, dark slacks, an eelskin belt with a gold initial buckle, matching eelskin boots.

"I'm sorry." He bent over to help Rita pick up the papers. "I didn't mean to startle you, Rita honey. And I didn't mean to sound harsh, either. It's just that—"

"Oh, please, Mr. Rand," Rita said, scrambling papers together. "Let me get these. You really don't need to—" Flushed, eyes fastened on him, she stood up and put the papers on the desk. She'd forgotten all about me. "Can I get you some coffee? I've made some, fresh. And I bought raspberry jelly doughnuts at the grocery. I thought maybe you wouldn't have had the heart for breakfast."

"That's my brave girl," he said, patting her hand. "Sure, coffee and a doughnut'll do fine. Bring a cup for our visitor, too." Rita opened a door behind her desk and disappeared into a small kitchen. C.W. turned to me with an appraising look, one eyebrow raised. He extended his hand. "I don't believe we've met. C. W. Rand."

"China Bayles." His hand was soft and warm and held mine a fraction of a second longer than it had to. "I won't keep you, Mr. Rand. A friend of Andrew Drake's has asked me to look into the situation, and I thought perhaps you might answer a question or two."

He folded his arms across his chest and checked me out, head to toe. "You a lawyer?"

"I'm assisting with the preliminary investigation." It wasn't a lie, just an evasion.

The hazel eyes were clear, candid. "Well, ask whatever you've a mind to. I've got nothin' to hide. Matter of fact, I'll be glad to help." He reached into his jacket pocket and pulled out a pack of Marlboros. He put one in his mouth, took out a lighter, and lit it. "Ask me, the sheriff's takin' the wrong road, goin' after Drake."

"Who do you think killed your wife?"

The answer came without hesitation. "One of those Mex'can witch cults, like the ones that killed that tourist down in Matamoros." He inhaled and blew out a stream of smoke. "I told Sybil and *told* her to stop messin' around with those stupid plants, all that tarot and astrology mumbo jumbo. Stuff like that, she was a perfect target for any crazy come over the border."

"Had you heard any rumors about your wife and Drake?"

He sat heavily on the edge of Rita's desk, shaking his head. "The husband's the last to know, I guess. But I wasn't totally surprised when the sheriff told me." He sighed, shoulders slumped, swinging one eelskin boot. "'Spose you heard she was gettin' a divorce."

"She told you about it, I understand."

"After she went to see her lawyer." A gold ring flashed as he flicked his cigarette ash into an ashtray. "Would you believe she even wrote it all down? Like she wanted to be sure I got the message. As if I'd miss it," he added with acid irony. "After all, I was bein' cut off. It's not somethin' I'd let get past without noticin'."

"But you'd have to say it was lucky, wouldn't you? That she wrote the note, I mean."

"I oughtta be glad to trade my cut for a clean bill of health from the sheriff?" He laughed shortly. "Maybe I'd rather have the money. Especially since I was in Atlanta when it happened. No way could anybody figure me for the killer."

"May I see the note?"

"Sheriff's got it." He rubbed his jaw wearily. "I tell you, it was a blow. I mean a *real* blow. Oh, sure, Sybil and I had our problems. I'm no saint, and she was your all-time superbitch. But it was good once, and she sure as hell didn't deserve to get her throat cut." He shook his head. "Believe me, this thing has messed up my life, no lie. I can't even get into my house. The police have it sealed up. I'm stayin' in one of the lease units."

"I'm sure it's rough." I looked at my watch. "Tell Rita I'm sorry I couldn't stay for coffee. And thanks for your cooperation."

"I gave you what I gave the sheriff," he said. "Drake's entitled to any help he can get. I just wish the sheriff'd stop screwin' around with him and go clean out that shantytown over by the freeway. That's where the cult's holed up, you ask me."

I drove back into town, chewing over what I'd learned. Despite Rita's denial, I guessed that she had already known there was something going on between her boss and her sister. I also guessed that she had a crush on him herself, the kind of hero worship that women sometimes lavish on a boss. He didn't even have to be handsome. Miss Texas might feel that way about Charlie Lipman.

But it looked like C.W. was off the hook. The typed note proved that Sybil had told him about the divorce. I shook my head. Something about that note rang a bell. I wished I could remember what it was.

13

It was one by the time I got back to the store. Leatha told me that Joyce Moyers hadn't called back, gave me an enthusiastic rundown on her busy morning, and then headed for the kitchen to make sandwiches. She had the radio on, and when I went to turn it off I realized that the program was Fannie Couch's "Back Fence." I paused to listen.

"I know everybody's on edge over what's goin' on," Fannie was saying, "but I'm bettin' you don't *really* believe in witches." She paused to give her question greater emphasis. "Do you?"

"Well, I do an' I don't." The caller was a woman with a high-pitched wheezy voice, like a harmonica. "I mean, there's people who think they're witches, and then there's witches." A cogent summation, I thought.

Fannie was skeptical. "But they wouldn't actually kill somebody, would they?"

The caller hesitated, cautious. "The ones who are, they wouldn't have to. It's the ones who *think* they are that's dangerous. They might kill somebody just to prove they can." She lowered her voice, as if they might be overheard. "If you ask me, Fannie, it was that photographer did it. I heard he had a black magic bible in his apartment and he used to dance butt naked in the—"

Fannie cut in hastily. "Sorry, but we've got to take a commercial break." Her voice grew heartier. "All you listeners out there, don't go 'way. We got a real treat comin' up. Pecan Springs Singin' Sweethearts are with us, just back from their big success in San Antonio. They're goin' to favor us with their rendition of 'The Yellow Rose of Texas.'"

I switched off the radio and began on the mail, sorting the interesting stuff from the bills. My copy of *The Business of Herbs* had come and I pushed the bills aside and opened it. Paula Oliver, the editor, is a friend of mine, and the magazine keeps me going when times get tough. In this issue, for instance, she was featuring an article on a small company named Hillside Herbs, which is owned by two sisters who have developed a unique herbal jewelry collection. It just goes to show how two women can team up to beat the odds. I was deep in the article when the door opened and Angela Sanchez came in, wearing jeans and a maroon CTSU sweatshirt, her dark hair in one thick braid down her back.

She held up a bag. "Maria sent you some dried epazote to trade for fresh hoja santa. Got any, China?"

"Sure." I took the epazote, handed her a sack, and she headed for the herb garden. Epazote is a native Mexican herb that's added to beans in the last fifteen minutes of cooking, not just to flavor them but to keep them from doing what beans normally do after you eat them. Hoja santa, holy leaf, smells like root beer, with a hint of sweet anise. Mexican cooks sometimes use the fresh leaves instead of corn shucks to wrap tamales in, and season sauces, beans, and shrimp with the dry herbs. To make sure I have it fresh, I keep a few plants by the cottage where it's shaded in the afternoon. Once it's started, you have to be very firm with it. It spreads like bamboo.

Angela was back in a few minutes with a full sack of leaves. "Thanks. Looks like you've got a good crop out there."

I looked at her. "What's the word in the community about the Santeros and Mrs. Rand's murder?"

Angela looked dark. "Everybody says that the Santeros had nothing to do with it."

"Maybe they're protecting somebody."

Angela shook her head, her mouth firm. "No, China. This is not Santeros. Not Palo Mayomberos, either. There'd be symbols, bones, coins, an altar. You can't have a sacrifice without an altar. Anyway, if it was Santeros, word would get around."

"What about the doll?" The threatening voodoo doll that Sybil had received was another weak link in Blackie's case against Andrew—unless he'd somehow managed to connect Andrew to the doll. Was that what he meant by rattlesnakes?

"I'm still asking," Angela said. "I'll let you know if I hear anything. But I *saw* something you maybe want to know about. I was out at Lake Winds last night, helping Mrs. Maxwell with a dinner party. I was driving past a row of condos—the D section—when I saw Jerri Greene getting out of that Mustang of hers." She paused. "You know Jerri Greene?"

I nodded.

Angela gave me a crooked grin. "Well, it was late and I was curious, so I stopped where she couldn't see me and watched. She stood outside this door smoothing this, straightening that." With suggestive tugs at hips and breasts, Angela pantomimed Jerri's preparations. "When everything was in the right place, she knocked. It was Mr. Rand who let her in. When I drove off, I saw his Le Baron, parked around the side." She looked at me. "I'm not saying this was wrong. I just thought you ought to know."

I raised my eyebrows. "Thanks." I paused. "Angela, do you know Andrew Drake?"

Angela tilted her head. "He came out to the Rand house a couple times when I was there. He and Mrs. Rand were . . . friends."

I heard the hesitation. "Just friends? Or something else?"

Angela lifted her shoulders in an eloquent Latin shrug that accepted and tolerated all kinds of relationships. "Maybe. The sheriff asked too, and I told him the same thing. Me, I think Drake did it. People are saying he killed a woman in New Orleans."

I was saved from answering when the door opened and somebody else came in—a six-foot-three-inch redheaded replica of Ruby. She was wearing U.T. orange sweats with "Lady Longhorns" across the front.

"Hello, Shannon," I said.

Angela lifted her bag of hoja santa. "*Gracias,* China," she said, going out the door. "*Hasta luego.*"

"*De nada. Hasta la vista.*"

Ruby's daughter looked around apprehensively, as if she was afraid she might step on something. When you're six feet three and used to charging up and down a basketball court, small spaces probably make you claustrophobic. She got right to the point. "What's this shit about Mom being mixed up with a murderer?"

"It's not clear that he's a murderer," I said carefully. "There are other considerations to be explored. The law—"

Shannon snorted. "Gimme a break. The jerk's in jail, isn't he?" On the basketball court, she uses her height to intimidate. She leaned forward, using it now to make her point. "China, I am very worried about my dear, sweet, loony mother. Every now and then she totally wigs out over some weird bozo. She's really gone out of her way to pick a loser this time. What are we gonna do?"

I dumped Maria's epazote onto a tray and inspected it carefully. It was clean, as usual, and smelled of camphor, with a touch of mint. "We might try locking her in the closet and dropping the key into the river."

"How about this guy she's gone bonkers over? Will he get the chair?"

"He hasn't even been indicted yet." I put the epazote into a clean jar and put it on the shelf. "Anyway, they don't use the chair in Texas. They use a needle."

"A needle? Gross." She paused for a moment, digesting this information. "Mom says you're going to be his lawyer."

"Definitely not." I brushed epazote leaves off the counter. "Anyway, this isn't a capital case. The most he could get is life."

Shannon's orange chest rose and fell in a heavy sigh. "I tell you, China, I am very, very worried about Mom. She's starting in on her third set of fingernails. But there's no point in trying to tell her to kiss this jerk off. She won't listen to a word. So if there's anything you can do to prove that somebody else did it—"

To that logic, there was nothing else to say except "I'll do whatever I can."

She enveloped me in a hug, and the top of my head bumped her chin. "Listen," she said, releasing me, "about the season tickets, don't worry about a thing. I put your name on the list. But you'll have to pay full price. The NCAA watches that stuff like a cross-eyed hawk." She made a face. "When they should be watching steroids, they watch tickets."

"How's the season shaping up?" I asked, glad to be off the subject of Andrew and Ruby.

"Not too bad. We're gonna stomp LSU." She shot me the hook-'em-horns sign, an obscene-looking combination of thrusting fingers that I never learned to display without embarrassment. "Fix it so the guy beats the rap," she ordered, and ducked through the door. On her way out, she narrowly missed charging into Leatha, who was coming in with a tray of sandwiches, salad, and drinks.

After lunch, I told Leatha I needed to leave again and offered to turn the shop over to Laurel Wiley, who was still tending the Cave.

Leatha shook her head. "Let me," she said. "I love it." She looked around. "Maybe I'll tell Sam I'd like to have a little shop like this. Where are you going?"

"To the gym."

"That's good," Leatha said approvingly, going to sit behind the cash register. "I worry that you don't get enough exercise."

✳ ✳ ✳

Jerri Greene was just finishing a class when I came in. In red leotard and red-striped tights, she stood out like a chorus girl in a crowd of female flabbies, jumping wearily to ear-splitting music. She waved me into the office and closed the door behind us, shutting out everything except for the rhythmic bass, which rumbled in the floor.

"Want to sign up for Early Sunshine Slim and Trim?" She cast a practiced eye over my black bulky sweater, which hides a multitude of sins. She was not deceived. "Three times a week, seven thirty in the morning. A good way to lose a few pounds before the holidays."

"I probably should," I said with no intention of actually doing it. "Listen, Jerri, I wonder if you could help me. I've been asked to do a little digging into the Rand murder."

"Oh, yeah?" She took a towel off the back of a chair, flipped up her ponytail and wiped her neck. "Going back to being a lawyer? Lawyers make good money, don't they?"

"Some do. But I'm just sorting through a few things, that's all."

She draped the towel around her shoulders. "Well, if you're working for Drake, you probably got your work cut out for you. Way I heard it, he and Sybil were getting it on. That's why he killed her."

"Does that surprise you?"

She headed for a small refrigerator beside the window. "Why should it?" She shot me a quick glance. "I didn't know her. Don't know him, either."

"Why do you think he did it? Not just because they were lovers, surely." *If* they were.

She took a bottle of cranberry juice out of the refrigerator and drank deeply. "Heard he owed her a big bunch of money." She wiped her mouth with the back of her hand and looked at me as if for confirmation. When she didn't get it, she went on. "Anyway, they must've been into some pretty kinky stuff. This girl who works at the Exxon station, her brother is a deputy. She says Drake had this big book full of evil spells and instructions for weird sex. And I know for a fact Mrs. Rand had poison plants." She shuddered. "A person could get killed, all those poison plants. God, if I'd been C.W., I'da been freakin' out."

I took my cue. "I'll bet it was hard," I said sympathetically. "Was he? Freaking out, I mean."

"C.W.?" She sat down, crossed her red-striped legs, drank again. "Well, he mentioned it a time or two. Wouldn't you freak out, if *your* wife was growing stuff that could kill you deader'n a doornail? I wouldn't stick around thirty seconds, somebody threatened me like that. I'd get the hell out."

"You mean, she actually threatened to *poison* him?" My voice was full of shocked surprise.

"If growing all that poison stuff wasn't a threat, I don't know what was," Jerri said. "Especially after he pleaded with her not to do it. He begged her to knock off that flaky stuff, told her it'd get her ass in trouble. And sure as shootin', it did." She sat back with a served-her-right look.

"I understand that you and C.W. are friends." I smiled warmly, to show I didn't mean anything by my remark. "Somebody mentioned seeing you drop in on him last night out at Lake Winds," I added, by way of explanation.

Jerri pulled off the towel and dropped it on the floor. "No kiddin'? Boy, you can't do *anything* in this town, can you? Yeah, sure, we're friends. He's one of my regular massage customers. He calls me whenever he's super stressed out, and I give him a massage. Usually, I go to his house or his office. But the cops locked him out of his place so last night I went to the place where he's staying." She laughed. "I better watch it, I guess. Never can tell who might get the wrong idea."

I laughed with her. "Yeah, you never can tell."

Jerri's assistant, an anorexic in silver leotard and tights, legs and arms like paper clips, opened the door. "I hate to tell you this, Jerri," she shouted over the music, "but the john's flooded again. Crap all over the floor. And the switch on the sauna heater quit working. It's stuck on broil."

Jerri shook her head wearily. "Thanks, Peaches." Peaches slammed the door, restoring relative quiet. "God, I'll be so *glad* to get out of this dump. Damn landlord won't fix the crapper, hailstorm punched the roof full of holes, and he stuck the insurance money in his jeans. Not to mention wall-to-wall roaches." She held up two fingers a couple of inches apart. "Big brown ones, about the size of a crocodile. Another two weeks, I'm gone."

"You're moving?"

"You got it. There's some space opening up in the mall, pricey, but worth every penny. Maybe I'll even get new equipment, too. Excuse me. Gotta call the plumber." She smiled at me. "Don't forget about Early Sunshine. Just what you need to trim off that flab."

The next aerobics class was taking the floor when I left the office. Peaches clapped her hands above her head, a bright smile on her face, her silvery body singing with energy.

"Okay, everybody," she called, bouncing onto the platform. "Let's start off with the dirty boogie. How about it, huh?"

A chorus of middle-aged laughter echoed across the floor, including mine. Flab or no flab, I guess you never forget the dirty boogie.

※ ※ ※

Back at Thyme and Seasons, Leatha was ready for an afternoon break. "I think I'll just run next door to the Emporium," she said. "Sara might like one of those candles I saw in the window."

I had to stop for a minute and think who Sara was. Oh, yes. My mother's step-daughter-to-be. "Have fun," I said, leafing through the pink phone messages. She was halfway down the walk when I found the one with Joyce Moyers' name on it. I opened the door and yelled, "Hey, was there anything special about the call from New Orleans?"

Leatha turned and shook her head. "Just call back. The woman said it was too complicated to put into a message. Anyway, she had something she wanted to ask you."

I sat behind the counter and dialed the New Orleans D.A.'s office. Busy. A minute later, I tried again. Still busy. I'd just put the phone down when it rang. It was Miss Texas. Frostily, she put Charlie through.

"I was thinkin' that maybe Ruby might like a little cheerin' up tonight," he said, "seein's how her friend Drake's got himself locked in the pokey. Think maybe I ought to take her out to dinner?"

"Sounds like a reasonable thing to do. When she comes in I'll—"

The door to the Cave opened. "I'm back," Ruby said. "Anything new?"

I held out the receiver. "Charlie Lipman wants to ask you a question."

Ruby took it. "Hi, Charlie." There was a pause. "Well, I don't know," she said doubtfully. "Shannon came down from Austin, and we were planning to—" Another pause, and some lip-biting. Then, decisively, "On second thought, Charlie, that sounds like fun. I'm sure Shannon would enjoy it. Yes, we'll see you at seven. Thanks." She handed me the receiver with a suspicious look. "Did you set that up?"

"Would I do something underhanded like that?" I hung up the phone. "I'm a little surprised that you decided to go."

She gave me a hard stare. "You and Shannon think I'm a flake, don't you." It wasn't a question. "A real looney-tune."

"Well—" I dragged it out.

"Don't give me a hard time, China. Shannon told me you two had a serious talk about me. About how weird I am."

"It was mostly Shannon who talked. She said she was worried and wanted to know what we should do. I suggested locking you in the closet and dropping the key in the river, but since that didn't seem practical—"

"—you sicced Charlie on me."

"I didn't. It was entirely his own idea. Anyway, you could have said no." I looked at her. "Why didn't you?"

"Because I don't feel right about Andrew seeing Sybil without telling me," Ruby said with dignity. "We didn't have an exclusive arrangement or anything like that. But I'm old-fashioned. I like to know who else is sleeping with the man I'm sleeping with, even if I am having safe sex. It's the principle of the thing."

"I take it you talked to Andrew this morning."

Ruby nodded glumly.

"Did he say they were sleeping together?"

"Not exactly. But he didn't say they weren't. My right brain still doesn't believe he killed her, but my left brain isn't so sure anymore. You said it yourself, China. He was at the scene of the crime, and maybe he had a motive, after all." She stopped, frowning. "Although I just can't see him trashing out my store and stealing my knife. I can't believe he'd want to incriminate me that way."

"You're not incriminated if your knife was stolen," I pointed out. "You'd hardly trash your own store."

"Whose side are you on?"

"Yours."

Ruby sighed. "It's all very confusing. Anyway, if Andrew's cleared, maybe I'll see him again. I'll decide that when the time comes. In the meantime—" She lifted her chin with a frosty smile. "In the meantime, I'll go out with whomever I please, even Charlie Lipman. And you and my wacko daughter can stop plotting to save me from myself. It's not necessary."

"We weren't plotting." I didn't want to show how relieved I was that she was being sensible about Andrew. At the same time, though, I felt a kind of perverse regret. Ruby gave so much of her self in love, was so beautifully open, so passionate. I was sorry to see her close herself off, be careful, be cool. And I couldn't help thinking that Andrew had lost something important when he lost her unquestioning support. Who but Ruby could believe so uncompromisingly in his innocence? I looked at her. "What else have you been up to today?"

She tossed her head. "Oh, just talking to a few people on the phone, doing a little research."

"Research? If you've decided to cool it on Andrew, why are you digging into—"

Ruby leaned forward and put both elbows on the counter. "I've been digging into the Reverend. I found out that he went to prison for six months for stealing that car in Abilene. After that, he went to Dallas and got religion."

"How'd you find that out?"

"My brother-in-law Raymond has a sister, Raynelle, who lives in Abilene. It turns out Raynelle and Bob Godwin went to school together. She knows a lot about Billy Lee. She dated his cousin Harpo."

I was trying to keep it straight. "Raynelle kept track of Billy Lee after he left Abilene?"

"Raynelle didn't," Ruby said, "but Harpo did. See, I called Raymond, who gave me Raynelle's number. Then I called Raynelle and she called Harpo. It took a little while, but she finally tracked him down through his mother. He raises ostriches over around Brownwood. Isn't that interesting? I thought ostriches lived in Australia."

"Africa, actually."

"Oh, really? Maybe it's emus that come from Australia. Anyway, Harpo raises them for the meat. He says they don't have any cholesterol."

I thought of the toll charges Ruby must have rung up to discover the virtues of ostrich meat. "So what else did you find out about the Reverend?"

"Well, after he got saved in Dallas, he went to work for Harvey Haines, that big TV evangelist who raised all those millions of dollars from sweet little old ladies who sent in prayer requests. I guess that's where Billy Lee learned how to preach." She paused, waiting for my reaction.

"Why is that interesting?"

"Haines is in jail, isn't he? For fraud?"

"That's what I heard. But I don't see the connection."

Ruby was patient. "If Billy Lee learned his trade from Harvey Haines, he could very well have learned a trick or two about how to take people's money."

"Ruby," I said cautiously, "exactly where are you going with this line of inquiry?"

Ruby was nettled. "Hell, I don't know. I just know that Bubba's not making any progress on finding out who trashed my store and stole my knife, and I somehow can't believe it was Andrew. I still think Billy Lee had something to do with it. Anyway, he got a girl pregnant back in Abilene and did time for stealing a car. That's enough ammunition right there to stop him from printing lies about us in his newspaper. Isn't it?" She put her hands on her hips. "Well, isn't it?"

"I just hope the Reverend's cousin doesn't call him up and ask him why some pushy person named Ruby Wilcox is digging around in his past."

"Are you kidding?" Ruby asked, incredulous. "V. I. Warshawski never gives anybody her real name. Harpo thinks I'm B. J. Jones, and Billy Lee and I went to school together." She looked at me. "So how about you? What'd you find out from New Orleans?"

"Nothing from the D.A.'s office yet," I said, "but I found out that—" I was about to tell her about Jerri's affair with C.W. and the note Sybil had left her husband when Laurel Wiley opened the connecting door and interrupted us.

"Ruby," she said, "Shannon's on the phone. Do you want to take it, or shall I have her call back?"

"I'll take it," Ruby said. "I want to tell her we've got a date tonight. See you later, China," she tossed over her shoulder.

When she had gone, I picked up the phone again. This time, I got through to Joyce.

"China!" she boomed. Joyce is a bulky woman, strong-willed and confident, with a voice that projects all the way to the back of the courtroom, even when she whispers. It could almost carry from New Orleans to Pecan Springs. "Hey, how're you and your plants doing over there? Working hard?"

I held the receiver an inch from my ear. "I don't know about the plants, but I quit every day at five."

"Oh, yeah? You've turned over a new leaf." She laughed uproariously. "I understand you're interested in Andrew Drake. He a client?"

"A friend of a friend," I said. "What've you got?"

"Not a lot. The case was closed three years ago. Seems that Drake borrowed thirty thousand dollars from some little old lady named Georgia Forgette. She lived uptown, east side of Audubon Park. *He* claimed it was a loan, anyway. She claimed fraud. But she died before the case got to the grand jury. End of story."

I'd already heard the broad-brush version. I needed the details. "What'd she die of?"

Joyce's chair creaked. "Funny you should ask. Unfortunately, I don't have an answer. I didn't have one for somebody named Blackwell, either, when he called yesterday. You know him?"

"Yes. Why don't you have an answer?"

Joyce's weariness was audible. "Because the file isn't complete. The autopsy report's missing. So are several pages of follow-up."

My skin prickled. "Somebody lost an *autopsy report*? How'd that happen?"

"Beats the hell out of me. It wasn't my case. Anyway, I told Blackwell I'd get the Department of Health to send us a copy of the death certificate, and one to him, and I've queried the coro-

ner's office about the autopsy report. But they installed a new
mainframe over in Health, and everything's in delay mode. The
coroner ain't too swift, either. I'll get back to you as quick as I've
got something."

"Judging from the file, what's your best guess?"

"Judging from the file, all I can say is that Drake was released.
But maybe I'd better add that while we do plenty of dumb things
around here, we don't usually let murderers skinny out."

I chuckled. "Want to bet?"

"Bet your sweet ass I wouldn't," Joyce said cheerfully. There
was the sound of papers rustling. "Hey, you want to do some
personal legwork, here's a little something for you. I didn't spot
this when I talked to the sheriff, so it's an exclusive. The dead
woman's older sister lived with her at the time of the alleged
crime. There's a note here says she now lives in Texas. Some
town called Fredericksburg. Your neck of the woods?"

"About eighty miles." I picked up a pencil. "Do you have
a name?"

"Virginia Forgette, 802 Dallas Street, age sixty-eight at the
time of the alleged crime. It might be worth talking to her. Or
you can wait until the coroner figures things out."

I jotted down the information. It might indeed be worth talking to Virginia Forgette. Of course, it wouldn't prove anything
about Sybil's death, one way or another. But if Virginia Forgette
accused Andrew of murdering her sister, it'd be one more indication that Blackie was barking up the right tree.

Joyce's chair creaked again, as if she were leaning back.
"Hey, I hear from Linda Corbey that you're hanging out with
some hunka-hunka ex-cop. Any truth to the rumor?"

I could hardly deny it, since Linda had taken McQuaid and
me to dinner when she'd been in Austin a while back. "Some," I
admitted. "The hunka-hunka part, anyway."

Joyce sighed gustily. "Boy, some people have all the luck.
Not only did you quit before the bear got you, but you grabbed
the door prize on the way out. When are you getting married?"

"I'm not."

She was intrigued. "Oh, yeah? How come? The way Linda tells it, he's got it all. Good looks, sex appeal, brains."

"Yeah, sure. But that doesn't mean I ought to marry him."

Joyce went on as if she hadn't heard me. "My assistant got married last month. Ripe old age of forty-five. First time, too, so I guess there's hope for the rest of us. Guy she married lives in Atlanta. They're commuting weekends to keep love alive." She chuckled. "I've been thinking maybe I'd take an hour or two off to look for the right man." She laughed again, louder, to let me know she was making a joke, and that she was perfectly okay single. But there was something about her laugh that made me think she wasn't perfectly okay. She'd paid a lot of dues to get where she was. Maybe she was looking at what she'd bought and counting what it cost.

I was closing for the day when McQuaid came in, looking good, sexy, smart, and exasperated.

I pushed the plant rack into the corner. "What's wrong?"

"Patterson," he growled.

"What's he done now?"

McQuaid paced up and down. "It's what he *hasn't* done. I asked him three months ago to set up the rooms and the equipment for this conference, and do you think he did it? Hell, no. He's been sitting with his thumb up his ass for three months, and this morning he tells me *I* have to do it. It took all day to fill out the paperwork, walk it through, get everything cleared—in addition to teaching two classes. Then, come to find out, somebody else is using the taping equipment, so I have to rent it, which will eat a big hole in the conference budget." He made a disgusted noise. "Jesus, what a twerp. I really think the guy's losing his grip."

I started clearing the register. "After all that, I think you deserve a day off. You're not teaching tomorrow, are you?"

"Nope. But I've got a lot to do. The conference starts Thursday night and—"

"Blow it off. Bag it. Tell the twerp you've been called out of town on an important investigation. Let him see what it's like when you're not there to say yessir."

McQuaid stopped pacing. "An investigation?"

"Yeah. Tell him you have to go to Fredericksburg to ask a lady whether Andrew Drake murdered her sister."

14

"You'll be gone again tomorrow?" Leatha asked as we finished eating the chicken chalupas I'd thrown together for dinner.
Chalupas make a fast meal—cooked chicken, mashed avocado,
cheese, lettuce, tomatoes, and chiles, piled onto a fried corn tortilla. Instead of sour cream, I use a spoonful of low-fat cottage
cheese on top.

"Do you mind?" I asked. It was a pointless question, actually.
I was going, whether she minded or not. And I wasn't going for
Ruby, either, who seemed to have stepped back from her
involvement with Andrew. I was going because I was tantalized
by the question of what had happened in New Orleans three
years ago, and whether it had anything to do with Sybil's murder. I frowned, thinking I should call Ruby and tell her about
what Joyce had said. But she was out with Charlie, and anyway,
I didn't want to. Ruby had had enough bad news. Let her have
an evening of fun.

Leatha pushed her plate back, a serious look on her face. "To
tell the truth, I feel like a fifth wheel, China. I like helpin' out in
the shop, but the rest of the time . . . I feel like you'd rather be
doin' almost anything else but talk to me."

I wished I could deny it, but I couldn't. I'd worked hard to
build a wall between us, and tearing it down wasn't going to be
the job of a minute or two. Hugs, kisses, the past is forgotten,
the old wounds forgiven—forget it. In fact, I didn't think it

could be done at all. I could never be the daughter she dreamed of, anymore than she could be the mother I had needed. We'd have to live with the givenness of our lives and get along as best we could.

"I'm sorry," I said. "Maybe—"

She was quick to pick it up. "Maybe I should go back to Houston? That's probably a good idea." She brushed a shred of lettuce off her pale blue lambswool sweater. "But first I have to say somethin'."

"What is it?" I avoided looking at her. I might feel guilty if she left, but at least there wouldn't be any more of these uncomfortable conversations. And she had Sara, the prospective stepdaughter, who sounded like a viable substitute for me. Under a thin veneer of natural jealousy, there was a lot of relief. Maybe Sara would do for her what I couldn't.

She put down her napkin and laced her fingers under her chin, intently determined. "The other day, I said you're a lot like your daddy. It wasn't a compliment."

That got me. "Oh?"

"I probably wouldn't be sayin' this on my own, but Marietta thinks I should just get everythin' off my chest at once, and then we can go from there. Dr. Neely thought so too. She said if I had anythin' to say to you, I should just say it."

"Well, then, *say* it." I felt the old bitterness coming up, acid in the back of my throat. Oddly, it felt good. It had been a real strain, dealing with a reformed Leatha. It was a relief to feel angry.

"Your father was an impatient man who didn't like to fool with people. He never wanted to be bothered with anybody else's problems—unless he was gettin' paid to do it in court, of course. When it was part of his job, he could be just as sweet as the next one. But as far as his personal life went . . . well, he just never could connect. With his mother, maybe, but not with me. Not even with you." She played with the string of blue beads that exactly matched her sweater. "Of course, back then I didn't know any better. I was glad for what little I got and thought I ought to be glad for that much. But now I realize how hard it must have been for you."

I frowned. It felt very strange, listening to my mother rehash our psychological history, giving the same explanations I'd often given to myself. Next thing you know, she'd be telling me I ought to—

"That's why," she said, "I really think it'd be a help if you got some therapy."

"*Therapy!*" I exploded. "*You're* telling *me* to get therapy?"

"Why not? What's so bad about gettin' help when you need it?" She leaned forward and put her hand on my arm. "You're what they call an adult child, China. That's the term people use to describe—"

"I know what it means," I said crossly. "And I don't need therapy. I'm doing just fine. I dropped out of the rat race, I've got a good business, friends—"

"China, China." Her voice was mild, her eyes pitying. "It's nice that you're not workin' as hard as your father anymore. It's nice that you're tryin' to slow down. But don't you think it'd be even nicer if you could have a real relationship?"

"I *have* a real relationship." I kept my voice level. "Two of them. There's Ruby. And McQuaid. Isn't that real enough for you?"

"Yes, but is it a *growing* relationship?" she asked. She leaned forward, her eyes as bright as one of the Reverend's flock. "To be in a real relationship means to make room in your life for the other person, China, even if you have to give a bit. Your daddy never could an' you're so much like—"

I dropped the last of my chalupa on the plate. I couldn't decide which was worse, a mother addicted to booze or to therapy. "Thanks for the advice, Leatha. I'll think about it."

Leatha looked at me. Then she looked at her watch. "If I threw my things in my suitcase and left right now, I could be back in Houston by eleven." Her tone was light, carefully casual.

"Sam called just before dinner. He got in today, unexpectedly. He's at the apartment."

I matched her tone. "Really? I know you'd hate to miss a chance to be with—"

"Of course," she said thoughtfully, giving me another chance, "he doesn't like me to drive at night."

"But you'd be taking the Interstate all the way," I said, refusing it. "I mean, there's really no—"

Leatha laughed. "I know. Aren't men just *terrible?* Sam's such an old fogey about my drivin'." She pushed back her chair and stood up. "I believe I will go back tonight, China. Can you find somebody to help in the store tomorrow?"

I stood up too. "Of course. And please don't bother about the dishes. I'll do them."

Leatha paused, wanting to get in one last word. "Your friend Mike is an awfully nice person, China, and he's got such a *sweet* little boy. I hope you marry him."

That tore it. "Why don't *you* marry him, if you think he's so great?" I shouted.

✳ ✳ ✳

"Where's your mom?" McQuaid asked when he came the next morning to pick me up. "Is she minding the shop?"

"She went back to Houston last night," I said shortly. "Laurel's taking care of things today."

McQuaid looked at me. "Did you two have an argument?"

"Whatever gave you that idea?" I'd pulled on my green corduroy skirt that morning, and now I added a green cardigan sweater. The gray clouds sagged like heavy pillows and the north wind was chilly with the breath of an early snowfall in the Panhandle. There would be frost by nightfall. "Come on, let's go."

"Did you call this woman?" McQuaid asked. "I don't want to drive all the way over there for nothing."

"I called her," I said. "She's expecting us."

We were walking out the door when Ruby phoned. "Just wanted to tell you that I'll be out this morning. I've asked Laurel to take care of the shop."

"Then she'll be watching both stores," I said. "McQuaid and I are going to Fredericksburg." I took a deep breath and gave her a rundown on our errand.

Ruby's voice was small. "Do you think he might have killed her?"

"I don't know," I said. "If he did, the N.O.P.D. and the D.A.'s office really screwed things up."

"Can I go with you? I'd like to hear that woman's story for myself."

I considered quickly. Ruby might *think* she wanted to hear, but she probably didn't. And there was the problem of logistics. I gave her that one. "Three is a pretty big crowd when you're questioning somebody."

"McQuaid doesn't need to go."

"I just don't think it's a good idea. You're involved. That's not to say you couldn't handle it. It's just that—"

She sounded resigned. "Let me know when you get back."

We took McQuaid's blue Ford pickup. I grew up in Houston, where you don't happen onto coyotes and rattlesnakes every day, so I'd never gotten used to riding with a loaded gun in the rack behind my head. In this state, it's legal to carry rifles and shotguns in your vehicle as long as they aren't sawed off and thereby concealable. McQuaid carries a twelve-gauge shotgun. When I first knew him, I thought this was a little strange, especially after I found that the gun was Dutch-loaded with 00 buckshot and rifled slugs. I wasn't exactly reassured when McQuaid told me it was his retirement insurance, protection against human varmints out of his past, rather than wildlife in the present. Ex-cops like McQuaid are always in season.

While he drove, McQuaid gave me the gist of the article he was writing on criminal profiling from crime-scene analysis. In return, I gave him an abridged version of my conversation with Leatha, leaving out the part about marrying him.

"Therapy, huh?" he said thoughtfully.

"Yeah. I'm glad that Leatha's getting herself straightened out, although I'm not sure it's any easier to relate to her sober. But I don't think therapy would do me much good."

"I guess it depends." McQuaid put his arm around my shoulders and pulled me over against him, like a couple of teenagers on a date.

"Depends on what?"

He rubbed the back of my neck. "Depends on what you want."

I shivered, liking the feel of his fingers. "What do you mean, what I want?"

McQuaid's answer, when it came, was studiedly casual. "Kids who grow up with a bad family experience, you can understand why they wouldn't want to have anything to do with family. If they get to the point where they think maybe they want family, a little therapy might help them figure out how to handle it."

I was silent. We were driving along FM32 between Wimberley and Blanco. The road follows the Espinazo del Diablo—the Devil's Backbone, the roughest country in this part of Texas. Driving west, you look down on mile after mile of white limestone cliffs, precipitated out of a shallow Cretaceous sea a hundred million years ago, studded with dense cedar brakes. Groves of live oak line the road and startled deer break for cover across rock-strewn meadows. It's awesomely wild and beautiful.

I broke the silence. "Are you saying I should get some therapy?"

He glanced at me, blue eyes serious. "Depends on what you want, China. Me, I'd like to be a family. You, me, Brian. We're good together, all three of us. I think it could be better if we'd make a commitment. A long-term commitment."

I sighed. We were coming to the M-word.

He grinned and smacked my shoulder lightly with his hand. "Hey, it's just a thought, counselor. Take it under consideration and don't let it bother you." He retrieved his arm and slowed to let a truck and horse trailer pass. "Drake's hearing was held late yesterday afternoon. First-degree murder. The D.A.'s taking it to the grand jury on Monday. Looks like they're not letting the grass grow under their feet on this one."

I was grateful to him for changing the subject, although I didn't like the new topic any better than the old. "Who did the autopsy? Travis County?"

Of the counties along the I-35 corridor, Adams County is the least populated, too small to hire its own medical examiner. It uses the services of two nearby large counties, Travis and Bexar. The J.P.s say they prefer Travis, which has a faster turnaround and where they can get verbal reports from the M.E. before the formal report is issued.

"Yeah, Travis. There ought to be something out this morning."

"Andrew found a lawyer, I presume."

"Some guy from San Antonio, according to Blackie. Apparently a friend with a small office who's willing to do the work cheap."

I frowned. A good defense doesn't come cheap. In our legal system, the state usually holds all the big cards, including money and manpower. If you're a small-time lawyer, you don't have the wherewithal to develop a case of your own, so you're forced to defend your client against the state's case. In most instances, what that buys you is a guilty verdict, or at best a plea bargain to jail time. My favorite law professor used to say that what's true for football is also true (if clichéd) for criminal law: the best defense is a damn good offense. Big or small, you've got to develop your own theory of the crime and convince the jury that it's a plausible alternative to the theory the prosecution is peddling. Without your own theory, you're at the mercy of the State.

McQuaid glanced sideways at me. "I stopped at the Doughnut Queen for coffee this morning. The breakfast crowd is making book that Andrew's guilty. It was the Satanist bible that convicted him. Mrs. Bragg says she's sure she saw him lurking around her chicken coop the night her chickens were killed. Everybody's convinced that he butchered Bob Godwin's goat and strung him up by the heels. A regular one-man Satanic band."

"Yeah," I said. "If it were my case, I'd petition for change of venue. You couldn't come up with an impartial jury in this county."

"That's the trouble with small towns. Most of the people have small-town minds." He looked thoughtful. "Come to think of it, though, it's not a lot different in the city. Once the grand jury returns an indictment, most people figure the law has done its job. The trial's just window-dressing."

I didn't say anything. McQuaid was right—people's attitudes about crime and punishment are basically the same, whether they live in Pecan Springs or Houston. But Andrew's situation gave me a glimpse of a Pecan Springs that wasn't as safe and secure as it seemed—not so much because a horrible murder had happened there, but because too many of its citizens were too quick to assign guilt. Like Pauline Perkins, who had chased off the demonstraters because they were testimony to a difference of opinion, the people of Pecan Springs wanted to get rid of Sybil's killer as quickly as possible—after they had squeezed all the sensational juices out of her death.

Once past Blanco, we took the shortcut through Luckenbach, a tiny hamlet that is remembered as the subject of a song—"Take Me Back to Luckenbach, Texas, the Home of Willie and Waylon and the Boys." We got to Fredericksburg about ten. It isn't a big town—only about six thousand—but like Pecan Springs it's a tourist town, so it looks bigger than it is. The main street is lined with businesses like Udderly Texas, which displays a six-foot fake saguaro cactus festooned with cow jewelry and neckties painted with cows, and the Plateau Cafe, where diners are surrounded by rusty ranch equipment and the skulls of dead cows. I often drive over to visit Sylvia and Bill Varney, who own the Fredericksburg Herb Farm, a much larger enterprise than Thyme and Seasons. Their shop is located in a lovely old house a lot like mine, except that it has a tearoom and B and B accommodations and is surrounded by acres of fragrant herb gardens, laid out in precise shapes and bordered by gravel paths. I covet the garden, and shake my head at the hard work and sweat Sylvia and Bill have poured into it.

Virginia Forgette's two-story white frame house sat behind a white wrought-iron fence, a couple of blocks off the main street. During the summer, the roses must have been spectacular, and a few blossoms still clung to the trellis at the end of the porch. When she answered the door, Miss Forgette appeared to be expecting company. She was wearing a white blouse with a lacy jabot, a pink cardigan, pink skirt, and pink-tinted glasses. Her pink-tinted white hair was frozen in glacial ridges, her furrowed cheeks were rouged with pink, and her pink lipstick had bled into the tiny age-cracks around her mouth. She was a tiny woman, not much higher than my shoulder, and her piercing voice was pure N'Awlins.

"Good mornin'," she said brightly. She glanced up at me and then at McQuaid, who was standing behind me. "Oh, good, you brought a photographer." She touched one gnarled hand to her hair and giggled. "I'm glad Bellah got such a nice do on my hair. All my friends are just dyin' to read this article." She held the door open wider. "Just come on in. You'll get chilled out there, no more'n you're wearin'."

McQuaid looked at me. "Photographer?"

"I'm afraid we're not from the newspaper, Miss Forgette," I said. "We're from Pecan Springs. I telephoned last night. Remember?"

She looked confused. "You're not from the newspaper over there?"

"No. We've come to ask you a few questions about your sister."

"Oh, I see." She sounded disappointed. "Well, maybe I didn't hear it right. I thought you were comin' to do a write-up on my hobby. The paper here did one last week."

"Your hobby?" I asked. "What's that?"

She smiled. "Thimbles."

"Thimbles?" McQuaid asked.

"My Aunt Mildred collects thimbles," I said. "She has dozens."

Miss Forgette's squeaky laugh lorded it over Aunt Mildred's paltry collection. "Dozens? I've got *thousands*! Three thousand and sixteen, to be exact. I counted 'em last week, ever' one, just to be sure I got it right for the newspaper." She led us from the hall into the living room. Two walls of the rose-papered room were filled floor to ceiling with wooden shelves, and the shelves were filled with thimbles—silver and gold ones, china ones, in all colors and with all manner of dainty decoration.

"My goodness," McQuaid said. "I'm impressed. No wonder the newspaper did a story on you."

Miss Forgette beamed. "Yes, I've been collectin' thimbles since I was a little girl. My grandmama gave me my first one, this one right here, on the middle shelf." She pointed. "She gave me the gold one and my sister Georgia the silver one—that's Georgia's right beside, you see."

It was the opening I was waiting for. "Actually, it's your sister we've come to ask about," I said. "My name is China Bayles, and this is Mike McQuaid. We're looking into a matter involving a man named Andrew Drake. Do you mind if we sit down for a few minutes?"

"Andrew Drake?" Miss Forgette sat on the edge of the cretonne-covered sofa. "Is there some problem? He's been making his payments very regular."

"Payments?" McQuaid asked.

"Ever' month. Isn't that what you wanted to ask about? At

the rate he's goin', the whole thing will be paid off in the next three or four years, even countin' the interest."

"The thirty thousand dollars he owed your sister?" I asked.

"That's right." She pleated her pink skirt between her fingers, shaking her head. "Poor Georgia, such a sight of trouble she caused, bringin' that boy up on charges, when the loan was on the up-and-up and he had every intention of payin' the money back." Her lips tightened. "I blame that old lady Jackson next door. Such a hypocrite, always findin' fault. She fed Georgia a mess of stories about handsome young men cheatin' innocent old ladies out of their money, and Georgia got all fretted and called the police. I told her not to worry, it was bad for her blood pressure, but of course it didn't do any good for me to talk, not with Miz Jackson pourin' all that poison in her other ear. I did feel sorry for that poor young man, though. It was a shame for Georgia to go, but at least it saved him from havin' a black mark against his name."

"I see," I said. I did, dimly. "Tell me, Miss Forgette, exactly how did your sister die?"

"Why, didn't you know?" She pulled a lace handkerchief from the pocket of her skirt and dabbed one eyelid with it. I couldn't see any sign of tears. "It really was the most *terrible* thing. She was ridin' the streetcar when a garbage truck ran into it at the corner of St. Charles and Prytania. It raised a big stink."

McQuaid coughed.

"Because the streetcar driver'd been drinkin', you see," Miss Forgette said earnestly. "There was garbage all *over* the place."

"That *was* awful," I said. "Was your sister killed in the accident?"

"No, only two was killed. But her leg was pretty well scraped up, and when they brought her home from the emergency room her blood pressure was higher'n fireworks on the Fourth and the next day she had a stroke and died." She waved her hand at the thimbles. "That's how I come to have so many thimbles, you see. I inherited at least half of 'em from her. I must say, though, I like mine best." She pointed to a glass tray of thimbles on the table beside her. "My niece sent me these. This one's got Charles and Di on it, and their wedding date. And here are the little princes. Aren't they sweet?" She heaved a mighty sigh. "So *tragic* about that family. How *can* his mother bear it, I don't know. If I was queen, I'd tell that Charles to stop his shenanigans, and if he didn't, I'd—"

McQuaid leaned forward. "Was Andrew Drake present when your sister had her stroke?"

"No, just Miz Jackson and me. I swear, that old lady just couldn't keep her nose out, had to come over and start talkin' about Andrew. Lord forgive her, if it wasn't the garbage truck that killed poor Georgia, it was Miz Jackson. But he was a lamb. Right away when he heard about it, he came to see me. He said, 'You don't have to worry about a thing, Miss Forgette. I'm a man of my word, and I'm goin' to see you get every penny of the money I owed your sister.'" She nodded fervently. "He is a good-hearted young man, I'm proud to say, and he takes care of his debts. Pays ever' fifteenth of the month, on the nose."

"Do you know why he borrowed the money?" I asked.

"He was goin' to start a photography studio over on Carrollton. Nasty business that was, too. Do you know about it?"

I shook my head.

She spoke pityingly. "Well, the way it turned out, his partner ran off with all the money they raised and left him holdin' the bag. It's a wonder he's ever recovered from that blow. He needed Georgia's money to get goin' again."

"Have you heard from him recently?"

"Just the check, regular as clocks. Couple months back, he dropped me a line and said he was openin' a new place here in Texas, over in Pecan Springs, and I could come over anytime and get my picture taken, free. All I can say is, I wish him better luck this time."

"Thank you," I said, as McQuaid and I stood to leave. "You've been very helpful."

"If you see him, tell him I'll be over someday soon to get my picture made." She smiled. "There's a young man who deserves to have things go right."

✳ ✳ ✳

"Well," McQuaid said as we drove down the main street, "are you surprised?"

"To tell the truth, yes," I said. "I didn't know Andrew had it in him." I pointed. "There's a parking place. In front of the Auslander."

"Is German food okay?"

I laughed. "In Fredericksburg, do we have a choice? It's German or Tex-Mex." I was exaggerating. We could probably find some barbecue if we looked. But like Pecan Springs, Fredericksburg was settled by Germans, and traces of German culture are evident everywhere.

We turned down the outdoor beer garden, with its jukebox and blinking neon Lone Star sign, in favor of the dining room, which was decorated with German travel posters, German wine bottles arranged along the plate rail, a framed collection of beer coasters, and an oil portrait of somebody's grandfather wearing a green jacket and a green felt Tyrolean hat with a feather. The waitresses wore blue aprons over blue-and-red print smocks and white ruffled blouses, with white sneakers and white socks. I ordered a Reuben. McQuaid got a plate of knockwurst, sauerkraut, and fried potatoes. We both had steins of Shiner Bock.

"Kind of changes the angle on Drake, doesn't it?" McQuaid asked, slicing off a hunk of knockwurst.

"Yes," I said thoughtfully, "it does. I guess I've been as guilty as the town. I got it into my head that he was using Ruby."

"Maybe he was. Maybe he was planning to borrow money from her. Does Ruby have any money?"

"Some, from her grandmother. She used part of it to buy the house. And it didn't help that he was so evasive about his past.

Remember the night the four of us had dinner together? I remember thinking then that the only things I knew about him were that he was left-handed, and that he didn't like talking about himself."

"But he *was* at the scene of the crime," McQuaid pointed out. "And there was something going on between him and Sybil. The fact that he's making good on a loan doesn't have a lot of bearing on whether he killed Sybil."

"I know," I said. "But—" I was about to take a sip of beer when the waitress came around to my right to serve me. We connected, and beer splashed onto the table.

"Sorry," she said, putting down the plate from my left. "I'm new at this job. I've got to remember that everybody else is right-handed." She wiped up the spilled beer.

"That's okay," I said. "No damage done." When she'd gone, I sat there, staring thoughtfully at the pickled chile that was impaled on my Reuben with a toothpick.

McQuaid looked up, his mouth full of knockwurst. "What's the matter? A beer-soaked Reuben doesn't appeal to you?"

"Did you say the autopsy report would be out today?"

"Blackie was expecting it. Matter of fact, I wondered why he charged Drake before it came in. I guess he figured he had probable cause, what with the fingerprints and the eyewitness testimony."

I stood up. "Back in a minute." I took my purse and headed for the pay phone in the beer garden. I dialed information, got the number, and dialed again. Blossom answered.

"We-ll, I don't know," she said in reply to my question. "The sheriff sure hates to be bothered while he's eatin' his lunch."

"Why don't *you* ask him for me. He probably won't mind the interruption nearly so much if you do it."

"I guess," she said, resigned. "What do you want to know?"

I told her. She was back in less than a minute with the answer.

"Sheriff said to tell you that the killer was right-handed. According to the Travis medical examiner, anyway," she added. "The report came in just a little bit ago."

"No kidding?" I said, drawling it out. "Listen, maybe you could do me one more favor. Tell the sheriff that Andrew Drake is a southpaw. And then tell me what he says."

This time, the answer came back in thirty seconds. "He said—" Blossom hesitated. "Actually, you don't want to hear what he said. It wasn't too nice."

"I can imagine. Hey, thanks, Blossom."

She sighed. "Does this mean I did all that paperwork for nothing?"

Back at the table, McQuaid blinked when I told him about the autopsy report. "Well, if it wasn't Drake," he said, "who the hell *was* it?"

"*I* don't know," I said. "Maybe Ruby's right. Maybe it was the Reverend."

"Billy Lee? Oh, come on now. The guy's a jerk, but I don't think he's up to killing somebody."

"Yeah, but who's left? The husband was better off with Sybil alive than dead. The note proves that he knew he'd been cut out of her will."

"That note," McQuaid said. He finished his knockwurst. "It seems familiar, somehow."

"You too? The trouble is, I can't quite place it."

"Some case or another, a couple of years ago," McQuaid said, staring into his empty beer stein. "But it wasn't something I—" He snapped his fingers. "I've got it! It was an article in *Texas Monthly*. This woman was accused of poisoning her estranged husband for his insurance. The trouble was, a few months before he died, he changed the beneficiary on the policy."

"Yeah, that's it!" I was so excited I slopped my beer. "At the trial, the defense introduced a letter the husband was supposed to have typed and sent to his wife, to the effect that he'd made the policy over to his brother. If the letter was genuine, it meant she had no reason to kill him. But the prosecution dug up a witness who testified that the husband couldn't type, and a hand-writing expert said the signature was a forgery. The jury figured that a wife who could forge a bogus note to clear herself could also do in her husband."

"You read the same article I did, huh?"

"No, I heard about the case from a friend who was on the defense team. But C.W. could have read about it." I snapped my fingers. "There's a bunch of magazines on the coffee table in his office. What do you want to bet there are some old *Texas Monthly*s?"

"If he read the article, he probably wouldn't make the same mistake in forging the note. Sybil typed, I suppose?"

"Yes. When I was there on Saturday, she was typing a plant list on the typewriter in the kitchen."

McQuaid nodded. "Okay. Then suppose that C.W. *doesn't* know about the divorce and the new will. Suppose he pays somebody to kill Sybil while he's out of town. He comes home and the job's been done. So far so good. But then he finds out from Blackie that she was planning to get a divorce, and she's cut him out of her will."

I stared at him. "You don't really think the sheriff would be dumb enough to just *give* him that information?"

"It's not a matter of smart or dumb. You're closeted with a suspect for three or four hours, and you aren't Perry Mason. You don't have a scriptwriter feeding you a bunch of great lines. Sometimes things just . . ." He left it with an eloquent shrug.

I nodded, understanding. I'd committed my share of bloopers. "So Blackie—or maybe a deputy—says something careless, like 'When did you find out your wife was leaving you a big divorce settlement but cutting you out of her will?' And C.W. pops up with 'Why, before I went to Atlanta, of course.' He remembers the article in *Texas Monthly* and offers to confirm it by digging up the note."

"Then he goes home and types it and hands it over. Voilà—no motive, no opportunity, he's home free, with half the community property. What do you want to bet Sybil's name is typed on it, not signed?"

"Maybe," I said, "he didn't *hire* the killer."

McQuaid raised both eyebrows. "Oh, yeah? What are you thinking?"

"That maybe he sweet-talked somebody into doing the dirty work. His girlfriend. Jerri Greene."

"A woman?" McQuaid scratched the scar on his nose. "In all the time I was on Homicide, I never heard of a woman slitting somebody's throat. Stabbing, yes, slitting, no. It's just not a woman's M.O."

"There's got to be a first time," I said. "And Jerri's certainly got the muscle for it. What's more, she was bitching just last week that she couldn't afford to move, and yesterday she tells me that she's planning to lease some of that pricey space in the mall."

McQuaid was still doubtful. "Maybe she's planning to get married and let her husband set her up. C.W. might not be inheriting a couple of million, but half the community property won't be small change." He drained his Shiner. "Or maybe C.W. never got around to telling her about Sybil's financial arrangements, and she thinks he's going to inherit."

I pushed back my chair and reached for the check. "Well, we're not going to figure it out sitting here. Let's head back."

McQuaid brought his hand down on mine. "My turn. You bought the night we went out with Ruby and Andrew."

"Yeah, but you fed me last Sunday. And it was my idea for you to come along."

McQuaid released my hand with a grin. "You're pretty convincing, counselor. Anyway, my mother always told me never to argue with a lady with a check."

❋ ❋ ❋

The return trip seemed slower, maybe because I was in a hurry to get back. But I wasn't sure what I was going to do when

I got there. Blackie probably wouldn't show me the note Sybil was supposed to have written, but I was hoping he'd let McQuaid take a look at it, in honor of the brotherhood. Maybe I should have another talk with C.W. Or maybe it would be better to find out what kind of alibi Jerri had for Saturday night. Or maybe . . .

"I think we should turn this whole thing over to Blackie, and let him handle it," McQuaid said, anticipating my third maybe.

I swiveled in the seat, facing him. "He's already put his nickel on Andrew."

"You don't think he'd listen to another theory of the case?"

"Why should he? The fact that the killer was right-handed is certainly compelling. The defense will use it to argue reasonable doubt. But it isn't conclusive, given the weight of the other evidence. Blackie might be a little more nervous than he was before lunch, but five gets you ten he'll stick with Andrew. Have you ever seen a cop book one suspect, then go after a totally different one without a major piece of new evidence? And Blackie's got the county commissioners looking over his shoulder. How's he going to justify all the man-hours he'd have to commit to a new investigation?"

McQuaid didn't have an answer, and we fell silent. We were driving along the Backbone about fifteen miles west of Pecan Springs. It was an overcast afternoon, typical November weather. I was watching the scenery and mentally ticking off my questions for Jerri, when I saw a flotilla of turkey vultures sailing in a lazy spiral, six, eight, maybe a dozen of them. Vultures feed on carrion. Something was dead in the depths of the canyon below, a steer maybe, or a deer. Bow season had already started, and archers who don't get a clean kill sometimes fail to track the wounded deer.

The Devil's Backbone is good country to lose a deer in. The cliff on my right was maybe fifteen degrees off the vertical, falling sixty, seventy feet to a wide, rocky ledge, then another sixty to a dry creek bed at the bottom. But it wasn't a dead deer the vultures were celebrating. On the shoulder of the cliff, halfway down, I saw the wreckage of a car, the smudge of a fresh burn like a black halo in the grass around it.

"Hey!" I craned my neck for a better look. "There's a car down there!"

McQuaid slowed, braked, and pulled over to the side. "Where?"

"Back up. I'll show you."

"Must be an old wreck." He put the truck in reverse and backed along the wide gravel shoulder. "I didn't see any skid marks."

I reached into the glove compartment for McQuaid's binoculars. "I don't think so," I said as he stopped. "Looks like a fresh burn." I jumped out and trained the binoculars on the wreckage. The car, a convertible, had landed wheels-down on the ledge, the crumpled hood pointed uphill. The rear end was blackened and scorched. There were three or four vultures working eagerly on something in the driver's seat, others on the ground and the car, impatiently waiting their turn.

My mouth was suddenly dry. "Jesus, McQuaid, the driver's still down there!"

McQuaid snatched the binoculars. "Not moving. Listen, China. You take the truck and bust ass to that Fina station up the road. Call the D.P.S. Tell them we've got a red Mustang down here and that the driver—"

"A red Mustang?" I grabbed the binoculars back and refocused them on the buzzards feasting on the huddled shape in the front seat. "That's Jerri Greene's car!"

"Well, if that's Jerri Greene down there," McQuaid said grimly, "she's not a live suspect any longer."

✳ ✳ ✳

When I got back from the Fina station, I clambered down the incline to join McQuaid. He was right. Jerri was dead. Head

lolling loose, eye sockets empty, the flesh hanging in bloody gob-
bets from her once-pretty face and arms, meat stripped from
bone by greedy vultures. The scene reminded me of pictures of
airplane crashes where the victims were found still strapped in
their seats, smashed like plastic dolls. Falling off that road up
there must have been like falling out of the sky.

"Looks like a broken neck," McQuaid guessed. He glanced
back up the cliff. "Probably flipped a time or two and rolled.
That's why the car's pointing uphill. Must've been here all day
at least, judging from the damage those vultures have done.
Maybe happened last night—everything's cold." He took off his
jacket and put it over what was left of Jerri.

I turned away with a shudder. My knees felt rubbery, my
palms clammy. The animated, energetic young woman I remembered, *tsuyoki*, full of *ki*, brimming with life and driven by ambi-
tion and the urge to get somewhere, *be* somebody—that person
was gone. All that was left was a broken body, soft flesh rib-
boned by beaks and talons.

McQuaid looked at me. "You okay, China? You look kind of
green. Maybe you'd better find a rock to sit on."

I wanted to sit, but I couldn't. It was better, now that Jerri's
face was covered. I walked around the car. The hood was
smashed shut, the windshield totally gone, the right front caved
in. The rear end was less heavily smashed, but it was blackened
from fire. The fire had spread behind the car and down the hill,
charring the short grass for a dozen yards.

The Mustang was an automatic, with the shift on the console
between the seats, an empty Gordon's gin bottle wedged in
beside it. Vulture droppings crusted the seat.

"Car's in gear and the ignition's on," McQuaid said. "It must
have stalled out when it crashed. That's why there's almost no
fire damage up front. The gas tank's probably ruptured."

"And the car's on an incline, so the gas ran out behind and
caused the grass fire?"

"Yeah," McQuaid said. "Lucky the whole thing didn't go up.

But a lot of the fuel was absorbed by this porous caliche soil. And it's pretty hard to catch a car on fire unless it's sitting in a puddle of gas."

"She must have gone over at a high speed," I said, reconstructing the scene in my mind. "She finished off the gin bottle, was drunk out of her mind, and didn't make that curve up there."

McQuaid frowned. "Let's go back up. I want to check on something."

On the road, McQuaid walked for thirty yards in both directions, looking carefully at the blacktop and the gravel on both sides. I walked beside him, bent into the chilly wind, trying to figure out what he was looking for.

"I don't see anything," I said finally.

"That's because there's nothing to see. No skid marks, no tire marks on the shoulder, nothing to show where she left the road."

"She must have been really flying."

"I don't think so." McQuaid turned to look back and down at the car. "If she'd been heading west, she'd have gone off somewhere around here. But there're no tire marks."

"What if she was coming the other way, toward Pecan Springs?"

"There'd still be tire marks. But there aren't any. No skid marks, no broken bushes or underbrush, no nothing."

I walked back down the road another twenty yards and noticed a small patch of scorched grass and weeds. "Look at this," I called to McQuaid.

McQuaid joined me. "Could have been a match or a cigarette, started a little fire." He paused. "Did Jerri smoke?"

"I don't think so. Why?"

"I was wondering if she parked here and had a last cigarette to go with her last drink."

I huddled into my green sweater, shivering. "You mean, she drove off the road *deliberately?*"

"That's how it looks to me, China. There's no evidence that she lost control and went off the road—and there should be, if that's what happened. So what's left? Suicide makes sense."

I scuffed at the gravel, thinking. "It adds up. Maybe things didn't work out the way she planned. She killed Sybil to marry C.W., but maybe he had different ideas. Or maybe C.W. talked her into doing it, then she had an attack of remorse and decided to end it all." I bent over to look at a worn-out Nike, a few feet from the burned patch. A Coors can lay a foot away, along with a McDonald's bag and an empty Salem pack. The "Don't Mess with Texas" campaign only works part of the time. I straightened up as a Department of Public Safety black-and-white skidded to a stop and a gray-uniformed trooper climbed out.

"What we got here?" he asked. He was a stocky, mustached man with a pockmarked face and a jutting chin. He wore a broad-brimmed Stetson, standard wraparound sunglasses, and a holstered .357 on his hip.

"Hey, Callaghan," McQuaid said. "How're things on the hubcap patrol?"

The trooper grinned, showing crooked, tobacco-stained teeth. "Say, buddy. Goin' great. How's life in the ivory tower?"

"Couldn't be better," McQuaid said. I wondered if they would give one another a high five, but they only shook hands. I wasn't a member of the fraternity. McQuaid didn't bother to introduce me. "Fatality," he said, nodding in the direction of the wreck.

The trooper walked to the incline and peered into the canyon. "Shee-it," he said disgustedly. "This makes three in the last month. Folks get high and drive this road like they're ridin' the Rattler at Fiesta Texas. You been down to the car?"

"Yeah. That's my jacket on the body. Vultures were after her. They already had breakfast and lunch, working on dinner." I shivered. McQuaid has always seemed to me a gentle man. Was this gritty nonchalance a coverup for feeling or a cop's working style?

Callaghan nodded. "Any sign of booze?"

"Empty gin bottle."

"Figgers. The others were D.W.I.'s, too." The trooper turned to go to his car, brushing past me as if I were invisible. "I'll put in a call to E.M.S. You don't need to hang around, McQuaid. I'll see you get your coat back."

"'Preciate it," McQuaid said. We got into the pickup and drove off.

I huddled into my sweater. "You didn't mention the thing about no tire marks. Or the burned patch by the road."

"Me, trespass on Callaghan's turf?" McQuaid flipped on the heater. "Hey, he's a friend. I'd like to keep it that way. He's got eyes, he'll dope it out."

"What if he doesn't?"

McQuaid shrugged. "Then it'll go down in the record book as one more D.W.I. She's dead, China. Suicide or accident, it's all the same to her. Callaghan's paid to handle it. Let it go, or it'll eat you up."

I leaned my head on the back of the seat, suddenly tired, feeling the weight of the gray afternoon, the dead thing in the rocky ravine. Maybe McQuaid was right. If Jerri had killed Sybil, maybe it was just as well that she'd taken care of things this way. And maybe it would be better for Rita and the rest of Jerri's family if her death was treated as an accident.

But that left Andrew, still in jail for Sybil's murder. And with Jerri dead, the chances of finding out whether or not she'd killed Sybil were very remote.

Suddenly the bleak afternoon seemed even bleaker.

✳ ✳ ✳

Coming out of the raw, chill wind, the shop seemed cozy and inviting, fragrant with spices and warm with the colors of dried flowers and autumn wreaths. Laurel told me that we'd had a halfway decent day. The wreaths were going fast, and we'd sold out of the new line of herbal soaps I was trying. I phoned a reorder, and while I was at it asked for some samples of bath herbs and sachets—comforting things to think about after what I'd seen in the wrecked car. I closed out the register and locked up the shop. I went to my kitchen, put on the kettle, and fixed myself a cup of hot mint tea. I had just finished it and was still sitting at the table, thinking wearily about Jerri, Sybil, and C.W., when Ruby knocked at the door.

"Tea?" I asked.

"Sherry," she countered, and pulled a bottle out of her jacket. "What did you find out?"

"About Andrew?" Had it only been this morning I'd talked to Virginia Forgette about her sister? It seemed like a century ago. I got out glasses and Ruby poured. "Georgia Forgette died after her streetcar got rammed by a garbage truck," I said. "Andrew's been paying back the money he borrowed, a little bit at a time. To the sister, who says he's a conscientious young man."

Her breath came out in a big rush. "So he's innocent!"

"He didn't kill the woman in New Orleans, if that's what you mean." The sherry was warm inside me. "And I doubt very seriously that he killed Sybil. The autopsy report came out this morning. The killer was right-handed."

"And Andrew's *left*-handed!" Ruby lifted her sherry glass in a triumphant toast. "I *knew* it! I knew he didn't kill her! Has he been released yet?"

"Released?" I downed my sherry and poured another. "Ruby, I said *I* don't think he killed Sybil. I have no idea what the sheriff thinks."

"Oh, but he—" She stopped. "Won't he?"

"Blackie's the only one who can answer that question." Khat came in from the bedroom and jumped up on my lap, kneading at my green corduroy skirt and purring his approval. Corduroy is his favorite. "There's more. On the way back, about fifteen miles west along Devil's Backbone, McQuaid and I found Jerri Greene's car in the canyon. She was dead."

Ruby caught her lower lip between her teeth, her green eyes wide with surprise. "Dead? Dear Jesus. How did it happen?"

"When I left, the D.P.S. trooper had all but decided she was D.W.I. There was a gin bottle in the front seat."

Ruby ran her fingers through her orange tangles. "You don't agree?"

"No skid marks, no sign she went over at high speed. McQuaid says maybe she *drove* over. Deliberately." Having permitted me to stroke him, Khat jumped down and sauntered over to his bowl. When he discovered it was empty, he sat down, put one paw in it, and stared at me, unblinking.

Ruby shook her head wonderingly. "She committed suicide?" Her voice was hushed, awed. "But *why?*"

I went to the refrigerator and found the gourmet dainty that Khat had agreed to eat this week. As a connoisseur of kitty food, he's as finicky as Imelda Marcos trying to decide which pair of shoes to wear. "If Andrew didn't kill Sybil, who did? We know that C.W. and Jerri were having an affair, which makes her the Other Woman. And when you and I talked to Jerri last week, she was moaning about not having any money to fix up her gym. Remember?"

Khat removed his paw from his dish, permitted me to fill it, and then sniffed the food suspiciously, with the air of a cat who thought someone was trying to put something over on him. Satisfied, he settled down and began tucking into his meal with feline gusto.

"Yeah, I remember," Ruby said. "She said it was a dump, which surprised me a little. I mean, it's not the Taj Mahal, but I didn't think it was bad, as gyms go."

I sat down again. "Yeah, well, when I saw her yesterday, she was talking about moving over to the mall and buying new equipment."

Ruby's coppery eyebrows shot up under her hair. "That space costs an arm and a leg. Where was she getting the money?"

"Maybe she was expecting to marry it."

"You think she killed Sybil so C.W. could have Sybil's money and she could have C.W.?"

"That's one way to look at it."

Ruby frowned. "But she'd gotten away with it. The sheriff charged Andrew with the murder. So why would she kill herself?"

"I don't know. Remorse, maybe." But the woman I'd talked to only hours before her death hadn't seemed remorseful. She'd been excited about leasing new space, buying new equipment. She'd looked like a woman for whom the world was a golden oyster, and she was poised, knife in hand, eager to open it. What had happened?

Ruby considered. "Maybe she was wrong about C.W. wanting to marry her. Or maybe he found out she'd killed Sybil and got cold feet." She shuddered. "What man in his right mind would marry a woman who'd slit his wife's throat?"

"It's possible," I said slowly, although I couldn't help thinking that Jerri knew how to get what she wanted. If she'd been determined enough to kill Sybil, she wouldn't have taken no for an answer from C.W.

Ruby reached for the sherry bottle and began to pour. "If Jerri killed Sybil, and Jerri's dead in an accident, and nobody figures her for the killer, what'll happen to Andrew?" She looked at me. The glass was full and she was still pouring. "I'm not asking because I'm emotionally committed to him, China. I'm just asking as a . . . well, as a friend." She looked down at the puddle of sherry on the table. "Shit," she said. "Why did I do that?"

I got a sponge and wiped up the spill. "You were thinking. It's hard to think and pour at the same time."

"Have they got enough on him to get an indictment?"

I tossed the sponge in the sink. I couldn't pretend optimism.

"Probably. Fingerprints, eyewitness testimony putting him at the crime scene, Andrew's statement that he was there, which he never should have made. It's probably even enough to get a guilty verdict, if the prosecution plays its cards right." I paused. "Hell, even if they *don't* play their cards right. That damn Satanic bible is pretty potent. In a jury's mind, it'll be sure proof that Andrew's sold his soul to the devil."

Ruby picked up her sherry, careful not to spill, and sipped it. "So we have to find out who *really* killed Sybil."

"Not us," I said. "His lawyer. That's the business of the defense."

Ruby wasn't going to let me get away with it. "But what if his lawyer doesn't? The sheriff and the D.A. aren't going to look anywhere else—they've got enough to convict Andrew, and that's all they want." Her voice turned bitter. "The truth be damned."

I had to admit that Ruby was right. It didn't sound like Andrew had hired somebody who'd make it his business. Unless I was mistaken, his lawyer would sit back and wait for the state's case before he began to develop a defense. By that time, the trail would be stone cold. Worse, it would have the state's tracks all over it, muddying up the truth.

I sat looking into my glass as if it were a crystal ball, not liking what I saw. To deflect my thoughts, I said, "What did you do this morning? Didn't you tell me you were taking off?"

Ruby nodded, still preoccupied with Andrew's situation. "I made a half-dozen phone calls to Abilene."

"Still on the trail of the elusive Reverend?"

She looked at me. "He's not so elusive anymore. I found what I was looking for. I found the name of Billy Lee's first wife. He married that sixteen-year-old girl he got pregnant."

"He did? But doesn't his church say you're not supposed to get divorced?"

"What do you want to bet that none of them know?"

"Now that *you* know it, what are you going to do? Snitch on the guy?"

Ruby was annoyed. "Stop trying to distract me, will you?" She leaned forward, her voice vibrating with urgency. "We can't count on anybody else to dig out the truth and make the sheriff cough up Andrew. Come on, *think*, China. We have to come up with something."

I came up with two things.

The first was talking to C.W. But there was no answer at the office. Angela had said he was staying in the D section at Lake Winds, but I had no idea where. I could make the rounds of the happy hour places—there weren't that many of them—but I'd probably end up missing him. C.W. would have to wait until tomorrow.

The second was having a conversation with the dead woman's sister. But right now didn't seem like exactly the right time. Rita had probably just learned about Jerri's death and she was still coping, not only with grief but with the inevitable details that attend death. I'd have to wait on that, too.

But not for long. Rita called about nine thirty the next morning. Her voice was frayed, her breathing uneven. She'd been crying.

"I didn't know who to call," she said. "Then I remembered that you used to be a lawyer. Could you come over to Jerri's house right away? There's something . . . " She stopped, swallowed, getting hold of herself. "I have to show you something."

"Sure," I said, and got the address.

"I'm coming too," Ruby said, when I went next door to tell her I was leaving. "I'll call Laurel and ask her to run over and stay with both shops until eleven thirty. I have to get back to do a phone interview with Fannie on the 'Back Fence.'"

Thinking of Rita's fragility, I was doubtful. "I don't know, Ruby. Two of us . . ."

"There were two of you yesterday and you did all right." Ruby reached for the phone, while I went to get a denim jacket to top my denim skirt and sweater. Today was a repeat of yesterday's gray skies, but the air had chilled down and the rain felt icy. Winter was ripping out of the Panhandle like a locomotive roaring south.

Fifteen minutes later, we were pulling up in front of Jerri's house. It was a boxy pink frame ranch with fake rock plastered to the front and black make-believe shutters on either side of small windows. The entry was hung with a limp bougainvillea that had been stripped of most of its foliage by an army of leaf-cutter ants, in a hurry to make off with the last of their booty before the freeze. A thin, wavering column of ants marched down the wall and across the sidewalk and into a neat round hole under an anemic juniper. This morning's *Enterprise* lay in the doorway, a photo of Jerri's car plastered across two columns on the sodden front page. The headline was terse. "One-Car Accident Kills Spa Owner."

Rita answered our ring. She was wearing a too-long black dress with padded shoulders. She looked thin and lost inside it, like a child playing dress-up in her mother's clothes. Her mousy hair was pulled back from a center part and fastened with red plastic barrettes. Her face was the color of pie dough, puckered where tears had furrowed her cheeks. Her eyes were puffy slits behind her blue-rimmed glasses, and her lips were trembling. She looked pummeled by guilt, as if what had happened to her sister was her fault.

"Thanks for coming," she said. Her voice faltered. "I . . . I wasn't sure I should call. But I had to . . . to tell *somebody*."

"We're so sorry about your sister," Ruby said. She put her arm around Rita's shoulders and led her into the living room. They sat on the sofa, Ruby comforting softly while Rita sobbed, not ladylike sobs but hard, wrenching paroxysms that shook her whole frame.

I went into the kitchen, ran tap water into a pan, and put it on the stove. I was surprised when I looked around. I'd supposed that an exercise teacher would be interested in good nutrition. But the counter was littered with single-serving cereal boxes, an open package of chocolate cookies, a empty can of macaroni and cheese, several empty Coke bottles. The remains of a Kentucky Fried Chicken dinner were scattered across the table. Behind the counter was a rack of professional-looking knives that appeared out of place in a kitchen where the food was cooked somewhere else.

When the water was hot I made instant coffee, extra-strong,

and carried a mug of it into the living room. If Jerri didn't cook in the kitchen, she didn't really live in the living room, either. It was bare and undecorated, with a minimum of furniture—a tweedy sofa, two plastic-laminated lamp tables and gold-colored lamps, a brown chair, a glass-topped coffee table littered with dishes and exercise magazines, and several paperback books with titles like *You Can Make a Killing in Real Estate*. A cheap stereo center and a television stood against the wall. Clothes were tossed carelessly on the chairs, and a wood-burning stove squatted on a square of red tile, a trail of ashes leading from it across the worn carpet to the sliding glass door. Beyond the door was a cement patio the size of a napkin and a dreary, featureless backyard.

On the sofa, Rita had subsided into hiccups, trying for control. She straightened up when I came in and took the coffee gratefully.

"Thanks," she said. She reached into her purse and took out a cigarette, holding it awkwardly and fumbling with the cheap plastic lighter as if she had only recently learned to smoke. "The last twelve hours have been just horrible. Indescribable. Mama's acting like the world's come to an end. She blames me."

"Blames you?" Ruby asked. "But why?"

"Because . . . " Her face twisted like a gray rag. "Because Jerri's dead and I'm alive, that's why." She tried the coffee, winced at its bitterness, tried again. "Jerri was her favorite. Dad's too. She was the one who knew how to get things done, even if she didn't always . . . I just can't believe she's . . . dead." The tears welled slowly out from under her eyelids and followed the furrows down her cheeks. She had the lost and lonely look of an abandoned child.

"What did you want to tell us?" I needed to hear more about Jerri, but that might mean more tears.

She was silent for a moment, her face working. "I . . . I don't know whether I can . . . "

Ruby traded glances with me. She put her hand on Rita's.

"It's hard, I know," she said. "But there are some things we just have to do, whether we think we can or not. They may be awful, but doing them makes us stronger." Coping 101, abridged version. It worked.

Rita straightened her hunched shoulders. "I guess I can't actually tell you," she said. She set her coffee mug on the table and jabbed out her cigarette in a dirty saucer. "I have to show you." She put on her glasses and got up, walking unsteadily. We followed her down the hall.

The blinds in Jerri's bedroom were down and the room was dark and close, with a slightly musty smell. When Rita turned on the overhead light, I saw that the floor was strewn with clothing and magazines. On the table beside the unmade bed was a lamp and a green glass florist's vase jammed with withered yellow roses. Through the bathroom door I could see a counter piled with makeup and used towels. A red leotard hung on the bathroom doorknob and a pair of hand weights lay on the floor, mute reminders of Jerri's intense physicality.

"I was . . . going through Jerri's stuff this morning, to get something Mama wanted." Rita bent over and pulled a pair of dirty white tennis sneakers out of the closet. They were heavily splattered with red. "I found these." She held them out.

"*Blood?*" Ruby whispered.

"Is it really?" She dropped the shoes as if they burned her hands and sat down on the bed, her face hidden from us. Her voice was thick, her hands clenched. "I just don't know . . . I can't imagine . . ." She shook her head from side to side as if she was trying to clear it.

I looked at her. "Did you find anything else?"

Mutely, Rita leaned over, opened the table drawer, and handed me a small doll. It was dressed in black, with black yarn hair and a bit of copper wire twisted around its throat.

Ruby's eyes widened. "Sybil's voodoo doll!"

"No," I said, "Blackie took Sybil's. This is another one, just like it."

Rita pressed her lips together. "I'd never in the world have known what it was, but Angela Sanchez came into the office yesterday morning to pick up her check from Mr. Rand. While she was there, she told me about the doll Mrs. Rand got before she died. This one looks like what Angela was talking about." She put it back in the drawer and looked up, her eyes large and dark. "You don't suppose Jerri's death was caused by the same evil force that killed Mrs. Rand, do you?" She managed a weak laugh, chiding herself. "No, that's silly. I don't really believe that. But . . ."

I frowned. There was something about all this that didn't feel quite right. "Do you mind if we look around?"

Ruby took the two bedrooms and the bathroom, and I went back to the kitchen. I spent ten minutes looking through drawers and cupboards, but all I turned up was more junk food. There was nothing in the trash but empty packaging. The refrigerator freezer held a half-dozen frozen dinners, stashed next to a gallon of Bluebell triple-chocolate ice cream, three boxes of Sara Lee cheesecakes, and a plastic grocery sack filled with Hershey bars. I wondered if Jerri had kept that great shape by bingeing and purging.

I turned from the freezer and stood for a long moment in front of the knives. There were four of them: a heavy cleaver, a substantial-looking butcher knife, a long, sharp boning knife, and a smaller fillet knife. The blades were gray, with a soft, dull sheen, the cutting edges honed silvery sharp. The handles were of unfinished wood, dark with use, and studded with brass rivets. "Greene's Custom Meats" was stamped on the handles.

I went into the living room and rummaged through the litter of magazines and dishes on the coffee table, then through the clothes on the furniture. Nothing interesting came to light until I opened the stove. It was cold, but inside, I saw the remains of a fire and what was left of a gray sweatshirt and pants.

I turned from the stove as Ruby came into the living room. "Did you find anything?"

"Only this." Ruby held out a scrap of envelope on which was jotted "LW C7, 2:30." "I copied it from the florist's card that came with the roses. Does it mean anything to you?"

"Not yet." I stuck the scrap in the pocket of my skirt and opened the stove. "Take a look at this."

Ruby bent over and peered into the stove. "Burned sweats," she said finally. "Is there enough left to test for bloodstains?"

"Bloodstains?" Rita asked from the hallway. "More *blood*?" Her face was white and pinched, her hands and lips trembling. She sagged against the wall as if she might fall.

Ruby went to her. "You've got to get hold of yourself, Rita," she said firmly, as if Rita were a child. She slipped an arm around her waist and led her back to the sofa. "Whatever happened, we have to get to the bottom of it. You must know that, or you wouldn't have called us to help you."

Rita collapsed against the seat cushions, arms limp, head to one side. "Yes, but Jerri would never have done anything . . . bad," she whispered hoarsely. "Sometimes she didn't show consideration for . . ." She swallowed. "Sometimes she pushed people around a little. But I can't believe she'd do anything . . . criminal."

"Rita," I said, "those knives in the kitchen. Did they belong to Jerri?"

She spoke with her eyes closed, wearily, as if she were almost too tired to get the words out. "They were my father's. He owned a meat locker in New Braunfels. People would bring pigs and cows they wanted butchered. He was proud of his work. He was proud of the knives. They were his tools."

A recognizable shape was beginning to emerge out of the confusion, like a hidden image in a child's puzzle picture. I leaned forward. "Did Jerri work in the locker when she was growing up?"

Rita opened her eyes. "Yes, we both did. Mom and I took care of the customers. Jerri mostly worked with Dad. She killed the animals and helped cut them up. That's why she got Dad's

knives when he died. She was good with them." She stopped
and looked at me, then pushed herself straight. Ruby put both
arms around her. "Why are you asking these questions?" she
cried, trying to push Ruby away. "What are you *saying*?"

I spoke softly. "Your sister may have been involved in Sybil
Rand's death, Rita. The sheriff needs to make an evaluation of
the things we've found here."

"No!" Rita shrieked. "No, no, *no*!" She pounded her fists on
Ruby's restraining arms.

I stared at her. Something didn't feel quite right. What was it?

Ruby held her tightly. "An innocent man is charged with
something Jerri may have done. She's dead now, and nothing
can hurt her. But you have the power to save *him*. Please call the
sheriff."

"I can't," Rita moaned. She doubled up over Ruby's arms,
clutching her stomach. "Jerri was selfish sometimes . . . and she
was . . . infatuated with Mr. Rand, but—"

I watched her narrowly. My sense that something was out of
place was growing stronger. "When did you find out that your
sister and C.W. were lovers?"

A tangle of hair had fallen over her eyes. "Lovers?" She
seemed dazed. "Jerri and . . . Mr. Rand?"

"Yes," I said. "How long have you known?"

She rocked back and forth against Ruby's arms. When she
spoke, her voice was thin and high, a child's voice. "Since . . . the
day before yesterday. When you came into the office."

"She told you then? Just before I came?"

"Yes, but that's just what she *told* me." The little-girl voice
was laced with bitterness. "She always bragged a lot about the
big, important things she was doing. She always had some
scheme for impressing people, for making them like her, for getting ahead. But if you listened real close, you'd know she was
lying."

"Did she tell you that she and C.W. were going to be
married?"

Rita looked up at me, widening her eyes, incredulous. "Are you saying she killed . . . because she thought she could marry . . . " She lowered her eyes again, but not before I had seen it. An elusive flash of glee, of triumph, so swift that I almost didn't see it, almost didn't recognize it for what it was.

But then it clicked, and I understood everything. Rita knew that her sister had killed Sybil, and she wasn't going to let her get away with it, even if she was dead. Out of bitterness, out of her lifelong anger at always being forced into second place, she was finally getting even. When she discovered the evidence, she'd deliberately called us here. She had wanted to show us what Jerri had done, and by showing us, she was showing her mother that her precious Jerri was a bad girl. It was all very complicated, but I knew I was right. And having seen them together, knowing something about their relationship, I could understand her feelings of triumph at finally having got the best of her sister.

I pulled in my breath, getting back on track. "Did Jerri tell you that she and C.W. were getting married?" I repeated.

There was a long silence as Rita struggled to hold on to the only illusion she had left. Finally she dragged out the words. "That's what she *said*. But it wasn't true. Mr. Rand was nice to her. But I know he'd never . . ." She shook her head. "But I guess she thought maybe she could talk him into it. And when she couldn't, she . . ." Her hands clenched into fists. "When she couldn't, she got into her car and drove off the cliff."

I straightened up. There was no point in trying to get Rita to come to terms with the full truth. It was kinder to let her live with her image of C.W., flawed as it was. "If you don't call the sheriff," I said quietly, "I'll have to."

She clutched Ruby's hand as if she were going down for the last time. "I *can't*," she whispered. "Mama would never forgive me if I were the one to . . ."

Ruby touched her cheek gently. "Then I will."

❋ ❋ ❋

"That about wraps it up, don't you think?" Ruby asked, as we got into my Datsun. It was almost eleven thirty.

"Looks like it." We'd spent the last fifteen minutes with Sheriff Blackwell. He hadn't been too happy to learn that we'd searched Jerri's house, but he had to accept my explanation that we were there at Rita's request and that we really hadn't expected to find anything. When we left, a deputy was bagging and tagging the bloody shoes, the clothing from the stove, and the doll, while another was conducting an official search for additional evidence. Rita would be spending some time with the sheriff, giving her statement, but I didn't think he'd make the questions too tough. I didn't think he'd dig out her secret, either. Rita had buried it pretty deeply, maybe even so deeply that she couldn't admit how she felt or what she'd done. Anyway, he was focusing on Jerri. When I left, he was calling the D.P.S. to request a report on the wreck and find out where the body'd been autopsied.

Blackie looked relieved, and I wondered if something besides finding that Andrew was a southpaw had taken the zing out of his case. If so, no wonder he was relieved. With a murder-suicide, the county would be spared the expense of a trial. It wasn't a minor consideration. Getting a verdict, especially if there is a change of venue or the jury is sequestered, can cost the taxpayers upward of a hundred thousand dollars. The county commissioners would be happy to hear that they wouldn't have to pony up. They might even be so happy that they'd give Blackie that budget increase he was asking for.

Ruby leaned toward me with a quizzical look. "It *is* wrapped up, right? Won't the sheriff have to let Andrew go?"

"He'll probably wait until he gets the lab work back, to be sure that the bloodstains are Sybil's. If they aren't—"

"Well, I think they are," Ruby said positively.

"I think so too," I said. "That bit about the knives, and Jerri working at the meat locker—it all fits. If her father taught her to cut up meat, he must have taught her to bleed an animal."

"To slit its throat, you mean." Ruby's voice was very small.

"Yes." We were both silent as I negotiated the town square. Mayor Perkins was coming out of the old bank building that's been turned into a city hall. There were several people with her—the site team, I guessed. She waved at us and I reminded myself that I was taking them to lunch tomorrow. It felt good to think of homely things like that, after what I had seen the past few days.

"So it was Jerri who broke into the Cave," Ruby said thoughtfully. "I guess she did it to cover up—to make it look like a cult."

I turned the corner onto our street. "That's probably why she made the voodoo dolls too. But I don't think she deliberately set Andrew up. It was just bad luck that he walked onto the crime scene and ended up in jail."

"Maybe that's why she committed suicide," Ruby said. "To take him off the hook." She frowned. "No, if she'd wanted to clear him, she'd have left a note. She wouldn't depend on people to dope it out."

That was the part that was bothering me, even after the rest of the package was neatly wrapped up. "Something still doesn't feel right, Ruby." I pulled up in front of the shops and turned off the ignition. "I talked to Jerri just a few hours before she drove over that cliff, and she didn't seem suicidal to me. She acted like a woman with big ideas, big plans."

"But if her death wasn't an accident and it wasn't suicide, that only leaves—"

I laughed shortly. "Well, at least Andrew's in the clear. But I think I'll talk to C.W."

Ruby turned to stare at me. "You think *he* might have done it?"

I shook my head. "You're way ahead of me again, Ruby. I'm

going to ask him why Jerri might have wanted to kill herself, that's all."

"I want to go with you." Ruby was decisive. "I'll phone the radio station and say I can't—"

I started the car again. "And leave Fannie Couch holding up the back fence alone for a whole hour? She'd never forgive you."

❋ ❋ ❋

Like any other central Texas resort on a weekday in November, Lake Winds was deserted. As I drove into the complex, past landscaped mounds of pampas grass, shrubby cotoneaster, and bright red bayberry, I noticed painted signposts, pointing like accusing fingers in different directions. A1–A10, one of them said. A recollection flashed into my mind, and I pulled over and fished in the pocket of my blue denim skirt. I pulled out the envelope on which Ruby had scribbled the number from Jerri's notepad. "LW C7, 2:30." I looked up, the hair prickling on my arms. Ahead was the signpost for the C units.

C7 was a posh condo built of limestone and cedar, perched on a bluff overlooking Canyon Lake. The water was bright and sparkling under a sunny, postcard-blue sky, and the north breeze whipped up whitecaps like meringue on a pie. A thirty-foot sailboat was motoring out of the yacht basin. As I watched, the helmsman cut the motor and brought the boat into the wind. A young woman in white pants and a white jacket, blond hair flying, ran forward along the deck and hauled up the jib, then, with the assist of a motorized winch, the main. As the helmsman cleated the mainsheet, the sail bellied out with a snap and the boat heeled over smartly, brass fittings glinting against the polished teak of the deck. Texas money out to play.

As I went around to the back of C7, I wondered if Jerri had hoped that marrying C.W. would admit her to the privileged world of Texas players. If so, it could have been a powerful

motive for her to kill Sybil. And what about C.W.? What kind of
hand had he played?

I stepped up on the concrete stoop at the back of the condo.
Yes, what *about* C.W.? Had he been the totally innocent spouse,
unaware of his girlfriend's plot? Or had he played a different
hand? Had he been a coconspirator? I remembered the note.
Maybe he'd been more. Maybe the whole thing had been his
idea, and Jerri his agent.

But that was a square-ten question, and I was still on square
one. Jerri's statement to Rita that she and C.W. were lovers was
the only proof of their relationship, unless you counted Sybil's
statement to Judith. But both were hearsay, inadmissible. If a
prosecutor wanted to make a case against C.W., there'd have to
be something more substantial than that.

The fact that the back door of C7 swung open when I
knocked didn't mitigate the fact that I was breaking and entering. But I'd take the risk. I put my head in the door and yelled
"Leasing company inspector, here to check the premises.
Anybody home?" The empty condo, with its sound-deadening
drapes and plush carpets, didn't even give me back an echo.

The kitchen was like a kitchen in a TV commercial—coun-
ters bare, stainless steel sink and cooktop spotless, refrigerator
empty except for a box of Arm & Hammer baking soda. Ditto
utility room, downstairs bath, and luxurious living/dining, furnished with color-coordinated furniture and wall art straight
from the showroom. The pale silver carpet bore the long sweeping print of a vacuum cleaner. Sharp and clear on the freshly
vacuumed rug were footprints—a man's shoes and a woman's
high heels. One set led from the hallway to the stairs and up.
The other set led from the stairs to the hallway and out.
Whoever had made them was gone.

Upstairs, there was the same feeling of luxuriously furnished
emptiness, like a vacant soap opera set. I followed the footprints
down the vacuumed hallway to the bedroom. The drapes were
drawn, darkening the room, and I flicked on the wall switch

with my elbow. Somebody had straightened the bedspread, but I could see the shadows of indentations on the pillows. It looked like a pair of somebodies had made love on the bed, bedspread and all, and had left in a hurry. Maybe that was why the vase of faded flowers still stood on the bedside table, beside a lipstick-printed Styrofoam cup, a quarter full of amber liquid that smelled like scotch. The flowers were the same yellow roses I'd seen beside Jerri's bed. This time, though, there was a card.

"To Jerri, with all my heart, C.W."

I shook my head. Love, oh love, oh careless love.

Downstairs, I found a chair and wedged it under the front doorknob, to make sure it couldn't be opened. Then I wrapped my fingers with a tissue and closed the back door. I stood for a moment looking at the lock, then reached into my purse and found my keyring. All the keys on it are keys I use, except for the key to Leatha's house, which she had given me to use in an emergency. This was an emergency. I pushed her key into the lock as far as it would go, then bent it sharply with the heel of my palm. It snapped off.

Nobody was going to get into C7 without going to a great deal of trouble.

❋ ❋ ❋

The woman at the front desk looked up when I came into the outer office. She was petite and dark-haired, with artfully made-up brown eyes, carved cheeks, and a soft, full mouth. Her cobalt-colored feminine suit had a sweetheart neckline that showed substantial cleavage, softly framed by a white chiffon scarf. The nametag on her left breast pocket announced that she was LouEllen Lamour, Sales Agent, and she was working on what looked like a sales report. Rita's desk was vacant, the top cleared off, a cover over the typewriter. The door to C.W.'s office was closed.

"Welcome to Lake Winds," LouEllen said with a smile and a

practiced head tilt that gave me her best angle. "How may we help you?"

I perched on the corner of her desk and swung my loafered foot. "You haven't heard from Rita today, have you, LouEllen?" I shook my head. "Poor kid. I don't suppose she'll be in for a while, under the circumstances."

LouEllen's smile faded. "It was a tragedy, wasn't it? Jerri was such a gorgeous person, so much life and energy. Rita probably won't be in all week."

I stood up. "Well, in that case, I'll just have a quick word with the boss. No need to buzz him." I headed toward C.W.'s office door.

LouEllen stood up and came around the desk. Her skirt was *very* short. If my legs were that good, I'd probably wear short skirts too. "I'm sorry," she said protectively, "you can't see him this morning. He's not taking—"

But I was already opening the door to C.W.'s office.

He was seated behind a large expanse of gleaming walnut desktop, the sleeves of his white shirt rolled up, tie loosened, heavy gold Rolex on his thick wrist, a shock of gray hair falling perfectly across his forehead. A handsome man, if fleshy. He looked up from the papers he was studying.

"Most people knock." His voice was rich and deep and familiar. He smiled, showing those white-white teeth. "Sheriff's still got your client in the lockup, I understand. I figured you'd have him out by now."

Some witnesses you lead along, gently and gradually. Others you hit fast, aiming to short-circuit the story they've been rehearsing. With C.W., I aimed to shock.

"The sheriff's at Jerri's, bagging up bloodstained sneakers, clothes, and a voodoo doll. He thinks it's your wife's blood."

C.W. didn't shock. He sighed heavily and threw down his gold pen. "I was afraid she did it," he said. He pushed back the boyish shock of gray hair.

I sat down across from him. "What made you suspect her?"

He rubbed a well-cared-for hand across his eyes, shoulders slumping. "You've got to understand, Miss Bayles. China." He glanced at me from under the long dark lashes that framed pale eyes. "This whole thing has been very hard. I'm in a difficult position."

"The two of you were sleeping together. Is that the difficult position?"

The hand dropped and he sat up. "I know that's what Jerri told her sister. But she was lying. She *wanted* us to have an affair—she'd been after me for three or four months, calling on the phone, stopping in here, leaving notes at the house. I wasn't having any."

I wasn't convinced. "A reformed man, huh? The paternity suit in Dallas—put the fear of God in you, did it?"

C.W.'s voice roughened. "Did Sybil tell you about that?"

"If you'd reformed, why did Sybil want a divorce? Why did she tell a friend that Jerri Greene would end up costing her money, like the others you'd been involved with?"

He put his elbows on his desk, clasped his hands in front of him, and made a tent of his forefingers. The large diamond glittered in his heavy gold ring. "I'll tell you the honest-to-God truth, Miss Bayles. I've had a few problems in the past, where women are concerned. My wife *was* troubled about the Greene woman. But I told Sybil, and I'll tell you, she had no reason. There was never a personal relationship between Jerri Greene and me, I swear. Sybil had her own reasons for wanting a divorce." He leaned back in his swivel chair and took a cigarette out of a gold case on the shelf behind him. "Sybil didn't tell me at the time and I didn't suspect, but now I know she wanted to get rid of me because she had the hots for Andrew Drake. That's why she was willing to make that big settlement. After the crap she'd handed me about other women, she felt guilty. She was buying me off." He flicked a gold lighter, inhaled deeply, and exhaled a wreath of smoke. "Not pretty, but there it is. God's truth."

Why didn't I believe him? I went back to my earlier question. "What made you suspect that Jerri Greene killed your wife?"

"The last time we talked—Friday, before I went to Atlanta— Jerri told me she loved me. She said she'd do anything to make it work between us. I told her to blow it off. I didn't want anything to do with her." He gestured with his cigarette. "But Jerri Greene was one hard-ass lady. She wanted something, she took it. Anybody stood in her way, she'd climb right on over. When I got home and Sybil was dead, I knew she'd done it."

I took a different tack. "When you and Jerri talked on Friday, did you tell her that your wife planned to get a divorce, or that she'd cut you out of her will?"

"Why should I? It wasn't any of Jerri's business."

"And you lied to me when you said you believed Sybil'd been killed by a cult."

"What'd'ya want? I should confess that my wife was killed by some flake who wanted my body?" He shook his head, amused. "No way."

"And you let the sheriff arrest Andrew Drake."

"I wouldn't've let them stick him with it. But I figured, a day or two in jail, no harm done. And I kept thinking that they'd check Jerri out. I wouldn't have to get involved."

"And now she's dead."

"And now she's dead." He brought his chair upright emphatically. "Period, paragraph, the end. All she wrote. Right?"

"I doubt it." I couldn't help it, I was beginning to hate the guy. It was his slick, smooth arrogance that turned me off, his ability to write two women out of his life because it was inconvenient or uncomfortable to be held accountable for his relationships with them. "If you didn't want anything more to do with her, why did you invite her to your condo room Monday night?"

He was wary. "You get around some."

"Why did you invite her?"

"I did not invite her." He mimicked my clipped tone. "She

called me up, said she wanted to come over and tell me how sorry she was about my wife. I told her to forget it, I was totally zonked, a zombie. She came anyway. I got rid of her as fast as I could."

I changed the subject. "What were you doing Tuesday night?"

He looked surprised. "Tuesday? I guess I did what I did Monday night. That was before the cops let me back in the house. I was in the office until four, four thirty, then I worked out at the gym for an hour."

"Jerri's gym?"

"That dump?" He grinned, flashing his teeth. I wondered how much money he had spent to get his mouth to look like that. "Are you kidding? I've got the weight room here set up just the way I want it. I happy-houred for a while at Santiago's Cantina, then I got something to eat at the Steakhouse over on I-35. Then I went back to the condo and watched television."

"Alone?"

"Of course," he said indignantly. "My wife had just died. What kind of a louse do you think I am?"

I gave him an acid smile. "I guess that's the question, isn't it?"

He pressed his full lips together. "Let me put this in words of one syllable, Miss Bayles. I would have to've been crazy to kill Sybil after I found out how things stood with that divorce settlement. But I wasn't entirely surprised to read in this morning's paper that Jerri Greene had tanked up and driven herself over a cliff. Not to speak ill of the dead, but she was an unstable bitch with a hyperactive imagination. She was capable of anything—including both homicide *and* suicide." He glanced at the Rolex. "If you don't mind, I need to cut this short. Sybil's funeral is tomorrow, up in north Texas, and I've got things to do."

I was dismissed. As I left, I took pleasure in slamming his office door behind me, startling LouEllen, who was entering numbers from her sales report into a calculator.

I jerked a thumb over my shoulder. "Tell the boss I'll send the newspaper a copy of our interview," I said, out of sheer malice.

"Super." LouEllen jotted down a total and started on another column. "Mr. Rand is always glad to get publicity."

I strode down the walk, fuming inside. I was trained to quarry the truth out of people who wanted to hang on to it, and I've developed a nose for a liar. I smelled one this time. C.W. was lying about his relationship with Jerri—the proof was in a bedroom in C7. I could have sprung that on him, but it seemed like a good idea to hold something in reserve. What's more, I was convinced that he hadn't known about the will or the divorce settlement before somebody let it slip during the questioning.

Getting in my car, turning on the ignition, I could see the whole scenario, clear and simple, with C.W. standing behind the curtain like a puppeteer, pulling Jerri's strings. He expected to inherit his wife's money. He promised Jerri to marry her as soon as his wife was out of the way. He had conspired with her to kill Sybil—had probably even come up with the idea and talked her into it. And Jerri, trained by her father to slit throats with dispatch, had done the job while he was out of town.

But the fact that C.W. wasn't standing at Jerri's elbow meant absolutely nothing in the eyes of the law. When two people plan something illegal—the law calls it "acting in concert"—each person is responsible not only for what he or she does and what the two do together, but also what the other does alone. If C.W. conspired with Jerri to kill his wife, his hand was on the knife as well as hers. He was as guilty as she was.

I drove through the gates and out onto the highway, heading toward Pecan Springs, still sorting through the ugly can of worms Rita had opened with her bloody discovery of Jerri's shoes, burned clothing, and back-up voodoo doll. Once Jerri had done the job C.W. assigned her, she was no longer an asset. In fact, she was a hell of a liability. If I was right, sometime on Tuesday night C.W. had taken steps to remedy the problem.

He'd got Jerri drunk and pushed her car over the cliff, intending it to look like one more D.W.I., wiped out on Devil's Backbone.

But I had learned a long time ago that it's one thing to know the truth, but another thing altogether to be able to sell it to a jury. Now that I knew the truth, I had a big job. I had to prove that Jerri hadn't acted alone in her murder of Sybil. *And* I had to prove that she'd been killed by her coconspirator.

It wasn't going to be easy, but I knew where to start asking questions.

17

On the way back into Pecan Springs I stopped at the Exxon station and called the nearest D.P.S. district office. Two holds and three clerks later, I asked my first question—where was Jerri's wrecked Mustang? The answer: the wrecking yard behind Hank's Auto Repair, on the east side of Pecan Springs.

I got back in the car, noticing that it was half-past lunchtime and feeling distinctly empty inside. It was time to ask my second question, and I headed for Maria's Taco Cocina, on Zapata Street. The restaurant is crowded into a small frame house behind a bare dirt yard decorated with truck tires painted white and planted with yellow and bronze and red mums, silver dusty miller, and blue salvias, still blooming. Inside, the Cocina is wall-papered with community notices and filled with tables, mis-matched chairs from the Salvation Army Thrift Store, and noisy diners. Maria, Angela Sanchez's aunt, makes extraordinary tacos and tamales. Today I had chiles rellenos—fried chiles—stuffed with Maria's special mix of beef, coriander, cloves, garlic, and raisins. When I finished, I went into the kitchen where Maria's helper was cleaning up after the lunch rush, and Maria herself was starting dinner. Maria is squat and strong, and she maneu-vers her bulk in the tiny kitchen with the finesse of an astronaut docking the space shuttle. She was stirring a simmering pot of vegetable soup, thick with onions, carrots, corn, and zucchini in a richly fragrant chicken broth.

We exchanged greetings and a moment of friendly chitchat. I got around to my question as soon as I could. "What have you heard about Sybil Rand's murder?" I'd already answered it to my own satisfaction, but it wouldn't hurt to check the alternatives.

Maria shook her head and turned from the vegetable soup to a huge vat of chili. She tasted it, then added a few vigorous shakes of comino. "The Santeros, they didn't do it, China. No way. Nobody made any doll, neither. You tell the sheriff, *comprende*?"

"You're certain about the doll?"

Maria gave me a hard-eyed look. "You betcha. My sisters and my mother, they asked all their friends. Nobody knows anything about it. Anyway, anybody can make a doll that looks like a voodoo doll." She shook her wooden spoon. "You want to, you can do it, easy. You won't know how to make the magic, but you can make the doll."

So could Jerri. She could also make two dolls, and send Sybil the best one.

I thanked Maria, bought three pine nut cookies dusted with cinnamon sugar, and went off to ask my third question.

Hank's Auto Repair is at the end of Zapata, where it meets the southbound frontage road along I-35. Hank has worked on McQuaid's pickup, put new brakes in my Datsun, and keeps Ruby's Honda on the road. He's honest, knows everything there is to know about cars, and has the patience of Job. I polished off the last cookie just as I drove up in front of his shop.

Hank works in a large corrugated iron building behind a gravel apron, where an assortment of ailing cars and trucks are parked in some mysterious priority arrangement. Inside the double doors, three cars were lined up, one of them a Chevy van on a hydraulic lift. Hank stepped out, pocketed his wrench, and wiped his oily hands on a shop rag.

"Howdy," he said. "Haven't seen you 'round here in a coon's

age. That Datsun runnin' okay?" Hank is lanky, blond, and fair-skinned, pushing forty. He wears grimy khaki coveralls with a red-white-and-blue Perot for President button on one lapel (once a Perot supporter, always a Perot supporter, Hank insists) and a neon yellow gimme cap that says Hank does it FAST. He chews spearmint gum, a considerable improvement over the Red Man tobacco he used to chew. Now, he pulled out a stick, unwrapped it, and doubled it into his mouth.

"She's running fine," I said. "D.P.S. says you've got Jerri Greene's Mustang."

Hank stuck the shop rag in his back pocket, where it hung like a red flag. "Yep," he said, chewing. "Back there." He jerked his head toward the three acres of wrecking yard behind the garage. "Shit-pot of trouble, too, gettin' it up that hill. Second in two weeks. First one was drinkin' Southern Comfort. This one was gin. Think people'd learn, wouldn't ya?"

I agreed that people ought to learn, even if they died trying. "Wonder if I could take a look at it."

"Not much to look at." Hank scratched his chin thoughtfully. "You know what you're lookin' fer?"

"Yeah, I'm the one who called it in. McQuaid and I happened to spot the wreck on our way back from Fredericksburg."

"Must of been pretty grim."

"You can leave out the 'pretty.' Would you mind taking a minute to look with me?"

Hank glanced at the Chevy as if asking its permission, then shrugged. "Might as well," he said. "Time to take a break, anyway."

We walked through a gate in the chain-link fence and into the wrecking yard, which was piled with cars in varying states of decomposition. Hank pulls off the high-demand parts, holds onto the hulks until he runs out of space, then puts in a call for the crusher, a big machine that travels from one wrecking yard to another. A forklift skewers the derelict through the windows and drops it onto the crusher, which looks like a giant drycleaner's press. It flattens the auto into a foot-high hunk of accordion-pleated scrap.

Jerri's Mustang was in a separate area, where Hank holds towed cars until the owners claim them or the police tell him how to dispose of them. I recognized it immediately. There was a pile of vulture shit on the seat and a few more gouges where it had been dragged up the hill.

"What're you lookin' for?" Hank asked. "There ain't nothin' on this baby worth salvagin', 'cept the tape deck and radio. Anyway, I ain't got a release from D.P.S."

I stared at the smashed, scorched hulk for a minute, wondering exactly what I *was* looking for. Maybe Hank could help. "If I wanted to send this car over the edge of a cliff and make it look like an accident, how would I do it?"

Hank took off his cap and scratched his head. His blond hair was mashed flat against his scalp, and there was a ring at the back where his cap fit tight. "You mean, like, to collect the insurance?"

"Something like that."

"Well, if that was what the lady had in mind," he said judiciously, "she sure as hell messed up. To make somethin' like that work, you gotta be around to collect." He guffawed. "Ya don't have to be a rocket scientist to figger that out."

"Forget the lady," I said. "If *I* was doing it, how would I do it?"

"Well, now, don't reckon I know how you'd do it." He put his cap back on. "But seein' as how it's an automatic, which means it creeps in drive if the brake ain't on, what *I'd* do is I'd stand by the driver's side with the motor runnin'."

"In drive?"

"In park for now. Mebbe I'd take me a screwdriver and set up the idle." He looked at me, judging my knowledge of the car's insides. "If I was you doin' it, mebbe I'd forget the idle and wedge the gas pedal with a stick or somethin'."

I bent over. There was no stick or anything under the gas pedal. Maybe it had fallen out. Maybe it hadn't been there. "Would the car creep without the gas pedal being wedged?"

"Yep. It'd creep slower, but it'd creep."

"Okay. So now what?"

Hank posed next to the Mustang, demonstrating. "Well, I'd reach on over, like this, and shove it into drive, like—"

I grabbed his hand. "Don't touch that shift," I said, thinking of fingerprints.

"Oh, yeah?" He tipped up the bill of his cap, really interested now. "Well, once I got it in drive, I'd just step on back and watch 'er creep, right on over the edge. Simple as hell."

I remembered the burned spot beside the road. "What if I wanted to make sure the car burned when it got to the bottom? How would I set it on fire?"

Hank pondered for a minute. "It's tougher to burn a car than most folks think. Me, I'd put a hole somewhere in the fuel system, so it'd keep runnin' and pumpin' gas. This is what, an eighty-two? When this baby was built, there weren't no automatic fuel cutoffs, the way they got now. 'N even now, them things don't always work. Or they work when they're not s'posed to. I had a brand-new Le Baron in here just the other week for that very problem."

"C. W. Rand's Le Baron?" I asked. My skin prickled. There it was. The evidence I was looking for. Well, close.

"Yeah. Sure couldn't be nobody else. He's got the only one in town. Had to tow it in from his office out there at the *re*sort." He laughed. "That Rand feller, he was kinda hot under the collar when I told him it was a malfunction in a safety device that kept his car from runnin'. People get kinda upset when it's somethin' like that. But hell, it weren't no skin off his nose. Chrysler dealer in Austin picked up the tab."

"Could I have a look under the hood?"

"It's jammed down tight." Hank looked at me. "You really wanna do this?"

"It could be important."

He heaved a big sigh and sauntered back to the shop. He returned with a rusty iron bar, which he inserted under the crumpled hood. "Guess it won't hurt if I bend things a little more," he said, putting his weight on the bar. The hood popped up with a screech. He wedged the bar under it to keep it open.

The engine was a smashed, scorched mass of parts and half-melted hoses. I frowned, trying to make sense of the mess. "Where's the fuel pump?"

"Down here." He pushed some debris out of the way. He frowned. "Hey, looka this." He was pointing at a melted blob of plastic in the line that ran from the fuel pump to the carburetor. "Ask me, the fire started here."

"How can you tell?"

"That glob is what's left of the fuel filter. Say it got punctured while the engine was runnin', the fuel would just keep on comin' out. When it gets on somethin' hot enough, mebbe the exhaust manifold, you got yourself a dandy fire."

"Could I puncture the fuel filter myself?"

"Don't see why not. Just take yourself a sharp screwdriver or an ol' ice pick, somethin' pointy like that, and stab a couple holes in it. When the gas starts spurtin' out, light yourself a match and Katie bar the door."

I frowned. "But why didn't the car burn up?"

"Like I say, kinda hard to actually burn up a car, 'less a course you get rear-ended and the gas tank goes wha-boom. This case, I'd guess the engine stalled when it crashed, so you got no gas pumpin' up front. And from the look of things, the fuel tank ruptured and the gas ran downhill."

"Causing a grass fire," I said, remembering the burned patch on the hill below the car.

"Might not of been much fuel in the tank, neither."

"And I could punch a hole in the fuel filter up on the road, before I put the car in drive, and light it then too?"

"If you was aimin' to torch it, that's what you'd do." He bent over and peered at the engine, then straightened, frowning. "Thing that gets me is it'd almost have to happen that way. No reason why this fuel filter should've ruptured in the crash. The line's flexible, and I don't see no damage in this area." His frowned deepened. "Them highway patrol guys got the same ideas you got?"

"I doubt it," I said. "The investigating officer seemed to think it was just another drunk driver. And when you pried open the hood just now, it was the first time it'd been opened since the crash jammed it shut."

Hank spit out his gum. "Prob'ly I should give 'em a call."

"It probably wouldn't hurt to give them the benefit of your thoughts on the subject," I agreed.

"Prob'ly won't listen." Hank got out another chew. "Hardly ever do." He jerked the bar out and the hood fell with a crash. "But mebbe I'll do it, when I finish up the Chevy. Don't reckon this Mustang's goin' anywhere."

Hank stepped back under the van and I got into my car and sat there for a few minutes, thinking. Question number three was the real pay-off. It looked more and more as if Jerri had not been the victim of an accident, but of a plot to kill her and conceal the murder. C.W. could have gotten the idea for the fire from Hank when he brought his LeBaron in for repair. But unless he'd left prints on the shift console—and I'd bet he hadn't—there was no physical evidence to connect him to the wrecked Mustang. I'd have to look somewhere else for proof that C.W. was the killer.

But first I had to check on something. C.W. might not have waited until Jerri got drunk and passed out before he did his dirty work with the car. He might have knocked her out before he sent her over the cliff. I stopped at a gas station and called the Travis County Medical Examiner's office, hoping to find out whether Jerri had suffered any injuries not accounted for by the accident.

"This is Mattie," I said, "at the sheriff's office in Adams County. You got anything on the Greene autopsy yet?"

The clerk left the phone and came back a minute later. "We don't have a Greene autopsy here. You sure you got the right county?"

"Oops," I said, "I meant to dial Bexar. Sorry I bothered you." I dialed the Bexar County M.E. and repeated my question.

"Didn't Pete get through to the sheriff this morning?" the clerk asked, sounding confused.

"I guess not," I said. "Sheriff Blackwell just got back from lunch and asked me to call. He didn't say anything about talking to Pete."

"Well, the report won't be ready until tomorrow," the clerk said. "We're backed up here. Noon, at the earliest, and no orals. Sorry, but we're swamped."

"That's okay," I said. "Everybody gets behind now and then. I'll tell the sheriff."

I hung up. That line of inquiry would have to wait until tomorrow, but there was something else I could try in the meantime.

✳ ✳ ✳

I was back at Thyme and Seasons by quarter past two. Ruby was gone, and Laurel was watching both shops. Things were looking up. She'd sold a seventy-dollar grapevine wreath, plus three or four flats of plants, quite a few toiletries and dried herbs, and a half-dozen books.

"I hope Ruby did as well on Fannie's talk show as we're doing on the register," I said.

Laurel laughed. She's a slim woman in her late twenties, dark-eyed and demure, with a dimple in her left cheek. She was wearing her dark hair in twin braids laced with rawhide strips, and a checked cotton shirt with jeans and a tooled cowboy belt. Her full name is Laurel Walkingwater Wiley. She and her husband—an environmental engineer—are from Albuquerque.

She's studying herbs of the Southwest. "Ruby did pretty well," she said, "even when she was accused of being a witch."

I shook my head. "Somebody actually called her that, huh?"

"Yes, but Fannie blew the whistle." This was not a figure of speech. When a caller says something Fannie thinks shouldn't go out over the air waves, she whistles into the mike. It drives the sound engineer crazy and he keeps telling her not to do it, but she does it anyway. Fannie is a law unto herself. "Ruby was very cool," Laurel went on. "She said she wasn't a witch, and if the caller wanted to come to her shop and bring a frog, she'd show him she couldn't turn it into Bubba Harris. Fannie thought that was pretty funny."

So did I. I'd have to ask Ruby how she planned to prove a negative. "Where is Ruby?" I asked.

"She said to tell you she'd be back about closing time. She's ordering stock this evening, so she'll be around kind of late."

I asked Laurel to stay for the rest of the afternoon and went through the connecting door to my house. I got out the phone book and looked up Rita's number. I had a feeling that Rita knew more than she was telling, both about C.W. and about Jerri. Or maybe she knew things she didn't want to know about their relationship and hence had forgotten them, not deliberately, but because she couldn't face them. Whichever way it was, getting through to the truth would be tough. She'd defend C.W. as long as she could.

Rita answered. When I asked if I could come over and talk to her, she said, "I can't just now. Mama's here, and her two sisters." She paused, and I could hear high, chattery voices in the background. "Can it wait a couple of hours?"

"How about four o'clock?"

"I guess." She sighed. "Mama's got to go home for a nap sometime or other. But you'd better call first."

I said I would, and then dialed McQuaid's office. My ideas about the case had firmed up, and I wanted to talk them over with him so he could point out the flaws in my logic. When there was no answer, I tried the criminal justice department. Lucille Sweet, the departmental secretary, told me McQuaid had gone to the airport in San Antonio to pick up some people who were attending the conference.

"What time will he be back?" I asked.

"Not before six thirty," she said. "The last plane gets in at five, and he'll have to hurry to get here in time for the banquet and the first speech." She lowered her voice. "Listen, China, if you see him before I do, tell him that Patterson's got another burr under his tail."

"God," I said. "What is it this time?"

"The copy machine." Lucille sounded resigned. "McQuaid didn't pay for his copies. If he can sneak ten bucks into the money box before the chairman comes in tomorrow, I'll say it got dumped on the floor and I found the ten behind the radiator."

I grinned. Poor Lucille bore the brunt of the chairman's bad temper with a good grace. I left a message for McQuaid to call me and tried Ruby, thinking that maybe it would be good to take her with me to talk to Rita. But there was no answer, and by now it was pushing two forty-five. I went back out, got in the Datsun, and drove to Jerri's Health and Fitness Spa.

※ ※ ※

The front door was posted with a red-crayon sign that said "Closed Today," but it was unlocked, so I went in. Peaches was in the office, bare feet propped up on a desk. She had pulled purple sweatpants and pink leg warmers over a gold-striped purple leotard, and she wore a petulant look on her hollow-cheeked face. Plastic rollers, like fat pink worms, curled all over her head. She was blowing the worms with a hand-held hair dryer.

"You decided to close?" I asked.

"So? Whatta ya think I should do?" she asked over the

wheeze of the dryer. "Take over her classes? Let people in to use the equipment? Or what?"

"Better ask Jerri's mother," I said. "Or Rita. I suppose somebody in the family's making decisions like that."

Peaches turned off the dryer and swung her feet to the floor. "Forget it. I just came over to sit in the sauna for a few minutes and unwind. Now I'm gonna pack my gear and my tapes and split. I'll probably never see another paycheck. And I sure as hell don't want to deal with that Rita. She may look like a Miss Goodie Two-Shoes, but looks are deceiving, believe you me. I've seen her and Jerri get into it a time or two."

"Oh, yeah?" I was interested. I'd often wondered how things would have been different if I'd had a sister, somebody to talk to, to share things with. But I probably idealized the relationship. Sisters were probably like everybody else, they tore into one another from time to time.

"Yeah," Peaches said emphatically. "Jerri'd get pissed off and throw things around, smash a few glasses, kick a wall or two. Ten minutes later she was cool again. But that Rita—" She pulled out a curler, testing her dark hair for springiness. "Kissy face, sweet as pie, but watch out. Scratch your eyes out behind your back."

Peaches' view of Rita was cast in some interesting metaphors, but I was more interested in dates and times. "Were you here on Tuesday night?"

Peaches looked into a mirror over the desk and began to pull the curlers out of her hair. "Was that the night she ran off the road?" To my nod, she said, "Yeah, I was here. Didn't plan to be, but Jerri called and asked could I take the Seven P.M. Steppers and close up afterward, so I did. Meant a little extra money, or so I thought." Her mouth twisted. "Doubt I ever see any of *that*, neither."

"Was Jerri here when you got here?"

All the curlers out, she began to fluff her hair with her fingers. "Yeah. She left after the class started. I know, because I saw her leavin' and like waved good-bye." She dropped her hands and gazed at herself in the mirror. Her eyes grew solemn and a little frightened, as if she were looking at her own skull. "I been thinkin' about that. Wavin' good-bye, I mean. Like what would I of done if I'd of known I'd never see her again? It seems sorta . . . well, sorta *puny*, don't it? Just a wave, when somebody's about to cash it in." She shrugged and fluffed some more. "Good thing I didn't know, I guess."

"How did she seem?"

She picked up a jar of mousse and dug in with both hands. "Seem? How'd ya mean?"

"Was she up that evening? Was she down? Had she been drinking?"

She rubbed her moussed fingers through the curls until they were shiny and oily-looking. "Maybe some. She always kept wine in the fridge. But she wasn't like drunk. And she sure as hell wasn't *down*. She'd been talking about movin' over to the mall, goin' big time, maybe even sellin' franchises." She leaned forward, arranging the curls around her face so that they looked disheveled. "Shit, I really walked into that one, didn't I? That girl, she had this way of making big plans that never panned out, and I got so I didn't listen much. But this time it was different. She had me convinced."

"Did she say where the money was coming from?"

Peaches laughed wryly and reached for a big-toothed comb. "You kiddin'? She never told me *nothin'*, 'cept when my check was goin' to be late." She teased out the hair on the side with the comb. "Then she'd piss and moan about the rent and the bills and stuff, and how the bank was goin' to take this, that, the other. Then she'd tell me I'd have to wait."

"When she left Tuesday night, was she on her way to meet somebody?" I paused, and took a long shot. "C. W. Rand, maybe?"

Peaches fished in her bag for a small mirror and used it to inspect the back of her head. "She didn't like say where she was goin'. But she talked to C.W. earlier, 'cause I happened to pick it up when he called."

I leaned forward. "Did he call often?"

She put the mirror back in her bag. "Once, twice a day, maybe. Who keeps score? But about that evenin', I don't know about her seein' him then. When she left here, she was with her sister."

That was a break. Maybe Jerri had told Rita that she was planning to meet C.W. later.

Peaches turned to me, tilting her head. "How does it look?"

"Curly," I said. "Wet."

"Good," she said, satisfied. She reached for her bag. "Listen, you mind? Friend of mine told me there might be a job at the gym over in San Marcos. I'm outta here."

"Good luck," I said.

She glanced around. "Yeah, well, wherever I land, it's gotta be better than this rat hole. This place gives me like"—she shuddered—"the creeps."

18

My conversation with Peaches had turned out to be unexpectedly profitable. Not only would she be able to testify that Jerri had not seemed suicidal, but had talked with C.W. on the phone on Tuesday, and often. Pushed, Peaches might even be able to recall other evidence of their relationship. I was betting that Rita knew that Jerri had seen C.W. later that night.

I stopped at a pay phone and called Ruby. Her answering machine was still on. When I dialed my machine to see if Ruby had left a message, what I got was Leatha, telling me that she and Sam and Sara were going down to the ranch at Kerrville for the weekend. If I wanted to join them I was more than welcome and so was Mike and that "charming little boy of his." I had to admit that a weekend away from Pecan Springs sounded like a good idea. Brian would enjoy stalking the animals, McQuaid could get in some hunting, and I was curious about Sam and his family. But it was out of the question while I was still trying to piece together the proof of C.W.'s involvement in Jerri's death.

By the time I finished listening to both answering machines, it was nearly four and the sky was glazing over with a wintry twilight. I couldn't wait for Ruby. I phoned Rita. "Is it convenient for me to come over now?"

"I guess." She sounded tired. "Mama's gone home to take her nap. If we've got to talk, this is the best time." She gave me her address.

Rita lived in a small ground-floor apartment about four blocks from Jerri's house. She answered my third ring, still wearing the loose black dress she'd had on that morning. Sometime during the day she must have caught her heel in the hem and ripped it loose, for it was hanging. Her dark-blond hair was limp and stringy, the flesh sagged in dark crescents under her eyes, she was barefoot. She padded in front of me down a hall and into a small living room that looked out onto a postcard-sized concrete patio surrounded by a weathered six-foot privacy fence. The planting space between the fence and the concrete had been filled with chrysanthemums, blooming bravely against the chill gray afternoon.

Rita's living room was as small as Jerri's, but much tidier, and she had paid a great deal of attention to decorating it. A chair and a rocking chair sat at right angles to a sofa–coffee table combination. On the polished wood coffee table was a white hobnail vase filled with red silk roses, and beside it was a tinted porcelain figurine of a woman in a décolleté gown frothed with gold porcelain ruffles. On one wall was a collage of red foil hearts, red velvet ribbon, and lace. On the opposite wall hung a large framed poster for *Gone with the Wind*, with a swooning Vivien Leigh clasped in Clark Gable's passionate embrace. Beneath it was a bookcase filled with Harlequin romances, neatly aligned.

"Please sit down." Rita gestured at the red velveteen sofa, which was decorated with a half-dozen crocheted pillows. "Would you like a cup of coffee?"

"Thanks, I'm fine." I stood, waiting for her to sit. "How did it go with the sheriff this morning?"

"Pretty awful." She went into the kitchen, came back with a cigarette, her lighter, and a glass ashtray. We both sat down, I on the sofa, careful not to disarrange the pillows, she in the wooden rocking chair to my right. She closed her eyes briefly. "I haven't told Mama yet." She opened her eyes and lit her cigarette. "About that stuff in Jerri's house, I mean. Or about the sheriff and all those questions. I don't relish the thought."

I didn't believe her. I thought she very much relished the thought of destroying her mother's illusions about Jerri, the sister who had always come first. But I didn't need to make us both uncomfortable by digging into it. It was her illusions about C.W. that I was here to challenge. "It's probably best not to tell her until there's something definite," I said. I gave her a sympathetic look. "But that makes it awfully hard on you, carrying the burden all alone."

"Yeah." She pulled several nervous drags on her cigarette. "It's pretty hard to sit here and listen to Mama go on and on about how perfect her dear sweet baby girl was, how Jerri never did anything wrong. She refuses to believe that Jerri was drinking. She keeps saying there must of been somebody else with her, and that was his gin bottle in the car." Rita leaned her head back and began to rock. "Mama says they'll probably find another body in that ravine. Or maybe he crawled out of the wreck and ran off." She blinked away tears. "It's bad enough about Jerri. It's worse to hear Mama making up all these stories, just so she doesn't have to face the facts."

I murmured something. There was a tissue box on the floor beside the rocker. Rita put out her cigarette and pulled up a tissue. She wiped her eyes, pushing her glasses up on her forehead.

"I guess I'm like Mama, I don't want to believe it. She must of drove off that road on purpose, to keep Mama from finding out what she'd done." She blew her nose. "How am I ever going to tell Mama her baby *killed* herself?"

I leaned forward. "Rita, I don't think that's what happened."

Rita's head jerked up and her glasses fell back down on her nose. "It . . . wasn't? You mean, it really *was* an accident?"

"I don't think it was an accident, either. I think your sister was murdered."

Her face went dead white.

I reached for her hand. It was icy cold. "Are you all right? Can I get you some water?"

Her eyes were huge, pupils dilated like black holes drilled into her head. "*Murdered?* But . . . but *who?*"

I gripped her hand tightly. "Rita, I think C.W. did it."

Her eyes closed. Her hand went limp. I thought she was going to faint.

I let go her hand and went to the kitchen for water. I'd known this wasn't going to be easy. Rita would deny the truth as long as she could to protect her illusions.

I brought her the water and made her drink some. I put the glass on the table, sat down again, and waited for her to open her eyes. When she did, I said, "It's hard to understand why C.W. would do it, but you have to try. Maybe it will help if we start from the beginning. Jerri and C.W. were lovers. They—"

She sat up rigidly, hands gripping the wooden chair arms. "Jerri lied!" she cried shrilly. "She *wanted* him, but he wouldn't. He loved . . . He wouldn't do it, that's all."

"But she *didn't* lie. They made love in an empty unit at Lake Winds. You can see for yourself—there's a vase of flowers on the table there, just like the ones in her bedroom, and a card from C.W. to Jerri. And Peaches, at the gym, says that he called Jerri once or twice a day, every day. He called on Tuesday, the day she died. And that night, he took her out and killed her."

Small red triangles, like clown's makeup, appeared on Rita's paper-white cheeks. "No," she moaned. "Oh, no, no, *no.*"

It was hard to tell whether her no was another denial or the sheer horror of seeing her illusion dissolving like a shadow in the harsh, unforgiving light of reality. It was her faith that had held her together, had inspired her loyalty to C.W. Without it, she was coming apart, and I didn't know if there would be anything left of her when it was gone. To get at the truth, the illusion had to die, no matter how agonizing the death. I had to be brutal.

"I don't know whose idea it was to kill Sybil," I said, "whether it was C.W.'s or Jerri's. But they planned it together. C.W. would be the first one suspected, so he arranged to be out of town when Sybil died. Maybe they decided that Jerri would slit Sybil's throat because Jerri knew how to do it, or because it isn't a woman's crime. Or maybe they decided to do it that way to make it look like a cult killing. With the cult scare going around, that would be a good cover. It would also explain the voodoo doll, and why one of them—Jerri, probably—broke into Ruby's shop and stole her ritual knife. And it must have been Jerri who called Bubba with that tip about a human sacrifice."

Rita was shaking her head back and forth mechanically, like a wind-up doll. "Where are you getting this stuff?" she asked desperately. "It's crazy. You're making it up." She reached for another tissue. "The part about Mr. Rand, anyway." She gave me a look of passionate pleading. "Jerri did it, all by herself. He couldn't of had anything to do with it. Why would he? Mrs. Rand had already left him a note saying she'd changed her will."

"He didn't find out about the divorce and the will until the sheriff started to question him," I said. "Then he went home and typed the note, to make it look like he'd known all along. It was an idea he borrowed from a magazine article about a murder trial." All this was inference, but it was damned *good* inference.

Rita began to shred the tissue. "You just don't understand him," she said despairingly. "You can't, or you wouldn't be saying these horrible things. You're making him sound just *awful*. And he isn't. He's sweet and kind. He's been . . . a wonderful friend to me, in every way. He never yells at me, even when I do dumb things. He gives me time off. He . . . brings me flowers and candy, and cards. To show me how much he . . . cares." Her chin trembled. "Anyway, *he* was the one who was in danger."

"Danger? From whom?"

"From his wife, that's who." Rita's eyes came to life. "She was an evil, evil woman. She wanted him dead. Why do you think she started growing all those awful poison plants? Every day he'd tell me how afraid he was. Once she tried to kill him with a knife, and another time she came after him with the car.

He just missed getting hit. He was afraid she was going to put some of those plants in his food. It was only a matter of time."

I frowned. I couldn't imagine Sybil taking out after C.W. with the car or putting a handful of monkshood leaves and some lantana berries in his salad. And I certainly couldn't see him eating anything that remotely resembled a poisonous plant. But Rita's version of history did offer one advantage, and I seized it without hesitation.

"Don't you see, Rita? The fact that C.W. felt threatened by his wife makes it even more likely that he *did* want to kill her."

There was a long silence. All that was left of the tissue was a litter of papery shreds all over her black dress. When she finally spoke her voice was wounded, fragile. "But why would he want to kill *Jerri?* My sister wasn't always . . . a very nice person. But she never did anything bad to . . . him."

"Look at it from his point of view, Rita. With Sybil dead, Jerri was expecting C.W. to marry her—something he maybe didn't want to do. And she knew too much. It was dangerous to have her around. In fact, I believe he intended from the beginning to kill Jerri. He manipulated her into killing his wife, and once Sybil was dead, he got rid of Jerri."

Rita stared at me for a long moment without saying anything. Her pale lips were compressed in a thin line, and the light reflecting off her glasses kept me from seeing her eyes. I'd been pretty rough, but it was necessary. I had to get her to see that the man she cared for was a ruthless killer, all the more despicable because he'd conned a woman into murdering for him, and when she'd done what he wanted, he'd killed her. And not just any woman. Her *sister.*

Rita's voice was flat and toneless. "How do you think he . . . how was it done?"

I relaxed a little. I'd opened a chink in her defenses. "They drove up to Devil's Backbone on Tuesday night. They'd probably been drinking, and Jerri was a little drunk. He got her to stop the car, and maybe he hit her to knock her out. We'll know more about that when the autopsy report comes out tomorrow. Then he started the car in park, punched a couple of holes in the fuel filter, and lit the gasoline that was spurting out. He probably got the idea from Hank, when he took his Le Baron in to get the automatic fuel cutoff fixed. Then he shoved the car into drive and watched it go over the cliff."

The expression that flashed across Rita's face was a mix of disbelief, desperation, and fear. "How do you *know* all that?" Her voice was incredulous.

"You can read it in the evidence. There's nothing to indicate that Jerri's car went off the road at high speed. There's a scorched spot on the shoulder where the car was set on fire before it went over. But the fire didn't completely destroy the evidence. You can tell it was deliberate."

She bit her lip. "Who else knows?"

"Right now, only you and I." Hank knew part of it, but that wasn't really relevant here. "I need you to confirm what Jerri did after she left the gym with you on Tuesday night. Where did you go?"

The same expression again. This time, more fear. Fear and something close to panic. Hadn't I convinced her? Was she afraid of betraying C.W.? "We . . . Jerri and I went to her house. We sat and talked for a while, then we . . . I left, and came home."

She wasn't telling the truth—not all of it, anyway. "Did she say what she was going to do after you left?"

"No, not exactly," she said. "But she . . . she . . ." She put her hand to her temple, as if she were feeling light-headed. "I don't know. I just don't know. I'm confused. It's . . . too much."

I put my hand on her arm. "You're doing fine, Rita. Just take your time. We'll do it step by step. While you were with Jerri, did she get a phone call?"

Her eyes flickered. "I don't . . . yes, I guess. Yes, she did. She took it in the bedroom, though. I didn't hear."

"Did she tell you who the caller was?"

She leaned back and inhaled a deep breath. "Yes." She let it out again.

"Who was it?"

"She said it was . . . Mr. Rand."

"Did she tell you about the conversation?"

"Not really. She said they were . . . going out." She didn't meet my eyes. "I thought she was lying. I guess I just hated to think about the two of them being . . . together." She pulled in her breath again, let it out with a long, wavering sigh. "But if he killed her, I can't protect him. Whoever did it has to pay." She fell silent, staring at her hands. Finally she spoke. "Do you think we . . . could make him confess?"

Now it was my turn to stare, dumbfounded by her change of heart. I prided myself on being good with witnesses, but I didn't know I was *that* good. "You're willing to confront him directly?"

She straightened her shoulders as if she were steeling herself against something too awful to think about. "Can they prove in court that he killed my sister?"

"I think so," I said without hesitation, "and I think the sheriff will too, when he sees the evidence." That was a little misleading, because Rita herself was the best evidence I had. "This won't be easy, Rita. Are you sure you're up to it?"

"If they can prove C.W. did it, I don't have any choice," she said. Her face tightened, her shoulders firmed as she pulled strength from some hidden place deep inside her. "He's working tonight. Around six, I'm supposed to go to the office to help him find some papers for the board meeting next week. It would be a good time to . . . " She swallowed. "To do it."

I glanced at the clock. It was nearly five. If I could arrange backup, a face-to-face confrontation might very well put the quickest end to this bloody business. C.W. was no doubt feeling pretty secure, and Rita would be the last one he'd expect to accuse him. If she hit him hard with what she knew, it might just jolt a confession out of him. On the other hand, Perry Mason theatrics are always risky. C.W. might simply laugh off her charges, and we'd be nowhere. Or he might panic and somebody would get hurt. Blackie would have to be there, and I'd feel a hell of a lot better if McQuaid was part of the backup.

"Confrontation wasn't quite what I had in mind, but it just might work." I looked around for the phone. "Let's call the sheriff. He has to be in on this, and it's going to take a while to sell him on the idea." That was an understatement. I had the feeling it would be a damn sight harder to persuade Blackie of C.W.'s guilt than it had been to convince Rita. I'd appealed to her emotions with a story that was mostly speculation. The sheriff would demand hard facts, and all I had was Rita's testimony that Jerri planned to meet C.W. the night she was killed.

Rita shook her head nervously. "No. No sheriff."

"But what we're doing could be dangerous. It's crazy to go storming out there without the sheriff's—"

"If you call the sheriff, the whole thing's off." Her eyes narrowed, her voice became fierce and determined. Suddenly she reminded me of Jerri. She was a woman of *tsuyoki*, of unexpectedly great *ki* that had risen up out of some inner reserve of energy to fuel her for this ordeal. "This is just you and me, China. If you're not willing to do it my way, forget it." The corners of her mouth tipped in a tight smile, and she played her top card. "You can forget what I told you, too. About Jerri talking to him on the phone. I'll swear I never said it, and you won't have any way to tie him to her murder."

She had me. "But why not the sheriff? I can understand why you want to confront Rand, but why does it have to be solo?"

Her face wrenched painfully. "Because I . . . *love* him." She twisted her hands. "Haven't you ever loved somebody who hurt you? Can't you understand how I feel?"

I could. When I was a child, I thought that good triumphed over evil naturally, without anybody doing anything to make it happen. When I got a little older, I thought the legal system took care of justice. But then I learned that the system has big cracks, and we depend on it at our peril. Each of us is obliged to create our own justice, in small ways and large ways, every day of our lives. The man Rita loved had murdered her sister, and she felt responsible for seeing him brought to trial. I was pretty sure she wasn't telling me the whole truth, and I didn't like climbing out on a shaky limb without a safety net. But she didn't have a choice, and neither did I. I had to play it her way.

"We can take a tape recorder," I said. "That will allow us to substantiate the confession, if we get one. But it's not quite five yet, and I have things to do before we go out there. How about if I pick you up in about fifty minutes?"

She shook her head. "No. If I sit around here, I'll lose my nerve. I'm coming with you. Wait until I change."

She disappeared into the bedroom, leaving the door open. In a few minutes she was out again, wearing a pair of dark jeans and a navy-blue sweatshirt. She had pulled her hair back into an untidy ponytail, secured with a rubber band. She went to the kitchen and came out carrying a shoulder bag. "I'm ready."

Outside, the chilly twilight had deepened to a hazy dusk. We drove to the shop in silence. Rita rolled down the window a couple of inches and lit a cigarette. Normally I'd object to that, but I felt I had to handle her carefully. I kept my eyes on the streets as I negotiated the square, but my mind was already out at Lake Winds. I considered rehearsing her, the way I usually rehearsed a witness I planned to put on the stand. But she'd probably be more effective if she just spilled out her accusation in her own way.

Anyway, I had questions of my own to resolve. Should I be on the scene, or should I stay out of sight and let her confront him? If I hung back, she'd have to take the risk of facing a suspected killer alone. Not just any killer, either. The man she loved. The man who might have murdered her sister. This wasn't going to be a piece of cake.

I stole an uneasy glance at Rita's profile. She was smoking with quick, jerky motions. Would she hold up? Could I count on her to pull this off? And what was she holding back?

Somehow, that was the question that worried me more than the others. Going into this blind, without backup, was risky. Going into it with somebody who was holding out on me was downright dangerous. For two cents, I'd pull up in front of the sheriff's office, haul her out of the car, and march her in for a little talk with Blackie. But if she made good on her promise to deny what she'd said about Jerri's plan to meet C.W., I was out of ammunition. Without her corroboration, Blackie wouldn't buy my conjectures. Like it or not, confronting C.W. was the only choice. But my stomach was twisted into a cold knot. Courtrooms I can handle, but I'm no Kinsey Millhone. Where I'm concerned, "C" is for Coward. My palms were already sweaty, and we hadn't even started yet.

Laurel had closed the shop and left. I checked the cash register, looked through the phone messages for something from Ruby, and turned to Rita. "I have to look things over next door. Ruby's still out. My tape recorder's there, too."

Rita nodded nervously. I checked the Cave's front door, then went to the counter. The week before, I'd loaned my minirecorder to Ruby. Luckily, I found it in the first place I looked, along with a couple of tapes and the thimble-sized auxiliary mike. I checked the batteries, loaded a tape, and hurriedly scribbled a note to Ruby. I stuck it on the cash register, where we usually leave messages. The phone was at my elbow, but Rita had come to the connecting door, where she stood leaning against the jamb, watching me. I ignored the phone. There was no one to call, anyway. Blackie'd give me the big hoo-hah, and McQuaid was somewhere between here and San Antonio.

"I guess that pretty much takes care of it." I went past Rita, into my shop. There was one more thing in my mind—the nine-millimeter Berreta that was hidden in the secret cubby behind my laundry hamper, a sad, unsavory reminder of a tragic event in my former life. I'd sworn off guns four years ago, and I wasn't going to perjure myself now, no matter how uneasy I was feeling. Better to leave the weapon where it was.

"Ready?" I reached for my brown jacket.

Rita looked outside. The dusk had turned to dark, and the wind had risen, whipping the trees. "We'll be early, but I guess it doesn't matter."

We got back in the car. I put the key in the ignition and turned on the lights. As we drove away, I had the anxious feeling that I'd overlooked something—something that just might get me in a hell of a lot of trouble.

19

We didn't speak. I was thinking, hard. Mostly, I was thinking about what lay ahead. But Rita's sudden urgency about confronting C.W. still bothered me. Did she know something more incriminating than anything *I* knew? If she did, what was it?

I thought back over the evidence against C.W., which I had to admit was pretty flimsy. In the case of Sybil's murder, everything incriminated Jerri—the choice of weapon and method; the bloodstained clothing; and the cult-killing coverup, including the voodoo dolls, the theft of the knife, and the anonymous tip about a human sacrifice, in a woman's voice. She and C.W. had been very careful. Nothing pointed to him, except the bogus note, which was obviously damage control. If he was innocent of Sybil's death, he didn't need the note.

But in the hands of a clever prosecutor the note could be as devastating as Andrew's Satanic bible. And there was plenty to tie Rand to Jerri's death. The flowers and the card carelessly left behind in the bedroom in C7, and probably fingerprints too, were evidence of their relationship. Hank could testify that C.W. knew about the potential auto fire danger, Peaches to his frequent phone calls to the gym, and Rita to the fact that Jerri planned to meet him just before her death.

I sorted through the facts again, one at a time, frowning. Something, some recollection, was trying to elbow its way through the busy, clamoring crowd of thoughts. I relaxed, stopped chasing it, and there it was, vividly, as if it were wearing neon. The day before yesterday, in the office at Lake Winds. Rita, flustered and anxious, arms full of the papers she'd retrieved from the floor, insisting that Sybil's death had to have been the work of Santeros.

"They're the ones who've been slaughtering animals, aren't they? And there was that tip some woman phoned in to Chief Harris."

But Bubba had kept his promise—there hadn't been a word about human sacrifice in the *Enterprise*. Not even the ol' boys at the Doughnut Queen had gotten wind of it. How did Rita know about the tip?

Rita turned. "We can park behind the office. That way he won't see the car." Her voice was taut with compressed energy, like a spring squeezed down and tied.

I skirted the parking lot and swung the Datsun down a lane. It was almost full dark, except for the lights that spilled golden puddles on the black asphalt. Three months ago, it would have been daylight at this hour. People would be heading for the tennis courts, the marina, the pro shop, the restaurant. But this was a midweek night in November. The parking lot was empty, the restaurant and pro shop closed, the tennis courts deserted. Somehow, I hadn't expected the place to be so empty. There was a chunk of ice in the pit of my stomach.

I stopped the car behind C.W.'s office and turned off the ignition.

"Let's wait inside," Rita said. She got out.

I got out too, and stuck the tape recorder in my jacket pocket, wishing—almost—that I'd brought the Beretta. The chunk of ice in my stomach felt colder, heavier. We walked around the building, under the shadow of the trees. The questions were flying around inside my head like black bats in a cave. I wasn't sure whether I should duck or grab one and hang on.

How did Rita know about the phone-in tip? Who told her that the caller had been a woman? Jerri? If Jerri had told her that much, what *else* had she told her, and when? Or was it C.W.?

We were at the door, under the security light. I stood to one side while Rita took her keys out of her bag and unlocked the door. Inside, she flicked on the lights and walked across the room to her desk. I glanced around quickly. There were three doors. The door to the kitchen, behind Rita's desk. The door to C.W.'s office, beside it. The front door.

Rita gestured off-handedly at LouEllen's desk. "You could sit down. It might be a little while."

I sat down and put the tape recorder beside the typewriter. More black bats. If C.W. had told Rita, when did he tell her? After he killed Jerri? I shivered. Or before?

Rita sat down and put her purse on the desk in front of her. She pulled out a cigarette package. I glanced at it. Salem Menthol.

And then another black bat flung itself through my head. A burned patch beside the road. A worn-out Nike, a crumpled Coors can, a McDonald's bag, a Salem pack.

Another bat, another memory, bigger and nastier. Peaches, pulling fat pink curlers out of her hair. "Kissy face, sweet as pie, but watch out. She'd scratch your eyes out behind your back."

Surreptitiously, I slid my hand to the recorder and flicked it on. "It wasn't Jerri who plotted with C.W. to kill his wife," I said conversationally. "*You* killed Sybil. And you helped him murder Jerri."

Rita's shoulders firmed. "*Not* C.W." Her voice was fierce, tight-strung. "It was me. Just *me*." She reached into the top drawer of her desk and pulled out a vicious-looking small-caliber revolver with a long barrel and wooden grips. She pointed it at me. "I wondered if you'd finally figure it out. Was it something I said?"

I sat back slowly. "Chief Harris didn't publicize the tip, so you couldn't have known about it unless the tipster told you—or unless *you* were the tipster." I managed a half grin. "And smoking may be the death of you. You dropped a Salem pack beside the road, where you started the fire in Jerri's car." I paused, the sickness of it chill and sour inside me. "So Jerri wasn't the only daughter trained to be a butcher."

"No." Her mouth was twisted, bitter. "Not Jerri. *I* was the one Dad trained. She was always too good to get her hands bloody. She worked up front because she was good with customers. Especially the men, always laughing and flirting. She played in the band, she was a cheerleader, she had dates, she was popular. She was always dumping the dirty work on me so she could run off and have a good time."

"But I don't see—"

She cut me off. "At first I was scared to shoot the cows and pigs. I'd throw up when I had to cut their throats to bleed them. But after a while it didn't bother me. I got good at butchering. Even Daddy said I was good." She glanced fondly at the revolver. "This is his gun. He let me use it to do the killing. He left it to me. He left me the knives, too."

"The ones Jerri had on her wall?"

"The ones I put there. For you to find. You and the sheriff." Her smile faded. "Daddy said I was good, but he always perked up when she was around. When she was there, it was like I was invisible. It didn't matter what I did, it was like I didn't exist."

I stood up and started to turn. "I'm walking out of here."

"Then do it backwards, please." Rita raised the gun and pointed it at me. It didn't waver. "I really don't want to shoot you in the back. It'll spoil my explanation to the police." She pulled back the hammer.

I sat back down. "What about C.W.?"

She released the hammer gently. "I lied when I said he was coming at six. He won't be here until seven thirty. By that time we'll be finished. Or rather, *you'll* be finished." She smiled at her little joke.

I was sweating in spite of the ice frozen in the pit of my stomach. Mealymouthed Rita wasn't sweet as pie anymore. She was definitely in charge, and the gun gave her a new authority. She wanted to talk, maybe to brag about what she'd accomplished. I might as well give her a chance.

"So why *did* you kill Sybil?"

She looked at me as if I'd lost my mind. "Don't you know? Because she was going to kill him."

"How do you know?"

"I told you," she said testily. "Don't you remember?" She bit her lip. "Really, it was so terrible, I don't see how he stood it. She kept threatening him with those awful poison plants, and she'd put horrible stuff in his salad, leaves and berries and things, which he never would eat. Once in the middle of the night she tried to stab him, and another time she almost hit him with the car. He was so scared, *I* got scared, too. I was afraid she was going to kill him. I couldn't face life without him. I just couldn't." The grin she gave me now was little-girl proud, and so pathetic that I would have wept if I hadn't been so scared. "Don't you see? I was the only one who could help. I had to do something to protect him, and I did. I saved his life."

"But didn't the whole thing strike you as odd?" I asked. "C.W. is a big, strong man. If he was afraid of his wife, why didn't *he* handle it? Or if he couldn't, why didn't he go to the sheriff?"

She put down the gun, took out a cigarette, and lit it with a match. I tensed, estimating the distance between us. Six feet, maybe eight. Before I got the gun, she'd get me. I forced myself to relax.

"Because Sybil was blackmailing him," she said, waving out the match. "He'd forgotten to report some income, you see. If he went to the sheriff, she'd tell the IRS, and they'd put him in jail."

I felt like gagging. "Did he say *why* she wanted to kill him?"

"She wanted to marry that photographer. The one they arrested for her murder." She looked concerned. "Are they going to let him out of jail, now that they think Jerri did it?"

"You'll have to ask the sheriff," I said. "If Sybil wanted to marry Andrew, why didn't she simply divorce C.W.?"

"Because of the money, of course." Rita spoke with the patient tone of a first-grade teacher talking to a slow learner. "A lot of it was hers, but a big part was his, too. She wanted all of it. If they were divorced, she wouldn't get it. She had to have him dead."

I thought what an awful mess of lies C.W. had dished out to her, and how easily, unquestioningly she had accepted them, *still* accepted them. "Did C.W. ask you to kill his wife?"

Her answer was so quick and so horrified that it had the ring of truth—the truth as *she* saw it, anyway. "Of course not! He'd never do such a thing!"

I rephrased my question and offered it more gently. "Did he tell you he'd be better off if she was dead?"

She tossed her head. "Well, sure. I mean, that was clear, wasn't it? A couple of times he said it was the only way out, but he'd be a fool to do it. He was right, too. He'd be the first they'd suspect. Really, t was all my idea."

I persisted. "Did he say *when* it had to be done?"

"No, not really. But I couldn't put it off. I had to do it right away."

"Why?"

"Because she told him she was going to make a new will the next week. The money would all go to some old aunt up in the Panhandle." She frowned darkly and shook her head. "That Sybil, what a *cheat*. She'd already *made* the will!"

The whole thing was becoming horrifyingly, sickeningly clear. C.W. had all but written out a set of instructions for his wife's murder and handed them to the one person who would do anything he wanted, no matter how terrible, as long as she thought she was doing it for him.

"Were you and C.W. lovers?" I asked gently.

She blushed. "Not if you mean did we go to bed together. It went a lot deeper than just . . . physical stuff. He loved me, I mean, really *loved* me. He told me so, lots of times. Sometimes when we were here all alone, he'd kiss me." The lines of her face softened and her hand went to her mouth, as if she were remembering the touch of his lips. "He said he wished he'd married somebody who was loyal and faithful and cared for him like I did."

I changed tack. "You set Sybil's murder up as a cult killing. Why did you decide to shift the blame to Jerri?"

"Well, that photographer got to be a problem. I didn't mean for him to get arrested." Her mouth tightened. "And I was fed up with Jerri's lies, bragging about how she was going to marry C.W., how he was going to give her a lot of money. She was always a liar. She took what she wanted, without thinking of anybody's feelings. And I was the good little girl who always gave in." Her voice rose in acid mimicry. "'Oh, let her have it,' Mama would say. 'You don't need it, do you?' It didn't matter whether I needed it or wanted it, or whether it was *mine*, Jerri got it. Even C.W.—she tried to take *him*. But I fixed her. It's the last time she'll grab something that doesn't belong to her."

"So you sent her over the cliff?"

She nodded, intent on her story. "It happened pretty much the way you said it did, except that it wasn't C.W. Honest, it was *me*. I set the car on fire and put it in drive, and it went over."

"How did you know how to start the fire? Did your dad teach you auto mechanics too?"

She laughed, pleased with herself. "No, it was Hank. I went to pick up C.W.'s car after it was repaired. Hank told me about the automatic fuel cutoff, and what could happen if it didn't work."

"Or if the car didn't have one."

"Right. Jerri's Mustang was pretty old, so I knew it didn't. When it had gone over, I saw the fire and knew that was the end. I walked up the road, got my car where I'd left it that afternoon, and drove home. I got the shoes and the sweatsuit I'd worn when I killed Sybil, and the knives and the other voodoo doll I'd made, just in case, and took them over to Jerri's. You know the rest."

I regarded her thoughtfully. "Now that we've got the story straight, what's next?"

"That's easy." She stood up and motioned with the gun. "You need to walk over there by the door, then turn and face me. This is only a twenty-two, so it has to be fairly close range. I'll make it quick." Her voice became apologetic. "I'm sorry, China, honest. But I can't let you accuse C.W. of something he didn't do. It's better if everybody thinks Jerri did it."

Her polite, gravely composed earnestness made the whole thing almost absurdly surreal. Two women in an ordinary office, the one with the gun giving the other one instructions on how to submit to being murdered. It was like a scene in a movie. It was happening to somebody else, not to me.

I didn't get up. "But there'll be another dead body. Won't I be rather difficult to account for?"

"Not at all. I'll tell the police I was working late when I saw the doorknob turning. I was nervous because of Sybil's murder. I was afraid I was about to be assaulted. I took out my gun and pulled the trigger before I could see that it was a friend coming through the door."

Her scheme was a good one, and I couldn't for the life of me figure out how to thwart it. Rush her? She'd shoot. Try some tricky aikido move? She'd shoot. Anyway, there was an unnerving difference between facing a benign, unarmed opponent in white pajamas and staring down the long barrel of Rita's very real revolver. Shit.

The door behind Rita's desk edged open a crack.

"I *said*," Rita repeated, "go over to the door."

I groped for the only stall I could think of. "What are you going to do about the car?"

"What car?"

"*Your* car. You rode out here with me, remember? What are you going to tell the sheriff—that you hitchhiked? Took a taxi?"

I managed a grin. "Of course, you could drive my car back to your place and pick up yours. But that leaves my car at your house. The sheriff would be curious about that."

She frowned, thinking.

"And since the M.E. can establish time of death pretty precisely, you don't have a lot of time to play car swap. You might call a cab, but the driver would remember—"

"Shut up and walk to the door. I'll figure it out later."

Several things happened at the same time. I took a step backward, Rita took a step forward, and Ruby charged through the back door. With a thundering "A-*ya!*" she grabbed Rita's right hand and yanked it down. The gun discharged with an ear-ringing crack and went flying. Ruby hooked her left ankle around Rita's left leg, jerked, and pushed. Rita crashed to the floor.

I scrambled for the gun and stood up. "What *took* you so long?"

"What do you mean, took me so long?" Ruby demanded. "I hurried. After all, I had to change."

"Had to change! I'm facing a killer, scared shitless, and you're geting dressed?"

"How am I supposed to know you're scared? All your note said was 'Come to C.W.'s office. Back door.' I thought it was a party. I went home and changed clothes." She had, too. She was wearing a vampy jade-green dress with spaghetti straps and jade-green spike heels. She looked like somebody's gun moll.

Rita stirred painfully, moaning. Ruby looked down at her. "How about if we put her in a chair?"

"Fine," I said. "Then let's give Blackie a call."

Ruby helped Rita up and sat her in her chair behind the desk. As she reached for the phone, the front door opened behind me. I swiveled, gun on the door. Rita half stood and Ruby pushed her down again.

"What's going on here?" C.W. took in the scene at a glance. "What are you doing with that gun?" he asked me. He looked at Ruby, six feet tall and splendid, her ginger hair in a frizzy nimbus, her hand planted firmly on Rita's shoulder. "Who the hell are *you*?"

"I'm the one who's calling the police," Ruby said. She picked up the phone and began to dial.

I motioned C.W. to the sofa. "Sit over there, please. You have some explaining to do. Rita's implicated you in your wife's murder."

"No!" Rita wailed. "No! I *didn't!* Don't believe her, C.W. I'd never tell, never!"

"Rita," C.W. said softly, "shut up." He sat on the sofa and appealed to me. "She's crazy. Whatever she did, she did entirely on her own hook."

Rita stared at him as if she was seeing him for the first time. "But you said—"

"I never said anything to you." He folded his arms. "I was in Atlanta."

Rita's look might have flattened him if he hadn't been sitting down.

"It wouldn't matter whether you were here or on the moon," I told him. "An accessory before the fact is somebody who incites, counsels, or orders somebody else to commit a crime— which is what, according to Rita, you did. If she's guilty of Sybil's murder, so are you."

C.W.'s face paled. He sat back and folded his arms. "You can't prove shit."

"I don't have to. That's the D.A.'s job. But Rita's just given a voluntary statement, on tape, spelling out the details."

Rita gasped.

C.W. frowned. "You violated her rights. She's supposed to have a lawyer present when somebody asks questions about a crime."

"When the *police* ask questions about a crime," I corrected him. "What Rita gave me was a voluntary statement about her involvement in a crime. I'm not a law-enforcement officer. I don't have to play by the Miranda rule."

Ruby put down the phone. "I just talked to the dispatcher. A couple of cars are on the way. It may take a while to locate the sheriff, though."

"Oh, yeah?" I asked. "Where is he?"

Ruby grinned. "He's giving a talk," she said. "At the law-enforcement conference, up at the college."

McQuaid rolled over onto his back with a deep-throated sigh of satisfaction. I flopped onto my stomach and draped my right arm across his chest. The sheets were tangled around us. A room-service tray with a half-empty bottle of champagne and the remains of eggs Benedict for two sat on the floor beside the bed. The drapes were half open, the Sunday morning sunlight painting a golden band across the carpet.

McQuaid and I had taken a vote. It was two-zip against a romantic weekend with my mother, her fiancé, and a bewildering assortment of prospective family members, and in favor of a weekend of R and R alone. I called Leatha and thanked her for the invitation and asked her to tell Sam and the gang that I looked forward to meeting them. Then McQuaid and I drove to San Antonio, dropped Brian off to visit his mother, and checked into the Menger Hotel, across the alley from the Alamo.

The Menger is a far cry from the plastic palaces that have popped up like toadstools along the River Walk. Its history harkens back to the glory days of San Antonio, when cowboys galloped into the city bent on high jinks and high culture, when Teddy Roosevelt recruited Rough Riders in the saloon, and Carrie Nation took her hatchet to the bar. The rooms are luxuriantly opulent, the Victorian furniture is marvelously vulgar, and the lobby rises on Corinthian columns three stories to a glorious stained-glass skylight. It's the best place in town for a weekend of serious, all-out, no-holds-barred decadence.

By contrast, we'd eaten last night at Johnny's Mexican Restaurant on New Braunfels Street. Johnny's gives you real Tex-Mex, paper napkins, no frills. The vinyl tile floor is scuffed, the window air conditioner wheezes, and the phone wears a sign that says "three minute limit." There's no limit to the great food. We feasted on cabrito, which Johnny cooks Jalisco-style by simmering a whole goat (no kidding) with bay leaf, oregano, garlic, salt, pepper, chili powder, and cumin. The cabrito is then deep-fried and brought to your table by a cheerful waitperson in a pink vest-apron, along with ranchero sauce, rice, beans, guacamole (a little heavy on the garlic), and an endless supply of tortilla chips in plastic baskets. Afterward, we went back to our decadent hotel and made decadent love, last night and again this morning.

McQuaid pulled my hand to his mouth and nibbled my fingers. Last night's garlic was still seeping out of my pores, but he didn't seem to mind. "I can't believe you did it again," he said.

"It wasn't exactly *me*," I said modestly. "At least, not by myself. I kind of thought we did it together. Sex *à deux*."

"No, not that," McQuaid said. "The other." He pulled himself up and stuck a pillow behind his head. "Rand and that woman. Rita what's-her-name."

"Greene." I crawled up and cradled my head on his chest. I could hear his heart thump-thumping in my ear. It was a comforting sound, regular, reliable. "Why can't you believe it? You saw it yourself. The car, I mean, and the burned spot by the road. You said it couldn't have been an accident. If Blackie had questioned Rita about how Jerri died instead of treating her as a bereaved sister, he'd have known immediately that she was holding something back."

"That's exactly my *point*," McQuaid said. "You should have left it to Blackie. For God's sake, China, you know you're not supposed to mess around in an ongoing investigation."

I sat up too, yanking the sheet around me. "I didn't mess around," I said with as much dignity as I could muster, considering the circumstances. "As for the investigation, it was going in the wrong direction. Anyway, you can bet your sweet ass that I *would* have got Blackie out to Lake Winds if I could have. You, too, for that matter. But you cops were talking shop instead of minding the store. Do you think I really wanted to slug it out all alone with—"

He scowled. "And that's another thing. Going off like that, at night, with some wacko woman you suspected of—"

"I didn't. At least not then. I knew that Rita had maneuvered Ruby and me into finding the bloody clothes, but I thought Jerri and C.W. had killed Sybil and C.W. had murdered Jerri. I had no idea it was Rita until we were out there."

"Same difference. It was a killer, either way." McQuaid touched my face, gently, his eyes holding mine. "What are you trying to do, Bayles? Get yourself wasted by some maniac so you can get off the hook with me?"

I took his hand and put it on my bare breast. "Well, no," I murmured. "It wasn't that complicated. I didn't want Andrew to get to the grand jury, that's all. After that, it's harder to call off the dogs."

McQuaid sighed heavily. "Yeah. But I worry about you, damn it. I love you, China. I'd hate for you to get your fool head blasted off." He pulled me against him, searching for my mouth.

We were about to be decadent again when the phone rang. And rang. Finally, I reached for it. "Hello," I said blurrily.

"Hi," Ruby chirped. "I hope I'm not interrupting anything."

I looked up at McQuaid. "Ruby hopes she's not interrupting anything."

McQuaid made a rude noise, rolled over on his side, and pulled the pillow over his head.

"Uh-oh," Ruby said. "I wouldn't have bothered you, but I have some news."

"There was a jailbreak," I guessed, "and Rita and C.W. stole a car and took off for Vegas."

The pillow came up. "Vegas?" McQuaid asked, alarmed.

"Not. I made that up. Joke."

"Well, I'm not joking," Ruby said. "Andrew says to tell you thanks."

"Tell him you're welcome. You interrupted us for *that*? Andrew can be grateful tomorrow."

"He's grateful today. If you don't have anything better to do, you might drop in at the River Walk Gallery and see his exhibit. It's still hanging, but every photo has sold. That's where Andrew got the money to pay Sybil back."

"If we don't have anything better to do. Is that it?"

"I just talked to Becky Ellen."

"Becky Ellen?" I shivered. The pillow was off. McQuaid was tracing my breast with one finger and kissing my throat.

"The wife of the Reverend."

McQuaid moved his hand further down and kissed my mouth. When I could speak, I said, "I thought her name was Barbie. Wasn't that her in the church newspaper?" I looked at McQuaid. "We're talking about Billy Lee."

McQuaid moved his hand again. He didn't answer.

"*Her* name's Barbie," Ruby said. "The one with the boobs. I'm talking about his *other* wife. The one up in Abilene."

I was getting confused, but maybe it was because I wasn't paying attention. McQuaid was kissing my belly. "You mean his former wife?"

"I didn't know Billy Lee was divorced," McQuaid murmured, licking my bare skin. "Isn't that immoral?"

Ruby chortled. "I mean his *present* wife. The jerk never bothered to get a divorce. He's married to both women!"

"He's a bigamist?" I asked. "You've got to be kidding."

McQuaid raised his head. "A *bigamist*?"

"It's the truth," Ruby said, "so help me God and hope to die if I should ever tell a lie." She was laughing so hard she could hardly talk. "Here's his holiness, preaching that we're witches and not fit to wipe his boots on, and he's got two wives! That turkey is in it up to his eyebrows."

McQuaid put his head back down. "Yeah," I said, somewhat distracted. "Listen, Ruby, is that all?"

"Is that *all*? Isn't that enough?"

I looked down at McQuaid's dark head. "Enough? No, not hardly." I hung up the phone.

A little while later McQuaid poured us each another glass of champagne. "I really meant it," he said, poking around on the tray to see what else he could find to eat.

"Meant what?" I sipped my champagne and let myself feel simply, deliciously wonderful.

McQuaid sat up and reached for the phone. "How about lunch?" he asked. "I'm hungry again."

"Fine," I said lazily. I took another sip of champagne and drew my finger along his bare arm. "Meant what?"

"I'll have to keep a closer eye on you."

I gave him a vampy smile. "Just how do you propose to do that?"

He peeled off the sheet and looked the length of my body. Then he pulled it back up. "Why don't we move in together?"

"We can't," I said. "Howard Cosell hates cats."

References

I have consulted many fine herbals and herbalists in my research for this series. Among them are:

Michael Castleman, *The Healing Herbs*. Rodale Press, 1991.

The Business of Herbs, The International News and Resource Service for Herb Businesses. Published monthly by Northwind Farm Publications, R.R.2, Box 246, Shevlin, MN 56676.

Madeline Hill and Gwen Barclay, *Southern Herb Growing*. Shearer Publishing, 1987.

Hylton, William H., ed., *The Rodale Herb Book*. Rodale Press, 1974.

Ann Lovejoy, "Monkshoods and Wolfsbanes." *Horticulture*, June-July1992.